TRUTH GAMES

CAROLINE ENGLAND

PIATKUS

PIATKUS

First published in Great Britain in 2020 by Piatkus
This paperback edition published in 2021 by Piatkus

1 3 5 7 9 10 8 6 4 2

A CIP catalogue record for this book
is available from the British Library.

ISBN 978-0-349-42282-4

Typeset in Garamond by M Rules
Printed and bound in Great Britain by Clays Ltd, Elcograf S.p.A.

Papers used by Piatkus are from well-managed forests
and other responsible sources.

Piatkus
An imprint of
Little, Brown Book Group
Carmelite House
50 Victoria Embankment
London EC4Y 0DZ

An Hachette UK Company
www.hachette.co.uk

www.littlebrown.co.uk

Caroline England was born and brought up in Yorkshire and studied Law at the University of Manchester. She was a divorce and professional indemnity lawyer before leaving the law to bring up her three daughters and turning her hand to writing. Caroline is the author of *The Wife's Secret*, previously called *Beneath the Skin*, and the top-ten ebook bestseller *My Husband's Lies*. She lives in Manchester with her family.

To find out more about Caroline, visit her website
www.carolineenglandauthor.co.uk or follow her on social media:

Twitter: @CazEngland
Facebook: www.facebook.com/CazEngland1
Instagram: www.instagram.com/cazengland1

Praise for Caroline England:

'A compelling tale of love, jealousy, betrayal – and a devastating secret at the dark heart of a lifelong friendship. A great read with a twist that I didn't see coming!' T. M. Logan

'Incredibly twisty, beautifully written, evocative and deliciously satisfying. I cannot recommend it highly enough!' Claire Allan

'Kept me gripped and guessing' B. A. Paris

'Stunning ... dark undercurrents and sinister twists. A top-end read' Amanda Robson

'A taut, tantalising thriller ... full of passion and intrigue, sexual tension and desperate longing ... mesmerising storytelling' Sheryl Browne

'Truly terrific!' Martina Cole

'[A] fantastic novel, which holds you in its iron grip throughout. Enough twists, turns, and deftly drawn characters to keep even the most demanding reader thoroughly satisfied' S. D. Robertson

'Packs a knock-out final punch. Cunningly plotted and beautifully crafted, this is England on superlative form' Helen Fields

'An unstoppable thriller with more twists and turns than a corkscrew. This book had me gripped from the very first page!' Caroline Mitchell

'A taut and twisted tale of toxic relationships' Rachel Sargeant

For Elizabeth Rose,
who'll always be my number one!

'It has to be the truth, the honest truth. Everyone agree?'

'But what is truth?'

'It's only a game, man. Besides, another slug and we'll know.'

Six young adults in the high-ceilinged room, two cuddled on the sofa and four on the floor. A girl and two guys sit around a candlelit coffee table. Though late, it's still balmy, the leaded windows ajar. They're drinking Jack Daniel's from shot glasses.

The girl snaps open the second bottle and pours. Her nails are bitten, her nose pierced, her short hair dyed black. Her attention is focused on the man stretched out on the floor.

Lifting his dark head, he glances at her. 'Isn't there anything other than that American shit?' he asks, his accent distinct. He goes back to his spliff and takes a deep drag. 'OK. Then we'll use the correspondence theory of truth,' he says. 'A belief is true if there exists an appropriate entity – a fact – to which it corresponds. If there's no such entity, the belief is false.'

The fair-haired boy laughs. 'OK, genius, I'll start.' Blue-eyed and neat featured, he looks younger than his twenty years. 'A secret. A true secret . . .' He knocks back the whiskey. 'I'm in love with somebody in this room.'

The girl whips up her head, her stark make-up barely hiding her shock.

'Tell us something we don't already know!' This man is huge, his voice booms Home Counties. 'Come on, old chap. What did you say? The honest truth. Something you haven't told anyone before.'

'Right; here's one. My mum tried to snog me once,' he says.

1

Everyone but the girl laughs.

'No, it's true, I'm not joking. Dad had buggered off, so she spent all the time drinking and crying—'

'And snogging you?'

'Yes, Your Honour.' He guffaws. 'The truth and the whole fucking truth, eh? Only the once, thank God, when she got close enough. I can't do needy. Fucking disgusting.'

A silence of drunk embarrassment, then the eloquent voice again: 'Are you two lovebirds playing?'

They turn to the couple on the sofa. The young woman is asleep. 'We're living our secret,' her boyfriend says. 'But one you don't know ... Let me think. My brother and me, we used to spit in the take-outs. Special treat for the racists we knew from school.'

'Nice.'

'Nah. Good try, but it won't put me off your delicious—'

'I saw my father beat up my mum.' The man on the floor looks fixedly at the ceiling. 'Badly. Watched the blood spurt from her nose. Did nothing to stop him.'

The Goth girl stares, but doesn't speak.

The blond boy leans over. 'Fuck,' he says. 'How old were you?'

'Still a kid. But I blamed her. Probably still do.' He sits up and throws back his shot. Then he squints through the smoke at the girl, still sitting cross-legged and silent. 'What about you, nice middle-class miss? You're not saying much. What's your secret?'

Everyone is watching, all eyes are on her. 'A secret truth?' she asks, turning to him. 'With an actual fact to which it corresponds?'

The man snorts. 'Yeah. Come on, then; try me.'

She opens her inky lips—

1

'Mum, Mum, Harry's used my toothbrush again!'

Ellie shook herself awake. The dream had dissolved already but it felt familiar, warm. She hadn't been smothered or drowned, or whatever happened in that nightmare.

'Mum, did you hear what I said? Harry has used my toothbrush again. It's disgusting.'

She propped her head on one arm and listened to the thud of a slamming door. She was usually up before the boys, showered and dressed, Marmite on toast at the ready. But sometimes her middle son Jake beat her to it, and if he was awake, the whole house was too. She smiled and swung her legs out of bed; today's complainant was Toby, her eldest, so that was OK; even Harry knew better than to touch *anything* of Jake's.

She yawned deeply and shuffled to the bathroom. Glancing at her reflection, she raked her auburn hair with slim fingers. It needed its six-weekly trim; she'd make an appointment and drive up the road into Gorton. 'Over the bloody border to Chav Land,' as Cam would say, which was ironic, given that's where he was born.

She leaned further into the mirror and lightly touched the blemish on her cheek. It was barely visible these days, but still felt like a nudge, a reminder of her fortunate life. Her gaze swept over the rest of her face. The pale purple smudges beneath her eyes were evidence of her interrupted night. If only she could capture the dreams like a ghost on celluloid; freeze-frame the snowflakes before they melted. Perhaps then she could exorcise them, lay them to rest, have a whole eight hours' flaming sleep.

'Mum? Mum! Are you coming down? Someone's eaten all the Coco Pops.'

Harry's voice interrupted her thoughts. She groaned at the woman looking back. There was no doubt about it: she resembled a crumpled newspaper. It was time to iron out the creases.

Ellie looked around the doctors' waiting room, willing the latest patient to hurry out. With an indulgent smile, she'd watched a dark-haired little girl play with a bead frame, she'd read all the notices about pregnancy and HIV, and listened to two patients loudly whisper about the 'village oddball' sitting opposite them. As ever, the poor woman was wearing several layers of luminous pink clothing and holding a matching parasol. The open brolly was bad luck, Ellie supposed, but the obvious tittle-tattle about her wasn't on. Besides, she admired her quirkiness. She was once like that herself.

She frowned at the gossips. 'She's eccentric, not deaf,' she wanted to admonish, but she was trying very hard not to say or do anything that might embarrass her son more than he already was. Twenty-six minutes had gone by since they'd arrived. Toby was sitting three seats away from her, as silent and rigid as his hard plastic chair. When she'd attempted to make conversation, his gaze hadn't left the huge digital display that repeatedly reminded them of the importance of immunisation for flu and shingles.

They were here for a rash on his scrotum; no wonder he was grumpy. Remembering yesterday's embarrassment, Ellie winced. Toby had haltingly tried to describe the hives on his groin and she'd casually replied, 'Do you want me to look?', not for a moment expecting him to say yes. But he had, poor boy; no doubt petrified of deformity, leprosy or lice, or one of the other million things twelve-year-olds worry about. Not least, had masturbation caused it, like God's plague or locust wrath?

She hadn't known what to say as she stared. The rash was livid. Toby was nearly a teenager and it was both awkward and unsettling to discover that the nether regions of her firstborn were more man than boy.

Boys and their bollocks were really Cam's department, but he was working away again. 'It's only scrot rot,' he'd said with a snort when he'd finally telephoned late last night. 'All boys get it. Buy some cream from the chemist.'

She had cringed at his typically graphic epithet. Now he tells me, she'd thought. How was she supposed to know about that, or all the other testosterone-related joys of having sons? Ellie loved her boys, but at times they were a mystery. Men were a mystery. Thank goodness she had Mum.

Leaning across to Toby, she had another go. 'Maybe grab the jabs while you're here. "Preparation is all, young man", as Grandad would say,' she mimicked, in her best Maurice voice.

With a hint of a smile, Toby opened his mouth, but his reply was cut short by his name on the screen, shortly followed by the intercom. 'Toby Hastings. Room two, please.'

'We're up. Come on, love.' Ellie stood and covered the cringe with a smile. Oh hell, the announcer was female; she hadn't thought to ask for a man. Hoping she was wrong, she guided Toby to the door, knocked and entered. Oh joy: not only a woman, but young, far younger and prettier than a doctor should be.

'Hello, Toby and Mum. Sorry for keeping you waiting,' she said. 'How can I help you today?'

Pink and sullen when they left the surgery, Toby was still glowering when they arrived at his high school. He made no move to climb out of the car.

'Have a good day. See you later,' Ellie said, unintentionally adopting the sing-song tone of the doctor. Then, trying for a Cam-like chivvy, 'Come on, Toby, it's time for school now. Scrot rot isn't an excuse to stay at home all day.'

'Really? Can't I just—'

'Absolutely not! Get thee to the classroom . . .'

Though she wanted to hold him tightly, she pushed him playfully from his seat. A nasty scrotal rash might not be a reason to hide, but humiliation and embarrassment definitely were; she knew that more than anyone.

Telling herself she'd done 'the right thing', she watched him throw his rucksack over his shoulder and slouch into the glassy entrance. Pat on the back for Eleanor Wilson from Maurice! Her father Maurice, who'd instilled the importance of doing the right flaming thing in the baby, the child and above all the teenage Ellie.

Almost wanting her son to reappear, she stared at the door for several moments. Had she let Toby down? Trying to shake off the discomfort, she pulled the car out, but the journey was cut short by the peal of her mobile. She glanced at the screen, then did another take. Oh hell; it was Mrs Laverne from Jake's primary school. The familiar lurch hit her stomach; at only eleven o'clock in the morning, a buzz from the head teacher was not going to be for a friendly chat.

'Oh, ignore the ancient bat,' Cam often said. 'They'll get rid of her soon.' But *soon* wasn't soon enough. Mrs Laverne, purple perm and patronising intolerance, was there now.

'Have you considered that perhaps a specialist school would be more appropriate for Jake?' she said regularly. But Ellie wanted mainstream for her middle boy, almost as much as Cam did. The psychologist had agreed: 'Jake is at the very lower end of the autistic spectrum,' he'd said. 'He'll have some difficulties during his education, but nothing he can't overcome.'

'Too right,' Cam had responded. 'He's a Hastings! Bloody nanny state.'

Steeling herself for the call, Ellie now sighed. Her sons were indeed 'Hastings', but she wasn't.

She pressed the icon. 'Mrs Laverne. Hello. Is everything—'

'There has been an unfortunate episode with Jacob already,' the woman interrupted.

'Unfortunate episode? Why, what's happened?'

'I'll explain when you're here. I'd like you to come in straight away.'

Her jaw set, Ellie stood at the entrance to Purple Laverne's office. She stared at the plastic stopper that wedged open the door. Did she have the guts to kick it away and give the bloody woman a mouthful? It was fortunate Ellie didn't have a formal job, but these demands to turn up at a moment's notice for some minor Jake misdemeanour were getting ridiculous.

Mrs Laverne peered over her glasses. 'Do sit,' she started crisply. Then she leaned forward and sighed, apparently changing tack. 'Jacob, oh Jacob. What are we going to do with him?'

Ellie had heard that preamble before. In the past she'd made the mistake of asking Laverne what the answer was, and she wasn't going to fall for it again. Sure, Jake had stubborn episodes from time to time, even an occasional tantrum, but they could be resolved if handled properly. His current teacher was brilliant, but sometimes she was ill or on a training day. 'You said there had been "an episode" with Jake this morning?' she asked instead, folding her arms.

The brusqueness returned. 'Attacking another boy. An assault. And I don't use that word lightly. The boy had a nasty red mark on his throat, which the playtime staff can verify.'

Instinctively placing a hand on her cheek, Ellie felt an icy spread. 'An *assault*?' She pulled out the chair and sat. 'I'm so very sorry, Mrs Laverne. Please tell me what happened.'

2

The June evening sunshine lit the study through the slats of the wooden blind. Ellie swung in Cam's leather chair, a large gin and tonic in her hand. She felt vaguely guilty about drinking alone, but reasoned she had little choice with Cam being somewhere in the back of beyond, and it had been a pretty crappy day what with Toby and his scrotum, followed by the set-to with Laverne.

Squinting at the sooty printer, she sighed. She had intended to give the room a spring clean today, but paperwork was everywhere, so where to begin? Though she could've moved the mouldy coffee mugs, she supposed.

She pictured the joyless face of Cam's mother, Jaqueline, who would have clocked the lack of cleaning. The look was familiar, one of indifferent smugness, if the contradiction wasn't a stretch too far. 'For God's sake, call me Jaqs,' she always said, but Ellie struggled to get the pally abbreviation out.

Of course, *Jaqs* was right: Ellie should've tackled it ten days ago when Cam left, but she always felt resentful of his 'office' and stayed out until he was due home.

She glanced around. It didn't take a genius to deduce that Cam and his partner's business was in boxes. Tim had done the lion's share of globetrotting in the past, but his wife had objected eighteen months or so ago. She only had a chihuahua for company and the loneliness made her anxious, so Cam had taken it on. Still, when he was in the UK, he worked from home, so he had more time with the family.

That was the theory, at least.

Ellie took another slug of her gin, savouring its cold warmth before swallowing. The ice catching her throat, she turned to the tall bookcase and looked it up and down. She could fetch a cloth and attack the top layer of dust or ... Yup, idle procrastination was infinitely preferable. Moving a swathe of invoices aside, she climbed on to the desk, reached up to the top and tugged down a couple of sketchbooks. Until noticing them just now, she'd forgotten they were there. Her old oil canvases were stashed in the spare room upstairs, and though she looked at them occasionally, the strange clutch of pleasure and apprehension they evoked always left her unsettled. Blowing off the fine particles, she opened the first one. Fruit. Not just at the start, but dotted throughout the spiral-bound pages, there was an assortment of plump, fleshy produce in pencil, pastels and watercolour. She smiled. Vibrant and bright, the happiness shone from the parchment.

She pulled over the next pad and flicked through the first half. Mostly in graphite and charcoal, this was a darker affair. Avant-garde and experimental, certainly. Stark trees? Empty rivers? A sense of loneliness, loss? Then a more discernible, realist drawing of a girl looking towards a thatched cottage at the top of a hill. It reminded her of something; what was it?

Breathing out her surprise, she sat back. All the creations were good, even when the perspective was just a little skewed. It looked as though she had meant it. Whoever *she* was.

When had she last put pencil to paper? She couldn't remember. Oils were more her thing at university. Trying to think back, she flicked through a few empty sheets. She stopped at the sketch of a still, sleeping baby. Her first born, of course. Toby, precious Toby, her perfect boy; how she'd loved him, still did.

She pictured his hunched shoulders in the car this morning and berated herself yet again. Did he remember to use the prescribed lotion on his 'bits' before bed? She hoped so. She'd hidden a grab bag of Munchies under his pillow to cheer him up, and when he came to say thank you, she'd almost reminded him. But the chocolate had brought a small smile to his face, so she'd thought better of it. The mention of scrot rot was best left until his wedding; Cam was sure to bring it up then. If, of course, Toby ever got married.

Recalling that unique newborn smell, she smoothed her pencil-faced baby with a soft hand, then replaced her artwork where she'd found it. But the cottage picture still bugged her. Ah, that was it! The intricate drawing was a nod to *Christina's World*, the famous mid-nineties painting by Andrew Wyeth. Clever old Ellie, what a talent! The thought of a crippled woman dragging herself up a hill was a little disturbing, though. God knows when she'd drawn it.

When she returned to the chair, the telephone rang.

'How's my beautiful girl?' Cam asked. It's what he always said.

'Not so beautiful today,' she replied. 'And I'm a rotten mother and one of our sons is the new Boston Strangler.'

'Why? What happened?'

'A boy in the year above Jake took his football. Jake chased him, as you'd expect, but then he pulled the boy's hood until he let go.'

Cam guffawed. 'I'd have done the same if my ball was nicked. It's just a bit of rough and tumble; it's what boys do.'

'That's not how Purple Laverne saw it, Cam. The playtime staff said the boy had a red mark on his throat.'

Another laugh. 'Bloody thief. Serves him right. Good old Jakey, that's my boy.'

She sighed. As usual, Cam wasn't really listening; yet in this case Laverne *had* been unfair. The older boy had simply got to the playtime teachers first, the same bloody boy who constantly picked on Jake, taunting him and enjoying the spectacle of Jake 'losing it'.

The real problem, in her view, was that most of the staff had already labelled Jake as trouble, so they never made the effort to find out what had really happened. It was at times like this, when she was called into school and ordered to sit in front of the principal's desk like a naughty schoolgirl, that she wanted to wade in, to find the tormentor and strangle the little git herself. But then she *had* been a naughty schoolgirl once upon a time; more than naughty.

'Eleanor Wilson. Detention again. Whatever happened to that lovely girl we used to know?'

That lovely girl. When did it happen? How had it happened?

Her father, of course.

'Ellie? Are you still there?' Cam's voice brought her back to the sunlit study. 'Look, Jake'll be fine as soon as he sees his dad,' he soothed down the line. 'Don't worry, sweetheart. I'll be home in forty-eight hours. We'll go out, just the two of us, get drunk and have some fun.'

Shaking off the old shudder, she closed her eyes. 'Sounds perfect, Cam. I can't wait.'

3

It was a good start to the day. Ellie had managed to extract all three sons from the house without cajoling, shouting or bribery. They had even walked the length of their sun-dappled Heaton Moor road without the usual Toby–Jake scuffle. Jake didn't like anyone to touch his hair, so of course it was the last thing Toby did before diverting to his bus stop with a smirk.

Now at the school gates, Harry darted ahead and lifted his hand. 'Bye, Mum. Enjoy your Friday piss-up!'

'Why, thank you,' Ellie called back with a smile. She used to wonder what other parents made of her youngest's end-of-week farewell, but being the mother of a strangler, amongst Jake's other felonies, she didn't much care any more. Besides, two of those mums were founder members themselves.

Over thirteen years. How time had flown. She'd met Hen and Nina when they were 'expecting', as her mum always put it, a weekly get-together at their antenatal swimming group. They'd exchanged horror stories of birth, blood and gore while sipping scalding weak tea in flimsy plastic cups (a health and safety risk, surely, looking back) with an obligatory Basics Digestive biscuit. First pregnancies, of course. How would they know they were in labour? Would it hurt? A natural birth or every painkiller offered? How the fuck would they get it out?

Now older and wiser, the conversation at the Friday piss-ups had moved on: teachers (the handsome insomniac Mr W in Year Six), current affairs (just the headlines; Brexit talk banned, obviously), gossip (why was *everyone* living on Poplar Street getting divorced?), partners (sex only on birthdays – his birthday, of course), *Peaky Blinders* (parts had been filmed in Stockport, didn't you know?), all with crudités and wine (no more than two glasses when it was Hen's house. It *was* the afternoon and she had moved six miles away to posh Hale, so one couldn't stagger home).

Spotting Nina's spectacular afro in the distance, Ellie waved. Nina's eldest was four days older than Toby. Baby Faith, pretty and perfect from the moment of birth. From the shape of her bump, indigestion and the speed of his heartbeat, Ellie had just known she'd have a boy (with heartburn hair) and although she would never admit it out loud, she'd been a little jealous of Nina. Though Faith had been more stroppy teenager than sweet angel for a couple of years now, Ellie still secretly wished she'd had a girl somewhere along the line. It always felt as though the daughter she should've had was missing. It wasn't for want of trying: she hadn't gone back on the pill after Harry was born, but nothing had happened. Just as well, really, with Cameron being away so much. Besides, she did love her three boys enormously; she just didn't always understand them.

Letting out a long breath, Ellie finally stepped out from the bustling school corridor. Save for two mums with their prams at the far end of the dusty playground, it was silent and empty. Like a warm massage, relief spread through her shoulders. She'd managed to have a few sensible words with Jake's teacher outside his class-room without Purple Laverne throwing in her two-penn'orth, thank God.

She glanced at her watch. Only ten past nine. The post office and its surly counter staff had to be done first, but there would be enough time for a quick whip around Sainsbury's before driving on to Hen's house.

Hoping Jake would be OK, she shot a last glance at the door before moving on. Royal Mail parcels, then home for a quick splash of mascara and lippy before heading out in the car. It was funny, really, Cam liked her 'done up', but the boys always complained, Harry especially. 'You've got lipstick on,' he'd say accusingly. 'Take it off. You don't look like Mum.'

She shook her head. Just like her father all those years ago. Even when she'd used make-up to look pretty, the disapproval had been there: *Upstairs now, Eleanor. You're not going out of this house with that muck on your face.*

She cringed at the memory of the inevitable spat. And that dis-cordant scraping sound of a key against metal. But that had been much, much later. Why she was thinking about it now, she didn't know. She was off for her Friday piss-up and Cam would be home tomorrow. Today was a good day, after all.

'Ellie? Ellie!'

Though Ellie had already spotted Ciara Walsh and her young-est child ten minutes earlier, the sharp Irish tone behind her was unmistakable.

Looking suitably surprised, she turned. 'Oh, Ciara, hi.'

Not sure whether to air kiss, hug or shake Ciara's hand, she did the safe thing and spoke to the baby. What was this one called? There were so many Walsh kids, it was difficult to recall. 'Look at you! Haven't you grown? I bet you're walking now.'

It was clearly the right thing to say. 'Georgie is indeed. At eleven months to the day like his brothers and sister,' Ciara replied, almost waggling her head with satisfaction. 'And look at these teeth.'

Black-haired like his father, the baby didn't seem the least bit put out to have his mouth inspected by a virtual stranger.

'Wow, fantastic,' Ellie commented. Then, hoping Ciara might take the hint, 'I'd better get to it. I've only popped in for a quick shop before going on to a friend's house.'

Ciara didn't apparently hear; she was too busy scrutinising the contents of Ellie's trolley and, if she wasn't mistaken, sucking in her cheeks.

Good God; which was the offending item? She tried again. 'Nice to see you, Ciara, I'm in a rush so . . .'

Seeming to twig her imminent departure, Ciara turned her cart to face the same direction. Hers was piled high as though a famine was imminent; it was the price of having a million kids, Ellie supposed.

'Oh, a friend's house, did you say?' Ciara asked. 'Who might that be, then? Anyone I know?'

Sighing inwardly, Ellie smiled thinly and moved past the tinned tomatoes. Supermarket shopping on a Friday morning wasn't wise at the best of times and now she was a captive audience for 'Ciara the Pious', as Cam called her, diving in with her usual starter-for-ten.

'Why would you know any of my friends?' she wanted to reply, but she settled for, 'I don't think so.'

Almost feeling guilty, she watched Ciara's sculpted face as it fell. It wasn't unattractive; in fact, her pale, ginger Pre-Raphaelite appearance was rather exquisite. In truth, Ellie had been shocked that Sean Walsh, of all people, had married someone that seemingly pure, but after ten minutes of Ciara's interrogation and opining when they first met, the fragile beauty had dissolved, exposing the rather shrewish woman beneath.

In fairness, Ellie didn't know her that well. Ciara and the family had moved from the outskirts of Dublin to Marple Bridge nine or so months ago, and they hadn't been acquainted before then. Cam had met her; he'd been a guest at her and Sean's wedding and had visited his best mate at least three times a year since. Understandably, their boozy Irish get-togethers were at an inn or a bed and breakfast, away from Sean's home and his brood of noisy kids.

Ellie knew Sean Walsh a little more. Over eighteen years ago now, she'd shared a large Victorian house with him, Cam and others in their third year at the University of Leeds. Number 11 Alston Terrace had been a gathering of oddments, students who'd never met before that final September, but needed somewhere to live. She'd never got to the bottom of Sean's story, but that wasn't surprising. As a long-haired and opinionated philosophy student, he'd barely spoken to her unless he was drunk or high or on a political rant, and when he had, he'd made her feel shallow and uninteresting, a rebellious fraud, so she'd kept her distance.

Ellie now snorted at the memory. Things hadn't changed much: whilst Sean's long hair had been replaced by a dark beard, Ciara did enough talking for them both.

Hoping to shake off his wife and her chatter, she moved briskly along the aisles. What exactly had she come for? Coco Pops for Harry, lager for Cam. And something nice for the boys' tea. What would be a relatively healthy treat? She tried to focus, but Ciara's soft and persistent voice badgered her as they walked.

'Look at the price of those frozen French beans, won't you? We have a lovely little patch in the garden that Sean's dug, so I'll be growing my own like I did back in Dublin. Beans freeze beautifully, but they have to be par-boiled. Did you know that, Ellie? How's Jake getting on at school now? You have to be firm with these principals. They're there to serve you, not the other way around. Mustn't let a little incident or two put you on the back foot. Start as you mean to go on. That's what I'm doing with my children and the teachers alike. I won't be taking any nonsense, I'll tell you . . .'

What the hell? The bloody woman seemed to know a lot about Jake. The heat rising, Ellie stalked on, unsure who had irritated her the most: Ciara for lecturing her on how to handle Purple Laverne *and* her boys, or bloody Cam for obviously discussing it with Sean.

Ciara still hadn't drawn breath by the time they arrived at the checkout. 'So, what are your plans for this weekend, Ellie? I believe Cameron will be back.'

Relieved the quizzing would soon be over, Ellie decided to play nice. 'No plans, really. I think we're going to chill with the boys. It'll just be nice to have Cam home and do nothing.'

'You do know that you're coming to us tomorrow afternoon?' Ciara nodded to the contents of her trolley. 'The barbecue at ours?' She peered at Ellie, her face loaded with sympathy. 'Oh, Ellie, didn't you know? It's all been sorted between Cameron and Sean. Paul and Ruth will be there. Didn't Cameron mention it?'

Deflated and frayed from the overdose of Ciara, Ellie chucked the shopping bags in the boot of her car. Ciara the Pious indeed. Who grows their own flaming veg and freezes it? She'd like to see a set-to between her and Purple Laverne and see who wins. But there had definitely been a look of triumph on her face when she'd mentioned the Marple Bridge gathering.

Bloody typical Cameron, so much for his promises. Just the two of them, eh? He would be walking off the plane tomorrow morning, straight into the arms of his best buddy Sean. Why she always set herself up for the grand romantic reunion, she didn't know.

A police vehicle in the wing mirror caught her short. Sitting stock still, she watched and waited until it passed, then she puffed out a long breath and applied lipstick without censure. Her life was actually hunky-dory. Even better, right now she was off to Hen's for a good old moan.

4

The 'daily' let Ellie into Hen's sprawling Cheshire house. She found her and Nina in the conservatory, which, as Cam always pointed out, was larger than his entire childhood home.

'Hello, darling, do help yourself to wine,' Hen said. 'Just telling Nina about my latest "encounter". So where was I? Ah yes, my new lounge carpet. Very nice Axminster, Ellie. I'll show you in a mo . . . '

The sun warm on her back, Ellie poured a glass of chilled Chablis and sank into the sofa. Like one of Pavlov's dogs, just being here was a kind of therapy. Even now she could feel the tension travelling from her temples to her torso, through her limbs and diffusing through her toes.

'Ellie? Are you with us?' Nina asked. 'You don't want to miss this.' She widened her shiny chestnut eyes. 'The *encounter* was with a carpet fitter-cum-part-time model, no less.'

'Correct.' Hen raised her arched eyebrows. 'I think you both know I don't suffer from shyness when it comes to hunky workmen, but how does one communicate one's desires when there are three men on the job, two of whom are old, ugly or otherwise unacceptable?'

Nina snorted at Hen's dramatic pause. 'You're not really expecting us to answer that, are you?'

Hen sipped her drink. 'One solves the problem by taking off one's knickers, standing over the part-time model, duly busy with his Stanley knife, and asking if there's anything he would like . . .'

Wiping away her tears of laughter, Ellie eventually managed to speak. 'And was there something he'd like?'

Hen pulled a face. 'Shame on you for even asking, young lady.'

Ellie smiled and sat back. What would happen if Edward was ill or popped home early and caught Hen in the act? Not that she'd ask, and besides, she never knew whether Hen's stories were true. She didn't have a job, her successful banker husband worked long hours and her only child, Giles, was now at boarding school. Perhaps Hen lived in a fantasy world because she was bored and lonely.

Suddenly feeling a little sad, Ellie swallowed the flinty alcohol. *Lonely*, she understood. She had supposed she'd get used to Cam's absences, but the sense of loss was there each time. At least she had her lovely mum, Marian, only a forty-minute drive up the motorway near Chorley. And of course Nina and Hen, to whom she could grumble without reproach.

She filled them in about Cam and the Walsh barbecue. 'Of course he didn't mention it,' she complained. 'Typical. Leaving me to find out from Ciara Walsh. It clearly made her day. *And* it's our turn to go to the Hastings' this Sunday. I'm hoping Cam will have forgotten.'

'You were there the other week! Is that a whole month? Why don't you stretch out turns to six monthly? You hate it, Cam hates it . . .'

'Or so he says. But it's that old thing of slagging off your own

21

parents, but not being happy if anyone else does it. And they are his mum and dad, after all, so I have to behave.'

Ellie sighed. She could never decide which was worse: visiting Jaqueline and Stuart Hastings' house in Gorton and witnessing their pained expressions when Cam asked them to puff their cigarettes outside, or them coming to her and Cam's breezy home with its open patio doors and decking for the smokers. Though the strained lunchtime conversation at the former was excruciating, she could make an excuse and escape as soon as the sugary puddings were scoffed. But when they came over the border they stayed, sitting glumly on the sofa with their eyes glued to the television like a scene from *The Royle Family* until Harry's bath time at seven.

Jaqs and Stu hated visiting, clearly. Why did they come so regularly? Why didn't they leave earlier? It was a mystery, as was their relationship with Cam. Instead of applauding his success, his good job and comfortable home, or even praising him in any small way, they seemed to resent it.

Or perhaps it was her, *Nice middle-class Miss Eleanor Wilson*, as she'd been called way back when. They knew she saw them as lacking; it was written all over their faces. How she hated being the daughter of her father, but in truth she couldn't help it.

The genetic grip, she supposed.

She didn't mention *that* to Nina and Hen. She was grateful for her friends, but some things you didn't share, especially those you didn't understand yourself.

The sight burning her nose, Ellie watched Jake walk the length of the playground. Though the other kids congregated, noisy, chatty and joyful, he was alone, his whole bearing slumped. 'Is Dad home yet?' he asked, his first words to her all day.

Not wanting to embarrass him, she hugged him briefly. 'Not yet, but not long to go until tomorrow, love.'

Head down, he shuffled his feet as they waited for his younger brother. The last to emerge, Harry and his best pal burst from the blue door, shoulder to shoulder like Siamese twins. He released Saffi for Ellie, giving her a tight squeeze. The surge of affection was there as always. Happy Harry, so like his dad. Blond-haired, tactile and affectionate; easy-going, compact and sporty. And so easy to love.

Setting off towards home, Ellie laughed. 'You smell of grass, Harry,' she said, ruffling his hair.

Again, just like Cameron. Funny how aromas took you back.

Her memories of university were sometimes sketchy, but their first meeting at Alston Terrace was always clear in her mind. She had hoped the student house would be empty, to slip in as unobtrusively as possible, but there he'd been, lying on the shabby, orange-patterned sofa. Wearing grass-stained shorts and a plaster cast, his crutches were splayed on the threadbare carpet.

The twenty-year-old Cameron Hastings was chirpy and friendly but not particularly inquisitive. If he wondered why the new girl was moving in to number eleven at lunchtime in November, he didn't ask.

'You must be Eleanor Wilson,' he said without looking away from the small television screen. 'The landlord was here earlier, clearing the box room for you.'

'It's Ellie.'

'Not a box room as I know it, though. My bedroom *was* a box. Hello, Ellie. I'm Cameron, Cam to my friends. Sorry about the greasy hair.' He pointed to his leg. 'Showers are a no-no. Baths even worse. Fancy putting the kettle on? I can move, but . . .'

She'd liked him immediately. Though slighter than the boys she'd dated previously, his fair hair and regular features were appealing. Not to mention his relaxed attitude and disarming grin. And he was open, funny, incurious. After half an hour in the draughty lounge, she discovered he should've been in America for the third year of his sports science course, but he'd been stymied by injury, snapping his cruciate ligament when bowling 'like fucking Lillee' for the university team. His second-year housemates had gone to the States, leaving him behind, 'the bloody bastards'.

'I could've stayed in Manchester in my mum's tender loving care, but it wouldn't have been tender or loving. So, it seems I'm going to be a geologist.' That smile again. 'Don't worry; I've been going to lectures for five weeks and I still don't know what that means either. It was the only course with space for a crocked sporting genius.'

Listening to his words, Ellie had thought about her own mum. In all brutal honesty, as much as she loved Marian, her intense watchfulness over the past few weeks at their home in Lancashire had been claustrophobic. 'Perhaps we're both escaping,' she'd replied.

'Yeah, maybe,' Cam answered. He'd switched off the TV and turned with a grin. 'Wait until you meet Sean, Ellie. Now he really *is* a fucking genius!'

5

Seared with a death mask of white cream, Cam's face pops up like a jack-in-a-box, waking Ellie with a petrifying jolt. She flicks back her eyelids, but everything is black and opaque and she knows she is dead, entombed deep in the ground. Moments of terror pass, then reason kicks in, and with a tremendous effort she breaks through to the surface and screams—

A dream, just a dream. Her skin cold with sweat, Ellie carefully reclined, her heart thumping so hard it seemed to jump from her chest like a cartoon character's. God, oh God. Would she have a coronary from this recurring shock and die, really die, one day?

Tears seeped from her eyes. From self-pity and trauma and alarm. But she found them embarrassing too, these night terrors, hypnic jerks or whatever they were. She tried not to cry out when scrabbling from the 'death dream', but sometimes a piercing yelp escaped and one of the boys ran in from his bedroom, desperate to help, but more scared than her.

Cam had long since lost interest.

'What happens, exactly?' he used to ask. She'd found them difficult to describe. It was like layers of dreams, she tried to explain. She'd wake from one terrifying ordeal straight into another – the death dream – and then have to swim or dig out, to break free from the dark sticky depths.

'Like drowning?' he'd asked.

'Yes,' she'd replied. 'I suppose it is. Or perhaps like being buried alive.'

A balmy Saturday morning, all three sons were up and ready, even Toby, who seemed to have gone overnight from a boy who was out of bed and hyper at six in the morning, to a youth who could sleep until noon.

The house felt busy, the atmosphere euphoric. Harry was looping around the park opposite on his bike. At eight, he could just about get away with it, but Ellie felt tolerance was growing thin and that someone would soon point out the churlish 'no cycles allowed' sign at the entrance.

She glanced through the window to check Toby was still on guard. And there he was, her handsome – and surly – eldest son, lolling on the bench near the gate, his ears covered by huge headphones, his current prosthetic.

Jake was still in his bedroom, but that was the norm when there'd been an 'episode' at school. It seemed to knock out all the confidence he'd acquired over the previous tussle-free weeks, making him retreat into himself and stay away from the few friends he had. At least he was busy with his artwork, his head down and beavering away at his desk.

From the array of coloured pencils, crayons and glue, Ellie guessed he was creating a 'welcome home' poster for Cam. She wished Toby would be kinder to him. Toby could handle his middle brother well when he made the effort, but it was apparently

26

more fun winding him up. He tried to taunt Harry, too, but Harry was so chilled, he just shrugged it off.

She sighed. Sibling rivalry and arguments weren't something she'd had to contend with, yet she'd longed to have a brother or a sister when growing up, someone to dilute the intensity of home. Maurice had an older sibling in Canada and her mum's sister, Diana, had no children, so there weren't even any cousins. Just a father devoted to his wife, and the wife doing her best to referee between husband and daughter, who looked strikingly similar, but seemed to have nothing else in common.

Snatching a citrus-honey aroma through the open window, Ellie inhaled deeply and stilled. Magnolias? Or perhaps the hay-like tang was 'Lady's Bedstraw', the name her mum used for the yellow wildflowers. Why floral smells always invoked that broody imperative she'd had after Harry was born, she had no idea.

Pushing the old melancholy away, she spread out the bedding and laughed to herself. Funny how Toby hadn't lifted his face to the heavens and groaned when she mentioned this afternoon's barbecue. He would have complained long and loud had it been any other family without a son his own age. The answer, she was sure, was a girl.

Warmed by the rays shining in, she pictured their first visit to the Walshes last autumn. At the top of a leafy steep hill in Marple Bridge, their new home had surprised her at first glance. A sprawling sixties bungalow in an L shape, with stone cladding and huge windows, it wasn't at all what she'd imagined the left-wing and opinionated Sean Walsh would choose. Then again, he was a professor of psychology now and she hadn't seen him for a very long time, probably not since one of their infrequent conversations in the pub at university, which had always turned into spats.

'So, what's really behind the . . . alternative façade, nice middle-class

27

Miss Eleanor Wilson? Anything more than skin deep? Come on, tell me, I really want to know.'

Skin deep; he'd always said that. How she'd hated it.

'That chip must be weighing you down, Sean.'

Her response was always weak. In the hours that followed, the reply was much better in her mind. The patronising, arrogant bastard. And yes, with a huge bloody chip on his shoulder. But even if she'd tried to shape her thoughts into clever words, she knew he'd still have derided her.

Nineteen years on, those thoughts had still loitered. She'd been tense and on guard when he opened the door.

'Ellie! Nice to see you. Come in. And this must be Jake.' Sean had been affable and smiling, his eyes as green as she remembered, his beard very black. Cam had followed with Harry and Toby, Harry rushing through to investigate somewhere new, Toby standing upright, polite, his 'Grandad face' in place.

'Sean the man. About bloody time you moved closer,' Cam had said with a hug and a grin. 'Let's say hello to the team, then.'

The 'team' had started with fourteen-year-old Katrina, her face free of make-up, her hair severe in a plait, and went down in size through to red-cheeked, curly-haired baby George, slotted on Ciara's hip.

'My Katrina wants to join the Sisterhood as soon as she's of age,' Ciara had announced proudly as though the poor girl wasn't there.

Ellie's gaze had flickered towards Sean's then. Could this really be the same person who would rage for hours about 'insidious Catholicism'? By some instinct she'd then turned to Toby behind her. She'd had to resist taping his mouth closed as he ogled at the teenager.

Coming back to the present, she smiled. Yup, definitely a girl. But there was nothing wrong with a little romance – her good-looking guy would be home very soon. She caught her reflection in the mirror. Pleased to see her own excitement was reflected in her face, she stood closer and swept gentle palms over it. Her freckles were out in full force, camouflaging the slight dent. How she'd hated them when she was younger, trying to hide them under layers of foundation, but she liked them now.

'Your freckles are out,' Cam would say, kissing her nose. 'It's the start of summer.' Of course, they were always there, but she knew what he meant.

The warm spread of anticipation increased. Ellie looked at her watch. If Cam's flight was on schedule, she had time for a coffee and a flick through the newspaper before rounding up the boys and loading them into the car.

Cam was right; it really did feel like the start of summer.

6

The call came just as the kettle popped.

'Ellie!' There was something in the way Cam said it, she later thought, or perhaps it was the absence of the usual Manchester Airport noises, but disappointment hit her chest the moment he spoke.

'Sorry, babe,' he continued. 'I've been in meeting after meeting, so couldn't call before now. A small hiccough with production, so I'll have to stay until tomorrow, maybe Monday. If there was any other way, sweetheart ... Well, you know that. But, hey, just a couple more days until I'm home, three at the most. Makes it all the more sweet. Look, I'm wanted. Phone you in a bit. Oh, and say hi to the Walshes.'

What? Really? Dumb with shock, she didn't speak for a moment. Then the need to yell and ask a million questions set in, but he'd already gone with a 'speak later'.

She glared at the screen. Cam had let her and the boys down dreadfully, and his main concern was for her to say 'hi' to the bloody Walshes? Like hell she would. Outrage replacing dismay, she flung the handset to the table. It skidded and dropped to the ground with a smack. Oh hell, she'd probably broken the damned thing. Did she care? No. Right at this moment she willed it to be smashed into a thousand pieces so she'd never have to speak to Cam again. Silly, she knew, and it would cost her a fortune to replace, but she was so very angry.

Fighting hard not to scream, she rested her head in her palms. Cam had altered plans a few times before and she had accepted it grudgingly. She had no option, after all. Yet this one felt different; like a shadow, there was a nagging concern in her mind that she couldn't quite grasp. And why did he have to wait until the last minute to tell her? Why did he think it was OK to casually move the goalposts, to always put work before the family?

Like a fucking doormat; it felt too, too much like Maurice and her mum.

Without moving, she gazed at the open doors to the decking, waiting for the rage to quell, for her face to clear sufficiently to find the boys and break the news.

'If not for me, then what about your sons?' she wanted to shout. How good it would feel to gather them and say, 'Your dad is a selfish bastard. I didn't want him to work abroad; I asked him not to go. He couldn't wait to escape. The nightmares have got worse since he's gone. He's only ever thought of himself.'

But that would be unfair to them. And, with Jake, wholly unproductive.

Headphones around his neck, Toby sauntered in. 'Mum, shouldn't we be leaving to collect Dad by now?' He jerked at the sight of the phone on the floor. Picking it up, he peered for a second. 'The casing's dented, but it looks OK.' His eyes searched her face. 'Hey, Mum. Are you all right?'

Ellie shook her head. His look of concern had brought a clot of emotion to her throat, preventing her from speaking.

He gave her a quick, tight hug. 'It's OK, Mum, I'm here. You can tell me.'

His attempt to be manly stung her eyes. 'It's nothing to worry about,' she managed, blinking back the tears. She took the proffered mobile. 'That was Dad, I'm afraid he's been—'

The phone abruptly rang, surprising them both. Like a hot potato, Ellie tossed it back to Toby and shook her head. She wasn't ready to talk to Cam again, wouldn't be for a very long time.

'Hello?' Toby asked. And then, politely, 'It's Toby. I'm fine thanks. Yes, I'll put her on,' he said, handing it over.

Who the heck was it? 'Ellie speaking . . .'

'It's Sean,' a voice said. 'I'm just checking about today.'

Still fuming, Ellie couldn't help herself: 'Cameron isn't coming home today and as far as I'm concerned, he can stay in Stockholm or Copenhagen, or wherever he is,' she said crisply. 'So, thank you so much for the kind invitation, but no we won't be coming. Oh, and don't pretend you didn't know, Sean. You can do me a favour and fuck off too.'

She threw the mobile again, but more gently this time, into Toby's lap. A wave of hilarity struck. She'd regressed years, but it felt strangely liberating.

Suddenly anxious, she glanced at her son. For a beat he looked astonished, then he started to laugh, a deep belly chortle. A moment later, she joined in.

'Sorry, Toby,' she said after blowing her nose. 'I know it was funny, but I was bang out of order.'

'It's OK, Mum. I guess Dad isn't coming home yet.'

Looking at him carefully, she nodded. She hoped her behaviour hadn't damaged him somehow. She and Cam rarely argued, and certainly not in front of the boys. Cam dodged, charmed and evaded; she silently fumed; that's how it worked.

Mostly, at least.

'And my language . . .'

Toby rolled his eyes. 'Words I've *never* heard before, Mum.'

She smiled a small smile. 'Yes, but still.'

A recollection abruptly surfaced, one from university she'd all but forgotten. Bloody Sean Walsh in her box bedroom. Blithely raking through her paintings without permission. She had told him to fuck off that day too.

'So what's the plan, Mum? Do you want me to tell Jake?'

'Sorry, love?' Shaking herself back, she focused. Perhaps it was the loneliness, but she increasingly found herself in dreamland. From seconds to minutes, lost in thought and forgotten memories.

'Oh yes, Jake, poor Jake. No, it's fine, thanks. I'll tell him.'

She reached for Toby's hand and gave it a squeeze. 'Psychotic mother over. Let's have a drink, give it twenty minutes, then I'll go to Jake with a peace offering. Shall I take chocolate or chocolate? Talking of which, where's Harry?'

Toby grinned. 'Where do you think?'

His fingers and clothes gloopy with droppings, wispy fur and sawdust, Harry had been 'cleaning' out the rabbit hutch.

Even as Ellie scrubbed his dirty nails at the utility tap, it was hard to be cross. 'I know you're trying to help, love, but how many times, Harry? Not with bare hands! Right, clothes off, but leave them in here so I can give them a soak.'

At the bottom of the stairs, she took a deep breath. She had swilled the worst of the bunny dirt off Harry's arms and hands at the outdoor tap. He'd laughed as the icy water sprayed his face and his T-shirt; he'd shrugged at the news about Cam. If only her middle son was that easy.

She tapped on Jake's door and poked her head in, but the room was empty. Her heart already sinking, she took in the smell of adhesive and stepped in further. The collage of the word 'DAD'

33

was propped on his desk. Created from paper he'd clearly coloured himself, the scraps had been cut the same size, shaped and glued with precision.

Though she didn't turn, she knew her boy was behind her. His breathing shallow and fast, she could feel his excitement, his tense anticipation. She rotated slowly. His face was expectant, so heart-rendingly keen. 'Jake, that is so beautiful. Dad will absolutely love it, but—'

The ping of the doorbell cut in. Not now. Who was it? But before she took stock, Jake had flown from the room, his footsteps pounding the stairs.

The sound of Toby's chatter flew up, followed by a man's. For one glorious moment she thought it was Cam, that the earlier call had been some sort of wind-up, but as she reached the top of the landing, she realised it wasn't his voice, but the Irish timbre of Sean Walsh.

Shit and how embarrassing, were the first thoughts that came to mind, rapidly followed by the idea of hiding, which was truly pathetic. She peered down to the hallway. Toby and Harry looking on, Sean was crouched in front of Jake, quietly talking to him.

Alarm and self-consciousness swamped Ellie's cheeks and her chest, hell, her whole bloody body. Hoping it didn't show, she crept down towards them.

'Jake?' she asked. 'Is everything OK?'

Her son turned, but the agitation and upset she expected to see were absent from his face. Instead, his eyes were bright, his breathless words rushing out. 'Sean says that Dad can't come home today, but that if you don't mind we can go in his new car and have a sleep-over at the Walshes' tonight.' Then after a moment. 'It's an Audi Q7.'

Four pairs of eyes looked expectantly at Ellie. Bloody hell, Sean was still a clever bastard. But she reluctantly acknowledged he had handled Jake and the Cam situation very well. From her peripheral vision she could see Toby studying her with interest.

'Well, seeing as it's an *Audi Q7*. And if Sean and Ciara don't mind . . .'

The boys cheered and scattered, leaving her with no option but to look at Sean.

For an iota he gazed, those green eyes thoughtful. Then he smiled and seemed to blink the intensity away. 'It goes without saying that you're invited too, Ellie. The burgers and sausages are already cooking, with The Judge in charge.' He lifted his dark eyebrows. 'And you'll remember his culinary skills. Or lack of them. So speed is the thing.'

Accepting defeat with as much grace as she could muster, she nodded. 'Thank you, Sean. That sounds nice. I think I'll give the sleep-over a miss, though. I'm sure my offspring will have more fun without me keeping the evils on them. Just give me two minutes to grab my things.'

Her heart clattering her ribs, she searched for her shoes. Sean and Ellie. The Irish Beast and Miss Eleanor Wilson. Polite and civilised.

And so very surreal.

7

Bashful and exposed, Ellie climbed into the front of Sean's SUV. It wasn't just her ridiculous outburst on the telephone; sitting next to a man she'd only recently met after so many years felt both intimate and scary. Of course she knew Sean Walsh, the one with opinions and mocking eyes, the oracle who'd have his followers mesmerised with his rants, his dogma and erudite philosophies of life, none more so than Cam. But this Sean seemed different; still darkly attractive, still dangerous and hidden somehow, but kind too. She'd never thought of him as a caring person and it threw her. She preferred people to conform to type, so she knew what to expect. Like Cameron: charming and easy-going, but not always a great listener. Or her contained but affectionate mum. Even her intolerant dad: he might be dictatorial at times, but at least she got what was written on the tin. And he wasn't that bad; he was almost a little proud of her these days.

Berating herself for being so feeble, she pulled on her seat belt and tried for a smile. The old Sean had fenced with her undoubtedly; he'd derided her for being middle class; he'd tried to dig into her past. But was that really the reason she'd avoided him all these years? She shook the discomfort away. The sensation was similar to déjà vu, that was all; like a small earth tremor, the ground slightly shifting. Everyone experienced it sometimes, she was sure.

Harry's fretful voice interrupted her thoughts. 'The gate! Mum, the gate: it's open.'

'It'll be fine, love. No one will notice.'

'But the big rabbits are out, Mum. I can see Bubbles right now.'

'Not those *goddamn rabbits* again,' Toby said through the side of his mouth, mimicking his dad.

'Not funny,' Harry yelped. 'I'm going to—'

'Stay there, love.' Ellie could hear the wobble in her youngest's voice. A bunny death was the one thing he would not take lightly.

Keys in hand, she sprang from the car and ran up the path, through the porch and front door, belting across the kitchen to the patio, then down the decking steps. Checking Harry's 'goddamn rabbits' were still in the garden, she locked the gate and returned, all without breathing, or so it felt.

Panting, embarrassed and hot, she shuffled back into the car. 'Bunnies all accounted for – shame I can't say the same for my new tender fuchsia,' she managed. She turned to Harry's pink face. 'Panic over, love.' Then to Sean, 'Sorry about that. Let's hope the sausages aren't completely incinerated . . .'

The two brown and white rabbits had recently become eight, a surprise for them all, and rather seasonal, as Harry had discovered the babies hidden deep in straw and rabbit fur on Easter Sunday. He'd been mortified at first. 'But two boys can't have babies! How has this happened?'

She had glared at Toby meaningfully, but Jake was first to answer, surprisingly knowledgeable about same-sex couples. 'Gay people have babies all the time,' he'd said. 'The men have to adopt because they can't grow them. The woman can, but they need to go to a sperm bank.'

'Like a sperm whale?' Harry's eyes had been like saucers. 'You're joking? In a *bank*?'

Cameron had been away then, too – Easter bloody Sunday, of all days. She hadn't questioned it at the time, but as she squinted through the windscreen, it occurred to her that it was odd. Was Easter Day still Easter Day throughout Europe and if so, who would be trading boxes around a Bank Holiday?

'Ellie?' Sean's voice made her jump. 'You seem far away. Is everything OK?'

She nodded, forcing herself back to the present and the sound of bickering behind her: each son was clearly blaming the other for the open back gate. She thought of intervening, but the pull of anxiety was too strong. Both hot and goose-pimpled, she turned away and gazed through the passenger window. As the terraces and tatty shops morphed into pretty cottages and shades of green, the sense of movement and uncertainty increased, churning in her stomach.

Oh God, oh God. Had she been blind?

The moment the SUV was parked nose-to-tree on the Walshes' steep driveway, the boys stopped squabbling, thrust open the doors and scrambled out.

'You need good brakes here,' Ellie commented, sensing she should finally say something. 'But then there's the cherry tree to stop it running into the ...' She glanced at Sean, who was regarding her with a slight frown. 'Thanks for the lift. Can I join you in a minute?'

He stroked his beard. 'Sure,' he said after a moment. 'See you inside.'

Lowering her head, she tried to steady her breathing. Her heart was still racing, or was it her mind? Ridiculous, surely. For the last fifteen minutes her thoughts had been galloping in circles, trying to jump hurdles but falling each time, then starting again from the beginning, a cycle of stress and panic, prompted by flaming rabbits, of all things. But those babies were born on Easter Day, for God's sake. Cam wasn't home at *Easter*. What did that mean?

She inhaled deeply, but the rally started again. Who had decided Cam should work away from home? Did he swap with Tim by choice? No, it was Susie's demand. She'd suffered from anxiety with only her yappy dog for company. Cam hadn't wanted to do it; he preferred to be in the UK. That's what he always said. And yet, and yet ... Hadn't she once heard Tim thank him for volunteering.

Staring blankly at the late blossom, she felt an urgent impulse to go home, to inspect her desk diary and chart all the days Cam had worked away over the last year, just to see what it looked like. She'd believed him, she'd trusted him; she'd been so blasé with her absolute faith that she hadn't known where he was at any given time. Well, not exactly. Country, yes; town, maybe; hotel, rarely. They kept in touch by mobile, by text and FaceTime. She hadn't needed the name and number of a hotel, she hadn't required chapter and verse. And even now, there was nothing to make her suspicious, nothing but a motion, like a doorway breezing open, which was silly.

She was being stupid, that was all.

But why had Sean studied her so intently? Did he know something?

The sound of footsteps broke through, so she jerked up her head. Not Sean, but the lumbering form of Paul, dipping under the branches with a grin. That was right – Ciara had mentioned him and Ruth in the supermarket yesterday. But yesterday Ellie had been too irritated to listen properly; yesterday seemed a long time ago. Sean had spoken of him too, hadn't he? But it was difficult to focus; her mind was elsewhere, in dreamland. The rug being pulled, a dizzy sensation, like fainting.

Focusing her attention on Paul, she couldn't help smiling. Because he'd studied law and looked like one, they had named him 'The Judge' at university. Now resembling something between a butcher's assistant and an overgrown bridesmaid, he was squinting into the passenger window. Of course; he was in charge of the barbecue food.

He opened the car door like a concierge. 'Ellie, my favourite girl, you're here at last. Let me ravish you before Ruth catches up with me.'

Relieved to be back on solid ground, Ellie beamed. If she could have chosen someone to be her dad, it would've been The Judge. Or perhaps as a playful uncle. He'd been avuncular for as long as she'd known him, offering his broad shoulder more than once during that final year at university. For weeps of sadness, of frustration. And confusion.

About Cam, always Cam.

She climbed out and plucked the halo of pink blooms from his hair. Wrapping her arms around his striped apron, she held him tightly and cleared the emotional lump from her throat. 'I believe you're in charge of sausages,' she said into his chest. 'Should we be worried?'

He laughed. 'Put it this way: one hopes you like them *bien cuit.*' Then pulling away and lightly frowning, 'Something tells me you need a drink.'

She studied his affable face. The red flush on his hairline betrayed a few glasses of wine. An eloquent anecdote was sure soon to pop out. When they'd still lived in Alston Terrace, she and Cam had once slipped into the public gallery of the law courts in Leeds to watch him perform a mock trial, hoping to distract him with loud sighs, throat clearing and coughing. They had watched him give his long speech, then a break, a pulse of time as he adjusted his gown or his wig, before moving on, point made. It was very effective.

As if on cue, Ruth appeared. Wearing her sensible doctor's shoes, she held forth a tall glass topped with lemon and ice.

'Did someone say "drink"?' she asked in her gravelly Glaswegian. Without spilling a drop, she kissed Ellie on both cheeks and linked arms. 'Come and tell me all the gossip before Paul over-excites himself. Where on earth is dear Cam?'

8

Rocking gently on the hammock at the top, Ellie sipped her icy drink. The undulating lawn sloped down to a stream where the children had congregated in thin T-shirts and shorts, holding buckets and nets. All except Jake, who was swinging on a tyre tied by thick rope to a tree, apparently talking to himself.

The fragrant breeze swept her face as she listened to Ruth chat. Squashed in an old-fashioned stripy deckchair, the doc was describing the highlights of her working week. The sensible shoes had been discarded, revealing her plump, perfect toes.

'She makes an appointment each Tuesday morning at ten,' she was saying. 'We have a five-minute natter about what she's watched on the TV, then off she goes. Loneliness. It's worse than illness in some ways ... ' She knocked back the gin. 'A reminder to go home and see my old folk more. They won't always be here; we need to be kind.'

Her usual mix of parental emotions needling, Ellie nodded. She liked Ruth and her straight-talking ways. Get-togethers with the Walshes were a new thing for them all, but she and Cam socialised with Ruth and Paul fairly regularly, theatre trips or meals in pricey bistros. Their wedding had been a couple of years previously, second time round for them both. Ruth had worn a lemon trouser suit rather than a dress, and the ceremony had been at a Register Office, but still it had rankled.

Other people's weddings always did.

Cam had chuckled when the newly married couple posed for photographs. Paul was as tall as she was small; Ruth was as fat as he was thin. 'Look, a perfect fit.'

'Like Jack Sprat,' Ellie had replied, the niggle still there.

Ruth's voice now brought her back. 'Poor Robbie hasn't been himself this week; not that I blame him; who wants to diet . . .'

Ruth and Paul had no children, by choice. Taking into account the astonishing girth of their three basset hounds, it was probably just as well. 'Devoted, gentle, tenacious; friendly, sweet-tempered, affectionate,' Paul always said, straight-faced, when the dogs were mentioned. 'And that's just Ruth on a bad day.'

Closing her eyes, Ellie drifted. It was funny how the world seemed a better place after two stiff gin and tonics made Dr Ruth-style: 'For medicinal purposes, of course!' as she'd say. She smiled to herself. She'd been drinking gin when Cameron Hastings reappeared in her life after a twenty-month hiatus. Hoping double measures would buoy up the dreary conversation with BB (Boring Brett), she'd been on her second or third in a Manchester wine bar when Cam materialised.

A fellow student on her teacher training course, BB had been overly intense about military history. In fairness to him, the topic had been less pasty after a few drinks, which he'd always pay for; he'd driven her from door to door and wasn't bad-looking either. But on that particular evening, Cam had strolled in with a bunch of other noisy business types. His hair shorter and spikier, he was wearing a sharp suit.

'Bloody hell, Ellie Wilson,' he'd said, his grin immediate and exuberant. 'I hardly recognise you. Where did you go? You just disappeared, cleared out of the house without telling any of us. You bloody broke my heart, you did. Unbelievable, seeing you here. I come in all the time with the lads. Serendipity or what?'

He'd sat down next to Ellie and talked, the very same Cam she'd never stopped loving. Upbeat and chatty, he dished all the gossip: Sylvie was pregnant and Raj's family still didn't know. Sean had gone back to Ireland for a Master's in psychology. The Judge had been to 'Barrister's school' in London but was looking for a pupilage locally, and he himself was in 'piss easy' recruitment, but not for long. He had something up his sleeve, needed to get away from his mum and dad, who were driving him nuts.

Brett left the bar at some point, but Ellie didn't notice. Cam's friends teased loudly about Cam and his superpowers with 'yet another bloody woman', but Ellie didn't hear. Her black-and-white life had unexpectedly been filled with colour again.

'Look at you, you're stunning. Your hair! Wow, it's copper, it's beautiful. You're beautiful. I'd almost forgotten.' He'd laughed, his face open and handsome and joyous. 'This is meant to be, Ellie. I'm telling you, it's fucking serendipity! Come here, kiss me. Promise you'll never run away again.'

The fond memory now blurred. A perfect fit. They were the perfect fit.

They still were, weren't they?

With a sudden lurch like a ship, she sat forward. Ruth was still talking from her chair, but when she snapped her head to the rope swing, it was empty.

'Did Jake go down to the stream?' she asked.

'I'm not sure; I wasn't . . .'

Sudden fear setting in, Ellie slid from the cushions. Focusing on the slatted steps by the water, she began to pelt down.

'Ellie, hey.' A firm hand caught her elbow. 'It's fine. He's over there. Look.'

She followed the direction of Sean's arm. A black-and-white cat curled in his lap, Jake was sitting cross-legged by the shed on the other side of the garden.

'Next door's moggy,' Sean said. Then after a moment, still looking at Jake, 'Are you all right, Ellie?'

Stumped for words, she gazed at her son and didn't reply. She could smell the sandalwood aroma of Sean's deodorant or aftershave, and the damp from the grass was seeping through her toes, but she couldn't shape her sudden panic into sound.

As though realising he was still holding it, Sean abruptly released her arm. Then he turned to face her. 'Everything OK, Ellie?' he asked again.

'Of course,' she replied, embarrassed at the query, discomforted by his close proximity and that curious gaze with those same green eyes.

'OK; it's just, you seem a little . . .'

Alarm spreading, Ellie stepped back. *Please don't ask questions I don't know the answer to,* she wanted to reply, but she was saved by Paul, who was trotting towards them, his speed building as though he might not stop.

'I know you're irresistible to womankind, Sean, but you can't have Ellie,' he laughed, overshooting. Finally coming to a stop, he loped back up the hill. 'Ellie and I are virtually betrothed – she promised me a second-chance offer in two thousand and one.' Putting his hand to his chest, he caught his breath. 'I have been sent by the lady of the house to gather the guests. I'm giving Ellie and Ruth the heads-up before the locusts descend on my sausages. As the greatest chefs say . . ."grub's up".'

45

9

Sean didn't speak to her again through the long afternoon. Ellie helped dry his kids as well as her own with rough outdoor-dried towels; she made sure shredded lettuce was included in their hot dogs or burgers with at least one cherry tomato; she sat with Paul and Ruth and listened to their comical banter; she even managed polite chat with Ciara in the kitchen and helped with the coffees.

The children soon dispersed and the adults retired to the high decking, drinking chilled wine and chatting through the long afternoon.

'Mum?' She heard the call but didn't register her son's voice for a moment. 'Mum! Mum!'

Holding a large can, Harry was below in the garden, his saturated top stuck to his skinny chest. 'I fell in the stream, I'm freezing. But I did catch a tiddler. Come and look.'

As if by magic, Ciara appeared at the patio doors. 'I've got it,' she called, running back into the house and returning with a bath sheet. She disappeared again, her voice on the breeze. 'A clean outfit is on its way.'

'Good catch, Harry,' Ellie said, inspecting the tiny fish, then wrapping him in the towel.

Reappearing with clothes, Ciara tutted and took over. Almost mesmerised, Ellie watched another woman briskly strip, dry and re-dress her boy in a too-small Thomas the Tank Engine T-shirt and shorts. It felt like a reflection of her fears. And the worst was that Harry didn't mind; her Cam-like son simply shrugged it off and sauntered back whence he'd come.

Relief spread through Ellie's shoulders when she finally glanced at her watch. She'd evaded those searching eyes, and it was a reasonable time to escape and go home. She slipped away to the loo, then pulled out her mobile in the cool hallway to search for an Uber.

'No need for a taxi, Ellie.' Sean made her jump. 'I can drive you; I'm going near you anyway.'

Wanting to hide the anxious flush, she stared at her phone. 'Oh, thanks, but that's fine. I'm sure there'll be a cab somewhere fairly near.' Then, lifting her head and trying for normality, 'Even here in the flipping sticks. Besides, I'm sure we've all had too much to drink.'

Folding his arms, he leaned back with a quizzical frown. 'I gave up the booze a long time ago.'

The hot blush increased. 'Oh right, sorry; not thinking straight.'

Had Cam told her this? She doubted it; Sean Walsh without a narcotic of some sort, she *would* have remembered. And there it was again, that disorientation, the world at an angle.

She came back to him. Despite his dark beard, his jaw was clearly tight. She'd offended him and she really didn't want to. Covering her agitation, she smiled. 'It's beyond the call of duty when you've already fed and watered us all, but if you're going out anyway, a lift would be great, thanks.'

*

Lit by the evening sunshine, Ellie gazed at the hills, trees and rooftops as they sped towards Stockport. Not knowing what to say, she said nothing, and besides, the silence felt safer. Conversation was dangerous, like then in the hallway.

So Sean didn't drink; why had Cam never told her? And what about all those boozy weekends away at Sean's place in Ireland, at a pub or bed and breakfast, or wherever Cam had allegedly stayed?

No, she didn't want to talk; talking would open a can of insidious worm-words.

She glanced at Sean's hands on the steering wheel. He was as quiet as her; what was he thinking? And who was he, really? He didn't seem to bear any resemblance to the man who'd slept in a bedroom opposite hers. Weed, whiskey and women had seemed to be his raison d'être back then. Road to Damascus, or what? Pious wife and even more saintly daughter, a hundred kids, no alcohol and those strangely kind eyes.

A thought slapped. Oh God, was it *pity*? Did he know something about Cam that she didn't?

Her heart galloped again. Don't let him speak. Do not let him speak. If he did he'd say something she did not want to know.

Trying to rationalise the sense of danger, she stared through the window and wished the old Sean Walsh back. That brought a small inward smile. What the hell was wrong with her? At times, she'd detested that man.

Get out and fuck off.

Yes, she remembered *that* clearly. She had hated resorting to expletives rather than expressing herself cleverly like he did, but sometimes swearwords hit the spot. Momentarily, at least.

Her afternoon art lecture had been cancelled and she'd returned early to Alston Terrace to find him in her bedroom, his long mane tied back. Holding up a canvas, he was examining it closely.

He didn't flinch or turn when she cleared her throat noisily.

'Why are you so angry?' he asked instead, holding up the black-and-white abstract to the light.

'Well, funnily enough, I'm never particularly delighted when someone thinks it's OK to come into my bedroom and have a nosy at my stuff.'

He glanced at her. 'I meant all these paintings.'

'I'm not and they're not and anyway, it's none of your business.'

He put the canvas down. Holding her breath, she followed the movement of his dark head as he scrutinised her meagre possessions. The poster of Johnny Cash giving the finger, the box of tampons on the dressing table, the card in a heart shape from her mum; the unmade single bed, Cam's trainers on the floor.

'So, what did you want?' she asked, finally breaking the silence. Fearful he might tell her something she didn't want to hear, she willed him to leave.

'Looking for Cam. Thought that he might be in here. He usually is.'

'Oh, are you jealous?'

The moment the words were out, she knew how preposterous they sounded. He and Cam had all-night sessions, drunk on whiskey and debate. If the 'Irish Beast' clicked his fingers, Cam would dance; the other housemates, too. And occasionally, when she'd interrupted them mid-bottle, the room would fall silent and she'd just know from Sean's artful glance that he'd warned Cam off her for no other reason than spite. And there he was in her box room, gazing for a beat, then laughing. She'd never seen him like that before. It was almost worse than his verbal disparagement.

'Oh, fuck off, Sean,' she'd snapped. 'Get out and fuck off.'

'Ellie?' The echo of his voice tugged her back to today. His car was parked outside the house; he was looking at her quizzically. 'It's none of my business, but . . . Something's bothering you. What is it?' he asked.

49

That old guffaw of disdain was fresh in her mind. And the strange power he still had over Cam. She opened the door, glad of the cool breeze. 'Nothing. Really. I'm fine. Thanks for the lift.'

'You seem—'

She inhaled deeply. Did she want to yell or to sob on his shoulder? Neither would do. 'Look, Sean, I know you mean well, but we don't really know each other, so . . .' God, she hated the quiver in her throat.

He smiled. 'I think I know you a little.'

'For a few months, last year of uni. A long time ago. So . . .'

He seemed thoughtful. 'You never came to visit. With Cam, to Ireland. I thought you might.'

It was true, she hadn't. She really hadn't wanted to; but then again, had Cam ever asked her along?

Feeling emotional and tipsy, she shook her head. She wanted to sleep, to escape from this surreal little drama. She swung her legs from the car, but Sean touched her arm. 'If it's Jake, I can help. I'm lecturing full time now, but child behaviour is one of my areas, so feel free to ask. And Cam being . . .'

Unable to speak, she nodded and climbed out. Keeping her face averted, she strode to the porch and opened her handbag. Scrabbling for her keys, her fingers finally touched metal.

The door relenting, she stepped into the hall and let out her trapped breath. Cam being *what*? What, exactly, was Sean going to say?

10

Registering the lack of bumps, bangs and banter, Ellie stretched her legs and yawned. It was Sunday, that was why; even Harry had a little lie-in these days. Protecting her eyes from the bright glare through the window, she sat up and peered at her mobile. Ten o'clock. What? She fell back. Of course; the boys were at the Walshes' for their sleep-over and . . .

She groaned at the memory. Sean in the car and her irrational paranoia. What the hell had been wrong with her? She'd come into the house, had another stiff gin and that had done the trick, thank God: blissful unconsciousness until . . .

Snapping upright, she listened: the muffled sound of singing from the shower.

She let out a long breath. That was right. Waking from deep sleep in the night, she'd gradually become aware of movement, a slamming car door and voices outside. Though she couldn't explain why, the noises had brought on a spread of icy fear, and despite an urgent need to pee, she'd forced herself into a child-like cocoon of sleep, not surfacing again until Cam pulled back the duvet.

All had been fine; the clatter, the *danger* had been him, arriving home in a taxi. Time must have passed, but at some point he'd been there in the bed, slipping his arms around her waist and kissing the back of her neck. She would've normally turned over and welcomed him home, however briefly, but this time had been different. She'd found her pulse racing. Suddenly anxious he might smell different, she hadn't wanted him to get close. So she'd feigned unconsciousness, which inevitably hadn't come, as Cam's breathing had slowed into light snoring.

Typical Cam with his 'innocent sleep'. Soothing away all worries. And now morning was here, her suspicions seemed stupid. No, more than that; they were pretty damn ludicrous.

Drying his hair with a towel, the man himself walked into the bedroom. 'What are you smiling at, young lady?' he asked.

Ellie pulled up her knees and chuckled. Just like Harry, Cam had no shame. 'The curtains are open and you are, to use your own delicate phrase, stark bollock naked, Cam.'

Confidence, she supposed. Cam was born sanguine, happy with his lot. Except, perhaps, with his mum and dad. They were the only people who could really rile him, especially when Jaqs harped on about other people's achievements.

'More interested in fucking television than me,' Cam would snap. But then again, sometimes he and his parents laughed – easy communal laughter – which always took Ellie by surprise.

'I see you've had all your business meetings around the pool,' she said, trying for lighthearted, but noticing the tan on Cam's chest, arms and legs in comparison to his pale bum.

The rope burns on his back from a sailing accident were still visible too. Another foreign 'work' adventure he'd relayed with a grin.

'Have to treat the locals to my budgie smugglers,' he replied easily. He raked back his hair. 'Right, I'm here and I'm all yours. What do you fancy? Your wish is my command.'

Despite the residual unease, Ellie laughed. At times Cam was so open and childlike, it was difficult to be cross with him for long. Besides, he was clean, toned and handsome, as golden as the sunlit room and clearly ready for action.

Cameron Hastings was the glue of the oddment house. Funny and friendly, always up for a laugh, he was rarely moody. And if he was, he'd animatedly talk through whatever was bugging him with whoever happened to be there in the old-fangled kitchen or the draughty lounge, before laughing: 'You look fucking bored! Don't blame you; I'm bored of it, too. Let's go to the pub.'

He was also generous, the pints flowing, never appearing to notice whose round it was next.

'Hey!' Ellie would exclaim. 'Cam bought the last ones. It's your turn,' to anyone who took advantage.

'Cam's feisty little foot soldier,' Sean would remark, if he deigned to speak to her at all. 'But she's right, Cam. You paid the last time.'

But Cam would shrug. Till the grant runs out. Life's too short. What goes around, comes around . . .

Ellie was hopeful during that run-up to Christmas, confident even, that Cam would ask her out. Not that people *asked* anyone out, they 'got together'. But she and Cam were already a couple in a way. He was tactile with everyone in the house, but he spent most of his time with her in the box room, lying on her single bed, his arm draped around her shoulders, listening to music, chatting, eating, sleeping.

Easy, safe, undemanding.

'No, listen again, Ellie. That riff. Makes the hairs on my neck stand up,' or, 'Write this down quickly. Pure poetry,' or, 'I'm knackered, wake me up when it's Christmas.'

And sometimes they'd kiss, soft delicious kisses that never went further.

For a long time it was frustrating. Ellie knew she was attractive, underneath the heavy make-up, at least.

'What a delightful face! Those red curls! Those freckles! That perfect button nose!'

Eleanor Wilson had spent a whole childhood hearing people in the butcher's, the newsagent's or Spar comment on how pretty she was. It had carried on at high school, the compliments shrugged away like water and a duck. Ignored because it didn't *mean* anything to her.

Being sweet-looking hadn't helped her feel beautiful inside.

Finally escaping to university, she'd dyed her hair a different colour every other week, worn bright make-up, quirky shoes and kooky clothes. But in the third year she stuck to black; ebony hair, inky lipstick, dark kohl around her eyes. Yet still head-turning and slim, surely? Other students wanted her; she only wanted Cam. He liked her, she knew. It was just a matter of time . . .

'Come on, share with the class, Cam,' Sylvie said one evening in the chaotic kitchen. Raj had cooked a delicious Middle Eastern dish for them all. 'What's Ellie got that I haven't?'

Her heart thrashing, Ellie looked up quizzically from her food. It seemed an odd question; Sylvie had her own bedroom, but shared a bed with Raj. His family were in the throes of arranging his marriage to a girl from a 'good family'. Not that Sylvie wasn't from such a family herself, if the landed gentry counted as 'good', a suggestion hotly contested when the Irish Beast was on song.

'I used to get the Cam cuddles before you arrived, Ellie,' Sylvie explained. 'He forgot where his own bedroom was.'

'Didn't Raj mind?' she asked, hot and embarrassed as she glanced at Cam.

'God, not at all. We thought it was a "Mummy" thing going on. And we're not talking Egyptian.'

Cam threw a piece of chapatti at Sylvie. 'The meds talking crap again.' But his voice was relaxed, he was smiling.

With a suitably assiduous expression, The Judge sat forward. 'I rather think I might have a *Mummy thing* if Sylvie or Ellie would be so kind . . . '

Cam slapped his back and laughed. 'Come on, girls, The Judge was sent away to boarding-school borstal at the age of three; this man really does have a *Mummy* thing. Who's up for some charity cuddles?'

The Judge stroked his chin theatrically. 'And perhaps one could mention it to the Irish Beast's bevy of endless cast-offs, too.'

'OK, Mission from Mars, people, is to get The Judge laid before Christmas.'

Everyone laughed except Ellie. Just pals, then, she thought. But she didn't believe it. A pipe dream born of love was still firmly there. Hope, cheeriness and optimism; as plump, wholesome and shiny as the fruit she was painting.

She just needed to be patient.

Ellie and Cam ate breakfast in companionable silence, hers a seeded bagel, his Lurpak on toast.

'God, I miss proper butter,' he sighed as he flicked through the newspaper.

Chewing her food, Ellie gazed at him. It was strange, just the two of them at the table. A couple more days, he'd said on the telephone yesterday. She didn't ask, 'Is butter all you miss when you're away?' She didn't want to enquire why he'd come home so much sooner.

His eyes still on the sports page, he absently picked up another slice. He buttered it lightly, then added some jam, a dab from the end of his knife between bites.

'Is this what you eat each morning when you're away?' she wanted to say.

A silly question, she knew. The whole family went on holidays, really nice breaks to all-inclusive hotels in Turkey and Greece. They ate breakfast together. Sometimes Cam went for the full Turkish, sometimes cereal, sometimes pastries. Why the hell did it matter?

It *mattered* because she suddenly needed to know what Cam did when he was without her. Was he on his own? Did he sunbathe by himself around a busy pool? Eat alone, sleep alone?

The need to be a fly on the wall of those hotels was suddenly inexorable. But what she might discover left her breathless.

Inhaling deeply, she waited for the nausea to pass. Here was Cameron, her partner and lover, relaxed in their breezy kitchen, smiling and easy, home a day or two earlier than she'd thought. She should be pleased; life should be grand. But why was that voice still there in her head? Recurrent; unremitting.

Have I been blind? *Have I been blind?*

11

The alarm woke Ellie at seven thirty as usual. 'What day is it?' she asked, still groggy with thick sleep.

Cam sprang from the bed. 'Friday,' he replied.

'God, so it is. How on earth did that happen?' Time just flew when Cam was at home.

He kissed her nose. 'No idea, but you can lie in. In fact, I insist. I'm fed up of bloody paperwork, so I'm in charge today. Boys, breakfast and supermarket.' He grinned. 'Maybe I'll get lucky and bump into the delectable Ciara.'

Ellie obediently stayed under the covers, but as the minutes passed by, her ears were finely tuned to the noise: the sound of three boys still in the house at eight twenty when Toby's bus left the main road at ten past.

Knowing better than to interfere, she flopped back against the pillow. She didn't like to be late for anything and had to dampen the flare of irritation when it looked as though time was slipping, even though it was another thing she had hated about her dad when growing up. His military precision was legendary.

'Where the hell are you, Marian?'

'I'm here, Maurice, I'm here!'

Ellie's paternal grandfather had died when she was a baby. It was all his fault, apparently. But he *had* been a Military Man, so had an excuse.

Perhaps it was in the genes – a worrying thought that she had too often. Had she acquired the worst of both parents' foibles? Military precision and red flipping hair. Though perhaps that wasn't fair; the ginger gene did come from Marian's side of the family, but her arty talents came from there too.

She tied a mental knot to phone her mum later. She had been incarcerated in Woodlands, the family home, by Maurice for years, but she'd broken free at sixty to work part time, running her own craft stall in an 'antique village' not far from where they lived in Chorley. Thanks to Ellie, the business was now online too, selling the artwork as well as DIY greetings card sets, personalised gift wrap and birthday banners created by her at Jake's desk. Every now and then she contributed a still life of flowers or a landscape watercolour to the booth, but it was done to a formula of what people liked to see, rather than the dark layered abstracts she used to create during her pregnancies. Her friends had strange cravings for food – sweet, salty, spicy and sour – but hers was to put paintbrush to canvas. God knows why, though. It always made her feel unaccountably sad.

She glanced again at her watch. Eight thirty-one. Toby's school assembly started at eight forty. *Jack Sprat*, she mused, fighting the urge to jump up and intervene downstairs. A burst of conversation flew up. Hadn't they gone yet? Bloody hell; sometimes it was easier when Cam was away. But then the front door slammed and as she reached the window, all three boys were climbing into Cam's car. Laughing, of course.

What to do with her unexpected free hour? Last night's horrible dream tumbled back and she shivered. Action was the thing; it stopped stupid, dark thoughts. She strode to the bathroom and picked up Cam's abandoned clothes from the floor, glad the urge to sniff them for evidence of *something* had passed. Batting that concern away, she replaced it with another. The supermarket. How would Cameron fare this time?

'Do you want a list, love?' she'd casually asked when he mentioned it last night.

'Absolutely not,' he'd replied.

Expensive slabs of rump steak and oven chips were guaranteed, together with a host of miscellaneous foods that took his fancy. She chuckled to herself. Him bumping into Ciara might be a good thing; her *pious* inspection of his trolley might induce him to add a vegetable or two, even salad. The kitchen cupboard was still chocka with winsome jars. Anchovies and a pot of Picanto peppers stuffed with olives had been the highlights last time.

But Ellie didn't quarrel about Cam's occasional indiscriminate shopping sprees; she never argued about anything money-related. Not any more. There had been the once, just the once, when Cam had 'lost it', a shocking spurt of disproportionate anger, coming from nowhere. He'd arrived home from Waitrose with carrier bags loaded with inappropriate food for the boys, who were still very young, and she'd grumbled about him wasting money on items they'd never eat. He had slowly turned, his fists clenched, his neck a livid red, his face unrecognisable.

'Who the fuck pays for everything?' he'd roared in her face. 'I do and don't you ever forget it.'

12

Giving a friendly Airedale terrier a wide berth, Ellie continued to jog steadily. She'd already done her twice-weekly quota through the multifarious streets of the Heaton Hills, but a third could only be a good thing, especially on a Friday.

Now on the home straight, she felt re-energised. If only she could bottle this endorphin high at the final line of one run and take a swig at the beginning of the next, to remind herself of how good it felt. Like being heroically patient with Jake when he was having an outburst. Like sex when she really couldn't be bothered. Like the motorway drive to see her mum and dad. It was always worth the effort in the end.

As though practising for a selfie, Hen was sucking in her cheeks and rearranging her glossy hair in the porch glass when Ellie reached the gate.

'Hen! Am I late or are you early?' she called, leaning against the wall to catch her breath.

Hen turned and flashed a very white smile. 'I thought I might catch Cam in the house on his own and seduce him with my special charms,' she replied. Then, squinting at Ellie, 'Only joking, Ellie. Husbands of close friends are embargoed. You know that.'

Ellie unlocked the house door, her thought inevitable: Cam wasn't her husband. She kicked off her trainers in the hall. 'Would you, though, Hen, if Cameron wasn't mine?'

'You know I can't answer that. You'll be offended if I don't fancy him, offended if I do.' Hen frowned. 'A strange question, Ellie. Are you OK?'

Ellie's mind flittered to Sean Walsh's green eyes. They were hiding something, she was sure. Going back to Hen, she snorted. 'I'll answer that when I've inspected the results of Cam's trolley dash. I'm bracing myself for sugared almonds and capers again. Probably in the same jar. He's been out since eight thirty, so he'll be back any minute and you can have first dibs. Be a love and put the kettle on while I have a quick shower.'

Early afternoon drifted by, but Cam wasn't back 'any minute'. Even the distraction of Nina's gossip didn't stop Ellie watching the kitchen clock.

Was this a new thing, checking the hour, monitoring Cam's comings and goings? Or had it always been there, subliminally?

She sipped her wine and shifted in her seat. She rarely remembered her dreams, but last night's nightmare was still fresh, uncomfortable and raw: though she'd been blinded by a shower of snow-like feathers, someone wishing her harm had been there. She'd known it was Cam, the hatred of him burning in her chest. 'I hate you! I hate you! I hate you!' But the words hadn't come; she'd been dumb. She'd tried to strike out, kicking and punching and scratching, but nothing would touch him, he'd been just out of reach. 'Cameron! You bastard, don't walk away!' had pulsed in her head. Then he'd turned. It wasn't him, after all; it was her dad.

As if on cue, the front door finally groaned. Ellie glanced at the time: it was nearly bloody three.

Shouldering through, Cam appeared with four carriers and a grin. He slung the shopping on the work surface, pulled out a chair and thumped down.

'Who has started their periods?' he asked, helping himself to the wine. 'Surely not you, Nina, you look far too young.'

Nina shook her head, but her dark cheeks were flushed. 'Stop earwigging, Cam. Leroy does it all the time and it drives me mad because he only gets half the story and thinks he knows it all. Faith has started her periods, since you ask. This very morning.' She lifted her eyebrows. 'I know, Cam, that does make me worryingly old. Having a daughter of child-bearing age.'

He laughed. 'Bloody hell. Wish I hadn't asked.'

'She had already bought some tampons for when it happened, can you believe? I wasn't allowed to use them until I was eighteen in case they broke my virginity.'

Hen yawned and stretched. 'I lost mine on my sixteenth birthday to an uncle,' she said. 'Don't look so shocked, Ellie. He wasn't a real uncle, just a friend of my father's, and besides I wanted to do it. Don't you remember how randy you were at that age? I just couldn't wait to see what it would feel like. Sexual intercourse! And a close-up of a penis, of course. He was a rather overweight professor of something with bad breath, as I recall, but there was no one else available at the time. That was the problem with being the vicar's daughter: people assumed I was chaste and devout.' She shrugged and nodded at the bags. 'What have you bought, Cam? Flowers, if not a large bottle of gin for Ellie, one hopes.'

Taking a deep breath, Ellie finally spoke. 'Where have you been all day, Cam?'

He put his hands behind his head, rocked back in his chair and smiled broadly.

'Have a guess. Here's a clue. A little excursion to Oxford Road.' His eyes amused, he cocked an eyebrow. 'The university?' he added.

Trying to hold in her agitation, Ellie smiled at her friends. 'See what I have to put up with? Thirty-nine going on five. I've no idea, Cam ...'

'Professor Walsh, of course! Went to see the man in action.' He chuckled. 'It took me bloody ages to find his department, so I was late and had to sit on the front row like a swat. He was awesome, as you'd expect.'

Ellie tried not to gape. 'You attended one of Sean's lectures? Is that allowed?'

'Who's Sean?' Hen asked.

'Best mate. Genius, professor of psychology, father of six,' Cam replied.

Remembering yesterday's telephone conversation with Sean, Ellie looked at her hands. He'd called to speak to Cam, but he'd said, 'Ellie, before you get him ... Sorry if I ... the other day. I just care, that's all. For Cam, for you and the kids.'

She'd felt afraid and vulnerable and didn't know why. *Please leave me alone,* she'd wanted to say, but instead she'd simply thanked him and gone to find Cam.

She reverted to Hen's incredulous face. 'Six? Who in their right mind has *six*? Ah, I know. He must be the guy married to Ciara, the baby-making machine. So, what does he look like, this Professor Sean? Not overweight with bad breath? I might regress. Can we meet him?' she asked.

Cam rubbed his hands. 'You certainly can. I'm going to arrange a big bash for my fortieth next year. A huge fuck-off party for everyone. Assuming I reach forty, of course. What does Sean look like, Ellie? You describe him to Hen.'

But Ellie's mind had strayed, a blast of memory from the past. Periods. Aged twelve or thirteen, she'd started them on a Sunday and in those days most shops near their home were closed. They'd had to find the emergency chemist in the 'back of beyond' and her mum hadn't driven in those days, so she'd asked Maurice to take them. Midway through the *Sunday Telegraph*, he'd grumbled, irritated at having his peaceful routine disturbed.

She could remember her anger, even now. It had been a seminal day in her life. She'd been anxious, embarrassed, confused by the unexpected blood, and all he'd cared about was his flaming newspaper.

She'd lifted her chin. 'Then I'll ask Aunty Diana. She'll take me,' she'd said.

'Don't be ridiculous, Eleanor,' her father had snapped. 'Why on earth would you say that? We haven't seen her for ages. We don't even know where she's gone to this time.'

Ellie now absently turned her wine glass. She hadn't thought of Diana for years. The young Eleanor hadn't known her particularly well, but Aunty Diana's occasional visits had been cheery and fun, like it was Ellie's birthday whenever they'd landed. She'd loved that, of course, but it was more the *idea* of her that appealed – the exotic actress aunty who'd run away from home to join a touring theatre company when she was only sixteen.

Whenever her arguments with Maurice had become overwhelming, it was Diana she'd thought of. Eleanor Wilson could get away if she'd really wanted.

She pulled herself back to Cam and her friends. They were looking at her expectantly, waiting for a reply. Warm, loving faces. 'Sorry, what was the question?' she asked. Then, catching the clock, 'Heavens, look at the time, Nina. We'd better hurry or we'll be late for school.'

Throwing back the last of her wine, she breathed and smiled.

There was no need to escape. Not any more.

13

Hearing a noise, Ellie wakes with a start. A dull shaft is sneaking through a crack in the cherry curtains, creating a white stripe across her pink duvet. She lifts a skinny arm, moving it to and fro until it catches the light, then she peers at her watch. Her mum tells her to take it off at bedtime, but she still loves her new Timex, she doesn't want to be parted from it. She needs a pee, but she's too tired and too snug to get out of bed. Careful not to move into a cold patch, she turns and crosses her legs.

And there it is again: sound, movements, whispering. Then suddenly her father's voice, harsh and angry in the dark: 'You're drunk and you're embarrassing yourself. This has to stop!'

The reverberation of the front door; silence.

Squeezing her eyes shut, Ellie wills herself back to sleep. But she can't escape the wretched keen of quiet sobbing—

Another eight days of June had passed.

'Do you need any help, love?' Marian called from the dining room.

'No thanks, Mum. Everything's under control. Start helping yourselves to the veg.'

Sunday lunch at Ellie's roast-scented home. As taught by Marian, she was making gravy from the juices of the beef and the vegetable water, adding a little stock mixed with cornflower and plenty of salt and pepper. Though salt, like sugar, was deemed bad for you these days.

'It'll be like butter. Back in favour in a couple of years. Mark my words,' Maurice had said, before adding that a sprinkling of paprika on top of the prawn cocktail starter would've 'brought out the flavour more effectively'.

Lowering the heat, Ellie stirred the sauce, smoothing the lumps with the back of a wooden spoon. Wishing Cam was there to do the same with the conversation, she sighed. She'd had a lifetime of *marking* her father's words, and had no idea how her mum coped with someone who had to be right about everything, all the time.

Maurice excelled at being error-free. His wealthy clients were always full of lavish praise about his wise words and financial advice, his recommendations about certain investments, his warnings about others. Or so he repeated ad nauseam. Even now, Ellie could hear him regaling Toby with a detailed story about the excellent capital gains tax advice he'd given to so and so, and how pleased so and so had been. Cam would've listened because he was interested in making and saving money, but Toby was only twelve and Maurice was alienating him, just as he'd distanced Ellie at the same age. Like her, she could sense Toby was nearly there, on the precipice of saying, 'I disagree. You're boring. There are other points of view than just yours.'

She poured the glossy *jus* into a white china boat, a thank-you present from Nina for having Faith and her little brother Noah for a long weekend.

'Oh, Nina, you shouldn't have. It was no effort at all,' she'd declared. But in truth it hadn't been easy looking after five children under twelve years of age for a whole weekend. How on earth did Ciara Walsh manage to do it and still appear so serene and composed? She couldn't imagine why anyone would want six kids, though a little girl to make four would have been nice.

Finally shouldering the oak door, Ellie brought in the last tureen and sat down. Harry was the first to the potatoes, piling six or seven golden 'roasties' on his plate.

'Jakey was sleepwalking last night,' he announced. 'He came into my room looking like a dead mummy. It gave me the creeps.'

Toby snatched the serving bowl. 'You're only a kid, Harry, don't take them all.' Then, when he'd counted his to make sure he had more, 'Jake the zombie? Yeah, I've seen him too. Biter, walker, rotter—'

'No, I'm not,' Jake retorted. 'That's a lie! Tell them it's a lie, Mum.'

Rubbing Jake's hand, Marian finally spoke. 'Your mum used to sleepwalk when she was little,' she said with a soft smile. 'So, even if it is true, love, it's not so bad, is it?'

Surprised, Ellie turned to her mum's placid face. Well, that was news to her. She knew she was too brash, too shy, too loud; too quiet, too fat or too thin, but somnambulism made a change.

Her *military precision* dad, of course: even when she'd done well in tests or exams at school, he'd always make the point that she could have tried harder and 'excelled', comparing her to the daughters of his clients, who were inevitably brighter than her, or so it had felt. And each time there had been the add-on: 'Don't forget I'm paying for your education, Eleanor. On top of my taxes.'

She continued to gaze at her mum thoughtfully. Neat and trim at sixty-five, she seemed happier now than she'd ever been, but she was still subservient to her husband. Ellie didn't get it; she didn't understand why her mother put up with being patronised, even bullied at times, when she was such a bright and assertive woman in other aspects of her life. She loved her very much, but couldn't help the dregs of resentment for her failure to protect her only child from Maurice's all too frequent put-downs.

A memory resurfaced: *'What utter poppycock!'*

How old was she then? Seven or eight? Sitting on the top stair at Woodlands in her pyjamas, listening to the adult conversation float up from the lounge. It was Aunty Diana's warm and husky voice, of course: *'What utter poppycock! She's a wonderful, bright and undeniably beautiful child. You're very lucky to have her.'*

Ellie didn't catch her father's complaint that night, but she thought about it often during the following days and weeks, as ever imagining the worst.

He was now ensconced in the carver chair at the head of the table. Still handsome and distinguished, with a thatch of silver hair, he was talking amiably to Harry about cricket. He seemed to have a soft spot for her youngest, but perhaps that wasn't surprising. From the moment Cameron shook his hand, Maurice had been approving.

'Hold on to this one, Eleanor. He'll be good for you,' he'd said.

Well, that was one thing she'd managed to do right.

Back then she had wondered if he'd still be of the same mind when he met Cam's mum and dad from 'over the border'. A parental get-together before their wedding, she'd thought, a meal out in Manchester or even at Cam's tiny flat, because that's what people did, didn't they? But that never happened. No wedding, no christenings, no reason for their paths to cross.

The parents did meet eventually, at Toby's insistence. 'Can't I have a party with both grandads there? Everyone else does.' So the grandparents became acquainted in their perfumed summer garden. Jaqs wore a too-tight white mini-dress and an ankle bracelet, Stuart donned shorts with a garish Hawaiian shirt. And her mum and dad? Wearing linen trousers and smart navy jackets, they almost matched.

The two couples had stood in a foursome on the patio. Ignoring the clamour of children ducking and diving with water bottles, bats and lunch boxes, Stuart sipped Pimm's and Jaqs listened to Maurice's stories with a hand on his arm; Marian threw back her head and laughed at Stuart's jokes. All four of them unrecognisable, like people Ellie had never met.

As though sitting on the top stair at Woodlands, she watched them from the decking, those strangers. That old sensation of childhood alienation had swamped her, but Cam had appeared and put his arms around her waist. 'Bloody hell, they get on. Who would've thought?'

Cameron Hastings, her saviour.

'Hitler Youth. Tell me, Toby, why would you want to—'

Maurice's loud voice snapped her back from her memories. Her father was scowling and shaking his head. ' — look like a member of the *Hitler-Jugend*?'

'Maurice, I don't think that's appropriate—'

'The National Front, then, Marian. Why would a young and educated man want to look like that?'

Ellie turned to her eldest and glanced at his hair. Her fault really; she'd heard the humming sound of Cam's shaver from her en-suite bathroom, but thoughts of *that* rash had stopped her from investigating further. When the door finally opened, she'd tried not to gape. The patchy number-two cut clearly wasn't the result Toby had intended.

'You've just missed a bit at the back,' she'd said. Then, when she'd tried her best to even it up, 'Looks great, Toby.' But she had noticed Maurice inspecting it from time to time throughout the meal and knew a comment would be inevitable.

'What's the National Front?' Toby asked, apparent sullenness masking the hurt.

Her father's rant was immediate: Good God, didn't Toby know anything? What on earth *did* they teach children at school these days? Today's youth clearly spent too much time watching television and computers, playing with gadgets and bloody mobile telephones. Didn't Toby read newspapers, and if not, why not?

The tirade went on until Ellie interjected. 'I think you'll find they call it the English Defence League these days, Dad.'

The gathering went rapidly downhill. Being described as a thug and a hooligan by his own grandfather clearly riled Toby, and his surliness was replaced with a determination to disagree with every one of Maurice's pronouncements. Secretly proud of her son, Ellie glanced at her mum, who gave a small smile in return, but the ruddy exasperation on her father's face grew. Worried that he might actually combust, she thought of intervening, but the tension was abruptly broken by the rattle of the front door.

It was Cam.

'Something smells good.' Carrying an airport plastic bag, he breezed in. 'Marian! Maurice! How nice to see you both looking so well.'

He kissed Ellie on the cheek. 'Looks like I arrived in the nick of time,' he whispered.

Breathing in his patchouli-infused aftershave, she smiled. 'You have indeed.'

'Impressive buzz cut, son.' He lifted his offering. 'Come on, Toby, don't look so glum. I've arrived bearing gifts. Chocolate for you boys and perfume for Mum—'

'Not Toblerone again,' the boys grumbled, almost in unison.

Cam pulled out a chair and sat down. 'OK, what's left for me? Harry, give me your plate and I'll have your broccoli. Jake, I bet you can't finish that last roast potato. Is there any meat left, love?

So, Maurice, tell me all your news.'

The atmosphere calmed, Ellie focused on her Sunday table. The gravy boat was empty, the dishes almost clean. Cam looked tired, unusually so, but he was chatting to Maurice and Harry, and Marian was nodding, listening intently to Jake.

She nudged Toby with a smile. His face was pale and tight; she knew he was still angry.

'*You adored Grandad Wilson at seven*,' she wanted to say. '*He and Grandad Hastings were the most important guests on your party list. Give him a break*.'

But she'd adored Maurice too, at seven, at eight, even later, constantly trying to please him. But failing, always failing.

Absently stroking the scar on her cheek, she looked at her father. Where did she go wrong? She no longer felt sad about it, but it was a question she posed inwardly each time she saw him.

14

Ellie gazed at the dappled light on the ceiling. It was dancing in time with a soft breeze puffing through the curtains. Today's plan had been a day out in central Manchester with Hen. Mooching about the fashion stores, popping into Harvey Nicks and Selfridges, no doubt, then lunch at a patisserie in Spinningfields and possibly a matinee at The Royal Exchange if tickets were available. But Hen had called to cancel last night. Poorly, she'd said, which was worrying and surprising as she was usually hardy, loath to 'surrender' to illness of any kind.

'You go anyway,' Cam had said, earwigging as usual. 'Spend some dosh. Have fun. I've got tons of invoices to sort out tomorrow, so I won't be much company at home.'

'I might just do that,' she'd replied. It had seemed a good idea and she'd even thought of inviting her mum, seeing as it was her 'free Monday', but on reflection this morning, the suggestion of shopping was Hen's, not hers. She fancied the notion of busy silence and companionable solitude. The prospect of not having to make the effort of conversation with anyone was seductive, and she knew just the place.

Pleased with her scheme, she watched Cam's sleeping face for a few moments, then she slipped out of bed.

Still chirpy despite Toby's exit with a grunt and a slam, Ellie studied her other two sons. She wasn't sure which was worse: Jake's 'bed hair', which he generally refused to comb, or Harry's Mohican, which, like Tilikum's dorsal fin, was on the verge of collapse from too many layers of gel.

'I don't know why you bother,' Cam always said when she pulled out the hairbrush like a weapon. 'When they start fancying girls, they'll brush it or cut it all off.' Which, Ellie supposed after Sunday's shearing episode, meant that Toby fancied girls. Though she knew that already, didn't she? Sean Walsh's devout daughter.

Pushing *that* thought away, she reverted to Jake's frizzy mop.

'Seeing as it's photographs today, would you be a love and give your hair a good comb through?' she asked, lifting the brush hopefully rather than brandishing it. Then, glancing at her youngest and knowing there was nothing she could do about his melting middle so close to school time, 'And can you keep an eye on Harry, collect him from his classroom as soon as they call out your name?'

Flaming school portraits. How would the session pan out this time? Last year she'd stupidly looked forward to a photograph of her three boys together, but Toby forgot to collect Harry from his classroom, which unsettled Jake, and they missed their five-minute slot. She didn't find out until weeks later when all the other mums congregated in the playground to inspect their offsprings' proofs. She asked Toby where his were and the story tumbled out of Jake's mouth, the relief of finally confessing so apparent that it negated any desire on her part to reprimand him or his brothers.

She sighed at the memory. Jake didn't like to be snapped at the best of times, but he seemed to like the big brother role, so maybe, just maybe, everything would be fine.

Smiling at the image of Jake's neatly styled quiff, Ellie walked from the school gates to the stop, pleased a bus appeared moments after her. Hen would've been appalled at the idea of rubbing shoulders with the 'ghastly public', but she quite liked steady bus travel. So long as it was after the early rush of workers, its methodical reliability appealed. Today there seemed to be a glut of students, though, their rucksacks and bumbags taking up more than their fair share of space.

Why didn't they go upstairs? She always had, watching the world go by as the double-decker trundled from the university art department towards Alston Terrace, the excitement and anticipation of seeing Cam already building in her chest or churning in her stomach. Often mixed with confusion and exasperation, too. She'd never suffered from unrequited love before. Not with a boy, anyway. Indeed, the reverse was true. She'd dated plenty of guys, but never for long, finishing with them quickly and without remorse as soon as they got even remotely possessive, which made the Cam situation so much worse.

As the bus did its thing, Ellie watched the world go by. Despite the pronounced shudder through the seats, it was nice to spend twenty minutes staring through the smeared windows at the dusty antique shops in Levenshulme, the billowing market stalls in Longsight, the milling people and busy traffic, but seeing nothing. She liked these periods of nothingness. They allowed her mind to ramble and roam without the constant noise of her boys when they were there, or the oppressive silence when they weren't.

Would the school picture be an improvement on the portrait commissioned by her mum as a surprise for Cam's last birthday? The photographer was a friend of Marian's, but Toby had still looked sullen, Harry's hair had been sticking up (unintentionally, at age seven) and his eyes had been half closed. And Jake? Well, he hadn't looked anything like Jake.

Maybe that's what he looked like to strangers. Perhaps we all appeared differently to how we imagined ourselves.

Like Sean bloody Walsh. Back in their student days, she once emerged from the toilet after a pee in the dead of night. Sleepy and adrift, she walked headlong into him. She'd already been fearful about leaving her bedroom and couldn't explain why, so she was almost relieved when he flicked on a light. She began to walk away, but he called out her name. Thinking she'd dropped something, she turned. He stared without comment before stepping into the bathroom.

'What?' she demanded.

He turned to her; an intense gaze for a beat. 'I wanted to see what you really looked like,' he replied.

She tried to push the memory away. But it wasn't just him, was it? Didn't she once tell a college pal that she'd gone to an acquaintance's wedding, even though she didn't want to, because she felt that she should, because she'd been asked and it was the right thing to do. 'Oh,' she had replied, taken aback, 'I didn't think you did anything you didn't want to, Ellie.'

She'd been hurt and surprised. Her friend had seen something that Ellie couldn't see herself. The idea of it was disturbing.

As the bus crawled and vibrated towards town, her mind drifted again. Sean had been called the 'Irish Beast' at uni. She could picture him as he was now – thick dark hair, a beard and those steady green eyes she still couldn't interpret – but could no longer grasp the Sean he'd been, or perhaps the Sean she *thought* he'd been. And Cameron Hastings. Was Cam still Cam? Had his aftershave always smelled of patchouli?

15

Away from the town centre and down Oxford Road, the second bus was almost an adventure. Stopping opposite the giant statue of Edward VII, Ellie thanked the driver and climbed off. She was surprised to see how many supermarkets had sprung up. Talk about competition. Netto and Aldi, Tesco and Morrisons. Unlike her uni days, students here were clearly spoilt for choice.

She smiled at the thought of the Alston Terrace corner shop. Bread, milk and vodka at extortionate prices. She'd survived on baked beans and toast in those days, the odd Mars Bar thrown in as a treat. Cam and Paul had been pretty much the same, unless Raj and Sylvie had leftovers, which The Judge commandeered on the grounds that he hadn't tasted 'exotic food' until he was eighteen. And Sean? She couldn't remember what he ate – he was rarely in the kitchen, fed at the house of whichever girl he was 'with' that particular week, and sometimes Cam was invited too.

Searching for any change to its exterior since the renovation, Ellie now studied the large red-brick building as she waited for the lights to change. Though she hadn't visited for some time, the

Whitworth was her favourite local gallery. She loved the spacious, high-ceilinged exhibition rooms in the Victorian building. But even better, it was set in Whitworth Park, which made it feel magnificent and stately, yet warm and inviting too. Like a huge conservatory, the light and sunshine shone in through its large windows, making eyes human, giving art the gift of life.

Her gaze swept over the handsome façade as she crossed. Reaching the gate, she spotted a grey bird on a corner turret. Squinting, she leaned in. Not a peregrine falcon, surely? More likely an overfed pigeon, and there were plenty of them. Like a floating feather, she tried to grasp at a bird memory, but she couldn't quite catch it. So deep in thought, the tart ping of a bell didn't register until the bicycle had swerved to avoid her.

Jolting with shock, she stepped back. Then, realising she was on the cycle path, 'I'm so sorry,' she said, putting her hand to her mouth. 'I did hear a sound, but not until . . .'

Though the cyclist hadn't fallen off completely, her bike was still between her legs and skewed to one side.

'I'm so sorry,' Ellie repeated. She steadied the handles as the girl stepped off. 'Are you OK? Not grazed or bumped or anything?'

Dark-haired and pretty, the girl shook her head. 'No, I'm fine. I was stopping here anyway.' She narrowed her eyes and her forehead creased lightly. 'How about you? Are you OK?'

Knowing she must have looked crazy as she gawped at a bird, Ellie smiled wryly. 'I was in a dreamland. But yes, thank you, I'm fine. Apart from trying to topple people off their bikes, of course.' Then, trying to bat away that familiar sense of unbalance, 'You don't sound as though you're from here. A student?'

The girl grinned, a perfect even smile. 'Yeah. A long way from home but I adore Manchester. People say your uni town's like a first love.'

'True, but for me it was . . .' Ellie frowned. Leeds, bloody Leeds.

She was already spending too much time there in her head. 'Well, I'll let you lock up your bike.' Then, feeling she'd been too abrupt, 'I haven't been here for ages. I believe there's a new place to eat. Are you just looking around or—'

The girl flushed deeply. 'Meeting a friend, actually.'

'Well, have fun.' Ellie touched her slim arm. 'Sorry again. Glad you're still in one piece. I'll bring a pedestrian L-plate next time . . .'

Batting away the disquiet of another déjà vu daydream, she entered the cool building and selected a brochure from the reception table. 'Fall in Love Again', it was titled. Looking forward to reading it on the journey home, she slipped it into her bag.

Remembering the old café, she looked to the right. It had been replaced by two neat shops opposite each other. She strolled around the first, selecting small items for the boys: watercolour pencils for Jake, a writing pad for Toby, a pencil case for Harry.

'Please tell me you're not buying them junk again,' she heard in her head. Cam, of course, despite his own propensities. But Jake would use the crayons and she could hardly buy just one child a present. Besides, she had that lighthearted festive feeling of 'time out' and she wanted to share it. Like when the boys returned from their summer-term trips, their bright, loaded eyes belying the nonchalant shrug as they handed over a pencil sharpener or rubber from Alton Towers or Chester Zoo.

The thought made her pause. She remembered that, too, didn't she? Buying holiday lavender or lilac for her mum?

Almost smelling the memory, Ellie paid for the goodies and headed to the belly of the building. Discordant sounds bounced off the walls. She popped her head into the textile gallery. Parents sat on beanbags with toddlers on their knees, bashing triangles and drums, ferociously shaking a tambourine or a rattle. Happy noise, undoubtedly, but not the stillness she craved.

She side-stepped to a room on the left; this was more like it. A sparsely filled gallery with a small number of contemporary pieces labelled 'new acquisitions'. Her footsteps echoing, she moved from display to display, gazing approvingly at the oil of a Minotaur for several minutes, then almost laughing at 'twin canvases' – two Masonite sticks cemented to one canvas and the gluey marks where they'd been removed on the other. Even she didn't see the art in that.

'Most art is like the bloody Emperor's new clothes,' she remembered from long ago. *'But yours is good, Ellie, really good.'*

Heading towards silence, she moved on. A panelled walkway took her to the glass café. It had been built on a wing jutting into the park since last she was here. Inhaling the aroma of coffee, she was tempted to stop, but instead she glanced at the menu for later, then squared back along a parallel corridor to examine a wall of black-and-white prints by a 'society photographer'.

'Fucking parasites,' she could hear. *'Taking up a whole wall. Bloody nepotism. Who would be interested if the photographer wasn't a member of the fucking upper class?'*

Climbing a short flight of stairs, she reached a mezzanine level, heading with interest to a garden-type scene. It took her back to a childhood image of Woodlands – her dad's white handkerchiefs pegged on the washing line, surrendering to the trees beyond the greenhouse. She took a step closer. No hankies today, but a display of pencil, watercolour and charcoal artwork hung on thin metal cables.

Making a note to suggest a similar arrangement to her mum, she retraced her steps to the portrait gallery. Breathing in the familiar smoky scent of the room, she studied her favourite self-portrait, the ravaged head appearing from a deep abyss of black paint. Self-loathing, she'd always thought, and today was no different. It still resonated, still chimed. Squeezing out unhappiness through a tube of black oils; she understood that.

Wishing she could caress them, she followed the wall, gazing at each image, lost in awe and pleasure. And anticipation, somehow. She could do this if she wanted to. The escape was sublime.

Taking another staircase, she popped into a bright gallery of art from the sixties. Selecting a brochure from a metal pocket, it took a moment to work out which panel was which, but as she examined the first set of prints, her stomach rumbled so loudly a man next to her turned. God, she was starving, more than ready for a panini in the café downstairs. She stuffed the pamphlet in her bag, but stilled at a sound. Not just speech, but a distinctive voice. Really? It couldn't be. Spinning round, she stared. It was him, just a few metres away. His back turned, he was studying a huge canvas, his arm casually slung over the shoulders of a slim woman with long hair.

Her mind disbelieving, she ogled for a second. Then she recovered herself, quickly snapping back to the pop art she'd already seen. After a few moments, she stole another look. Laughing, grinning and pointing to the painting, he pulled the woman closer.

There was no mistaking it was him. Happy, relaxed and smiling. But as the woman pulled away and kissed his cheek, the realisation was immediate: the girl on the bicycle. Young, too young. An undergraduate, she'd said. And how she'd flushed with pleasure when she mentioned she was meeting a friend.

Twenty at most and clearly one of Professor Walsh's students.

A wave of sheer disappointment hit. Sean Walsh, married father of six, was having an affair with one of his charges. How horribly predictable. Not able to tear her eyes away, she gazed at the young woman. So pretty and fresh with that stunning white smile; too like herself at that age, the smooth-skinned Ellie before she was branded.

Turning away, she caught her reflection in a painting. Nearly forty and she looked it. Why wouldn't Sean be tempted by a younger woman? More to the point, why wouldn't Cam?

Her chest seething with anxiety, she made her way to the staircase. Halfway down she heard Sean call her name, but she continued to move steadily through the galleries and the reception towards the exit as if she hadn't heard.

Eventually blinded by sunshine, she stepped outside, but a hand caught her arm, so she turned.

'Ellie? I thought it was you.'

His expression tense and dark, it seemed the happy and relaxed Sean had been left with the girl in the gallery. He cleared his throat. 'Ellie, it's not what it looks like.'

Feeling stupidly like her mum, she pulled back her shoulders and stood tall. 'Sean,' she replied coldly, 'you don't need to explain yourself to me. It's none of my business.'

Trying to shake off the brimming panic, she walked up the patchwork path. Her heart thumping, she waited for a stream of cyclists to pass, then finally she was free to pace away along the pavement.

At the bus stop she glanced back. Though now partially obscured by the trees, Sean was still standing at the top of the gallery steps. A shadowy figure; too like the one on the high gallery wall.

Finally on the bus and pushed against the window by a member of the *ghastly public*, Ellie glanced at her mobile. There were five voicemail messages. Five terse statements from Mrs Laverne.

Jake had run away from school.

16

Wishing she'd run back up Oxford Road, so she could breathe, Ellie immediately called Cam. The dialling tone rang out. No reply. No bloody response from the house or his mobile. He was working at home today; where the hell was he?

Her thoughts flitted to what she'd just witnessed – a married man who wasn't where he should be – but she batted it away. Right now, the important thing was to concentrate on Jake. Focus on her son and find him.

Her mind racing, she cursed the bus for its one-speed sluggishness. Jake had often reacted badly when he'd felt anxious or frustrated at school, but he'd never run away before. Trying to calm herself and stop her mind lurching from one disastrous scenario to another, she darted from the bus to a taxi at the Piccadilly rank.

There was no point in speculating, but she couldn't help herself as she stared sightlessly through the passenger window. By the time she'd jumped from the cab, every word of self-reprimand in the dictionary had bubbled through her chest.

Mrs Laverne was waiting at her desk. She didn't bother

raising her plump body from the chair, but launched into her pre-prepared speech.

'Mrs Hastings, at last,' she began with a theatrical sigh. 'I'm afraid this situation is unacceptable. Jacob has gone too far this time and I will have to think carefully about his future at this school.' She took a gulp of air before continuing. 'Instead of making the improvements I asked for, his conduct has deteriorated. His behaviour is disruptive to the other pupils; he has little or no self-discipline . . . '

Purple Laverne liked to pride herself on her 'open door' policy and today was no exception. Vaguely wondering what the nearby classes were making of it, Ellie tapped her foot, desperate for the tirade to end so she could search for Jake, but the bloody woman was still speaking.

' . . . which I can only put down to a lack of parental skills.' The woman peered at Ellie. 'Or perhaps you are simply blind to his behaviour.'

Ellie had heard this sermon before and had responded with profuse apologies, but not today. Today Laverne had gone too far. She thought of her dad, ruddy from anger and frustration. Feeling herself step into his polished shoes, she closed the door.

I'm losing it, she thought, as she lost it.

'Don't you dare speak to me like that. I left my child in the care of this school. It was your responsibility to look after him and you have the audacity to imply that it's my fault you've lost him. Have no doubt, I will be taking this to the school governors and asking for a full inquiry into how a child can simply walk away from the premises without anyone noticing. I hope that's crystal clear. Now I'm going to do what you should have done an hour ago: find my son.'

Perhaps in time Ellie would chuckle and describe the look of astonishment on Laverne's dimpled face to Hen and Nina, but at that moment nothing felt remotely funny. Jake had disappeared, Cam hadn't returned her calls and she was shaking, endeavouring to gather her thoughts, to think calmly and logically, when all she wanted to do was scream.

She stalked from the office to the playground, crouching to slow her palpitations. Despite the self-reproach in the taxi, she'd convinced herself Jake would be here, found somewhere in a toilet or a boot room, under a desk or behind a gym bench, but Laverne had explained the school buildings and grounds had been thoroughly searched by staff and the caretaker. Where else would Jake go? Staring at the concrete, she realised the answer was obvious. Home. Of course. He knew Cam was working there today and in a time of turmoil he would've gone to his dad.

Ellie pulled off her shoes. Impervious to the sharp pinches of pavement stones, she sprinted home, only stopping for breath at the end of her own road.

Though their house was midway, she saw her son clearly. Hunkered down in his usual rocking position, he was waiting outside the gate.

'Oh, Jakey. I'm here,' she called as she paced the final stretch.

He lifted his head as she neared. His hair was tangled from anxious rubbing, his face dirty from tears. 'Where's Dad?' were his first words. 'His car isn't here. I thought he'd be at home.'

Her own bloody thoughts. 'I don't know, love; I'm sure he isn't far. You forgot your coat. Let's get you in. Biscuit and a hot drink?'

Once inside, she sat her son on the sofa and held him steadily until he calmed. Then she brought him malted wafers and warm milk. Lifting his head to her lap, she chatted softly until he slept. But she didn't move. She stayed as though frozen, her body completely still but her mind in overdrive as she stared through the bay window, only turning from time to time to squint at her mobile.

Where was Cam? Where was bloody Cameron? He said he'd

be working at home today. Invoices. Tons. Where the hell was he?

Despite the intervening years, the doubt, the anxiety and turbulence were there as though it was yesterday.

Number eleven Alston Terrace. Somehow the unrequited love had been bearable in the house. The two of them had still hung out there together, spending hours lying on Ellie's bed, listening to music, chatting and kissing, but as the days went by, Cam's injury had healed and he'd become much more mobile. Out and about at the campus and bars, she'd spot him from a distance. In a crowd, usually women, then with two or three girls, then finally one. A pretty, preppy girl, the same girl, several times. Enlightenment had popped like a firecracker, the dreadful 'why was I so bloody blind?' nausea she was experiencing right now in the pit of her stomach.

A hangover from childhood, Ellie had almost forced herself to sleep when she heard the creaking sound of car tyres on grit. She carefully lifted Jake's head and kissed his soft cheek. Aware of sore feet and cold anger, she padded to the front door and stepped out. Standing in the porch, she watched Cam through the glass with folded arms: climbing from the car, lifting the gate latch, turning to lock with his fob, then strolling up the path carrying a rolled-up newspaper. Casually, with all the time in the bloody world.

Unable to contain her agitation any more, she yanked open the door. 'Where the hell have you been?' she snapped.

But suddenly she was afraid, wishing she hadn't asked, fearful of his response. Suppose he said he was with Sean, watching him give a lecture at the university again? What then?

Cam's raised eyebrows showed surprise. 'Been in the pub; I fancied a pint. Why, what's happened?'

Instead of replying, she turned away and walked into the lounge. Covered in one of Marian's patchwork blankets, Jake was still out for the count.

Her voice emerged as a croak. 'They moved his desk, so he decided to come home. We'll have to talk to him, of course, but for now . . .'

'Ah,' Cam whispered. He shoved his hand in his jeans pocket and pulled out his mobile. He glanced, then handed it to Ellie. 'I didn't realise. It's on silent.' He held out his hand. 'Sorry. Come on. You look like you could use a drink.'

In the kitchen he made coffee, adding a large slug of brandy before sitting down. 'So how was the shopping?' he asked. 'Bought anything nice?'

'I didn't go to the shops in the end,' she replied.

She was still shaky inside. There were plenty of pubs within walking distance, but she wouldn't be asking him where he'd been or why he'd gone in the car.

He smiled. 'A secret assignation?'

She rubbed the table. 'The Whitworth Art Gallery, actually.'

Would Sean tell Cam what had happened? Did he already know? Perhaps they had a pact to cover for each other when they needed to go AWOL. Like those visits to Ireland?

'Ah, the Whitworth. Did you see the Lowry painting – the one of the outpatients' hall at Ancoats Hospital?' He topped up the coffees, his expression smug. 'Ha! Surprised you there, didn't I? Well, here's another: it was my dad who went to see the painting and told me about it. His mum worked there. At the hospital. Not sure if she's actually in the painting, though.' He laughed. 'I'd be surprised if my gran was ever that thin.' Grasping Ellie's hand, he pulled her to his lap. 'I'm glad I've made you smile. Come on, beautiful, cheer up. All's well, and all that . . .'

Sliding his arms around her waist, he pulled her close.

It didn't comfort her.

'*I can't do needy. Fucking disgusting,*' she heard.

Yes, Cam had said that, but she couldn't place when. Not that she needed to; Cam expected everyone to be like him, to shrug off irritations or worries. To 'crack on', as he often put it.

How she wished that she could; the anxiety and uncertainty were still churning in her stomach. '*Why do I feel so neglected, Cam, so abandoned, unloved?*' she wanted to ask, but she knew he wouldn't thank her for it. Besides, it was irrational.

Cam was holding her; he was there.

17

The clouds of foam popping, Ellie sighed. Though in the bath this time, she was lying motionless again, unmoving on the outside, but clattering within. Still, a physical standstill was a good thing. She completely understood Jake's need to bolt, and that sensation was dangerous.

Trying to analyse why she'd felt so panicked at school, she stared at her toes. A child of Jake's age couldn't go that far, surely? It was more a fear of someone taking him away, losing her boy for ever. The notion was still unbearable, physical almost, tugging her insides. When Jake had woken from his nap, Cam had sat him down and spoken to him seriously. He was a big boy now. Running away was not acceptable behaviour. If he was unhappy or anxious he was to speak to his teacher or an adult.

She had felt Cam's eyes on her, a quick frowning shot. Then he'd gone back to Jake. 'Unacceptable, Jakey. You're never to run away, ever again. OK?'

She now reached for the sponge, daubed it with 'therapeutic' oil and absently washed her body. Ridiculously expensive and paid for by Cam, the product was her Mother's Day gift from the boys. She'd read the description before finally snapping open the lid. It contained a combination of lavender, ylang ylang and petitgrain to 'calm and soothe the mind for a more peaceful, relaxing mood'. Well, wouldn't *that* be nice? She'd most definitely had enough trauma for today, but the aromatherapeutic miracle didn't seem to be working. A few glasses of wine would be more helpful, but she'd be drinking on her own. Again.

She stepped out of the tub and wrapped her hot torso in a towel. It wasn't so much that she was alone; it was more a question of being lonely. Was there even a difference? Cameron had taken the boys out for a pizza and then to Cineworld at Parrs Wood so 'Mum can have some time to herself'. It didn't matter that it was the start of a week, that Harry was far too young to see the chosen film or that the boys had school the next day. This was Cam's way and Ellie didn't have the strength to spoil the fun, even though she'd be the one to get the flack in the morning from tired and grumpy sons.

And she hadn't been asked along. It was silly, she knew, when she could've invited herself, but still she felt abandoned and friendless, left out from the fun.

Still only eight thirty, Ellie padded down the stairs and glanced around the tidy kitchen. What now? Lunch boxes for tomorrow was the thing. Though that was possibly bad parenting. She usually made them fresh in the morning, but lettuce went soggy whenever she prepared them and anything green was doubtless pulled out and binned by her sons. Judging by Toby's usual leftovers, she suspected he was cadging chips from his mates in the school canteen. But at least trying to feed her boys healthily made her feel better. Like keeping up appearances. That, and all life's other vital idioms, which had been drilled into her by Maurice. With *military precision*, of course.

How she hated not keeping them up, the appearances. Like with Sean and the barbecue telephone call. Like today at school. Perhaps that was why she'd occasionally absconded too. If she wasn't around to show the ugliness, then she couldn't fail to meet expectations.

Opening the bread bin, she sighed. The boring mum routine. What would happen if she went on strike and refused to prepare packed lunches? But she knew the answer: Cam would say fine, no problem, he'd stop at the newsagent's en route and send his sons on their way with a bought plastic sandwich, or sweets even, crisps and a can of Coke. And the boys would love him for it.

'Hey ho,' she said aloud, thinking that perhaps she should regress and rebel, just like when she was a teenager, flouting every Maurice adage. It reminded her of the inevitable confrontation with Purple Laverne tomorrow. She should probably apologise. Bawling at one's son's head of school was, perhaps, *letting the side down* and certainly *too close to home*.

The doorbell pinged. She put down the serrated knife and shook her head at the intrusion. Deliveries for Cam got later as the nights became lighter and she didn't like to answer the door in her dressing gown. There was no hiding from sight in the windows of the porch and it made her feel exposed. She pictured Hen sucking in her cheeks on Friday. And her quip about seducing Cam. Hen, who was never ill; Cam, who said Ellie should go shopping anyway.

Paranoia clutched her throat. No; the idea was both ridiculous and terrifying.

Batting it away, she stepped from the hall and peered through the glass. A man was standing on the path. His arms folded, he was looking towards the road where his SUV was parked. What the hell? What was *he* doing here?

Embarrassment followed surprise. Then annoyance set in;

irritation that he had turned up unannounced; anger for being the perfect father-of-six bloody fraud.

Aware of self-consciousness colouring her cheeks, she tapped on the pane. 'He's not in,' she said through it. 'They've all gone to the cinema.'

'I know,' he replied. 'I've come to see you. Can I come in?'

Could she really say no? She stood frozen for a moment, then nodded and stepped away, waiting for the burst of spring air to enter with this 'friend' who had too, too much influence in her and Cam's lives.

Feeling defensive and vulnerable, she tightened her belt. Why was he there? As though cold, she rubbed her arms and waited for him to speak.

He didn't. Instead he gazed, his expression thoughtful, as if determining something.

Panic hit Ellie's chest. What was there to decide? If it was something about Cam, she did not want to know.

He cleared his throat, his eyes still on hers. 'About today. I wanted to explain about today—'

Relief spread down her spine. His young lover, of course. 'Look,' she interrupted. Oh God; the girl's flushed cheeks, the anticipation in her shining eyes. She didn't want this conversation. She didn't need to know about who, about why. Most of all she didn't want to hear his justification. 'As I already said, Sean, it's none of my business.'

'It is, I wouldn't want you to—'

'To tell your wife that you have some pretty girl in your sights? Don't worry, I won't.'

A shadow passed across his face. 'Not just that. I don't want you to think badly of me.'

'*Badly* of you?' The words popped out before she could stop them. 'I've always thought badly of you, Sean. It makes no odds.

91

I won't say anything to Ciara. Now, I've had a difficult day, so please—'

He laughed then, his teeth white against the dark of his beard. 'And what did I do to deserve such a kind endorsement?'

Her eyes stinging with anger, she glared. 'I'm sure you can recall perfectly well.'

'Recall what?'

'University. The fact you put me down at every opportunity, for starters.'

'Did I? I was probably trying to get your attention,' he replied, amusement in his voice. 'That's what boys do. Have you never noticed?'

Suddenly deflated, she lowered her head. She no longer knew what to *notice*. She understood she was a bad daughter, that was set in stone, but she'd tried to be a good mother to the boys, a good partner to Cam. She wanted to sleep or to disappear, it didn't matter which, as long as she could escape from this, from him, from her increasing paranoia about Cam.

She took a silent, shuddery breath. 'OK, whatever. I've got things to do, so can you go now, please?'

Staring at her bare feet, she willed the anger to return, not this brimming self-pity, desperate to burst. She stepped to one side to open the door, but Sean blocked her way.

'Ellie? Hey. You're crying—'

She held out her palm to stop him. 'No, I'm not. Please just—'

No longer smiling, he wrapped her in his arms, holding her steady as she wept. Pathetic tears soaked his thin cotton shirt, but he still held her tightly. Aware of his stirring body, she pulled away then, wiped her face with her towelling sleeve and lifted her head to say something, anything to break the surreal moment.

His gaze was too intense, too serious. And there was something in his expression, a dark glint that made her stomach flip and her skin crawl. Her head loathed this man, but her body was responding, craving those arms, the heat and his smell. What the hell was wrong with her? He was still that dangerous, derisive student who'd turned everyone's heads. Cam's especially.

She pushed at a door in her mind, trying to remember, but Sean's gentle hand on her cheek caught her short.

'How did you get this?' he asked, his eyes on hers, searching, almost fierce.

She flinched, uncomfortable that he'd noticed. Disturbed by his touch. Was it so obvious? 'It's nothing.'

'You can't see it,' he said, as though reading her mind. 'I just know it's there. From then. From university.'

The tears pricking again, she turned away to hide her face. 'I thought it had healed by the time—'

'It had, but . . . How did you get it, Ellie? What happened?'

Skin deep, skin deep. His green mocking glare. Did he know? Had he always known? Her heart whipping with alarm, she shook her head and stepped away. 'I can't really remember. It was a long time ago. I think you should go now.'

'Ellie . . . '

'Please, Sean, just go.'

'Night, then.' He opened the door. 'By the way,' he said softly, 'the girl you saw at the Whitworth today—'

She turned. 'Please, it's fine. I really don't need to know.'

'Her name is Samantha. She's . . . ' He blinked. 'She's my sister.'

18

Even as she starts climbing the shallow rungs of the windmill, Ellie knows she should have stayed at the bottom and let the boys wave at her from the top. There's only enough room for a single procession of holidaymakers, and they're hot on her heels, so there's no going back. As the steps rise onwards and upwards to the sky, her heart beats faster, her limbs grow weak.

She's used to the dark humidity and smell. It's the height – the steep unknown with no escape – that terrifies her. Though her legs are leaden, she has to move; the bodies behind are pushing her on.

'You are special, you must know that.'

'It'll be over soon.'

'A nasty dream. Here's an aspirin.'

The bright sunlight strikes and for moments she's blinded. But there's her mum, her smile reassuring, reaching out her arms. Knowing not to look down, Ellie holds out her hand. Their fingers nudge, a soft feather touch. Then abruptly she trips and she plummets—

*

Ellie awoke with a sharp jolt. A dream, just a dream. And she was back in her dusky bedroom, so only one layer. Shaking herself awake, she quickly sat up; sometimes she fell back into the nightmare without catching a breath of relief or reality, plunging into hopelessness again. But there was Cam next to her in their bed, his face smooth and peaceful, snoring lightly.

After a disastrous start with Jake on Monday, the week had improved. She'd sat down and spoken properly to Cam about Jake and the school and the future. Despite his offer to turn up and brave the flak from Mrs Laverne, she'd done it herself, taking a middle road between apology and blame, describing why, from Jake's point of view, he'd walked away from the classroom. His teacher, Miss Myers, understood how difficult he found change without careful warning, but she'd been on a training course on the previous Friday, so hadn't been there to explain that the desks in the classroom would be rearranged for the Year Six SATS. If he'd been warned, he would've expected it and coped. His view of life was black and white; the grey areas were uncertain and confusing – not only for Jake but for many other kids like him, which a head teacher should bloody well know.

But Ellie had been on her best behaviour, she hadn't put it quite like that at her meeting. She'd even been rewarded with a too-soft wrapped toffee and a plump shake of Purple Laverne's hand.

She now glanced at the digital clock. Only just past midnight, but it felt like dawn, as though she'd been napping for hours. Her sleeping pattern was different when Cam was home. She seemed to spend more time awake, more minutes walking through the week's highs and lows, the nadirs getting precedence as night-time thoughts do. Strange really. But perhaps it was that old Woodlands thing. With Cam there, she was safe; she didn't have to force sleep to block out childish terrors. What on earth had they been? Fear of the dark and wetting herself had been two of them; conflicting worries that hadn't made for good bedfellows.

Turning the pillow, she contemplated the Friday piss-up at Nina's house. Today – yesterday now, she supposed – Hen had looked as elegant and coiffured as ever; no sign of illness. But then four days had passed since she cancelled their trip into town and Ellie hadn't liked to ask how she was feeling or what had been the matter, just in case.

Just in case, what? Ellie stared into the dark void and sighed. Just in case Hen had blushed, or her eyes had slightly flickered or blinked? She shook her head. The momentary paranoia had been preposterous. She knew that now. She'd known it as soon as she was embraced by Hen, her close and affectionate friend Hen.

'You look different,' she'd said, studying Ellie's face. 'Beautiful as always, but different. I can't work out what it is. Have you done something with your hair? New lipstick? Or have you finally got round to shearing your eyebrows?'

It was an 'in' joke. 'I like the Neanderthal look,' she'd laughed in reply. 'Liam Gallagher for one—'

'And that Cara What's-her-name has brought the mono-brow back into fashion, so you're fine,' Nina had added.

'Just for the record, girls, I never had a mono-brow!' Ellie had laughed. 'Possibly the reverse. Not sure you'd even see one in dreaded ginger.'

'Blame the mirror. I do . . .'

The ragging and quips from her two closest friends had continued. Her only close friends. What would they think if they saw a photograph from her Alston Terrace days? The nose and multiple ear piercings, the black hair, black eyeliner, black lipstick. She smiled to herself. Black eyebrows, too. Everything black as pitch until she washed it off late at night and became nice Miss Eleanor Wilson again, that pretty girl she had grown up with, the one everyone had admired but didn't really know. Only Cam had seen her face naked at university. And Sean, that one time in the bathroom. But she wasn't thinking about him or his lies.

'I've told Faith not to pluck her eyebrows or shave her legs, because once you start, you can't stop,' Nina had said.

'A bit like smoking, then,' Hen had replied.

'Or Pringles.'

'Or a multi-pack of Tunnock's Caramel Wafers,' Ellie had added with a chuckle.

Hen had shrugged her slim shoulders. 'Or affairs, for that matter.'

The shudder had been there, but Ellie had ignored it. 'Will Faith take any notice, Nina?' she'd asked.

'Probably not,' Nina had mused. 'In fact, definitely not. After all, did any of us take notice of our mothers' advice? Well, not until we were thirty, and then we became them.'

'Or fathers,' Ellie had replied, recalling her Maurice-like tirade on Monday. 'Purple Laverne was so taken aback at my rant, and no doubt worried that the school could be in trouble, she's decided to take Jake on as a cause. She's been reading up on autism, apparently. Poor Jake, if she's going to cocoon him in kindness and understanding, he will be confused.'

'Isn't that what all men want?' Hen had asked, taking another sip of her wine. 'For us to be their mothers? Oedipus and all that?' She'd laughed. 'Seems to me they deserve to be smothered.'

There had been an uncomfortable jolt then, too. Something in the imagery of her words. It strangely disturbed Ellie, even now.

She turned to Cam. Her eyes accustomed to the night, she gazed at the contours of his closed face. It was symmetrical and quite perfect. The innocent sleep, she thought again. Didn't Macbeth say that? *Innocent.* Perhaps that was why she was awake.

'Hold on to this one, Eleanor. He'll be good for you.'

Had she 'held on'? Desperately holding on, as opposed to being held?

'Which idiots need a public ceremony and a certificate to show they're committed or part of a family?' Cam had said at some early point in their relationship. 'The Church of England are hypocrites for allowing couples to have the whole religious debacle at the drop of a hat. Why be a sheep and do something just because the middle classes do it? And then label the poor bloody kids if you have them?'

She'd absorbed his speech and hadn't commented, but her eyebrows had been raised; she didn't for a moment believe Cam really invested in his unexpected diatribe, so she hadn't thought twice when she raised marriage, not long after Toby's birth. Cosy and loved up, she'd been sure of the answer.

'Why don't we get hitched, Cam? Wouldn't that be great? Mr and Mrs Hastings in our finery; invite family and friends; make the three of us a proper family?'

'No ta. Not for me.'

'Really? Are you joking?' She'd seen from his expression he wasn't. 'But why?' she'd asked, both floored and gobsmacked.

His jaw had been set. 'I just don't want to, so that's that.' He'd lifted a hand to stop her further protest. 'We're really good as we are. OK?' he'd added.

The shocking and deeply disappointing reply had brought back his earlier Sean-like rant. It had felt as though the 'Irish Beast' himself was in the room with them. She'd been deeply unsettled at the idea. Had Cam been under the oracle's influence, even then?

Sean, bloody Sean. She was not going to think about him.

She explored her cheek with gentle fingertips. Right now the scar felt quite deep but, hidden amongst her freckles, not so much to look at. Or so she had assumed. Thinking back to university, some things were hazy – from too much alcohol or dope probably – but the cigarette burn, that she could clearly remember.

19

Ellie glanced at the Saturday breakfast table. Packets, boxes, bottles, tubs and jars. It seemed Harry had emptied the contents of the fridge and food cupboards, yet had still stuck to his usual Coco Pops.

'Anyone up for keeping me company in the car this morning?' she asked, even though she knew the answer. Jake had become pretty solid as a goalkeeper, so he and Cam would be practising scoring and saving at the local sports fields as usual, and Toby was still in bed.

Harry sprinkled a layer of sugar on his remaining brown milk. 'I'll come.'

Cam pulled back his chair. 'Time to go, Jakey.' He ruffled Harry's hair. 'Good lad. You can show Grandad your new cricket bat. A Newbery Krakatoa, like he recommended.' He gave Ellie a peck. 'A great all-round bat for slow, low English wickets. Which means?'

She smiled. 'Not a clue.'

'That the ball doesn't bounce too high. Weave that into the conversation and your dad will love you for ever.'

'I doubt it, but thanks for the tip. Enjoy the footie.'

She turned back to Harry. It seemed her youngest could multi-task. He was apparently reading about the nutrition of Bran Flakes, humming along with the radio, slurping milk with one hand and trying to smooth his Mohican back into place with the other.

'Thanks for coming, love.' Giving him a quick hug, she made a mental note to buy him sweets and a comic before they hit the motorway. She increasingly found it helpful to take one of the boys when she visited her parents, a distraction from their forced mundane conversation, and often an excuse to leave.

The habitual mix of love, exasperation and anxiety prodded. Indicating right, Ellie waited for a car to pass before entering the drive of her childhood home.

She smiled at Harry. 'I can still smell those white mice. They were my favourites too.'

He'd rolled up the comic 'for later' and his pick 'n' mix sweets were long gone. He'd chatted amiably on the way about school. Like his dad, he had a knack of collecting all sorts of information and gossip without appearing to listen, then pass it on randomly to the rest of the family: 'Really? You're joking! Who on earth told you? When did you find *that* out, Harry?' was oft heard.

Today she had learned that the mousy middle-aged teacher from Year Two had treated herself to a sporty Mercedes '*as well* as having her teeth whitened', and that the new male teacher (who all the mums fancied) 'batted for the other side'. She hadn't liked to ask Harry if he knew what that meant. Besides, her cricket knowledge was clearly not as good as it should be, so perhaps he'd meant it literally.

She was glad to have her youngest with her today. It wasn't only his sunny tolerance, he felt like a shield – although from what, she didn't know. Her dad hadn't held back on poor Toby at the last gathering, after all. So perhaps it wasn't him but Woodlands itself, her fabulous former home. Nestled in a half-acre plot, the old house was surrounded by neat gardens to one side and . . .well, *woodlands* to the other.

Marian waved through the kitchen window. Taking in the reassuring sight, Ellie parked behind her dad's Jaguar and stepped out. The usual bouquet greeted her. Though the delicate fragrances from her mum's bedding plants were there, they were overpowered by the smell of trees, bushes and shrubs. Visual aromas, like art. Earthy, mossy, mildewed and piney. And if the wind blew, the musky, sweet and heady smell of juniper and eucalyptus.

Then there was birdsong. Always that.

They sat in the lounge as usual, Harry with a tall glass of iced squash and a china plate of custard creams, Ellie a coffee.

Searching for conversation, she absently gazed through the window at the bird table and the woods beyond.

Maurice usually had time for Harry. 'Come here, little chap,' he'd say, patting his knee. 'Tell me all about it. Are you still winning every race and coming top in class?' But despite the strong smell of linseed oil coming from Harry's cricket bat and him stroking it meaningfully, Maurice clearly wasn't in the mood for pleasantries today. Sat in the armchair by the hearth, his eyes remained on his newspaper; he wasn't saying a word.

Her father's silence meant he was angry about some minor misdemeanour, of course. Until she'd learned to ignore it at twelve or thirteen, it had been like walking on shards of glass as she urgently tried to work out what she'd done, *that* time at least. When he'd finally exploded, the angry words firing out, it had always been such a relief just to know.

Marian was chattering about her stall and the latest sales but, head bowed, Harry was gently kicking his bare heels against the sofa. Ellie felt the heat rise. The poor boy wasn't allowed to bring his iPad to Grandad's house, which he accepted with a shrug, but of course he got bored, and it still irked her that her parents never made the effort to have *something* child-friendly in their huge home. One of the bedrooms upstairs was filled with old junk, but there were no kids' books or toys, not a jigsaw, nor any of her old board games, let alone a swing or a slide in the wooded garden. Cam had once suggested setting up a rope seat from one of the sturdy high trees, but Marian had demurred on the grounds of safety.

'I'd never forgive myself if there was an accident, Cam. There's the park up the road. I can make up a picnic if the boys fancy going,' she'd said.

Bloody covering up for Maurice, as usual.

She supposed that Operation, Guess Who or Mousetrap were packed away with every other item she'd left in her bedroom when she departed for Leeds at eighteen. Not that her parents had given her those particular games. The more 'frivolous' ones had been brought by friends as birthday gifts, or by Aunty Diana on one of her surprise visits. Maurice always favoured Scrabble or Monopoly, but even those had disappeared.

Ellie had thought that was the norm until she visited the homes of uni pals for a weekend. She'd been surprised to find they still had their own bedrooms, complete with picture books, soft teddies, old dolls and outgrown clothes. When she came home in the holidays, Marian was delighted to see her, but always said, 'I've made up the spare room for you, love,' even though the *spare room* had once been her pink, special place.

She now shook her head. No wonder she'd never invited friends to stay at Woodlands. By the second year of university, she hardly went home at all, save for a few nights at Easter and Christmas, and day visits here and there on the train to see her mum when Maurice was at work.

Illuminating it like a grotto, the sunshine lit the greenhouse outside. But, of course, she did come home. Home to Marian at the beginning of the third year for several weeks. Home because she'd desperately needed her mum. She had climbed into the starched clean sheets in the spare room and closed her eyes. For hours she'd been too sapped to move, but eventually through the silence, she'd heard her mother's voice, an angry yell with an edge she'd never experienced before.

'Is it true that you cut off her grant money? Without even telling her? How was she supposed to live? To eat? To pay her rent? How could you, Maurice? How could you?'

She couldn't hear his reply, but she'd been glad. Too weary, too numb to absorb his excuses that final time.

'Do you know what you've done? You put this right now, Maurice, or I'm leaving and I mean it. Do you hear me? You make this right now.'

As she watched the twitch of the mantelpiece clock, her chest smarted with irritation. An hour or so had gone by and her father had said only one word – 'yes' to the offer of an omelette for his lunch. His eyes, it seemed, were fixed on the same page of the broadsheet. She looked across to her boy. He was still looking at the carpet, his precious new cricket bat bouncing on his knees. Whatever she or Marian had done to offend Maurice, it wasn't Harry's fault. She didn't want him to feel he'd done something wrong like she had as a child.

'Well, Dad,' she said crisply, standing up, 'if you've nothing to say, we'll get off home.'

No sound, no reply, no acknowledgement from Maurice, just a kiss on her cheek and a squeeze of her arm from her mum outside the front door. 'You mustn't mind him, love, you know what he's like when he has something on his mind. He's worrying about this HS2 train business, but I'm sure it won't affect us. He'll be as right as rain soon. See you next week.'

Bending to Harry, Marian placed a folded five-pound note in his hand. Then she covered his fist with hers. 'Now you're a big boy,' she whispered.

Hearing the scrape of metal against metal, Ellie snapped her head to the Jag. Shaking the old memory away, she turned back to her mum. But the door had already closed and the tinny sound was just her mum locking it. Not one turn but two.

Firmly locking her daughter out with her keys.

20

It was another of Cam's 'I'm in charge' Sunday mornings, or perhaps an, 'I'm going away for two weeks and I'm making the effort' day. The plan was for a family walk on the moors, Cam in charge of the route and the picnic. Though he insisted with raised eyebrows that Ellie have a nice 'lie-in' first.

She wasn't really in the mood for lovemaking, and there was always the worry of a child charging in, but Cam coaxed her with the usual non-PC humour before the boys stirred. 'You know you need it. Can't have you shag-absent crabby for fourteen whole days. It wouldn't be fair to Greater Stockport.'

'There is no such thing as Greater Stockport, Cam. And this is my *lie-in*, apparently.'

'Oh, so the lady's awake. That's a start.'

He kissed her neck and her shoulders, her feet, then everywhere in between, not allowing her to reciprocate as usual. 'No, this one's all yours,' he said, grinning. 'To make sure you really miss me.'

*

Inevitably it was drizzling when she and the boys clambered into Cam's car. The weather seemed to affect even his mood. As ever he drove too fast along the M67, having to brake sharply each time he caught up with a lorry. 'In the outside bloody lane. What's he playing at?' Then a groan at the usual nose-to-tail traffic at the Glossop roundabout.

To Ellie's surprise, rather than his usual ploy of taking his chances and pushing in, he stayed in the left queue, tapping the steering wheel. A grin abruptly replaced the frown and he swerved to the right. 'I've just remembered. Sean told me about a short cut.'

Uncomfortable at the mention of his name, she didn't reply, but Cam looked at her, still smiling. 'Sean the man, eh? It's a left turn after the roundabout. Look out for a Tesco. I don't know how he knows, but he does. Bloody fountain of all knowledge.'

She nodded. Cam wasn't even being sarcastic. Sean was still the seer who could do no bloody wrong. When did they have their tête-à-tête about left turns and Tesco's? And what else had they talked about? Tall stories about attractive student-age 'sisters'? Though that was highly unlikely; surely Cam would have told her about *that*.

She threw the thought out. She didn't want Sean Walsh to infect a nice family day; she wanted to enjoy it, not think forwards nor back.

Cam slammed on the brakes. 'Fuck, it's the police,' he said, his eyes on the rear-view mirror.

Whipping her head to the wing, Ellie looked too. Oh God, he was right; the full beam of a police car was on their tail, getting nearer and nearer. As though fending off the inevitable, she scrunched up her eyes. When she opened them again, the boys had finally woken from their morning malaise.

'Wow, that was fast!'

'Do you think they're after a robber?'

'Or a gun, Dad? Do you think there's been a shoot-out?'

Whistling with relief, Cam manoeuvred the car from the pavement. 'No idea, but that was a close call,' he said. 'I was doing over fifty.' Then looking at Ellie, 'You're as white as a sheet. Feeling OK?' But before she could answer, he spoke again, 'Harry, look at the tiny doors of these cottages. They must have made them for . . . ' He laughed. 'What's the PC expression? People of restricted growth?'

'That's what you always say, Dad.' Harry sniggered. 'As well as "too many bloody pedestrian crossings".'

'Language, son. Though you're right: there are too many bloody pedestrian crossings.'

Finally through the chock-a-block town centre, the car popped out into residential emptiness the other side. Cam headed towards the Snake Pass but before hitting the hills, he turned down a side road and eventually pulled up at the side of a rickety corrugated barn.

'God, it stinks!'

'Smells, Harry. And don't take the Lord's name in—'

'We can't park here,' Jake interrupted. 'We're next to a red car. Mum doesn't like them.'

Cam looked at Ellie and crinkled his nose. 'Well, that's news to me.'

'We were walking to school the other day and a Toyota pulled up to speak to Mum. The man wound down the window and Mum's face went like a ghost and when I asked, Mum said it was because she didn't like red cars.'

His jaw tight, Cam gazed through the windscreen without speaking for a moment. Then the other vehicle moved away, so he turned to the boys. 'Seems Mum's luck is in; the car is leaving, Jake, so no need to worry.' He rubbed his hands. 'Come on, lads. The hills are a-calling.'

Harry jumped out immediately, Ellie giving chase with his cagoule. When she returned to her eldest, he sullenly peered at the sodden view. 'Really?' His only contribution all morning.

She cuffed him playfully on the chin. 'Come on, gorgeous,' she said. 'You'll be pleased when you beat Dad up that hill.'

With a crooked smile he relented and climbed out. 'I hate walking. Now, if we had a dog . . .'

A dog, Ellie thought, the cure for all evils. But in her case it hadn't just been an animal to love, it had been the glorious *promise* of one. The excitement and anticipation, the sure knowledge that the solemn pledge would be kept. It wasn't.

Inwardly she sighed. It was long ago, too long ago to dwell on now.

She reverted to Toby. 'I'm up for a puppy if you can persuade Dad, but I very much doubt you'll have any luck with that one.'

The sky cracked a smile. 'Ready, Toby? Boys? Race you,' Cam declared, making a head start up a mound. Ellie followed, the rucksack heavy on one shoulder, but content, happy to hear her family's laughter, surprised to see that Toby was nearly as tall as his dad.

They trudged steeper and higher up the Peak District hills, dodging thistles and tussocks, sludge and sheep. The wind damp on their faces, they reached a crest, which Harry claimed with a broken branch. Then the sun came out properly and Ellie spread her waterproof on a stone ledge to watch Cam and the boys wading up the sparkling stream. Leaning back, she closed her eyes, savouring the sensation of mellow warmth on her skin and listening to the different voices of the birds out of habit.

'*Listen carefully, Eleanor; that's a blackbird, slightly different from a thrush,*' Maurice used to say when she was small. '*Now concentrate on the sound. There! Did you hear it? Can you tell?*'

She'd wanted to please him, to say, '*Yes, Daddy, of course I can tell.*' But she knew that he'd test her and if she got it wrong he'd be disappointed.

More at ease than she had been for some time, Ellie now smiled to herself. The summer holidays were fast approaching, life was on an even keel with Cam and the boys and she wanted to keep it that way. Harry was just Harry, the happy, jovial little man he always was, and Jake had settled down again at school. Toby was quiet and a little mopey, but he was nearly a teenager, so it was fair enough.

Nina's Faith was 'dating', though apparently the label involved nothing other than *saying* it, and occasionally sitting next to the boy in question at the lunchtime break. Did Toby have a girlfriend? Ellie didn't think so, despite the shaved hair. Or maybe because of it. She doubted whether he'd tell her, but then again he'd told her about his rash, so maybe he would. Of the boys, she and her eldest were the most similar. Not only did they look alike, there seemed to be an intuition between them – words unspoken, but an empathy, an understanding somehow.

As the breeze brushed her eyelids, she pictured Toby's thunderbolt reaction when he first saw Katrina Walsh. Like a domino effect, another young woman flashed into her mind. The beautiful girl who'd kissed Sean. Dark shiny hair and such devoted eyes.

His *sister*? Really? There had been a definite falter in Sean's gaze when he'd said it; telling lies, she was sure. She sighed deeply. Yes, it was disappointing, and there was still the vague worry that unfaithfulness could spread to Cam through a kind of osmosis, but it wasn't something to dwell on any more. She wanted life to be smooth and stress-free.

'That's a curlew,' she declared, bolting upright.

Shielding her eyes from the sunshine, she searched the clear sky, finally spotting the bird high above a clump of glossy trees. Pleased with herself, her lips twitched.

The smile fell. God, she *had* to try harder with her dad. His behaviour had been appalling yesterday. But had hers been much better? Crisp and offended and reactionary, instead of asking him what was wrong and at least trying to understand.

'Ellie!' The sound of Cam's voice brought her back to the Derbyshire landscape. Ruggedly beautiful or dour, she could never decide. Like most things in life, it probably came down to the weather.

Cam scrambled up the slope. 'Two whole weeks without me. Will you miss me?' he asked.

His clothes were wet, his face smeared with mud. She could only imagine the soggy damage to the boys as they noisily clambered up behind him.

She squinted and grinned. 'Might miss the shagging. But otherwise, nah.'

'Hope you haven't been peeking at lunch,' he said, nodding to the rucksack.

'By the weight of it, I'm expecting a whole dead pig.'

He chuckled. 'So, you have been peeking.'

Warm and secure, Ellie laughed too. Why she'd ever doubted this man, she had no idea.

21

Ellie strolled up and down the aisles in Tesco's. Inspiration was the thing. It was fun to follow a recipe or to try something new when Cam was at home, but her sons were somewhat conservative in their culinary tastes. They all liked pasta, but the sauce had to be plain tomato, preferably out of a jar that didn't have 'bits' in it. *Bits* were the devil.

She had, from time to time, tried making her own passata with fresh tomatoes and veg, then blending it 'to buggery', but still the boys found a visible piece of onion in it.

'Ugh! What's this?' Jake would ask. 'It looks like a slug. I'm not eating it.'

'A slug? Brilliant,' Harry would reply, excited at the prospect, until deflated by Toby.

'It isn't a real slug, idiot.'

Once or twice she'd tried the 'Well, you won't get any pudding if you don't eat it up' routine, which had worked every time when she was a girl. But Toby had just laughed, setting off the other two and she had joined in, thinking that life was too short for rules.

But of course there were rules in life; rules were unavoidable. 'Ellie? Hello, Ellie.'

She returned the jar to the shelf. Flipping heck, she wasn't even in Sainsbury's today. Was this bloody woman tracking her? But she turned to Ciara Walsh with a practised smile.

'We haven't seen you for ages. Now, where have you been hiding?' Ciara declared. Her pale eyes had followed the Dolmio. 'It's much better to make the sauce yourself, Ellie. So easy too. I can give you a recipe. That one will be full of sugar, salt and additives.'

The smile stiffened. Yup, life really was too short for rules.

Ciara continued to talk. 'The tomatoes and onion go towards the five portions a day, of course, and I like to add mushrooms and olives and a good helping of celery. And anything else going,' she said without taking breath. Then, in the manner of someone about to expose a deeply buried secret, she stepped closer. 'It's so much cheaper, especially if you use the veg at the end of its life, if you follow me.'

Ellie chuckled inwardly. The Walsh clan clearly didn't have an allergy to slugs. She glanced in Ciara's trolley: fruit, veg and dairy; flour and eggs. Not a biscuit or a crisp packet in sight.

Those appraising eyes again. 'I get my meat from the butcher's, Ellie. I like to support the local shops and . . .' She leaned forward again. 'In contrast to places like this, you know where it's come from and, more to the point, how long it's been there.'

Wondering why Ciara was in a 'place like this' – other than for stalking – Ellie took a breath, but the woman carried on. 'Cameron's away, isn't he? Two weeks, I believe, this time.' She patted her arm. 'Why don't you all pop over at the weekend for something to eat? I'll be doing a casserole or the like anyway, so it'll be no trouble.'

Cow directly from the pasture with lashings of celery? Caught on the hop and irritated with the woman's usual *Camdar*, Ellie gritted her teeth. Yet she was being mean-spirited. Ciara's invitation was sweet, she already had a hundred kids; she didn't have to bother with an extra four mouths to feed. And she was right about the butcher's; Ellie tried to do the same herself.

The thought of Sean's 'sister' flitted into her head. Would she be invited too? Of course not: a girl nearly half his age was hardly going to be a sibling . . .

Reality hit; oh God, poor Ciara.

'That's really kind, Ciara . . .' she began. The boys would love a day at the Walshes' place, but could she really face Sean after her stupid tears and those excruciating moments in his arms? Not to mention what she saw in the gallery. Staring at his wife's placid face, she racked her brains for an excuse, but the sound of her mobile saved her. 'Oh, sorry, my phone. Do you mind?'

Ciara nodded, but didn't move. 'Not at all; go ahead.'

Glancing at the screen, Ellie smiled. Good old Mum, just in the nick of time. She stepped away from her 'pal's' curious gaze. 'Hi, Mum. What are you up to?'

'Oh, Eleanor, thank goodness . . .' Marian began.

The goosebumps were immediate. Oh God; what had happened? Something was clearly wrong.

22

Breathing through the usual claustrophobic dread of hospitals, Ellie strode towards her mother. Her hands folded in her lap, she was sitting straight-backed on a plastic bench outside Maurice's ward. Ellie hovered, but Marian's gaze seemed to be fixed on a fly silently battering itself against a window. She'd worn very well for her age, but today anxiety was scored on her face, making her appear fragile and old.

Abruptly registering her daughter's presence, she jerked. 'Oh, Ellie, you're here.' Then standing up and smoothing her skirt, 'He's napping, love. Best left for now. Shall we go for a coffee?'

It was a relief to hear her mum's words. For the last fifty minutes, Ellie had been terrified she'd arrive too late, that there'd be nothing to see but a lifeless body sprawled on a white sheet. Needing to check on her dad now, she opened her mouth to say so, but Marian had already slipped an arm through hers and was firmly guiding her down the corridor, away from the nurses' station.

Surprised at her mum's odd behaviour, Ellie left her at a grey canteen table, then went to buy drinks. The acrid smell of a fry-up filled the air. Ordering two cappuccinos, she tried to shake off that old association between hospitals, sorrow and death. It was illogical, of course; apart from her wisdom teeth, her only experience of infirmaries was the birth of her sons, and that was quite the reverse.

'Mum, what exactly happened?' she asked when she finally sat down.

Marian lifted her dewy gaze. 'I should've made him go to the doctor. Persuaded him, that is. He's been grumbling for a day or two. You know, dizziness and headaches. Saying that he was under the weather. Adding that I didn't care ...'

Ellie nodded. There was no point saying the obvious; she would still feel guilty.

'And occasionally his speech was slurred, like he'd had one too many. They think it's a stroke. I should've known, shouldn't I?'

'Of course not. It's just the benefit of hindsight, that's all ...'

Clutching her mum's weathered hand, a surge of emotion seeped out. She wished she'd done more in her adult life to show Marian that she loved her, but her father had always been there in spirit, if not in person. Out for a relaxing ladies' lunch, or even with the boys when they were tiny babies, Marian would soon look at her watch and say, 'Heavens! Look at the time. Your father will be home from the office soon. I haven't prepared dinner. I must get back before he does.'

'She's a one-person woman and it's no longer me,' a friend once said in some context or other, and Ellie had immediately thought, That's my mum. The one person, of course, being Maurice.

As the aroma of cooking changed from breakfast to lunch, the canteen slowly filled. Waiting for her mum's cue to leave, Ellie glanced around: a severely disabled child pushed in her wheelchair by a weary carer, an old couple bent double but still holding hands, a handsome youth struggling with crutches.

'A penny for them?' she eventually asked Marian, even though she knew the answer.

'I was just thinking about the day I met your dad at the town hall. So tall and distinguished. I was just eighteen and I couldn't believe it when he asked me to dance. All the good-looking boys usually made a bee-line for Diana. But he chose me.'

Her mum's eyes were shining; it made Ellie's heart ache. 'Why wouldn't he? I bet you were just as beautiful as Diana. You still are,' she replied.

Ellie tried to think back. What had her aunty actually looked like? The memories from childhood were of exotic beauty and musky aromas, but she hadn't seen a photograph of her for years.

'Oh, I was pretty enough, I suppose,' Marian replied absently. She fell quiet but came back after a while. 'You wouldn't think it now, but I was painfully shy in those days. Diana was just . . .' She seemed to search for a description. 'Well, she was everything – bright and clever and charming – so I paled in her shadow. Not that I blamed her; I adored her too. Everyone did, especially our father, and I accepted that was the way it was without any resentment. But with your dad . . . well, it was different. He said he found Diana to be "vain and shallow". Not terribly kind words, but it was rather nice for me, to be so . . . so special.'

'And so you are. Very.' Rubbing her mum's arm, Ellie smiled. She'd never heard the story before, but she understood. Being *special* had an edge on love.

'Shall we go and see Dad now?' she prompted. 'He might have woken up.'

Marian's expression was glazed; still dancing in the town hall with her handsome suitor, Ellie guessed. After a moment, the question seemed to land. 'You go ahead, love. I might just get another coffee. I'll catch you up.'

'Are you sure? Do you want me to wait?'

'No. I'll only be ten minutes.'

Hoping her arrangements for the boys would go to plan, Ellie

116

checked her mobile in the lift. With Cam being away, Nina was to collect the boys from school, drop them at the house, then Hen would take over from there. She hoped that Toby would arrive home at the usual time so Hen could let him know what was going on. She hadn't wanted to frighten him with a toneless text about his grandad being in hospital. She just knew he'd feel guilty, like she did.

She caught her tight expression in the mirror. Should she call Cam? Despite her pale, drawn appearance, she said no to her reflection. Vietnam was thousands of miles away, and there was no point worrying him at this stage. Besides, she'd never once asked him to come home early, despite being desperate at times, especially with Jake. She'd imagined him yelling, 'It's my job, Ellie, how I earn us a living. I can't just drop everything on a whim.'

That one argument about money still scared her. It seemed silly now, but at the time she thought he'd struggled not to hit her. She'd been wrong, of course, but his response was so out of character that she never wanted to revisit it. And she relied entirely on him financially, just like she had on Maurice growing up. That dependency had been frightening, too.

A breathless tension in her chest, she strode down the passage-way towards her dad's ward. Readying herself for the unknown, she glanced into openings and windows. Muffled silence and illness and loss echoed back. And that peculiar smell, a combination of cleanliness and decay. Shaking the nausea away, she forced herself back to thoughts of her chubby new babies.

'What's the best thing that's ever happened to you?' Toby once asked.

'You,' she'd replied.

He'd groaned but still grinned. 'I knew you'd say that.'

To impress her dad, she'd once said she wanted to be a doctor, but in truth the prospect of seeing a dead body had terrified her, still did. All the usual fears had swamped her mind: what would it look like? Or smell like? How did you know the person was really deceased? What if you made a mistake? Suppose they came to life like a zombie?

Now at the door, she put her hand to her neck. Was she going to see one now? How would she cope if she did? 'Not life threatening,' her mum had said. Why was she panicking?

With that old need-to-pee sensation, she entered. Her father was in the far-corner bed. Picturing a flash of blood red, she blinked it away and stepped closer. He was still, his eyes closed. Though grey and pallid, his face was smooth and unlined. Oh God, like a death mask? Stock still, she stared, only exhaling with a jump when his arms suddenly twitched.

A strangely comical moment; she wished Cam was there. She blew out and glanced around. What now? Her alarm had been replaced by a dull sensation of guilt. Maurice hadn't planned to be ill, but it felt like a reproof. She had definitely been 'off' with him when she and Harry last visited, and now he was in a hospital.

'Hello.'

She turned to the voice. A medic had picked up her father's nursing chart. 'How is he?' she asked as he studied the notes. 'Oh, sorry, I'm his daughter.'

The young man smiled warmly. 'I can tell. He's OK. It appears he's had a stroke but he was confused and upset when he woke earlier, so he was given a sedative. For now, he just needs lots of rest.'

A stroke. What exactly did that mean? She wanted to ask more, but didn't know where to begin in such untrodden territory. She began to formulate a question, but the guy had moved on, so she sat in the bedside chair and gazed at her father's non-father face. Would it be strange to kiss his sleeping cheek?

'Eleanor.' Marian's hiss was unexpected. 'Is he still asleep, love?'

Ellie turned to the entrance. 'Yes, he looks peaceful. Here, come and have this seat.' Her mum made no move, so she stepped to her. 'The doctor said he was confused and upset earlier. What was that all about?'

'Oh, I don't know. I suppose he was,' she replied, searching her handbag.

'How so, Mum? What did he say?'

She shook her head. 'I'm suddenly so very tired. I don't know what's come over me.'

'I expect it's the shock. Let's sit down and I'll drive you home later. I'm happy to stay for as long as it takes. Then when he wakes we'll be here, the first people he sees. It might help his confusion—'

'Now, Ellie, please!' As though on the verge of hysteria, Marian's voice was shrill. With an obvious effort, she tempered it. 'I really need home and some sleep, if you don't mind, love. And I'd like to go now.'

23

Ellie weaved through the teatime traffic and yawned. It wasn't that late, but her mother's exhaustion was contagious. Erect in the passenger seat, she was awake but silent, the agitation she'd shown earlier apparently all gone.

From time to time Ellie glanced at Marian's glazed gaze. She was astonished she hadn't wanted to stay at the hospital; she'd expected to have to drag her away. But who knew what she was feeling inside; save for her admission of guilt, she wasn't sharing it, that was for sure.

The crunch of pebbles seemed to bring Marian back. Peering at her handsome home, she finally dug into her handbag and passed the house key to Ellie.

'All right, Mum?' she asked as she opened the front door.

The usual aromas greeted her. The mix of her mum's craft products – resin, clay, paint and turps – topped with a cloud of household cleaning products to satisfy her dad's OCD.

Her voice sounded echoey. 'Come on, Mum. You go and lie on the sofa and I'll fetch you a cover, then something to eat.'

'Righto.'

Marian obliged, meek, like a child.

Watching her shuffle away, Ellie's belly churned. Oh God, what would become of them all if Maurice died? Though the thought had been prodding since Marian's phone call this morning, it wasn't one she could retain for long as it didn't feel real. Her father was too strong, too vital in her head to expire. The figure in the bed was an imposter, pretending to be ill. That's how it felt.

When she returned with a blanket, Ellie glanced at the settee, but her mum was sitting in Maurice's hearth chair, as though keeping it warm for him. 'What do you fancy eating?' she asked her.

'A sandwich will do, love; I'm not very hungry.'

'Okey-dokey. A cup of tea, too?'

Setting to work in the kitchen, Ellie reached for the bread board, but stopped to study Marian's display of craft on the pine dresser. The line of windmills seemed to high five with their blades, but the furling artwork and crumbling trinkets the boys had made over the years tugged her heartstrings. Had everything gone to plan with Nina and Hen? God, she hoped they were OK.

She pinched her nose at the sad passage of time, then turned to her task, preparing a ham and salad sandwich, remembering at the last minute that her mum didn't like butter. As she waited for the kettle, she gazed through the large pane. It felt curious to stand in Marian's shoes and watch life as she saw it – Maurice's Jaguar in prime position on the driveway, the glossy leaves of the high laurel bushes behind, now lit by the evening sun. And there was the sweet aroma of the floral disinfectant her mother always used. A childhood smell, which always made her feel inexplicably melancholy when she caught it.

Perhaps she missed Woodlands more than she realised.

Carrying the tray to the lounge, she stopped in the doorway and observed her mum for a moment. Her expression vacant, she was staring at the vibrant wooded area through the window.

Ellie's stomach lurched again. Marian's whole adult life had revolved around Maurice; she'd be terrified of losing him. Since she was eighteen, there had been that tight love and dependency. And if he died, she'd be alone, isolated in this rambling house with its nooks and corners and emptiness.

Ellie glanced at the ceiling. Playing hide-and-seek in the vast space upstairs with her primary-school pals had been fun but scary too. Woodlands wasn't ancient, but there were some parts that Marian hadn't got around to renovating and those rooms, while accessible, remained in their original state. They were cold and dank, crammed with dark musty furniture, artwork and junk. If one had ever crouched in there, one had wanted to be found PDQ.

'Must be worth a bob or two these days,' Cameron once commented when they stood in the garden looking up at the house. 'If a developer got hold of this plot, he'd build another four and make a killing.'

'Shh, Dad will hear you,' Ellie had replied. 'The only way he'll leave here is in his coffin.'

Oh God. Had she really said that?

She put the snack on a side table and settled down in the armchair opposite her mum. Silent but there, it felt like a peculiar role reversal as she watched Marian eat and drink, then close her eyes and slip into sleep.

Motionless herself, she observed the starlings and house sparrows fruitlessly pecking at the bird table. Why had Marian been so keen to leave the hospital and thereby Maurice? It seemed wholly out of character. But shock was draining, Ellie knew that. More than just *draining*. She'd experienced it herself, sleeping solidly in the 'spare room' for days. Barely speaking, barely eating, barely there, until by some miracle she'd forced herself together, stuffed her backpack and returned to her studies in the November.

To a new house and new friends in Alston Terrace.

The rasp of the stones accusingly loud, Ellie reversed her car from the drive and headed for the motorway. She felt bad for leaving, but she'd called the ward to check on her father and had left a note for her mum:

Mum – Dad is fine. They say he's comfortable and sleepy. Love you lots. Call you tomorrow.

Ellie loved her mum dearly, but her sons were her priority. Children should always come first. It was how it should be, surely? And Hen couldn't be expected to stay all night. As she watched the Lancashire hills turn industrial, it occurred that she could've asked Jaqs to help out, but it wasn't something she and Cam had ever done.

'Mum wasn't Florence Nightingale, put it that way,' Cam would say with a mock grim face if anyone asked about his childhood. 'But Dad was a good laugh, still is.'

Finally back in Heaton Moor, Ellie stifled another yawn, tiptoed up the path and quietly opened the porch door. She hoped the boys would be in bed, if not asleep. She was too weary to face all their questions just now.

Hearing voices from the kitchen, she put her head around the door.

'Oh, hello,' she said, trying not to show the alarm she felt. 'Is everything all right?'

Of course she had expected to see Hen, but her friend cosied up with male company took her by surprise.

'Everything is dandy,' Hen replied, her voice husky. She turned and lifted her eyebrows. 'Now at least.' Her cheeks lightly coloured. 'It's entirely my fault, Ellie. Everything was going swimmingly. Then, as the boys were saying goodnight, I said the wrong thing to Jakey. No idea what, but he disappeared upstairs and then reappeared fully dressed, saying he was off to the hospital. Walking, apparently. Sorry, Ellie, I didn't want to trouble you and the only deal Jake was prepared to make was to call the professor here so he could drive Jakey to . . .'

'To Chorley,' Ellie said, noting Hen's elegant fingers on Sean's arm.

'Toby was very clever and found the telephone number for me,' she continued. 'Then Sean turned up, managed marvellously to reason with Jakey within minutes. The boys went to bed, mission accomplished. About five minutes ago, actually.' She stood and smoothed down her fitted dress. 'And now, darling, I must love you and leave you. There are some dreadfully boring banking types at home and Edward is desperate to show off his spectacular wife to them. That's me, apparently,' she added, flashing a smile at Sean.

Ellie followed her pal to the porch. 'Thanks for everything, Hen,' she said, kissing her goodbye. 'You've been a lifesaver.'

'Oh, don't thank me,' she replied, stepping into the dusk and wafting her hand. 'Thank the professor in shining armour. So handsome. And not a bald patch in sight.'

Breath trapped high in her chest, Ellie turned back to the kitchen, but Sean was already in the hallway, car keys in hand. He was leaving, thank God.

'Thank you for coming over and sorting out Jake; it was very good of you,' she said, her voice emerging ridiculously clipped and formal. But she still stayed at the door, holding it open and willing him to leave.

'Mum! Mum!' An urgent call from upstairs. Jake, of course. 'Mum, is that you? Are you home?'

She smiled thinly. 'Motherhood, eh? Night, Sean. Love to Ciara and the kids. Thanks again.'

24

Lit by the dim landing light, Jake looked sleepy, his hair ruffled. Although he was tall for his ten years, he had an innocent air about him. A tiny part of Ellie wanted to shout, to tell him off for being so difficult, to demand he bloody well go to sleep. But that would be horrible and unkind. And counter-productive. If she wanted some rest before the early hours, she knew he had to explain what was troubling him.

Smiling despite herself, she sighed. In a funny way, her middle son had been good for her. He'd taught her patience.

She climbed in next to him, stroked his forehead and said those familiar words, 'Come on, Jakey, tell me all about it.'

A girl would have been nice, but Ellie was still delighted when Toby was born. A healthy son to start the family. Soon falling pregnant again, she secretly hoped for a daughter. Indeed, the pregnancy was so different, she convinced herself the baby would be a girl. No morning sickness and though she was tired at times, it was nothing compared to the overwhelming fatigue she'd experienced with Toby.

After a long labour, she'd been so surprised to see another willy that she wept and couldn't stop. It had felt as though her baby girl had been taken away.

'Relief and pleasure and hormones,' the midwife had said, laughing. 'Don't worry, cry all you like, it's perfectly normal.'

Ellie had glanced at Cam holding his second son, but saw no disappointment in his face. Then Jake was put in her arms. She looked at his exquisite features, took in the heady smell of a newborn, and was overcome with guilt. Calm and beautiful, he looked back with wide, inquisitive eyes.

'He's been here before,' the midwife said.

The perfect little baby, Jake fed well and slept well, keeping a watch on the world. People commented on what an angel he was, admiring his strawberry-blond curls and bright eyes. But when Harry came along, everything changed. Jake became withdrawn and difficult. He refused to share Ellie or his toys. If he didn't get his own way, he fell into uncontrollable waves of anger, hitting out and screaming until he exhausted himself.

The tantrums drained her. Not knowing how to handle an outburst in public, she stopped going out. Jake's behaviour was embarrassing enough at the village shops or in a supermarket, but felt even worse at the mum and toddler groups. She felt alienated from the other mothers with their perfectly behaved children and their disapproving faces. 'Look,' she wanted to shout, 'I brought up Toby, a perfectly nice and ordinary little boy. He's fine. He's normal. It's not my fault!'

Secretly, of course, she knew it was her fault. She should only have asked for a healthy baby when pregnant. She shouldn't have been so dashed when another son was born.

She now came back to her beautiful boy. His voice thick with sleep, he was telling his story. So tired, he struggled to prop open his eyes, but the need to vindicate himself was all-important. She understood that, though some truths were better kept to oneself.

'Hen told us that Grandad Wilson was under the weather, and that was why he was in hospital. I told her that I knew "under the weather" was just a saying, and that if she wasn't going to tell the truth, I would find out for myself.'

'Grandad is fine, Jake. Truly. I left him fast asleep in the hospital, which is how you should be too. Shall we talk tomorrow and I'll explain everything? I promise. A song for now?'

He nodded and Ellie sang quietly as his breathing slowed into sleep.

Eventually she stood and stepped away. The clutch of emotion in her chest, she gave him a last glance. Not a bedtime had gone by without replaying that dreadful evening, the night she'd realised she needed help with him. It had been a day consumed with his bad behaviour: crying, fighting, fits of temper. Cameron was working away. After hours of battling and calming and comforting, Jake had finally dropped off in the early hours.

In sleep, the peaceful angel had returned. Ellie spent a few moments picking up thrown Lego and teddies and torn artwork, and then his pillow, damp from snot and tears and discarded on the floor. Like now, she stood and stared at her boy, wanting to bottle the quiet and calm. Then she'd watched herself lean over his face, the tendons in her arms and hands protruding as she pressed hard with the cushion. He didn't struggle, but the fabric tore, spraying plumes gently around the bed, like snowflakes. And instead of worrying about the boy, she tried to catch the feather-snow – jumping, scooping and laughing – like a gleeful infant at Christmas.

The out-of-body experience had soon passed, thank God. She'd still been clutching the pillow to her chest; not a down-filled cushion, but polyester. And with a deep shudder of relief, she'd gently

127

lifted her boy's head, tucked the pillow beneath and kissed him goodnight.

She now blinked away the disturbing image. Everything was fine; Jake was settled and asleep. Though she longed to close her eyes and block out those snowy feathers, the windows and doors needed locking, just one final chore before bed.

25

Ellie padded down the stairs and made for the front door.

'Ellie?'

Though spoken quietly from the kitchen, the unexpected sound made her jump. A palm to her chest, she stepped in. What the ... ? Sean hadn't left; he was back in his seat, the 'Fall in Love Again' brochure from the Whitworth in his hands.

Oh God, he didn't want to talk about *that* again, did he? She had no energy, no interest. No bloody resilience right now.

He raked his dark hair. 'Sorry, I didn't mean to startle you. Thought I'd stay a couple of minutes to see if everything was all right.' He smiled with tight lips. 'It seemed wrong just to leave.'

'Oh right. Well ...' she started, then she noticed the bottle of whiskey and a single glass on the table. Cam's Jack Daniel's. Even the smell of it knocked her sick. Had Sean been drinking it? Had Hen?

American shit.

Who had said that? Like someone walking over her grave, she felt a shiver.

Sean's eyes followed hers. 'Still very beguiling,' he said.

'Are you never tempted?' she asked, trying to shake away the discomfort.

'Not the booze, no.'

Another shudder she couldn't quite describe. 'So, yes, Jake,' she said, deflecting that gaze. 'He needed to explain about the misunderstanding with Hen. He didn't like the expression . . .Well, he probably told you. He's fine now. Asleep, I hope. Sorry again for spoiling your evening. I'm sure you need to get back to—'

'And what about you? Hearing about your dad must have been a nasty shock. How are you coping?'

'What's this? *In the Psychiatrist's Chair*?' she asked. She had intended a jovial tone, but her throat was constricting. She took a silent breath and looked at her watch. 'Dad's fine. I'm fine,' she replied, shrugging. 'I'm just tired, so . . .'

She wanted him to leave. All through the long day no one else had asked how *she* felt and his concern made her want to cry. Privately, alone.

Showing no sign of moving, he didn't reply. Though her head was bowed, she knew he was watching, waiting for her to speak.

'Actually, I don't know how I'm coping,' she blurted after a beat. 'My father, who I've loved and loathed throughout my life, is in hospital and I'm not sure if I'm sick with worry or I simply don't care. All I do know is that I feel culpable. I feel guilty that I was cross with him the last time we spoke. I feel guilty for leaving Mum on her own tonight. Guilty for dumping the boys on Nina and Hen. Guilty that I'm still full of resentment towards my dad, which is ridiculous after all these years.'

Still leaning against the door jamb, she inhaled sharply, the need to say it imperative. 'He stopped paying my grant at uni. At the beginning of the third year, before . . . before I lived with you and Cam. He just cancelled the standing order without even telling me, and I had no money. Not a bean for rent, the bills or food. Over something I'd done, something so minor that I can't even remember what it was. I know it's pathetic – I should've moved on long ago – but I still think about it. I still feel resentful, angry, hurt . . .'

Deeply flushing and shamefaced by her pathetic self-pity, she finally puffed out the trapped air. 'God, I'm sorry; rant over. I don't know where that came from. You'd think I'd be over teenage angst by now. Or should I say early-twenties trauma?' She tried for a smile. 'Is it just me, or do all fathers fuck their children up?'

The cloud was immediate, a dark shadow that passed over Sean's sculpted face. Then the glower that had once been so familiar. She could feel his mocking eyes and hear his biting words as though it was only yesterday: *'Her paintings are angry, Cam. Do we think it's real? Or are they just fake avant-garde crap? Shall we ask Lady Eleanor to explain what they mean?'*

She stared. Yes, on reflection she had been a spoilt middle-class girl who'd been wholly dependent on her daddy. But that's the way she'd been brought up, and it didn't mean her feelings of shock, rejection and, yes, rage, had been any less valid. And what the hell had she said to needle the chip on Sean's shoulder this time?

'Do all fathers fuck their children up?' Realisation hitting, she dropped her gaze. Oh God, the girl at the gallery. She *was* his lover. Did that make him a crap father who'd fuck his children up? Yes, probably. But only if he left them. Or if he was found out. Bloody hell; did he think she'd tell Ciara?

Swinging from embarrassment to indignation, she pulled out a chair and sat down. Taking a shuddery breath she rubbed the table. 'I wouldn't dream of telling Ciara.' She glanced at him. 'Or Cam, if that's what you're worried about.'

His expression perplexed, he dipped his head to meet hers. 'About . . . ?'

Oh hell, how to put it? She stumbled on. 'Look, it was just a stupid quip about fathers. I didn't mean anything by it. And I've already said it's none of my business.'

As though the penny had just dropped, he sat back and folded his arms. 'What are you saying, Ellie?'

'Nothing. I don't know. What you said about being tempted just now and ... I'm just knackered. I need to go to bed, so if you wouldn't mind ...'

Her heart clattering, she rose and made to pass him, but he caught her hand.

'Tempted? You think Samantha's my—'

'No, of course not.' She lowered her head to hide the brimming tears. 'I'm confused; I don't know. I just felt so, so ...'

Disappointed, let down, jealous. But she couldn't say any of that. And his incredulous face right this moment ... Oh God. The girl *was* his sister. Why was her judgement so impaired? Perhaps she had reason with this man and their hostile history, but Cam and Hen, even her mum. She had to stop the paranoia and get a grip.

With a huge effort she pulled herself together and looked at him straight. 'I'm sorry. I'm just a bit of a disaster at the moment.' Conscious his warm palm was still fastened to hers, she carefully withdrew it and tried for humour. 'See – what did I say about guilt? Now I feel guilty that I've offended you.'

Leaning back, Sean rotated the pamphlet from corner to corner. 'Well, you're probably right. In all likelihood we've all fucked Samantha up.' He sighed. 'I didn't even meet her until she was five years old.'

It was Ellie's turn to fall quiet. She didn't know what to say. She couldn't imagine having a little sister and not seeing her until she was of school age. Children were shaped by then, personality already set in.

'I'm sorry,' she said finally, wanting to know more, but sensing it wasn't appropriate to ask.

'Well, there you have it. I'm pretty much an expert in regret and all that goes with it myself.'

Scrabbling for kind words, she smiled. 'She seemed thrilled to see you.' Then, 'She was nice, very pretty.' She didn't really want to think of the chance meeting at the art gallery and how it had affected her equanimity, in all sorts of ways.

He stared at the brochure and frowned. '"Fall in Love Again",' he muttered. 'What makes it acceptable to give in to temptation? Is love enough? And what about the guilt?' Seeming to shake himself back, he stood. Then he reached out a hand to her cheek.

Holding her breath, Ellie stilled as he lifted a stray strand of hair.

'But sometimes you don't feel remorse when you should,' he said. 'You pretend it isn't happening. What about you, Ellie?'

'So what made you decide to meet Samantha?' she asked, stepping away from his touch.

He was silent for moments. 'Things happened; I grew up. And when I held Katrina . . .'

Ellie nodded. She didn't know what had occurred, or why he hadn't met his sister until then, but that powerful, evocative smell of a newborn she did understand.

Sean looked at his watch. 'I was here to listen to you and I've . . . I'll go.'

Ellie's mind flitted to the Maurice angst. How many times had she tried to explain it to Cameron? But the: 'he's a good guy really', 'just set in his ways', 'he means well' platitudes always slid from Cam's tongue before she'd even finished her sentence.

'You did listen,' she replied. 'Thank you.'

Keeping her distance, she followed Sean to the front door. He put his fingers on the latch and turned, his eyes dark and unreadable. 'I don't tend to talk about Samantha. Some things are too personal, you don't ...'

A prickle of anxiety and danger caught her breath. What did he mean? Troubled and confused, she searched his face for an answer. Then he moved towards her.

'Night, Sean,' she said, quickly moving back.

Why she wanted to feel his strong arms hold her tightly, she didn't know.

Those arms weren't safe, were they?

26

Sainsbury's again, the trolley so heavy. Up and down the aisles, then back to the start. Scouring pads, disinfectant, aspirin. Scouring pads, disinfectant, aspirin. The smell sweet in her nostrils, the shopping piled high. Scouring pads, disinfectant, aspirin.

Leaning her weight against the trolley, she heaves it slowly towards the checkouts. Her mother is waiting behind the till. She's wearing a nurse's uniform and yellow Marigold gloves.

'It's really for the best, I promise,' she says.

But a gentle hand catches hers and she meets troubled eyes. 'What makes it acceptable to give in?' a man asks.

Torn between the two, she turns back to her mother. Her soft face folds in disappointment. 'Eleanor Wilson! You're naked.'

Ellie sat bolt upright in her bed.

'Mum, you're bare, that's yuk.'

Harry covered his eyes with his fists. He was standing in the doorway, lightly kicking the jamb, dressed and ready for school.

Her heart racing, she pulled up the duvet. 'Well, whose

bedroom is this anyway?' Expecting Cam to be there, she turned to his pillow. Oh God; he was in Vietnam.

She came back to Harry's scrunch of disgust. 'Can't anyone have five minutes' peace around here, cheeky chops?' she asked as she slumped back against the mattress.

'Not when it's half past eight,' Toby called from the landing. He popped his head around the door. 'We had a debate and decided it was best to let you have a lie-in. If it hadn't been for goody-two-shoes here, we'd have got away with it until lunch.' He lightly smacked the back of Harry's head. 'Look, Mummy's boy even put on his uniform.'

'Right.' Trying to throw off the grogginess, Ellie shook herself. 'Everyone out and let me get dressed. Toby, thank you, darling boy, but get to your bus!'

'I was only trying to help by staying,' he replied. 'I couldn't leave goody-two-shoes on his own with weirdo.'

'Toby! How many times have I told you . . . ?' But he had already gone, bounding down the stairs, the front door slamming.

She peered at Harry. 'Don't tell Jake what Toby called him, love.'

'I know,' he replied, rubbing his head as he left.

A hundred worries were jabbing, most of them guilt. *Guilt*, oh God, her father. She looked at her watch and tried to calm herself. Get up, wash, clean teeth, don clothes, take the boys to school, then ring Mum. The rest could wait.

'Harry,' she called as an afterthought, 'has anybody had breakfast?'

Appearing calm and composed, Marian was waiting at the door. She'd made up her face and taken care to look her best. Like going for an interview, Ellie thought. Her jumper was cashmere beneath her blazer and she'd softly curled her pale hair around her cheeks; she looked pretty.

'How are you this morning, Mum? You look nice,' she said as she bent to kiss her.

It was funny how children outgrew their parents. Toby was as tall as Ellie and Jake was catching up, too. Had her eldest arrived safely at school? She took it on trust that he did actually go. She had, every day, on the bus from the top of their road to her fee-paying school near Preston. The trouble was that she hadn't always stayed.

Marian didn't say much on the way to the hospital. Not that it mattered; Ellie was distracted herself, trying not to internally obsess. She'd phoned Cam four times before leaving home and there'd been no reply. She hadn't left a message at first, but by the third she'd felt sufficiently exasperated to say, 'Cameron, it's me. This is the third time I've rung. Why have you turned your bloody phone off? It's important; call me.'

Her unease was interrupted by Marian's firm voice. 'Did you hear what I was saying, Ellie? I said that if Dad's still a bit confused, you mustn't mind.'

From her mum's rigid stance, Ellie was sure there was more. 'OK. So . . . ?'

'Well, when people are ill, they become disorientated, and say silly things, don't they?'

Ellie nodded. Did they? Yes, she supposed they might, but her father wasn't the type to say 'silly' things. The childhood apprehension prodded, faded but not gone. What had he been saying about her this time? A vague worry, but thoughts of Cameron and why he hadn't replied to her messages and texts were more dominant right now.

The car hummed at the temporary traffic lights. They seemed to stay on red for an aeon. 'The tram lines,' Marian eventually stated, breaking the silence.

'Right,' Ellie replied, but her attention had slipped back to this morning and poor Harry's pink cheeks and indignation. The boys were undoubtedly as keen as she not to witness bare flesh. They knew to knock before entering the bedroom. Perhaps Harry had; maybe she'd been stuck in a dream, forgotten now.

The funny side not quite there yet, she shook her head at the faux pas. 'I saw Mum's boobies this morning. It was disgusting,' Harry had pronounced to his teacher at the blue school door. The day had started badly: naked boobies, absent Cam and a 'confused' Maurice. Whatever that meant. She sensed it wasn't going to improve.

'When do you think they will finish these roadworks?' Marian suddenly asked. 'A client of Dad's designed the original bridge, you know. Clarence Thorpe's his name. He and his wife never had children, but they've always kept Siamese cats. Dad says that he sneezes whenever he goes there. We went for dinner, just the once, and it was very embarrassing, not because of the animals, but because the food was terrible. They served baked beans as the veg. Most peculiar.'

Surprised, Ellie glanced at her mum. 'As long as they were Heinz,' she replied with a smile. She'd heard this tale before. From Maurice, of course. He was a good raconteur and his version, although somewhat embellished, was quite humorous.

In fairness to her dad, he could tell a good yarn when he was in a jovial mood, but too often it'd evolve into a 'how well I've done for a client', or, 'how clever I was getting the better of the tax man' anecdote. One had to repeatedly hear the same account, playing the appreciative audience each time. Marian didn't seem to mind, but eventually Ellie had learned to cut in quickly: 'Yes, Dad, you've told me.'

Culpability rose again. Uncharitable; she was unkind to her dad. Was it really so hard just to listen for a few minutes?

Her mind softly landed on last night. A needy release in a way.

An exchange of private information, of secrets, almost. It had helped, hadn't it? Everyone needed someone to pay attention once in a while, to sound off and not be judged or dismissed. And yet the fluttering concern was there in her belly. She'd shared too much. She regretted telling Sean about Maurice and money. She had shown her hand, gone too far. Secrets should remain secret and hidden. Letting hers spill over made her feel vulnerable and exposed.

And Sean; why didn't he 'tend to talk' about his sister? Did Cam know about her?

The naked dream from this morning suddenly surfacing, she peeped again at her mum. She'd try harder with Maurice. She definitely would.

27

Ellie pushed at the ward door and held her breath. The same imposter body was in the far corner, but today the two beds opposite were occupied. Her chin held high, Marian click-clacked across the linoleum, softly stroked her sleeping husband's fringe from his forehead, then sat. Though her mum's shoulders didn't move, Ellie felt them slump.

Disappointment, relief or anxiety? It was difficult to judge.

Not sure what to do, Ellie loitered around the footboard and picked up her father's chart. Her mum was in the allocated chair and sitting on the mattress felt impertinent, not only from a health and safety perspective (hadn't she read that it wasn't allowed any more?) but in respect to her dad. Around the age of eleven, it had been made very clear that she was sufficiently mature to cope with the bad dreams by herself, and that the comfort of her parents' divan was banned.

'Turn over the pillow and go back to sleep, Eleanor. Ghosts and bogeymen don't exist; you're old enough to work that out for yourself,' she remembered.

And when she'd protested, her mum's soft voice: *'Just try it, love. Dad's right. Waking up is a habit you've fallen into.'* Then she'd give her an aspirin before bed. *'Here, love. This will help you get off.'*

A placebo, of course. Even at eleven, she'd known that, but it had felt like a sign of Marian's love; despite Maurice's way or the highway, she had understood.

Ellie glanced around the room and then wished that she hadn't. The old guy opposite had milky eyes and was breathing heavily; the tube from his mouthpiece appeared to be full of blood. The other poor bugger was asleep on his stomach, the vent of his gown revealing saggy, white buttocks. The third bed was neatly made up and empty. There had definitely been someone there yesterday. Hadn't there? Oh God, here today, gone tomorrow. To home or to his grave, she didn't know.

The thought made her think of Cam again, so she dug in her handbag. She stared at the empty screen; still no response to her blinking texts. She composed yet another.

'Now come on, Maurice, it's time you woke up,' Marian said suddenly and loudly.

'Mum!' Surprised at her mother's imperious command, Ellie sneaked a look over her shoulder. An elderly cleaning lady was sweeping under the beds, and a couple of nurses were chatting at the entrance, but nobody seemed to have noticed. She tried to hide the bubbling snigger. 'I don't think you're supposed to badger the patients. Besides, library rules apply in a hospital.'

Matching pink circles had appeared on Marian's cheeks. 'Well, it's time he woke up.' She pushed hard at Maurice's shoulder and he half opened his eyes.

'Oh, there you are, Marian,' he croaked, sounding far older than his sixty-eight years. Clearly dazed, he swallowed. 'Is there a—'

Marian thrust a baby-type beaker in his hand and he sucked

greedily at the spout. Feeling something between pity and hilarity, Ellie stayed back and watched.

'I'm glad you're here, Marian.' The water had apparently revived her dad like a plant, as his brisk voice returned. 'Yes. I'd like you to find the manager. This bloody hotel's lost my briefcase and it contains an important file that I need to read for this afternoon's meeting.'

He sounded and looked so preposterous that the need to laugh out loud grew, and it was all Ellie could do to hold it in. But it wasn't just his ridiculous self-importance, it was relief; she could feel the tension oozing from her jaw, her shoulders and limbs. Maurice was back with them. He was indeed clearly confused, but thank God he was back.

She opened her mouth to say something, but Marian turned and gave her a stony look. 'You're not at work, Maurice,' she said with loaded patience. 'You're in hospital. They say you've had a stroke.'

'Well, that can't be right,' he answered firmly. 'I've had an hour with Andrew Maher today; he's been headhunted again. Wants me to take a look at his finances.'

'Now, Maurice—' Marian started.

'Mr Wilson, you're awake! Here, let's get you a wee bit more comfortable.'

A formidable-looking nurse with an incongruously soft accent had appeared. She lifted Maurice's head to remove the pillow, which she battered into shape.

Ellie blinked, thought of Jake, hoped he was having a good day at school.

'I trust you're going to be in a better mood today, Mr Wilson,' the nurse said. As though it was Marian's fault, she looked at her sternly. 'He was more than a wee bit stroppy when he woke up this morning. He refused his cup of tea or to eat his breakfast. I had to read him the riot act.'

Exchanging looks with her mum, Ellie walked into the huge space the ward sister had left. 'Hello, Dad,' she said cheerily. 'How are you feeling?'

He studied her for a second, then turned towards Marian, his pale eyes cold. 'What's she doing here?'

'Eleanor has come to see you, of course. She's been very concerned about you,' she replied with a steely calm about her.

Ellie moved aside as the cleaner approached. The smiley woman brushed all around them, wiped over Maurice's side table, then spoke to him. 'There we are, my love, all nice and clean now.' She nodded at Ellie. 'Now this must be your pretty daughter. There's no mistaking the two of you are related.'

Maurice shook his head, his face defiant. 'She's not mine. I don't have one.'

'Of course you do, Maurice. It's Ellie.'

'No, Marian. I do not have a daughter.'

Not knowing what to say, Ellie swallowed as the poor cleaner shuffled away. What the hell? This was more than *confusion*. Exactly how bad was the stroke? But her father's expression was so hostile, her concern morphed into the usual smarting hurt. Her instinct was to bolt, but she remembered her silent vow in the car.

'Oh, come on, Dad, I'm sorry if I've done anything to upset you. I don't like to see you poorly. Let's be friends. The boys have been asking after you.' She fished in her bag. 'Jake got up early and made you a card before school.'

He continued to fix his belligerent gaze on his wife. 'Marian, I have no idea who this woman is. Could you ask the manager to deal with the situation? She's causing a nuisance.'

'Maurice, you're being ridiculous; you're not at work now, and that's no way to speak to Ellie. She has many other things to do, but she's driven all this way to see you because she's worried about you,' Marian said, an edge of panic in her bark.

'Now what is going on here?' The ward sister had appeared from nowhere again. Belying her gentle tone, her eyebrows were knitted over dark flinty eyes. 'I'm sure I don't have to remind you that Mr Wilson has suffered a cerebrovascular accident, ladies. He shouldn't be over-exciting himself.'

Marian inhaled to protest, but Ellie caught her short. 'It's all right, Mum, she's right. I'll go. Give me a ring later.'

She looked to her father, but his arms were folded like a truculent child's. 'Bye, Dad, get some rest. I'll come and see you tomorrow, should I?'

No reply, no reply; how she'd always hated that. But today she had to see the bigger picture, to swallow the hurt and humiliation, for him and her mum. Her chin raised like Marian's, she collected her handbag, moved to the door and stepped outside. Resisting the urge to run, she took a deep breath.

'I'm telling you, Marian. I do not have a daughter!' she heard as she walked briskly away.

28

The darkness feels brutal tonight. Oppressive and scary, but she doesn't know why.

It's silent, too silent. Holding her breath, she listens for voices, angry sound. But she knows that's just stupid. A cuddle or a hug, that's all she needs. Of safety and reassurance, that she's OK, that the world's OK.

Not shifting, slipping, out of control.

She steps to the open curtains to block out the night.

He's still there, in the car. As she stares, he looks up, but she scrunches her eyes.

Yes, she can feel them; those lips burning a necklace around her neck; his torso slick with sweat and moving against hers. And that rhythmic pressure intensifying, mounting and building.

Special, so special, she knows that she's special—

Rousing from the dream, Ellie opened her heavy eyelids before closing them again. It was daylight and she was alone. She tried to focus through the grogginess. That was right. Maurice; her father;

his rejection, yet again. Weary and numb, she'd come back from the hospital; she'd tidied the kitchen and lounge, then trudged upstairs. One more time, she'd thought as she lay on her bed, I'll call Cam one more time . . .

Unconsciousness had been instant, that dangerous drug of daytime sleep.

Almost expecting to be naked, she now put a hand to her belly. The sensual fantasy was still fresh, arousing and uncomfortable. Flushing at the recollection, she rocked her head and smiled wryly. What the hell, Ellie? And there were more chores to do; she needed to get on. But her limbs were still immobile, her mind stuffed with sand. Drowsy, so drowsy. She'd get up in a bit; just a few moments longer . . .

The world was still black, but an alarm was shrilling. Swimming hard to the surface, Ellie surged from the sludge.

She'd fallen asleep again. And the sound . . . ? A phone. The telephone on Cam's side of the bed was ringing. She snatched it up. 'Hello?'

'Ellie? You sound muzzy. Have I woken you up?'

'Cam, where have you been?' she managed through the wooziness. 'I've phoned about ten times.'

'Oh, it's my mobile. I'll have to get a new one. Everyone has been complaining.'

She shook herself awake. *Everyone, someone*; Cam's usual generic evasions. But she didn't have the energy to tackle that right now. Still winded, she took a breath. 'Dad's had a stroke. It was yesterday. He's in hospital.' Then, 'Don't worry, he's not dead. It's . . .' What word to use? She didn't actually know *what* was going on. '. . . it's manageable, I think.'

Cameron had finally called, but she felt flat. Flat and deflated, wanting to go back to that evaporating dream. She could no longer quite catch it, but her skin was still tingling.

She heard Cam's surprise, his intake of breath. 'What? Maurice has had a *stroke*? You're joking.' Then, after a beat, 'Oh sweetheart, that's awful. You poor thing. You should've telephoned the hotel.'

A clever bluff? The random *flat* thought passed through Ellie's mind.

'Bloody hell, poor old Maurice. I'm really sorry to hear that,' Cam continued. 'He'll hate not being able to get out on the golf course. How's he feeling?'

She pinched the burn at the top of her nose. 'He's well enough to give me a mouthful of abuse. Apparently I'm not his daughter.'

Cam snorted. 'Well, that's silly. You're the spitting image of him.'

'I'm not entirely sure that's a compliment, Cam. Anyway, I don't expect he meant it literally. Metaphorical madness. The crap daughter who's fallen below his expectations, et cetera, et cetera. Just the usual put-downs, but presented differently this time.'

'Oh, come on, sweetheart, he isn't that bad. He'll just be a bit out of sorts because he's in hospital. Bloody hell, who wouldn't be? Don't worry, he'll get over it. How are my boys?'

The usual bloody platitudes. Ellie tuned her mind to her sons. Bare boobies, slammed doors. But earlier than that? Yesterday seemed a lifetime ago. 'Jake had a turn when Hen was looking after him last night and . . . ' She paused. Did Cam already know? What had Sean said before he left? *Too personal?* What counted; what didn't? 'Well, she called Sean and he came over to reason with Jake. It was very kind of him.'

'Good man. If there's anyone you can rely on, it's Sean.' She could hear a muffled tone in the background. A female voice? 'Oh, someone wants me, Ellie. I'll give you another ring later. Keep your pecker up.'

Someone. She fell back on the bed. Flat and riled; not a good combination. The tears stung her eyes. Typical bloody Cameron. As ever, there had been no point trying to tell him how *she* felt. She wished she hadn't tried.

29

The weekend was roasting hot, even for late June. Ellie spent the early morning in the garden with the boys, heroically making up the numbers in a two-a-side football match, but cringing each time the ball thwacked next door's fence. Neighbourly relations were Cam's department. She didn't know which of the two women it was, but 'Valerie' had their phone number and when she called to complain (most weeks), Ellie didn't engage, but passed the handset to Cam, laughing at his ability to smooth the most ruffled of feathers.

'Do you think Valerie and the blonde are a . . . a couple?' he had asked with a grin when they first moved in.

'Very tactfully put for a Hastings,' she had replied. She'd kissed his cheek. 'But don't think for a minute I can't read your mind.'

At thirteen goals to nil, the match was abandoned. Harry stayed out to play with the rabbits but the other two disappeared, pleased to skulk back into the cool house, Jake to some intricate artwork and Toby to his mobile, his headphones and music.

'Whatever happened to good old fresh air?' she asked no one in particular. She sounded worryingly like Maurice.

Stretching out her bare legs, she sat in Cam's deckchair and watched Harry chat to the family Leporidae. He had names for them all, but as he presented each one, they looked pretty much the same. Except for Lulu, a beautiful pale grey bunny imposter, a throwback in the gene pool, it would seem.

She snorted. Like her, but she didn't even have that bloody excuse.

Her skin slightly sizzling from the relentless sun, she ambled to the kitchen and made for the tap to splash her face. But a voice from the open door stopped her in her tracks. Toby was talking on the hall telephone. Or at least, a polite faltering version of her eldest son was.

Was it a delayed Valerie tirade? She put a hand on her hip and watched him carefully replace the receiver. He stared for a moment, then excitement took over, flooding his face.

'Jake! Harry! It's the Walshes,' he hollered, almost deafening her. 'We're invited to a picnic at Lyme Park. They're on their way. They have all the food and equipment, we just have to follow.'

Barely ten minutes later, Ellie found herself in the open-windowed car, following the Walshes' SUV along the A6. Though there was little point, she pulled down the mirror flap at the traffic lights and attempted to rake her windswept hair into some semblance of respectability. Her reflection was pink and freckled. She'd probably spent too long in the sunshine already, but what the hell. Though a slightly annoying fait accompli, she conceded the invitation was thoughtful of Ciara. It had got the boys out of the house and into 'good old fresh air' again – nod to Maurice – and was a welcome distraction from the saga of his continued hostility towards her.

And, of course, her partner's absence.

'Isn't this the way to the Walshes' house?' Toby asked from the front seat.

'Yeah, they must have come all the way to collect us from Heaton Moor, only to double back,' Ellie replied. 'Isn't that nice?'

'So do you like Ciara now?' Jake asked from the back.

Ellie laughed. 'Who said I didn't?' she replied.

The sun prying its green hands, Ellie sat beneath a horse chestnut tree. She stretched out her legs and watched Sean and the boys play tag rugby. It felt odd to be doing nothing. She usually joined in the rounders or cricket with her clan, but gathered that boys were boys and girls were girls in the Walsh household.

It felt strange. Though she tried to grasp it, the fiercely political and opinionated man she'd shared a house with was slipping through her fingers. What was going on? The long-haired Sean had hated isms before they'd existed. Or that had been his propaganda, at least. Just once or twice she had tried to rail against it. Unsuccessfully, of course.

'*You say you're a feminist; you hate sexism. Really, Sean? Men and women are equal, are they? So you think that squares with the way you treat women?*'

'*You have no idea how I am with women.*' Green eyes offended, hostile and challenging. '*But if you'd like to discuss hypocrisy, Miss Eleanor, let's look at you, shall we?*'

Thinking he'd touch her cheek, she'd flinched. But he hadn't, and instead of rising to her tenacious – '*You haven't answered my question, Sean*' – he'd walked away.

She shrugged off the teetering discomfort. What did Cam always say, somewhat rudely, to Paul or Ruth if they brought up university days? 'Old news; we were different people then. Move on.'

In fairness, he was right.

She turned towards her host. 'Can I help with anything?'

Laying out the picnic on a sun-dappled tablecloth, Ciara appeared to be talking to herself. 'Sandwiches and wraps, chicken legs and potato wedges.' With a mild frown, she carefully opened a foil-wrapped item and nodded. 'Still warm.' Then, seeming to hear Ellie's question, 'No, it's all grand. We have salad *and* fruit. Strawberries mixed with mango, cherries and grapes. Oh, and dark chocolate kept chilled with the drinks. Ninety per cent cacao never did anybody any harm.'

Ellie gazed at the multicoloured spread. Churlish. She'd been churlish about Ciara. She really must stop. 'Looks wonderful. Thank you so much. You've done us proud.'

Her lips twitching, Ciara tucked a stray ginger curl beneath her scarf. 'It's no trouble. It's what us women are here for, don't you think, Ellie? To look after our men?'

Glimpsing Toby and Katrina from the corner of her eye, Ellie didn't reply. She watched them stroll around the perimeter of the playground, deep in conversation.

Ciara followed her gaze. 'Now there's a lovely thought. Wouldn't it be sweet if those two fell in love? They'd make such a handsome couple. Then we'd be related.'

Ellie covered her desire to snort loudly with a polite smile. Flaming heck; here to look after men. Marry poor Toby off at twelve. So much for the churlish check. If only Cam was around with a 'get thee to a nunnery' quip, which only he could get away with.

The humour dissolved. Cameron bloody Hastings who was 'somewhere' with 'someone' and 'everyone'.

Ciara's shrill voice brought her back. 'Georgie! Dirty!' she exclaimed, jumping up and racing towards her youngest child, who had managed to crawl several metres towards a pile of litter.

'Everything good?' a voice asked.

With a lurch Ellie turned to Sean's toned and tanned legs. Glossy with perspiration, he was squinting against the sunshine. He crouched down beside her.

Glad to hide behind her sunglasses, she nodded and looked away. 'Great, thanks. It was kind of Ciara to think of us.'

'How's your dad?'

'Oh, he's fine.'

He didn't respond. Though she couldn't look, she knew his eyes were sharp, attentive.

'Well, physically he's fine,' she continued. 'Seems he's Lear and I'm Cordelia, though that's hardly a fair comparison to the King's saintly youngest daughter. But you get the gist.'

'Ah, I see,' he replied. 'Cognitive issues can be quite common after a stroke. Problems with concentration, difficulty with recall both verbally and visually.' He looked at her intently. 'The short-term memory loss can be quite comical at times, but not so funny when it's directed at you.'

Turning, she stared. How did he know this? His intuition, his job or . . . ? The heat rose through her chest. Cam must have told him. That bloody hold Sean still had.

Harry flew up, coming to a stop with a skid. 'Mum,' he said breathlessly, 'Aidan's stuck at the top of the tree.'

Ciara followed with the little one tucked on her hip. 'Now I do like to see lads having fun,' she said with a tight smile. She passed the baby to Sean. 'You'd better save Aidan and then change Georgie. I'll keep our guest company.' Seeming to read Ellie's soul, she peered. 'Will I be getting us a soft drink while we have a nice chat?'

Sweaty and tense at Ciara's offer of companionship, Ellie watched Sean and Harry walk away. Her latest faux pas had tumbled back. Before leaving home, she'd grabbed a bottle of bubbly from the fridge, her only contribution to the picnic, which she'd proffered to Ciara when they'd arrived in the car park.

'Sean and I don't drink alcohol, Ellie, and you won't be wanting it yourself seeing as you're driving. Pop it back in your car, why don't you?'

Ellie had wanted to slap her own forehead. The Walshes didn't drink booze, she knew that. On the spur of the moment, she'd simply forgotten. And though it was said quite nicely, she'd felt reprimanded.

Wishing she could shrug off criticism like Cam, she absently watched two brown-grey birds swoop from their high perch, grab a flying insect and return to the same spot. Ah! Spotted flycatchers. What had her dad once said? 'Spotted flycatchers are like Mum: beautiful in an understated way.'

She smiled to herself, but the fond memory was pierced by Ciara's conversational tone.

'He's a very good-looking man, my Sean, isn't he?' She was readjusting the yellow scarf around her head. 'My Sean, he's a very good-looking man,' she repeated, as though Ellie might not have heard the first time.

Not sure how to respond, she nodded. It reminded her of Hen's reply to a similar question posed by her, which made her think of Cam and his increasingly sparse calls.

Ciara was still speaking. 'A lot of women have chased him, you know, Ellie, but no one will ever succeed in taking him from us. Never.'

Her lips fixed, Ellie smiled politely but remained silent and tense. Where on earth was this 'chat' going? Her churlish check was being sorely tested; it wasn't the sort of exchange people who only vaguely knew each other had.

Ciara patted her head. 'That's better. The sun burns my scalp if I'm not careful.' She peered at Ellie's hair. 'Though you're a red-head too, of course. Darker than mine, though. Do you use any special products?'

Relieved the conversation had reverted to the mundane, Ellie took a breath to reply, but Ciara carried on without taking a breath: 'Best keep men in your sights, don't you think? You must worry about Cameron being away so much. He could be doing anything, and you wouldn't know. I'm sure it would stress me.'

Behind her shades, Ellie stared, searching for meaning, but Ciara's expression was guileless, placid and friendly.

'Oh, don't you go worrying yourself,' she went on amiably. 'It's just me having a girlie gossip. We don't often get the opportunity. Now then, will you be having lemonade? Homemade, and so simple. I can give you the recipe if you like.'

30

The humidity didn't ease through the evening and into the night. Ellie had opened the upstairs windows and thrown off the boys' duvets, replacing them with crisp cotton sheets. It seemed to be working for them, but not for her. She'd had a stiff gin and tonic when they arrived home, but still couldn't sleep. Too warm with the duvet, too cold with a sheet.

Swinging from thought to thought, blowing hot and cold, hot and cold.

Dull street light lit the swirls on the ceiling. They seemed to whirl and pirouette as she stared. Like Marian and Maurice at the town hall dance. Bloody Dad. She quickly tossed that thought away, replacing it with her plans for the spare room. It was supposed to be her art studio, a grand but inappropriate tag. Like the huge bedrooms at Woodlands, it had become a store-room for junk.

Woodlands ... Her errant mind flipped back to her father. She'd made two more attempts to visit him at the hospital during the week, but he still hadn't managed to say a civil word to her. Wearing new striped pyjamas, he'd sat upright in the hospital bed, flicking officiously through papers. 'All he'd needed was a bowler hat,' she'd said to Cam when he'd finally called for a chat.

She didn't mind Maurice's odd behaviour so much for herself, she was getting used to it, and his obsession with the cleanliness of his nails was slightly humorous, but she could see that her mum was becoming increasingly distressed. And then there were the pyjamas. The blue and white stripes had taken her back with an uncomfortable jolt to an angsty time she couldn't quite pinpoint.

Hoping for the cool side, she turned the pillow. Cam had once whacked her with his after she'd woken him in the night. He'd only been fooling, but it had hurt, an unexpected assault adding to the horror of her dream.

She inhaled deeply. Cam, bloody Cameron. Every attempted distraction came full circle to him, still thousands of miles away with someone, somewhere.

What exactly had Ciara Walsh been implying today? The possibilities were tenfold, it seemed. A hint that Cam was unfaithful? A genuine attempt at girlie chatter? Causing trouble? A 'keep away from my man' warning? Or perhaps nothing at all.

She continued to stare upwards. The spirals felt like tiny cyclones of hot air puffing down. Sighing, she swapped her pillow with Cam's. *'Oh come on, Ellie; I was messing. It's only a soft cushion; stop being such an attention seeker,'* she remembered. In the morning there had been a red weal near her eye where the piped corner had caught it, but he hadn't commented or said he was sorry.

She flicked her head from side to side. God, she so wanted to sleep, but her mind wouldn't rest. It's something, it's nothing; something, nothing, something, nothing.

Ciara's innocent and yet knowing face bobbed in again. And her flaming husband? How Ellie hated the way Cam confided in him. Did Sean then run to Ciara and tell her? Even more loathsome. The bloody woman seemed to be very knowledgeable about Cam's whereabouts; she'd known about him accepting the barbecue invitation before Ellie had. Oh fuck. Perhaps Sean had told his wife a secret that Ellie really didn't want to know.

Cam, absent Cam.

Something, nothing, something, nothing.

Oh God. She needed to find out.

Sitting up, she unfurled the scrap of paper in her hand. Taking a quick, sharp breath, she picked up the phone and jabbed in the number with a trembling forefinger. She had no idea what time it was in Vietnam, but she supposed the hotel reception was open twenty-four hours, most decent ones were, and Cameron wasn't one to slum it, especially on expenses.

Needy and anxious, she listened to the ringing tone halfway across the world.

'Pathetic woman, get a grip,' she declared out loud. As she lifted her hand to cut off the call, it was answered.

The conversation was soon over, but still Ellie held the receiver, deaf and dumb for several moments. Putting it down eventually, she stayed upright, cross-legged on the bed, trying to think logically. But paralysed by alarm, her brain was refusing.

She didn't hear the soft knock or notice Toby's presence until he spoke, half asleep. 'Mum? Are you all right, Mum? I could hear talking.'

Emotion stole her voice. 'Oh, Toby, are you too big to give your old mum a hug?' she managed to croak.

He gave her a quick squeeze before climbing in to Cam's place at the furthest side of the bed, then turning away. 'You're not old. You're still in your thirties. Jason's mum is old. She's about fifty.' Then, after a moment, 'Why have you been crying?'

Ellie didn't answer. She wasn't aware that she had been, but when she touched her face, her fingers were wet. Thankful her son's breathing was already regular and deep, she lightly stroked his hair, then she fell back and pulled over the duvet.

31

The room is solid black. She can't move, she can't breathe.

She's in the layer of a dream, she tells herself. She just has to push out. But her body is pinned. She can't sit up, she can't move. She can't even scream. Oh God, her windpipe is being crushed, thrusting her down and further down into the depths of inky death.

Her fingers tingle. Yes, her arms are free, she can shove him away! She gropes for his shoulders, but her hands rest on his face. She immediately drops them, the fight all gone.

It's too dark to see him, but she knows it's her son—

'Mum! Please, Mum, wake up.'

Toby's quavering voice broke through the thick tar of the nightmare. 'You're frightening me, Mum. Please wake up.'

Gasping, Ellie opened her eyes. Her heart thrashing and almost sightless by the glare of the bedside lamp, she squinted at her son.

His face was pale, tears threatening. 'God, Mum, you scared

me. You were making choking noises and I couldn't wake you up. It was horrible.'

She squeezed his arm and sat up. As though somebody had actually compressed it, her throat was sore and dry. She swallowed. 'So sorry, love . . . ' She tried again, 'I'm really sorry to frighten you, love. It was just a nasty nightmare.'

His eyebrows knitted. 'What was it about?'

'It's gone; I can't remember.'

Feeling guilty for frightening him, even more about the boy in the dream, she gazed at his troubled frown. Then like a sharp slap, recall struck her. The call to the hotel in Vietnam, the one Cameron had said he was staying at.

'Same hotel I always stay at in Ho Chi Minh City. Why do you ask?' he'd replied when she'd casually enquired last week.

After returning from the picnic, she'd looked it up on the internet and jotted down the number on a notepad. The Park Hyatt Saigon, five stars with all the amenities. It had looked nice. She'd torn off the sheet and crammed it in her pocket, feeling better for having it there, but never intending to use it. That would be spying, showing distrust, going a step too far. But she'd weakened in the night; she'd called the number, changing her mind at the very moment the receptionist answered. Holding her breath, she'd given his details. Cameron Hastings, the company name too. Dates of his stay, his UK address.

Mr Hastings was a regular customer, the man had replied in perfect English, they knew him well, but he wasn't there now.

Suddenly aware that Toby was still watching her, she came back to him. She tried for a smile. 'Sorry, love. Crazy mum again. Are you OK now?' she asked, resisting the urge to clutch him and kiss him. The night terror had frightened him, but hugs and kisses would petrify the poor boy. 'Do you want to go back to your own bedroom? It's fine if you do.'

161

'No, it's OK. But no more of those freaky noises.' He turned away and curled under the covers. 'Oh, and a word of this to anybody, and you're dead.'

He was only twelve years of age, but Ellie felt calmer with her son beside her. Her thoughts were random but steady as the long minutes passed. What would she do if Cam just disappeared off the face of the earth? It didn't seem so very ridiculous. Cam was like a chameleon. Pleasant-looking but unremarkable physically, he could blend in anywhere, with anyone. With someone, somewhere. Like the day he'd attended Sean's psychology lecture. Still youthful and boyish, he could've passed for a student.

There was Alston Terrace, too. Occasionally he had gone missing for a night, sometimes more, his whereabouts a mystery. The Judge and Sylvie would speculate where he'd gone.

'If it was a woman he'd tell us,' Sylvie argued. 'He's gone home to his mum.'

'Cameron hates his mater. Surely, he wouldn't go there.'

'I don't know – he does have that Mummy thing—'

'Maybe he just needs time out,' Sean would interrupt with a shrug.

But Ellie never knew where he went; she'd never worked it out.

And his parents, what would they say if he vanished? Would they even care? 'Incapable of love; just selfish and needy,' Cam often said of his mum. And yet she was nice to the boys, giving them rough hugs and buying them huge quantities of sweets whenever they visited.

Still in her fifties, Jaqueline Hastings was probably ten years younger than Marian. 'Your dad was an accident,' she'd sometimes say to the boys and Ellie would tense, annoyed at her inappropriate comment and waiting for Jake to ask what she meant. The way she'd say it with accusing eyes on her son was hurtful, too. As though his conception was his fault.

But Cam would shrug if Ellie mentioned it. 'Mum was fifteen when she got up the duff. She had to marry a man she didn't love, have a baby she didn't want. She was trapped. What do you expect? It doesn't bother me, anyway.'

Was that really true? Who knew? He rubbed along with his mum and his sister, swapped jokes with his father by text, shared a pint with his dad's mates in his local over the border.

Chameleon Cameron, all things to all men. Where was he now?

Careful not to wake Toby, she sat up and listened to the dead night for several minutes. Nothing, no one. Not even the screech of a fox or an owl. She slipped from the bed and padded across the landing to the spare room. Some of her old canvases from university were there, stacked against the wall, facing in. She didn't usually like to look at them, to remember the unhappy girl she was, but today it seemed right.

She flicked through each moody oil painting until she reached the final canvas, the one kissing the dado. It was a large and joyous abstract of citrus fruit, the golds and butter yellows, the red and burned orange shades glowing and vibrant, the texture thick and shiny with layers of transparent glue. It was a fabulous painting, her best by far.

But the gaping hole was still there. From corner to corner, it had been slashed clean through.

Covering her mouth, Ellie gazed at the painting. As though it was yesterday, the anguish was there, lurching and hitching through her chest to her throat, desperate to escape.

Not worthy of love, of commitment, of honesty.

And here she was again: '*Same hotel I always stay at in Ho Chi Minh City. Why do you ask?*'

A slick and sickening falsehood; oh God, she needed to puke.

Her stomach soon emptied, she washed her face and scooped up the chenille toilet mat. The tears came as she stared at it. It was old-fashioned but functional in a house full of boys who didn't always reach their target. Cameron Hastings. Where the hell was he? And why had he lied? If not for her, then what about his beautiful sons?

The anger building, she strode back to the canvas, staring and searching for answers. A vital, colourful and optimistic painting. And the deep laceration of grief. She hid her face with trembling hands. Was she really back there? Had nothing changed?

32

A Tuesday in Leeds. Sitting in her usual upstairs spot on the bus to the art department, Ellie intermittently gazed out of the window. A brand-new year, the snow was still thick on the Yorkshire fields and hills. She and Cam were closer than ever. Save for Christmas Eve and Day, the two of them had stayed alone in Alston Terrace. She'd always felt a strange claustrophobia about thick falling snow, but she and Cam had fooled around in the white drifting garden, thrown soft flaky balls and built a snowman; they'd cooked together, eaten together, watched *The Wizard of Oz* together on the small television screen. They'd exchanged silly Christmas gifts, drunk too much brandy and as usual they'd kissed.

On that everyday January journey, life felt bloody good. The scar on her cheek almost invisible, Ellie had stopped being anxious about red Toyotas and was finally comfortable going into town after dark. And most of the time, Cam was with her.

She looked up from her book, a split second between chapters, and she saw them, the clearest of views from her top seat. Walking along the slushy pavement, Cameron Hastings was hand in hand with a girl. The same one she'd seen before. A pretty, smooth-skinned, preppy type with long swinging hair in a ponytail, a scarf wrapped inside the collar of her navy blazer. Chatting and laughing, their footsteps seemed to chime. Then suddenly they stopped and Cam put his palms either side of her face. He kissed her pink turned-up nose, then her mouth. So unbearably tender, Ellie had touched her own lips. Even when they'd moved on, she still felt it.

Her lecture hall was at the next stop but Ellie didn't move. Even at the terminus, she stayed dried-eyed in her place until the bus eventually turned and took her back to Headingley. Though deadened with dashed hope, she knew what she had to do. Walking quickly to the house, she nearly slipped several times, but a gash wouldn't matter, she wouldn't feel it, however deep.

Arriving at number eleven, she put her key in the lock, her limbs suddenly heavy as she trudged up the stairs to her box room.

Time slowed as she stared at the large canvas. A vital, colourful and happy painting. Joyful, optimistic; hopeful and *sure*. It had taken her weeks to perfect. What a fool, a stupid, stupid fool. She should have known she wasn't worthy of love; she should have known better.

Opening her art box, she considered the contents for a few moments. Then she picked out the red Stanley knife, carefully touching the sharp nib with her fingertips, numbly wondering what damage it could do to soft skin. A single slash to each wrist. In the bath it would be painless, and who would care anyway? Not Maurice, not Cam. But her mum, her mum? What about Marian?

She pictured her face, her horrified expression only weeks ago. And her astonishingly furious words: 'My precious, perfect girl. You put this right now, Maurice, or I'm leaving and I mean it.'

Undecided and anxious, Ellie stared at her creation. Too cheery, too jolly, too full of fucking hope. The tears finally flowing, she lunged. Wishing it was flesh, she ripped from corner to corner.

Ready to tear it again and again until it was obliterated, she took a deep breath.

'Ellie, don't!' The door had burst open. 'What are you doing?'

She stopped in surprise and spun around. She'd thought she was alone in the house, but from his tousled hair, dark stubble and soft face, Sean must have been asleep in the bedroom opposite.

Shaking her head, she turned back to her mission. Needing to slit and slash again, she lifted her arm, but a strong hand caught it firmly, peeling her taut fingers away from the knife.

'Just stop, Ellie, stop.'

She covered her eyes. 'I have to. It's too painful, too much of Cam. I can't bear to look at it.'

'Then I'll take it,' he replied.

33

Just another balmy morning in July. Because whatever curveballs the gods hurled, life inexorably marched on.

Outside the school gates, Nina gave Ellie a sidelong glance. 'Are you OK? You look tired,' she said quietly as they walked away. 'I do, of course, mean that in a caring way,' she added with a wry smile.

It was an old joke of theirs. They both came across too many women who gave insults with a caring expression. Some of them bordering on racism, in poor Nina's case. Ellie knew her friend well enough to understand the concern was genuine. Besides, she was aware she looked terrible. She'd been told as much by three small boys on the walk to school, two of whom weren't even her sons.

'Let's run ahead,' Harry had said to the twins they saw most mornings. 'My mum's *really* tired.'

'Holy crap!' one of the twins had declared, looking at her.

'What can you do?' their stay-at-home father had replied with a shrug. 'I blame the mother.'

But at least it had brought a weak smile. Perhaps she shouldn't have mentioned it so often yesterday.

'What's up, Mum?'

'Nothing, love,' she'd replied. 'I slept badly; I'm just a bit tired.'

In triplicate. It had been nice of her boys to ask, to show their concern. But sometimes it was difficult to hide.

'The trouble with you, Ellie, is that everything shows on your face,' Cam often laughed when his parents finally departed after the monthly Sunday lunch. 'You'd be a crap poker player.'

'So, you're good at poker, are you, Hastings?' she'd ask.

And his reply, always: 'That would be telling . . .'

Oh God.

She'd spent yesterday attempting to act normally. Obviously not succeeding, but trying nonetheless. A Sunday roast for lunch, even though it had been so hot outside. But the boys liked their meat and roast potatoes. 'Beef every time and don't forget the radish horse!' Harry always said when offered an alternative.

Ellie had decided not to call Cam on his mobile and definitely not to try the hotel. Ever again. The whole episode had left her winded, shaky and afraid. She hadn't touched on finances through the night, but it had struck her like a blow to the stomach immediately she'd awoken in the lounge after a couple of hours' sleep. 'What would I do about money? What would I do about money?' running through her head in tandem with the thrust of her heart. She'd thought of nothing else since.

She'd been without it once. Stranded, afraid and alone. She was a proper grown-up now, but the notion of it recurring still terrified her.

Nina's voice brought her back to the humid morning. 'Do you fancy a coffee?' she asked. 'I've half an hour to fill before driving Mabel to her dental appointment. We could go crazy and have a

169

mocha frappé with vanilla syrup or the like at that posh new café in the village. My treat.'

'I shall forsake the ironing just for you, Nina,' Ellie replied, trying to lighten up. 'Thanks, lovely friend.'

Making the most of the sunny breeze, they sat outside the café. Despite the impressive canopy above them, the Heaton Moor pavement below wasn't exactly Mediterranean.

'So, why are you looking so . . . ?' Nina pulled in her chair to allow a pram to pass. She looked thoughtfully at Ellie's face. 'Sad? I hope your dad isn't getting you down. It'll be post-something-or-other confusion. Mabel was like that after her varicose veins and it turned out to be dehydration. Look at her now; she's as right as rain. More's the pity.'

Ellie smiled. Nina's mother-in-law was officially a battle-axe. She interfered with her life constantly. So, perhaps it wasn't that bad having laid-back lazy *Jaqs* as a . . . What was she? A mother-in-common-law. The thought made her hyperventilate again. She and Cam weren't married. Not even a divorce settlement. If he ever made an appearance again.

Lost in her panic, the words escaped in a whisper. 'What would I do about money?'

'Money?' Nina asked. 'It's fine, I'm paying; you don't need—'

'Oh sorry, it wasn't . . . I was thinking about Dad,' she replied, blowing her nose to distract her friend's curious gaze. 'The doctors don't seem unduly worried. He's coming out tomorrow or Wednesday. They've done the tests and say his problems with memory and thinking are routine for his type of CVA. They can and do get better, apparently, especially over the first three months, so that's good. In fact, it sounds as though he got off pretty lightly.' She tried for a smile. 'Still, madness in great ones, and all that . . . I just hope he behaves for Mum. And at the blinking golf club.'

'She'll just be happy to have him home, I bet. Talking of which, when is Cam back?'

Ellie sprinkled brown sugar on the top of her cappuccino, her head down as she stirred. 'Oh, he's due at the weekend.'

'You don't sound very enthusiastic. Do I detect a hint of exasperation?'

Ellie laughed. 'Now why would I be infuriated with a man?'

Nina's husband was an obsessive sports fan. He watched it and played it at every available opportunity, much to her chagrin. She clearly knew about *exasperation*. She abruptly looked at her watch. 'God, look at the time. I'd better dash. Don't want to be late for mad Mabel.' She kissed Ellie's cheek. 'Cheer up, gorgeous pal. Whatever's troubling you might never happen and you know how much Cam loves you. He'd head into battle for you and the boys, that's for sure.'

'See you later – and thanks, Nina,' Ellie called to her friend's departing back.

She stayed for a while, breathing in the scent from the flower shop next door. Would Cam 'head into battle', though? Even before his bewildering disappearance, she'd had the sensation he was running in the opposite direction at times. Still, she was feeling a little brighter. Nina was a good friend; she asked all the right questions without prying too far. If she had given Hen even a hint of trouble and strife, she would've dug and dug until the whole story was revealed.

And Ellie didn't like digging. No good ever came of it.

34

The ironing lasted for most of the afternoon play. Ellie peered at the huge pile. How did Toby and Jake manage to get through so many T-shirts and hoodies when Harry didn't? He wasn't yet at that smelly stage, the stinky armpits and funky feet that had appeared overnight when his brothers reached ten, but still she made a mental note to encourage him to change his clothes – and his undies – more than once a week.

The radio drama was about an elderly couple and Alzheimer's, but despite the sound blathering out in the kitchen, Ellie had no idea what became of the old pair by the end.

Trying to shake off the constant sense of loss and rejection, she sighed. Perhaps it was dementia with Dad. It was a private worry she hadn't shared with her mum, but the hospital registrar hadn't thought so.

'Not dementia, no, it doesn't fit that pattern,' he'd said with a friendly, attentive smile. A nice man, younger than her and attractive. A good catch for all those nurses, she'd thought. Whether male or female, she couldn't decide.

Thank God Maurice hadn't made any inappropriate comments. Well, none that she was aware of. Her father could be a tad homophobic at times, but it was more a generational thing, she hoped. Like Cam's dad and his plethora of vulgar gags. She could never remember a joke, but Stuart always had one on the tip of his tongue, misogynistic or homophobic, racist or sexist. Or the whole bloody lot. But gay jokes were his favourite, at least one per Sunday lunch, many more by text and in the pub, apparently.

'That is funny, Dad, but you can't really say it,' Cam would laugh.

'Bloody hell, not you as well, son,' Stuart would reply. 'Whatever happened to good old humour?'

The scrape of keys in the front door interrupted her thoughts. With a spread of doom, she checked the time. Oh God, what had happened now? Why was Toby home half an hour early?

Busy with the iron cable, she didn't look up, but there was something about Toby's breathing, the lack of his usual clamour. She slowly lifted her chin. The person who'd entered wasn't her russet-haired son after all. It was her missing partner.

'Cameron! What are you doing here?'

So shocked to see him, it took a moment to marshal her thoughts. The touch of elation immediately evaporated. Cam's drawn face was pale and pasty. There was simply no way she could swallow any story that involved him having been abroad.

Air stuck in her chest, Ellie stared. After her chat with Nina, she'd almost convinced herself that everything would be fine, that Cam would come up with a reasonable explanation of why he hadn't been in the usual hotel. No room at the inn, a mix-up on the part of the receptionist, a computer glitch. She'd been willing to accept anything even half believable just to avoid facing a horrible truth. But his expression gave everything away. He looked apologetic. Guilt was written on his face.

With jelly legs, she sat down, any fight clean gone. 'Cam, where have you been?' she asked quietly.

'We need to talk,' he replied.

He walked to the sink and ran the cold tap for several seconds before throwing down a glassful of water. He didn't turn back, but stared through the patio doors to the world outside.

Ellie glanced at the clock. 'It's time to fetch Jake and Harry,' she said, her voice flat. 'Do you want to go or shall I?'

Cam usually jumped at the chance of collecting the boys from school after he'd been away. 'You should've seen Jake's face. It was a picture,' he'd say. But today he glanced over his shoulder, his jaw clenched. 'You do it, will you?'

Torn between staying and leaving, she stilled for a moment. She could call Nina and ask her to collect the boys, but would she burst into tears? And what would she say, anyway? Besides, she knew something irrevocable had happened; she needed to cling on to normality right now; today might be her last 'everyday'.

She bolted from the house, then had to stop, her fingers trembling as she struggled to tie the laces on her trainers.

God, oh God, it was so bad that Cam couldn't face the boys.

Another mum was standing at the gates with Harry. Ellie looked at her watch; she was a little late. She hated to be unpunctual. Military precision, and all that. But was tardy allowed when life was upside-down? When your partner, who'd never loved you enough to propose, was proving it by leaving?

The mum was smiling. 'Is it all right if Harry comes to play with Hamid? I'll make them tea too,' she said. 'Sorry about the short notice, but they hatched the plan at school.'

Was this a good idea today? Ellie's mind was too scrambled to think clearly. 'Yes, of course. Thanks very much,' she replied, relieved she wasn't being reprimanded, as she knew she'd weep.

She gave Harry a little hug and took his school bag. 'Have a nice time. Be good.'

She watched them amble away before realising Jake was absent. Where was he? He usually waited with Harry at the blue railings. By some strange telepathy, did he know about Cam?

Alarm bells jangling, she scanned the front of the building, searching for him along its length. Then she sprinted around the corner towards his classroom door. His hands in his pockets, there he was, strolling across the yard with another boy she didn't recognise. And he was laughing, easy and happy, just as she wanted him to be.

Absently watching the muted television, Cam was in the lounge when they arrived home. Jake lunged. 'Dad! You're back!'

'Take it easy, Jakey. I'm getting old.' Holding him at arm's length, Cam studied his boy, then pulled him down on the sofa and slung over an arm. 'Looking good, mate. What've you been up to, then?'

Ellie turned away. She'd let Jake have a few minutes with his dad. Life had shifted. It would never be the same again.

35

The sun had finally disappeared behind the distant Derbyshire hills.

It was gone ten o'clock, the boys calmed and in their bedrooms, hopefully asleep after the usual high spirits of Dad coming home. Until this minute, the house had been so busy and messy and loud, there hadn't been time to stop or think. But now here they were, Cam and Ellie, sitting either side of the kitchen table.

Ellie stared at the jug of water in between them. Like a business meeting, a negotiation, a dismissal.

Cam folded his arms. 'I haven't been to Ho Chi Minh City,' he stated.

She bowed her head. So, he hadn't been to Vietnam. She'd known he would say those words, but the blow still stung.

He cleared his throat. 'Look Ellie, I know I haven't been entirely straight with you, but I thought you wouldn't ever need to know. I've . . . '

She tried to breathe through the clamour of her emotions. Entirely fucking straight! Typical Cameron style. He paused, so she looked up. He was pale and seemed agitated, moving in his chair, as though he couldn't get comfortable. Remaining silent, she waited. There was nothing to say and she was trying very hard not to embarrass herself by crying or demanding, perhaps even screaming like a banshee.

He took a deep breath and continued, his voice cracking, 'The truth is—'

The kitchen door flew open and Jake stormed in, clutching a thick roll of paper which he thrust at his dad.

His words tumbled out. 'I forgot to show you. It's meant to be a surprise at class assembly, but Miss Myers told me today so I'd know. Mums and dads can watch and you're back early, so now you can come. You will be there, won't you Dad? It's on a Friday. That's in four days.'

A sob bubbling to the surface, Ellie watched her son's expectant face. His eager eyes were bursting with excitement, trepidation and pride.

Cam unravelled the certificate and studied it, then he read it out loud: 'Jacob Hastings. Star of the Week.' He gently punched Jake on the shoulder. 'Good work, Jakey. Of course I will, mate. If I'm here, of course I will. But it's time you were asleep. Off to bed now.'

Ellie stood and held out her hand. 'Fantastic, love. We're so proud of you. Come on, I'll tuck you in.'

Jake trudged up the stairs, disappointment weighing down his shoulders like a cloak. She followed him up. 'Dad's just a bit tired after his long journey home, but he was really pleased. We both think it's amazing. Night, love,' she said before turning off his light.

Annoyance edging in again, she leaned against the door and closed her eyes. Couldn't Cam have just said yes? Was it really so hard to put someone else first?

Returning to the kitchen, she took her place opposite her partner. His face tight, he leaned forward, the words firing out.

'Don't look so fucking judgemental, Ellie. I thought I had cancer. I found a growth in my bloody testicle and I ignored it for weeks.' He sat back, his voice quieter. 'I couldn't admit it to myself, let alone tell you. Then the lump seemed to get bigger. It freaked me out and I was frightened that you'd notice.'

He pinched the top of his nose. Tears fell to his mouth and he brushed them roughly away. But Ellie was frozen. Whatever she had expected, it wasn't this.

'So eventually I went to the doctor,' he continued, his voice rushing. 'He sent me to a urologist. He talked about tests and biopsies. Step-at-a-time crap. But I wanted to get rid of it, whatever it was. It was getting uncomfortable. A constant fucking reminder. So last week I arranged to—'

She gazed, the penny finally dropping. 'You've been in hospital? This week? That's where you've been?'

'The Alexandra in Cheadle. It should've just been overnight. Then I'd go to Vietnam as planned. But then they wouldn't let me out. My temperature had soared. I couldn't move. Felt like shit. Long story short, I'd got an infection.' He took a breath, then snorted. 'Ironically. I should have stuck to the good old NHS.'

Cam had stopped crying and was trying for humour. But this wasn't funny. It wasn't the time for quips. Ellie was hot, irate, bloody livid, in fact. She'd swung from the debilitating fear of being betrayed and abandoned by this man to an astonishing anger that he'd put her through a horrendous wrangle of emotion for no good reason. And he hadn't told her he was ill. She'd been his partner for seventeen years. She'd given agonising birth to his kids, made fucking Sunday lunch for his ungrateful parents each month; she'd cooked every single family meal, scrubbed shit from the loos, hand-washed his underwear, polished his bloody shoes, but she wasn't trusted enough to be told he might have *cancer*. It was more than insulting.

'For God's sake, Cam. Why didn't you tell me?' she yelled. 'Have you any idea—'

Whipping from his chair, Cam glared, breathing heavily. Then he grasped the glass jug and hurled it against the wall where it shattered, the shards of broken glass and water spraying back against her face. 'This isn't about you, Ellie,' he roared. 'For once, just shut up. This isn't about you!'

Her heart clattered with shock and alarm, yet she still tried to protest. 'What the hell, Cam? I don't think it's about—'

'Yes you do. You think the world revolves around you. Fucking attention seeking, constantly.' Spitting the words, he leaned in towards her, his cheeks livid red. 'And if you don't actually *say* anything, it's there on your face. Me, me, poor little Ellie, cross little Ellie, misunderstood little Ellie. And if it isn't you pestering me, it's Marian. Even fucking Sean. In my bloody ear, like a brain worm. *Is Ellie OK? Is Ellie all right? Ellie, Ellie, Ellie . . .*'

He walked unsteadily to the door and leaned against the frame, his head down for several beats.

'I'm ill, Ellie. I'm going to lie down,' he said, his voice low and winded. 'You'd better clean up that mess.'

36

The clock in the hallway struck eleven times. Standing quietly at the bedroom door, Ellie peered at the double bed. Cam was on his side facing her, his eyes closed. After clearing up the glass, she'd tried to calm herself with a shot of whiskey, but her limbs were still shaky, her mind jangling.

The brandy had gone, so she'd had to resort to Jack Daniel's. It had made her even more anxious and woozy. *Fucking attention seeking.* The words made her shudder. Hadn't he said them before?

Cam's features looked young in the beam from the landing – childlike, almost. Perhaps that was why. He was still like a boy in many ways. Wanting life to be smooth and 'without bumps', he refused to take anything seriously; he shunned responsibility, preferring to walk away rather than face discomfort.

But he'd had to grow up fast, hadn't he? She blew out her breath as she stared. Was she making excuses for his behaviour already? Probably. But in fairness his dad had left the family home when Cam was in his early teens. Stuart had gone to live with another woman, an older woman, who lived only a few doors down their road. He'd just packed his bag one teatime and left.

She pictured her conversation with Cam. Back in the days when he actually told her stuff, of course.

His expression had been disgusted. 'He left me with *her*. With Mum. To pick up the bloody pieces. Self-indulgent sobbing. Boozing, nonstop. It was horrendous.' But his face had cleared. 'At least Dad and Monica were up the road to feed me, and she was a bloody good cook. So it wasn't all bad.'

Jaqs had eventually stopped crying and pulled herself together. She lost weight and started dating other men. 'Selfish undoubtedly, but she was still young, still attractive,' Cam had said. 'She just needed a reminder to look at herself in the mirror. And as soon as there was competition, Dad came running back.' He'd snorted. 'Probably regretted it a million times, though.'

'Wasn't that awful for you and your sister? Your dad just leaving like that?' she had asked.

'Nah. Don't know about Karen, but I knew he'd be back. There was no point getting stressed. He'd been fucking Monica for years. I caught them at it when I was a little kid and they pretended it was a game of "donkey". I remember because I went to a party where we played pin the tail on the donkey and I was bursting to say that wasn't how it was played. Anyway, it probably wasn't so much fun actually living with Monica. Everything wears off after a while, doesn't it? Sex, lust, love. Even good food.'

Ellie now exhaled long and hard. Humour as always, a big bloody joke.

Sighing at her contradictory emotions, she turned off the light and headed for her 'art studio'. Ironic; her escapes as an adult had always landed her in the 'spare room' at Woodlands, Marian hovering with love and concern.

'Ellie, come in here.' Cam's voice from the darkness made her start. 'You can put on the lamp. I'm not asleep.'

Trying to erase the image of his puce complexion from before, she climbed on the bed, pulled up the pillow and focused on it now. He did look ill. Pasty and drawn, with deep grooves beneath his eyes. He winced as he hitched himself up.

'What's this?' he asked, lifting her palm and nodding at the plaster. She had a small cut on her lip too. She'd had to pluck out a thin splinter of glass with tweezers and it had bled for ages, another red tear popping each time she thought it had stopped.

She shrugged. 'The jug was a bugger to clean up.'

And it had been; she'd had to be thorough: young bare-footed children lived here, for God's sake. But there was no point going there. There would be no apology, she knew. Cam rarely blew up, but when he did, it wasn't mentioned again. Not even much later as humour, when the dust had settled.

Neither Cam's anger nor his subsequent denial was normal or OK. But that was fine with Ellie. She could pretend it hadn't happened. Even to herself.

In times gone by, she'd asked herself why. Was her mother's subservience so ingrained she instinctively did the same? Ridiculous though it was, perhaps that was the answer. Or maybe it was that deep-rooted insecurity she couldn't quite shape. Those vague feelings of exclusion, culpability and loss. Either way, they added up to the same thing: the desperate fear of Cam leaving her.

He put down her hand and looked away. 'I just didn't want to tell you. OK?' The phrase was an echo of his words about marriage. But today he was answering Ellie's question from an hour or so earlier. 'That's how I wanted to deal with it. On my own. My body, my prerogative.'

They were silent for a while, then he sighed. 'I suppose you want to talk about it now?'

She nodded. She wanted to say, '*For God's sake, I am your wife, Cam!*' That's what Nina or Hen would say. Her mum, his mum. Bloody Ciara Walsh. But she couldn't say it because she wasn't a *wife*.

'The boys and I are your family, Cam,' she said instead. 'We all love you very much. We do need to know these things so we can help and support you.'

Seeming to relent, he yawned and smiled. 'Well, I've told you just about everything already. I went to see this urologist, Mr Chapman, and he scared the bloody shit out of me. He felt around my balls, which wasn't fun, I can tell you. He didn't have your fair touch, my love ...'

A cyst, the urologist had diagnosed, a cyst of the epididymis. But of course the doc couldn't be sure until there was a biopsy, so he'd felt obliged to explain the whole picture, just in case. Metastatic cancer, it was called, if it was cancer and had spread. Through the lymphatic system to the lymph nodes in the abdomen, chest and neck and then to the lungs. Relayed clinically by Mr Chapman to Cam.

'He wanted to do a biopsy to see what it was, and then a decision could be made what to do next. I said bollocks to that.'

He was doing what Cam did best, making light of it now, but Ellie knew he must've been scared, anyone would be. She felt a surge of love and concern, but it was tinged with sadness. Wasn't illness a time to confide in those you loved? If you loved them?

As though reading her thoughts, Cam leaned forward and looked at her through hollow eyes. 'If it is malignant, Ellie, and if it has spread, they'll open me up, take out lymph nodes and any other bits they don't like the look of. They cut the nerves that control ejaculation. It can leave you fucking impotent. If not dead, of course.'

Not knowing what to say, she nodded. There was so much to absorb. 'When will you know?' she asked.

He shrugged. 'Few days. God, I'm tired.' Turning away, he pulled himself down and put his arm under the pillow. 'But you don't get rid of me that easily. The surgeon said he was pretty sure from the look of it that it's just a cyst. So, everything's OK,' he said.

He reached back his free hand and touched Ellie's shoulder. 'Yeah? Ellie? Everything's OK?'

'Of course,' she replied and turned off the lamp.

37

Ellie woke early, immediately registering it was a Tuesday morning and that Cam was asleep in the bed beside her. Cameron Hastings, her partner, who was astonishingly in a mid-cancer scare.

She gently touched her sore lip. God, his sudden, explosive anger. A similar episode flashed in her head. The student house? Surely not. Too long ago, anyway. What mattered is now. How to go forward from here; what to say to their sons?

The world unsteady, she studied Cam's sleeping face a moment longer before slipping away.

With careful palms she checked the kitchen floor for glass, drank a strong coffee on the decking despite the soft drizzle, then she eventually woke the boys with a finger to her lips.

'Dad has the flu. He's getting better but he needs lots of sleep, so be as quiet as you can.'

Everything seemed muted: her sons, the radio, the weak July sunshine, even the Rice Krispies in the boys' milk-flooded bowls.

'We can chat now,' she said to Jake and Harry on the walk to school, but they were quiet. She'd noticed this before. Even when she tried to be chirpy, they reflected her mood.

The power of a parent; the labyrinth of guilt.

The thought brought her back to Maurice. He was due to return home from the hospital today. Although Marian had protested, saying they could take a taxi to save Ellie the long drive up the motorway and the inevitable waiting around, she had insisted that she wanted to help. She would collect Marian from Woodlands as usual, and they'd take Maurice home together. That was the plan, but the anxiety was there. As always.

Speeding past the dry Lancashire countryside and the shiny Macron stadium on autopilot, Ellie's thoughts oscillated between Cam and her parents.

'I understand a fury in your words, but not the words,' she remembered from school. Not mad King Lear this time. Maybe Othello? Paranoia and doubt. Yes, that seemed pretty topical, too.

The fury of words . . . Well, she was obviously Maurice's daughter, but what about Cameron's ugly speech? Was he right? Was she really so 'attention seeking' and selfish? Even against her mum's insistence, she'd made plans to collect her dad from the hospital, to be the dutiful daughter today. She'd been a pain in her teens, admittedly, but as an adult she'd tried to be a loving child. She really had. But perhaps it was that old thing of not seeing ourselves as others do. Maybe she was kidding herself.

She indicated left down the oak-tree-lined road and then right into the drive of her childhood home. Woodlands was not nearly as grand as some of the houses further down the private lane and it was in reality a semi, but still it was a very large house for a couple with only one child.

Cam once made a rare faux pas by casually asking her dad if he and Marian would eventually sell up and downsize, but Maurice's face had darkened and he hadn't replied. 'Bye, Maurice. See you soon,' Cam had said cheerfully as they left, but her dad had turned away without saying a word.

'See!' she had wanted to crow. 'I told you. That's what Dad can really be like.' Instead, she'd laughed. 'Perhaps he thinks you're after his money,' she'd teased a shocked Cam, just that tiny bit pleased that he had, for once, fallen foul of her father.

She now pulled up behind the man's Jaguar. Lit up by the bright weather, the navy blue enamel was dusty. She couldn't help a small smile – her dad would not be impressed.

Her mum was at the kitchen window as usual, raising her hand in an 'I won't be a minute' type of way, so Ellie turned off the engine and watched the tiny sparrows peck the bread crusts on the bird table. They were being fed; Maurice would be pleased about that.

She gazed at the thicket ahead. Shades of brown and vivid green splattered by sunshine. She'd loved to explore it, running to her dad with delight when she'd found a new hidden flower. Of course, she'd known not to pick them. 'Forget-me-nots, Daddy!' she had once called to him. He'd crouched down to look at the pretty cerulean flowers. 'No, they're blue-eyed Mary,' he'd replied. 'Clever girl. What else can you find me?'

Was that really why he had backtracked on the dog? How she'd longed for one, even as a toddler. And if not a dog, a cat or a rabbit: something soft and furry to cuddle and love. At eight or nine the answer from Maurice had always been, 'When you're older and you can look after it properly yourself, you can have a dog.' When she'd tried to plead, he'd say firmly: 'When you're older, Eleanor. A promise is a promise. When have I ever broken one?' And it had been true: her daddy was strict, at times he could be stern, but he always kept his vows.

The good-girl Ellie had patiently bided her time, secretly

expecting a puppy to arrive on her twelfth birthday. The celebration passed. 'I'm at high school, Dad. I walk to the school bus and walk home by myself. I can look after a dog properly now. Please, please can I have one?'

But Maurice said no, and when she'd persisted and reminded him of his promise, he'd flown into a rage.

'Dogs are dirty, they soil the garden. And they dig. A dog would ruin the plants, the wildlife, wouldn't it, Marian? The answer is no, don't ask me again.'

She hadn't asked again, knowing the answer from Maurice, and therefore from Marian, would be no. But then her best friend at high school managed to persuade her reluctant parents to allow her a pet, and it had given Ellie hope.

She stared at the bird table. That's when she turned; at twelve or thirteen, that's when she had finally rebelled. The dog was only symbolic, of course, but that was the moment; the hope and the disappointment had crushed her.

38

Walnuts were the best all round nut, *You and Yours* advised Ellie as she waited in the hospital car park. Marian had jumped out to see if Maurice was ready and thereby save the expense of a pay-and-display ticket.

The engine was running, but Ellie glanced around to check for a parking attendant. The tap at the window made her start, but it was only her mum.

'The doctor needs to discharge Dad and he's still on his rounds,' she said. 'I've brought us an Earl Grey while we wait.'

Sitting in the car on the verge like fugitives, they sipped their scalding drinks from polystyrene cups.

'The coffee is so much nicer in hospitals these days,' Marian commented. 'And so many tea options, I was spoilt for choice. Tea used to be tea. English breakfast, they call it now.'

'I didn't know you'd been in hospital, Mum. I was born at home, wasn't I?' Ellie grimaced at the family lore. It made her sound too much like her military-precision father. 'That's right; I was too impatient to wait for the ambulance. What were you in for?'

'Oh, tonsils, when I was little. And the food has improved, too. Dad has been very well fed over the past week.' Her lips twitched. 'I'm not sure that I like the competition.'

Ellie laughed. 'There's never any competition between you and anyone or anything when it comes to Dad,' she replied. 'You're the best wife anyone could ever have had.'

Marian looked a little sad and shook her head, making her soft curls bounce. 'But perhaps not the best mother?'

'Not true. You were always there when I needed you. And I knew I could be completely honest and tell you everything.'

'Eventually . . .'

Feeling a cramping discomfort, Ellie sighed. 'Yes, eventually, Mum.'

Still ticketless, Ellie waited again, but this time at the clinical collection point. Maurice eventually emerged from the double doors with Marian at his side, her arm slotted through his, the devoted little wife. He looked fit, tall and distinguished in a navy Pringle jumper and shirt. Feeling a flush of pride, she jumped from the car and opened the back passenger doors for them both, like a chauffeur.

'Hello, Dad, you're looking very well.'

Brightly said, almost holding her breath.

'Thank you, Eleanor. How are my grandsons?'

The warm glow of pleasure was immediate. 'Fine, thanks, Dad. They've missed you and can't wait to see you. Mum's worried that you may have got a taste for hospital food.'

'I think not,' he replied, kissing Marian on the lips. 'And I'm longing to get back in my own bed.'

Glancing at her mum's shiny face in the rear-view mirror, Ellie almost blushed. It did have its downsides, but she was glad to have such devoted parents. She supposed, in hindsight, that it took the pressure off being an only child. Hen frequently spoke of her warring parents, their semi-open marriage and often violent arguments. And even worse, their frequent attempts to get their children onside.

'But he's a vicar! An archbishop or whatever . . .' Nina would exclaim when Hen regaled them with shocking sexually charged stories from her childhood.

'Exactly. Religion – ethnic cleansing, torture, politics, crucifixion. All in a day's work,' Hen would say with a shrug.

The traffic fairly loose, they soon found themselves back at Woodlands. 'Are you staying for a bite to eat, Eleanor?' Maurice asked when she pulled up on the drive.

Silly though it was, the flash of delight was there again. 'Thanks, Dad, I will.'

She followed him in, watching with a calm and fond feeling as he stretched in the hallway, then roamed around the house, downstairs and up. He strolled through the wooded garden to the greenhouse, spent a few moments watering, then he sprinkled peanuts and seeds on the bird table. His mission accomplished, he finally settled down in his lounge chair for a corned beef sandwich which Marian had produced like magic on a tray. He napped then, his face peaceful and content, if a little pallid.

'Have five minutes too, Mum. It'll do you good,' Ellie said, carrying the plates back to the kitchen.

She rinsed the dishes, studying the dresser ornaments as she put them away. The knick-knacks were always there, of course, but she never looked at them afresh. Like Cam and his cancer scare. He must've been so worried and yet she hadn't noticed, hadn't seen anything amiss. A lump, he'd said, one so large he'd been frightened she'd spot it.

Oh God. Perhaps he was right; maybe she was selfish.

Feeling that familiar hint of the world moving, she focused on

191

the trinkets: an Egyptian mummy and the distorted clay head of a woman she'd made at school; the boys' creations and artwork; china plates for each month of the year and that whole section of windmills. Varying shapes, size and colour, but their intricate blades always waving.

She'd always thought it strange that Marian bought other people's pottery when she could make such beautiful items herself. And the windmills slightly disturbed her with their claustrophobic slits for windows.

Of course, it was Jake who had counted them then rearranged them in order of height. 'Why have you got eighteen of these, Grandma?' he'd asked recently.

'To celebrate my first sale. I buy one each October when I visit my friend. She has a gift shop and she bought some of my pottery when your mum and I went on holiday all those years ago. Do you remember, Ellie?'

Marian's once yearly *escape* from Dad, yes, that was something to bloody celebrate, Ellie had thought at the time. But now she felt ashamed as she looked through to the lounge. Both her parents were asleep, the relief of their reunion like a mutual sleeping draught.

Gathering her keys and handbag, she stood in the doorway for a few moments. The glow was still warming her chest, she felt quite sentimental. Her flesh and blood; that innate connection one couldn't and shouldn't ever break. There had been ups and downs, for sure, but the deep love was there, she could feel it.

On impulse she tiptoed to her father and bent to kiss him on the cheek.

The shock of the sharp slap sent her reeling.

'Don't touch me,' he bellowed, his eyes snapping open. 'Get out! Get out of my house, you whore.'

39

*Her body's spent, immobile from the exertion and the waves of release.
She snaps her head to the pillow. He's still there on his back, his hair
dark and glistening on his chest and his belly.*

He searches her face. 'Are you all right now?'

*She blinks him away, but he tucks an auburn curl behind her ear
and kisses her deeply. 'I was tempted,' he says.*

Trying to remember, she gazes. Has she been here before?

*Still spaced from the spliff and the tears, she turns in her single bed.
With an exhausted sigh she catches the Johnny Cash poster, then she
closes her eyes and finally sleeps—*

Though still dark, Ellie woke feeling languid, the cinders of a
pleasant dream sliding from her recall as she turned towards
Cam. Then the memory of her father's word struck her, as sharp
as the slap.

It wasn't the first time 'whore' had been hurled. The beginning
of October, the start of her third year at Leeds. It had been spat
at her then.

Willing herself back to sleep, she squeezed her lids shut, but the vile recollection still sizzled behind her eyes, hot and searing.

Like a burning cigarette, crushed into soft skin.

Awake far too early, Ellie pulled back the duvet and slipped out of the warm bed. Ironic, really. Now she had time to dwell, she didn't want to. On her return from Woodlands yesterday, she'd parked outside the house, trying to gather her clash of emotions before facing Cam and the boys, but Toby had trotted out of the porch door in bare feet and quickly climbed in her car.

'Dad fetched Jake and Harry from school. Jake said he had to keep stopping to catch his breath. Is that normal with flu? Do you think he's OK?' he'd whispered.

'I thought Nina was collecting them today. She was going to drop them home to save Dad the trouble.'

Though Toby had shrugged, his tight angsty face had given him away. 'Dad cancelled. I don't know why. I suppose he wanted to do it himself.'

With Toby on her heels, she had rushed to the lounge, but Cam was awake and lying on the sofa. Cross-legged on the new rug, Harry was about three inches away from the TV, watching *Terminator*.

'How's everything going?' she'd asked.

'Fantastic,' Cam had replied. 'We deployed the three critical evasion tactics to escape the old bat Laverne, came home via the park and Toby fetched chips from the Fish Bar, so we're fed. Except for a treat. We need chocolate, don't we, Harry? What have you got hidden away for us, Ma?'

Despite his chipper pretence, she had seen he wasn't well, but there had been no point in arguing, cajoling even. Cam did exactly what Cam wanted to do. He did it with deflection and charm, but at the end of the day, it was always his way.

She'd reached up to the top kitchen cupboard and extracted an old biscuit tin heavy with confectionery saved for weekend treats. Cam's way was to allow his eight-year-old son to watch an 18-certificate film and eat sugar on a school night. But she'd had no space to argue or care as she carried the box to the lounge. The word 'whore' had been too prominent in her mind; it'd been aflame in her ears and on her face. Though she planned to bat it away with brisk activity this morning, it was there still.

Determined not to think about Maurice, she marched the boys to school in the unexpected drizzle and busied herself in the house as Cam slept. She changed the towels and bedding, tidied as much as Harry's chaos allowed, hung up Toby's astonishing number of hoodies and dusted around Jake's artwork; she vacuumed and polished every room in the house, then finally knelt down on the kitchen floor and scrubbed, reaching beneath the units for any stray shards of glass.

'Whore', repeated in her head. Whore, whore, whore. Such an ugly word. Old-fashioned, too. Slag or slut would be the word these days. Unpleasant ones also, but *whore* seemed so much worse. Prostitute, sex worker, call girl, it implied.

Fuck, fuck! The word hissed and stung far more than the slap.

The kitchen door swung open eventually. Wearing a dressing gown and jogging bottoms, Cam shuffled in. 'Morning,' he muttered.

Grateful for the interruption, Ellie smiled. 'Afternoon, more like,' she said, nodding to the clock. 'Cup of tea? Are you hungry? I can make you some lunch.'

'Not yet. I still feel like shit. Bloody freezing. Have you got some paracetamol?'

She looked at him carefully. Despite his upbeat behaviour last night, she had seen he was wilting. He'd made a pretence of sharing a Twix with Jake and she'd found his cod and chips in the kitchen, hardly touched. After a couple of hours with the boys on the sofa, he'd given up the charade, with her at least. 'I feel like crap,' he'd said in a low voice. 'I'll say goodnight to the boys and then I'm going to bed.'

He looked much the same now, eighteen hours of sleep later, his face almost grey. 'How did it go yesterday? With Maurice?' he asked, throwing back the pills with a slug of hot tea.

Relieved she was turned away as she emptied the dishwasher, she shrugged. 'Fine. Settled back at Woodlands.'

No good would come of talking about her dad. Nor dwelling on that bloody word. Instead, she changed the subject, trying to overcome her shortness of breath by bringing Cam up to speed with life in Heaton Moor over the last week or so as humorously as she could manage. She was still astonished he'd been here all that time, not trading boxes in Vietnam, but down the road, having a potentially cancerous lump removed in a private hospital. But the mix of concern and mistrust, rejection and shame were swelling like a huge cotton-wool ball of anxiety in her chest; she had to swallow them all down to stop herself from retching, combusting or choking.

No quips or non-PC comments today, Cam sat at the table and sipped his drink, his eyes almost closing. After only ten minutes, he retreated to bed.

40

Every thought-distracting chore duly completed, Ellie programmed the washing machine and looked at her watch. It was the expensive Tag Cam had smuggled through duty free when he'd first begun to travel more.

'A bribe, perchance?' she had asked with a beam when Cam presented it to her.

'To remind you that I'm missing you every time you look at it,' he'd replied with a hug. Then he'd grinned. 'And to get rid of that tacky Timex.'

Her Tag still gave her a little fillip when she looked at it, but the Timex wasn't going to be thrown away any moment soon. Over the years it had come out of hiding whenever an old watch or its battery had died. More expensive timepieces had come and gone, but the child's Timex was still in her jewellery box upstairs and it worked whenever Harry delicately wound it up, as though precious treasure.

A fond sensation now pierced her agitation. She was lucky, so lucky to have her little men. And it was nearly time to collect them from school; she'd quickly check up on Cam, then buy them a treat from the Co-op on the way. She made for the stairs, but the doorbell rang. She frowned; what now? She didn't feel that great herself: tired and listless, her energy zapped. From errands, from Maurice and Cam. From all the bloody turmoil.

Wearily plodding to the door, she pictured Cam throwing back all those painkillers. A pill would be nice to make everything better. Nina had tried St John's wort when she was going through a low patch, and the only obvious change had been a ferocious appetite for sex on her part. 'It came between Leroy and his sport so I had to give them up,' she'd laughed.

Still smiling at the story, Ellie pulled back the latch. Her smile fell. Sean Walsh was waiting through the glass. Cam was ill, so of course he was. Didn't the bloody man have a job? Lectures to give, students to teach? Her jaw set as another thought landed. Oh God; what information, and when, had passed from Cameron to him without her knowing?

'Oh, it's you,' she said, opening the porch door. 'He's upstairs, asleep.'

'Can I come in and wait?' he replied with a puzzled frown.

'Do as you please,' she replied. 'I'm off to collect the boys.'

God, she was being rude. Yet still she grabbed a thin coat and brushed past him, leaving him standing on the path. The door clicked but the sound of footsteps followed her. Moments later Sean was striding alongside her.

'I hope you've got some keys,' he said amiably.

She didn't reply, but continued to walk briskly through the light shower, trying to analyse why she felt so cross with him.

Disappointment? Betrayal? Lies? Or simply paranoia? She increased her speed through the park.

Catching her elbow, he pulled her to a stop. 'Ellie, what's wrong? Why are you so angry?'

Blood rushed to her cheeks. His question was an echo from the past, but even as she answered, she knew her words were illogical; she was blaming Sean for Cam's shortcomings because she wasn't allowed to blame him. 'You knew that Cameron was in hospital, didn't you?' she fired out. 'You were fully aware he wasn't in Ho Chi Minh or working.'

He let go of her arm. 'I didn't know anything, Ellie. Not until your text.'

The heat spreading, she looked at the ground. God, she'd almost forgotten about that. Too agitated to sleep after her call to Vietnam, she'd gone down to the lounge, pulled out her mobile and sent Sean a message with fumbling fingers. The moment it had whooshed away she'd regretted it.

'Sorry. I shouldn't have sent it. It was just . . . It felt like a horrible dream to find Cam wasn't at the hotel. Then I did have a nightmare and frightened poor Toby . . . ' The strangling dream pelted back, shortly followed by the one she'd woken to this morning. Both disturbing in very different ways, she tried to shake them off. 'Sorry. I just needed a reality check, something, someone solid to—'

'It's fine. Really. I didn't mind. I don't mind.' He breathed a smile. 'Any time.'

She watched the raindrops glisten on her bare toes. She had to say it. 'I wouldn't have called the hotel normally. I'm incredibly embarrassed about it. Checking up on your other half is just so . . . I don't do that. I never have.' She looked up. 'But this time I . . . '

'You had a reason?' he asked. 'What was it?'

His eyes swept her lips. God, the cut; had he noticed it? She lifted her hand to cover it.

'Nothing; something and nothing.'

'What was troubling you, Ellie?'

God, why had she started this conversation? Illness had

prevented Cam going to Vietnam; why did she still need to know more? Because she'd been blind once, hadn't she? Yes, it was years ago, but Cameron Hastings had form; she'd been so sure and so wrong.

She cleared her throat. 'If Cam was attracted to – or even in love with – someone else, would he . . . ?' she began. She took a quick breath and attempted a smile. 'Actually, ignore that. I'm all over the place. Lack of sleep . . . ' She glanced at her watch. 'It's past three; I should get to school.'

Sean dipped his head to meet hers. 'Why would you—'

'It was just something Ciara said about him in conversation at the picnic,' she replied quickly, cutting him off before he said anything she did not want to hear. His expression was tight; he was frowning. 'But it was just . . . ' Oh God, he was angry. Hardly surprising when she was speaking out of turn about his wife. 'It was just girlie chatter,' she finished, using the bloody woman's own expression. Feeling foolish, she tried again. 'I warned you about lack of sleep . . . '

His face seemed to relax. 'We were pretty isolated in Ireland. I think Ciara's enjoying having people to chat with. She likes you very much. Look, I'd better get back to Cam.'

'OK. The door's on the latch.'

He began to walk away, then stopped and turned back, his expression intent. 'I never tell her anything I shouldn't. OK?'

41

Though she'd tapped her foot in the Co-op queue, a second till hadn't been opened, so Ellie arrived late. Miss Myers was waiting with Jake at the open blue door.

'Could I have a quick word, Mrs . . . ?' she asked.

Her heart sinking, Ellie nodded. 'Sure.' Then to Jake, 'Will you find Harry for me, love? Put up your hood and wait for me at the rails. I'll be no more than three minutes. OK?'

Jake flattened his hair, but nodded eventually.

Stepping back, the teacher smiled apologetically and lowered her voice. 'I hate to give you a hard time, but I'm concerned that after positive strides forward, Jake has taken steps back over the last couple of days. He's been particularly uncommunicative and moody. Is anything troubling him at home? I asked him and he didn't want to talk about it.'

Ellie swallowed. Slick bloody lies. They slid off Cam's tongue like honey. 'I'm afraid his dad isn't well. He had to come home early from his business trip. One of those flu-type viruses has floored him.' She spied Purple Laverne soaring down the corridor towards them. 'Would you mind bearing with him for now, but keep me posted? Thanks so much . . .' she replied hurriedly, escaping to the playground just in time.

Surrounded by a group of kids, Harry was animatedly telling a story – bare boobies, same-sex rabbits or *Terminator*, who knew? Jake was kicking the wall. Taking a deep breath, she smiled reassuringly. Perhaps it was just to her own ears, but the flu tale had not sounded very convincing. What could she do, though? Cam had made it clear that he didn't want people, or even the boys, to know the real reason for his illness. It was understandable, and his call, after all. But her middle son had a talent for picking up on fibs; Cam called it his 'fibdar'.

'You don't miss anything. The CIA would employ you in a blink, Jakey.'

'What do you mean by blink, Dad?'

'Like your eye. It means fast. Like when you blink.'

'Ready to see Dad?' Ellie asked him now. He barely lifted his head. She dug in her bag and pulled out the sweets, hoping the delay in the Co-op had been worth it. Three packets of fizzy strawberry laces for a pound and twenty pence. She felt like Cam, using the medicine of sugar to cure all ills. But it brought a grudging smile to Jake's face and Harry was elated.

'I bet you're glad you have three children, Mum. I mean, if there were only two of us, who would eat the third packet?' he asked.

Ellie chuckled. 'Who indeed?'

The drizzle had stopped, so they sauntered home, Harry's chatter about the 'wow words' he'd used in today's composition interspersed by sucking sherbet off his fingers. Finally at the end of their road, Ellie glanced up its length. Perplexed, she squinted at the flashing vehicle halfway up. The ice-cream van? She did another take. No; God, no. It was an ambulance, a strobing ambulance parked outside their house. What the hell? Flinging off her sandals, she sprinted then, Jake and Harry close behind.

'What's happened?' she asked, scanning the scene and breathing heavily.

Propped up on a stretcher but white-faced and sleepy, Cam was in the back of the van, Toby by his side.

His hair ruffled, Sean stepped forward. 'It's a good job you left the door on the latch,' he said quietly. 'I got back here and waited in the kitchen, then I heard a thump. He'd fallen out of bed. Boiling hot and convulsing. But it's fine, he came round.' He gave a wry grin. 'I stripped him and cooled him down with a damp towel. Felt a complete berk. Let's hope he doesn't remember that part.'

He nodded towards the paramedics. 'They think he's got an infection, that he probably had a febrile convulsion because he overheated. They're taking him to Stepping Hill for observation.' He looked at Ellie steadily. 'Don't worry, he'll be fine. He's already on antibiotics intravenously. You go with him. I'll stay with the boys. Give me a ring later.'

Back from the hospital four hours later, Ellie slumped heavily on the settee next to Toby. 'Dad's fine. Sends his love. Have you guys eaten anything?'

Toby nodded, his pale hazel eyes on the television screen. 'I helped Sean make spag bol, Harry washed up and Jake wiped. Sean's upstairs with them now.'

She smiled. 'So I'd better scrub the dishes again, then?'

Though hesitant, his lips twitched. 'Yup,' he replied. Then he added quietly, 'I'm glad that Dad's OK. It was scary coming home and seeing the ambulance.'

'I can imagine; poor you.' She wanted to hug him, but sensed he was holding on to his emotions by a very thin thread. Instead, she gave him a playful punch. 'Do you know, though, I'm absolutely shattered and your dad is sitting up happily in bed, flirting with all the pretty nurses.'

Toby didn't reply. Then, 'Mum?' he asked, frowning. She could tell by the long pause it would be a big question. 'What's really wrong with Dad? It's not just flu, is it?'

Wishing she could be honest, she swallowed. 'Dad will tell you himself. He'll be home tomorrow or Friday, so you'll be able to ask him all about it then.'

With a huffing noise, Toby folded his arms and looked away. Ellie didn't blame him. Cam had put her in a difficult position by asking her not to tell the boys the truth. It wasn't fair on any of them. She hated secrets. She could remember all too well the whisperings between her mum and dad when she was a child. She supposed all parents did it, but being the only one, there had been no one else except *her* to whisper about, and no siblings to dilute it or distract her.

She now tried for a compromise. 'It's nothing to worry about, Toby. Honestly. It's men's stuff, if you know what I mean.'

Scrot rot seemed to loom like a phantom. Toby quickly stood. 'I think I'll crash out. Night, Mum.'

She followed him to the stairs. Sean was on his way down. 'All right now?' Sean asked him, but Toby continued upwards without speaking.

Sean stretched his broad shoulders. 'Harry's asleep and Jake's reading,' he said. 'I said you'd be up in a while. I'd better get off home.'

'Thank you,' she said simply, pleased she'd have the house to herself so she could collapse and think. Or perhaps not think at all. It was easier that way.

She opened the door and Sean stepped into the porch. He looked uncharacteristically tired. 'Oh, I forgot to mention,' he said, turning back. 'Marian rang. Marian – your mum – phoned. She asked you to call back when you have a chance.'

Oh God, the slap and that word. Trying not to betray the pelt of anxiety, she nodded. 'Thanks,' she said again. She wanted him to go, to close him out of her home. God knows why, but the image of him stripping another man's clothes had stuck; it had been playing in a loop ever since he'd mentioned it. But he didn't stir. Not moving, not speaking, just there.

'Your lip. It's cut,' he finally stated.

She put her hand to her mouth; she had almost forgotten.

'Was it . . . ?' He peered at her intently, concern in his eyes. Expecting him to say 'Cam', she tensed, but he continued to speak. 'Was it your father? Did he—'

'No. No, it wasn't.' God, she wanted to cry. The smack had caught the split and it had bled again, though. She hadn't realised until she'd noticed the tissues she'd been using to mop her tears were stained pink. She took a gulp of air. 'No, it was just an accident – I broke a glass and it caught me.'

Apparently unconvinced, he frowned. Willing him to wrap her in his arms, she held her breath, but he finally nodded and strode away. 'Text or call if you need me,' he said over his shoulder.

She stepped back in the house.

'What was that all about, then?'

Starting at the unexpected sound, Ellie snapped up her head. Toby was crouched at the top of the stairs.

'Toby! You made me jump. Nothing. It was nothing.'

'Then why were you talking in the porch? With Sean?' he demanded in a shaky voice. 'You were together, whispering the other day too.'

She felt herself blush. 'Really? I don't think Sean and I *whisper*—'

He glared. 'And don't say *nothing*, when it clearly isn't. If it was nothing you wouldn't need to bloody mumble so no one can hear.'

'Please don't swear, Toby; we were just—'

'You were talking about me and Katrina, weren't you?' he blurted. 'I don't fancy her, you know.'

Ellie breathed. Why she'd felt guilty, she couldn't say. She'd only wanted a hug. Hadn't she? 'Of course we weren't talking about you. Katrina's a lovely girl but I know you're just friends.'

The relief of his comment and its sweetness almost made her smile. But overheard words could be painful. Not only as a young child, but an older one too. Even at twenty-one.

'What's she doing here again, Marian? She's finished university now. Shouldn't she be looking for a job instead of locking herself in her bedroom all day? I can't pretend that I miss all the arguments and the ugly black make-up, but when I see her she's like a ghost. It isn't normal. She isn't normal.'

The conversation had gone on for some time. Yet *'she isn't normal'* were the only words that Eleanor Wilson heard.

42

A warm Friday morning, the boys were up early, a hum of excitement in the house. Today was Jake's big moment at school assembly, it was the last day before the summer break and Cam would be home from the hospital by teatime.

'You do know that Grandma rang three times yesterday?' Toby said, as he bolted down the stairs in his 'dress down' attire. 'You are going to call her back, aren't you?'

'Of course,' Ellie replied. And she was going to, she really was. She felt bad about ignoring her mum's calls over the last couple of days, but she hadn't felt ready to speak to her yet. Silly though it was, it felt as though Marian had colluded in the slap. But today Ellie had woken with a desire to do a Cameron Hastings manoeuvre: to smooth things over with her parents and him. Sure, he had asked her to fib about his illness, but on reflection, his other 'misdemeanours' weren't actual lies. They were more like omissions. *Omissions* felt manageable in her head, a way to slide into happy-holiday mode with him and their sons.

The sunshine streamed in the hallway. Leaning into the mirror, she examined the cut on her lip and touched it tentatively. A little sore but it was healing fast, barely noticeable. No one else had commented. She shook the thought away and concentrated instead on applying a dab of concealer beneath each eye to hide the lilac-tinged smudges.

The boys were bickering, but it was a happy squabble, if that wasn't a paradox. They stopped and ogled when she entered the kitchen.

'Where are you going?' Jake demanded. As usual he had smeared the strawberry conserve on his toast with care, ensuring it reached the furthest edges before biting a quarter.

'Only Hen's, why do you ask?'

'Then why are you wearing a skirt?' He bit to a half. 'You only wear them on holiday.'

'She's got lipstick on, too,' Harry added, his jam having spread to his cuffs and his face. 'Maybe she fancies Mr Hall.'

'Or maybe it's a nice summer's day and *she* is looking forward to *someone's* star award, then Dad coming home?' Ellie said with a smile. She hoped that would satisfy Jake. He hated change unless there was a good reason for it.

'Oh Lord, you're not going to snog Dad, are you?' Harry groaned, *snog* being his latest favourite word.

'Well, I might do, you never know. And, don't say, "Oh Lord." You're only eight, not eighty.'

'Nearly nine,' he retorted. 'At least I didn't say *bloody*.'

'If you try really hard, Harry, you could say snog and bloody in the same sentence,' Toby interjected, giving his brother a little kick.

'You bloody want to snog Katrina!' Harry shouted triumphantly.

There was no doubt about it, her youngest was a smart little chap. Trying not to smile, Ellie waited for Toby's retaliation, but instead of the expected retort, he glared at her and stalked from the room with a slam.

Her fault as usual; oh well. 'Now, who wants more toast?' she asked brightly.

Enjoying the breezy warmth on her face, Ellie took off her sunglasses. 'Oh, this is heaven,' she said with a sigh. Hen passed her a glass of chilled wine. 'Thank you. Just the one, though. I'm collecting Cam at two.'

Hen eyed Ellie's legs, stretched out from the deckchair. 'So we do have legs, then, do we? And no corned beef marks from living up North. I'm impressed.'

'I thought that I'd take a leaf out of your book, Hen. You know, try to attract the attentions of a carpet fitter or two.'

'And a butcher, a baker, a candlestick maker,' Nina added, chuckling.

'You forgot about Fred,' Hen replied, examining her own long and tanned limbs.

Ellie and Nina looked to the end of the kidney-shaped lawn. Fred the gardener had rolled up his shirtsleeves, but his waistcoat and flat cap were still firmly in place.

'He must be at least eighty-five,' Nina exclaimed as they laughed. 'Harry accused me of fancying Mr Hall from school, who-ever he is.'

'Oh, he's the new teacher in Year Four,' Nina replied. 'Very attractive and very young. I'd be tempted to dig out my herbal pills for him any time, though I suspect he might be gay.'

Remembering Harry's comment, Ellie chuckled. 'Ah, the teacher "batting for the other side".'

'Talking of *education*, Ellie . . .' Hen turned with raised eyebrows. 'The handsome professor . . . Now he is sexy. The moody dark beard, the green, green gaze . . .' She fanned her face with a graceful hand.

Nina frowned in puzzlement. 'The professor? Not *your* professor who . . . deflowered you?'

209

'God, no. Ellie's friend from uni—'

'Ah, got it.' Nina put a finger to her chin. 'What did Cam say? Genius, professor of psychology, father of six—'

'And knight in shining armour. As for the soft "come to bed with me" Irish accent . . .'

Feeling the heat of another blush, Ellie snorted. 'Well, I can't say that I've noticed. And he is *not* my friend. He's Cam's. The two of them were joined at the hip. I never liked him. In fact, it's fair to say that—'

An old memory suddenly struck. Sean's words one day in the student house, uncharacteristically kind. *'Cam doesn't know what he wants yet. You've got to pick yourself up. Paint the sorrow on canvas. You're a beautiful girl, Ellie. Don't let it beat you.'*

Hen's voice brought her back from the shiver. 'Maybe not, darling, but he only had eyes for you the other night. I was quite put out; I must be losing my touch.'

Feeling both friends' scrutiny, a pulse of time passed. 'Well, if you're a good girl, Hen, I might invite you for a threesome,' she replied. Was this normal, the answer she should give? That image of Sean and another guy was still there; but this time they were partially naked.

Nothing felt 'normal' at all.

43

Another hospital car park in the sunshine. But this one was in Stockport and today Ellie paid for the parking. Cam was waiting for her in the lobby. She gave him a peck. 'Ready to go home?'

He gave a weary smile. 'Yup. I'll be glad to see the back of bloody doctors for a while. I've had enough prodding and poking to last a lifetime. Let's go.'

Unusually quiet, he held her hand as they ambled to the car.

A silent Cam freaked Ellie out. 'Is everything OK? You're not saying much,' she asked eventually. 'No complications or anything medical to report?'

'Nope. I'm just tired. Private may balls-up the balls, but at least you can sleep.'

'And eat delicious, gourmet food, according to Hen when she went in for her mole.' Cam's eyes follow a young nurse with swinging blonde hair in a high ponytail. It brought back a jolt of disquiet. Ellie focused on her summer resolution: an omission, that was all. She smiled. 'But I see the NHS staff are just as attractive.'

'No one is as stunning as my woman.' He put his arm around her waist. 'And she has very sexy legs.'

She raised her eyebrows. 'Well, I'll have to meet her then. In the meantime, I'm going to be extremely strict and stand over you until you've taken all your medicine. I don't want to visit a hospital again for a long, long time.'

He grinned. 'Strict, eh?' Then he glanced over. 'You didn't really tell me about Maurice, how he was when you collected him.'

She touched the ridge on her lip with a finger. True; she didn't. She hadn't wanted to get into questions she didn't know how to answer. 'Oh, it was fine,' she replied with a shrug. 'He looked surprisingly well and was happy to be home.'

For God's sake, what was she doing? She hated evasions and secrets more than anyone. She took a sharp breath. 'And then, when I was leaving Woodlands . . .Well, he was still hostile towards me. Put it that way.'

Parked up outside the house, Ellie turned to climb out.

'I think we should book a holiday,' Cam said.

She flipped back to him. He was frowning thoughtfully.

'I should think so,' she replied. 'The boys are expecting sun, sand and sea as usual. I was waiting for your work dates before checking out hotels online. I thought I'd see if the travel agents in the village would price match.'

Work. Hotels. Doubt and mistrust. The flip of agitation was there.

'I didn't mean our main holiday. I was thinking of a week somewhere before then, just the two of us.' Taking her hand, he kissed the plaster. 'I think it would be good for us.'

Like a bouquet of flowers out of the blue, Ellie felt on alert. It was a lovely idea but where had it come from? She cleared her throat. 'That would be nice. But realistically, Cam, leaving Jake without us for a whole week? Who would we ask to look after the boys anyway?'

'I could ask my folks.' He grinned. 'They might die of sugar poisoning, but why not? It'd do them good to see how the other half lives.'

She laughed unsteadily. 'What, over the border? Really?'

'Why not?'

Smooth life without bumps, she remembered. 'OK. Let's do it. But maybe start with just a weekend?'

'You're on.'

She caught Cam's wince as he swung his legs from the car.

'You don't think I'll actually organise it, do you?' he said. 'Well, you'll just have to wait and see, young lady. But for now I'm dead beat. I need to lie down.'

Still fingering Cam's surprise suggestion, Ellie glanced at the clock. There was time for a hot drink before the school run. She spooned in coffee and groaned at her stupid discomfort. Cam had done what she'd always been willing him to do; like with the Tag watch, he'd been romantic and spontaneous, that was all. She sighed. But in fairness it was odd. He usually wanted the boys to be with them on breaks and she agreed. She hated the vague sensation that something or someone was missing, even when they were all there. And besides, she enjoyed being 'the eleventh man', as Cam called her.

'But there's only five of us, Dad,' Jake would comment, his shorts stained red by excessively rubbing the cricket ball.

'Ah, but if there were eleven of us, then Mum would be it.'

The old sunny, warm feeling of holidays surfacing, she smiled and sat down. Crazy golf, tennis or basketball, followed by a sunlounger with a book, the boys hurtling off to cool down in the pool. Chilled relaxation; no cooking or housework; smooth days without bumps. Mostly.

Yup, an easy, stress-free life ... Which included her parents. The call had to be made sometime. Putting down her mug, she scooped up her mobile and quickly pressed the icon before changing her mind. Marian answered immediately, but her voice sounded tinny and distant.

'Woodlands 6275.'

'It's Ellie, Mum.'

'Eleanor! Hello, love.'

Ellie took a quick breath. 'Sorry I haven't got back to you sooner but Cam came home unexpectedly. He brought flu with him and everything's been upside-down. Oh, and Jake had his special assembly this morning. He was Star of the Week for the first time ever. You should've seen his face ...' God, she was gabbling. Get to the point, Ellie. 'I'd love to see you both soon. How about tomorrow? I'll bring one of the boys with me.'

A pause, then Marian's thin tones. 'No, please don't, love, not yet. Let Dad get settled back in. He's still a little confused, which makes him frustrated, and then ...'

Ellie waited for more, but the line was silent. 'Then what? Mum?'

'Oh, nothing I can't deal with. A broken plate, that's all.'

Picturing the mark of a hand on her mother's soft cheek, Ellie's heart battered her ribs. 'Has he hurt you, Mum? You must tell me. Has Dad hit you?'

'No, of course not. But after the last time you were here, I think it's best you don't visit just yet.'

It didn't feel right. Her mother was saying all the correct things, but her voice was peculiar. On the verge of tears? No, more exasperation. Whichever it was, it definitely sounded strained.

Ellie swallowed. 'Still a little confused.' 'A broken plate.' What did one do in these circumstances? Call the police? She doubted they'd get involved in a domestic situation, especially with illness. The obvious answer was to contact Maurice's GP.

His bizarre behaviour had to be connected in some way to his stroke.

'Mum,' she said, trying for measured and calm, 'I really think we need to get Dad to the doctor's, even back to hospital. There's clearly some sort of complication if he's still disorientated. Nina said Mabel's confusion was from dehydration. And I've heard urinary infections can cause it too. It could be as simple as that. I'm sure it can be sorted with medication of some sort.'

No reply for several beats, but eventually Marian spoke, her articulation flat but firm. 'I'm not going to the doctor, Ellie. I know what it is; I know exactly what's wrong.' She sighed. 'It's really very silly, but when Dad, when he . . . Well, when you accidentally awoke him, he thought you were Diana.'

44

It's a balmy night, the cherry curtains closed, the window open a crack. Though it's too dark to see them properly, Ellie's favourite birthday cards are still on the bedside table. Feeling a little guilty, she touches the new watch on her wrist; she hasn't taken it off like she's supposed to.

She needs to pee, but there are sounds: shuffling, tapping. And angry whispers. She covers her ears, but she can still hear them. Murmuring voices and sighs. A low moaning, too. She's heard it before; it makes her heart clang, but she doesn't know why. If she just squeezes her eyes she'll be—

It was still only noon, but it had been a busy morning, the first Saturday of the summer holidays in full swing. Boys of various shapes and sizes had called at their house. There had even been one or two newcomers. Not that Ellie minded one jot; she positively encouraged waifs and strays. It was one of the reasons she had insisted her kids go to the local state schools. She had gone private, and though she had friends there, they'd been scattered miles around the Preston area, so they couldn't just call at her door. And of course when they had visited Woodlands by prior arrangement for tea or a sleep-over, there had been the inevitable grilling by Maurice. Where exactly did they live? What did their parents do for a living? Did they know so and so?

At times he could be a frightful snob, which was why his high opinion of Cam had been a surprise.

'Perhaps Dad just wants you to be happy,' Marian had said when she'd voiced it all those years ago. 'Ever think of that, love?'

Most of the callers were for Harry. They were officially playing football in the park opposite, but more often than not the ball appeared on the road and stayed there, hoofed up and down with ferocious enthusiasm. The elderly neighbour a few doors down complained whenever he saw Ellie, but didn't bother with Cam. The last time he tried, Cam had shrugged and said pleasantly, 'Well, boys will be boys, won't they? I expect you did the same when you were that age. Bet you had a good left foot, Cyril.'

It had made Ellie smile. Cam's way, with charm.

Toby had grunted at his caller, a spotty school friend called Daniel. They had stalked upstairs to 'listen to music', whatever that entailed when both wore huge headphones. As for Jake, two pretty little girls had appeared for him. They were in his bedroom 'doing gluing and sticking'. Cam had laughed when he saw them. 'Girls? Bloody hell. What a dark horse. Must take after his dad.'

Ellie now moved the newspaper out of his eyeline. 'Cam, are you listening?' she asked.

'Of course I am, my love, I always listen to your dulcet tones.'

'No you aren't. You know you're not programmed to do two things at once. Look at me and then I'll know you *are* listening.'

He closed the page and picked up his Biscotti. 'I'm all ears.'

Although exasperated with Cam's inability to listen when there was the sports section of a rag at hand, she was pleased to note that after sleeping half the day, he looked much brighter. His hair was wet from the shower and he was still in his dressing gown, but he'd eaten a bacon butty and colour had returned to his cheeks. It was nice to have him at home.

Her dreams rarely stuck, but last night's had followed her around the house since she woke. So perhaps it was a memory and not her imagination. How old would she have been then? Ten or eleven? Still in her special pink bedroom and untouched by cynicism, not knowing one day it would be whitewashed.

She shook her head. Why the recall felt significant, she didn't know, but it did make her anxious about Marian's safety.

She eyeballed Cam to ensure he was still with her. 'Should I just turn up at Mum's or wait until she calls? If Dad, even intermittently, is so confused that he thinks I'm some aunty we haven't seen for decades, he could be, I don't know, mentally unstable. And if he strangles Mum in the middle of the night, it'll be my fault if I don't do something.'

'Maurice the Ripper? I hardly think he's equipped for murder. Except at golf. He's bloody good for his age, to be fair.' Cam waved his arms theatrically. An attempt at a crazed doctor from an old film noir, she supposed. 'Though the madness might be hereditary. Let me examine you, my precious . . .'

'Cam, be serious.'

'But, my dear, I—' He stopped and listened. 'Not the bloody bell again?'

'Sounds like it. I'll get it.'

Opening the door again, Ellie took a step back. The visitors were Sean and his eldest son this time. Liam was a little older than Toby, already huge and starting to look eerily like his father. Her mind leapt to Sean's sister. So much else had gone on, she'd almost forgotten about the attractive young woman, but there was definitely a resemblance. She was Liam's aunty, of course. Like flaming Diana, her long-lost relative, who was, for some reason, a whore. The thought made her hot.

Sean cleared his throat. Oh God, had she been staring?

'We've come to see the invalid,' he said. He followed his son in. 'Do you want to find Toby, Liam?'

He made a grunt similar to Toby's, and ran up the stairs in four strides.

'Will all the boys eventually communicate like cavemen?' she asked, willing her deep blush to disappear.

'Less of the bloody invalid,' Cam called from the kitchen. 'Come and have a drink while we discuss the moral maze of Ellie's parents.'

Rising slowly from the chair, Cam cupped his groin. 'Nuts with the beer?' he quipped. 'And before you say it, Ellie, I'm sure one won't hurt me. They only tell you to stay off the booze to be cruel.'

He busied himself in the fridge, eventually producing two bottles of lager and a glass of wine. 'Chablis for the lady,' he said, presenting it with a noticeably shaky hand.

They sat around the kitchen table, the three of them. It felt like a night in the pub in the early days at university, when Ellie had still gone, Sean spouting his angst.

One discussion stood out in her mind: how opinions had changed.

'Why would anyone want to get married?' Sean had demanded to know. *'Social and financial bloody bondage? Free love is the answer.'*

'Promiscuity, you mean, Sean,' Cam had replied. *'You just want to shag all the women in England. Punish them for the potato famine.'*

'Seriously, Cam. We need freedom from state regulation, freedom from religion, the Church, from the interference in personal relationships.'

'What about monogamy? The existence of real love? Fidelity and commitment; that's why people marry.'

'Don't tell me you'd marry, Cam. Your dad left your mum—'

'And that's the point, Sean. He was married, he returned.'

Like an echo, Sean's voice brought her back. 'So, what's happening with your parents, Ellie?' he asked.

'She thinks they're both going insane,' Cam replied for her. 'See, Ellie. I was listening.'

She frowned; she'd made light of the Maurice situation with Cam, but he was taking it to frivolous extremes as usual, and besides, she might not want to share it with a stranger. And she could feel that stranger's gaze, quizzical, appraising.

'I don't think *insane* is the description I'd use . . .'

She mused on yesterday's second conversation with her mum. Marian had backtracked by then, saying everything was 'actually fine', that Ellie had caught her at a bad moment and that perhaps she'd made assumptions about what was going on in Maurice's head.

Diana, by all accounts, was bohemian, artistic and unorthodox, which, Ellie was sure, her dad would interpret as a 'good-time girl', a woman without morals. The fact he saw her in that category wasn't something she wanted to contemplate. She suspected her mum had reached the same conclusion.

'Has he hurt your mum or himself in any way?' Sean asked quietly, rotating his beer bottle, but not drinking it.

'She says not. He's thrown a plate in frustration, apparently. But . . . ' Should she say it? 'Well, I surprised him with a peck on the cheek the other day and he . . . ' She put her hand to her face. 'He cuffed me. But it was really my fault; he was napping and I startled him. I shouldn't have woken him . . . ' Embarrassed, she trailed off. Repeating the incident made it sound trivial.

'You didn't tell me that Maurice had assaulted you,' Cam said incredulously.

'No, Cam, that's too strong a word. It was more a . . . '

The two men looked on as she contemplated how she might phrase it better, but she was saved by Jake, who had appeared at the kitchen door. His face looked tight and she wondered what was coming.

'Can Lorna and Laura have a sleep-over tonight?' he asked.

The two girls appeared next to him, both solemn faced.

'We need to finish the project,' one said with a lisp.

'Sticking and gluing,' the other said.

'And we're being very careful with the edges,' Jake added, as though that explained the need for an overnight stay.

Ellie smiled, flummoxed. Was it usual for girls of ten to sleep-over at a boy's house? Children she'd never met before today? She started to think of a way to say no.

'We'll ask your mums what they think, and if they say yes, then of course you can,' Cam replied for her. 'Do you have their phone numbers, Ellie?' Then, as though the intermission of the last half-hour hadn't occurred: 'In answer to your question: yes, you should just turn up at your mum's. Sean will go with you, won't you, man?'

45

Inhaling the sweet vanilla scent, she tromps up the slope, the never-ending hill. Badly needing to pee, she clutches her groin. Holding it back gives her stomach cramps, but she scrunches her eyes, willing the danger away. Sleep, Ellie, sleep. It'll be over very soon.

Her Dr Martens too heavy, she trudges on and on. The car is getting closer, she'll have to obey. The window winds down and she tenses. It's her daddy, thank goodness, kind and friendly. But when she steps closer he's sobbing. His face is white and frozen in terror. And he's opening his mouth to scream—

'Wake up, Ellie. You're having a nightmare.'

She dragged open her eyes. Cam was glaring back. Even in the shadows, she could see *his* face wasn't friendly or kind. It was fair enough, really; she'd disturbed him in the dead of night and he was ill; he needed his rest.

The dream had almost evaporated, yet the horror was sickening and real. She felt a surge in her stomach and knew she would—

'I think I'm going to be sick.'

She bolted to the bathroom and knelt at the loo but nothing came. Just a need to spit, then spit again and again. Pulling herself on to the seat, she breathed deeply and waited for the spasms to pass. As her heartbeat slowed, its thud was overtaken by the pure sound of birdsong through the open window. The dawn chorus, so it wasn't that early after all.

What was it her dad used to say? *'Those bloody birds. They wake me at dawn and then I can't get back to sleep. I like them in the fields and hills where they belong. You shouldn't encourage them here by feeding them, Marian.'*

It was funny how things changed: Maurice had become the keeper of his feathered friends, feeding them every day, watching them at the table from the lounge window. Starlings, house sparrows, blackbirds; blue and great tits, robins, greenfinches and collared doves. Young Ellie had learned to name every one.

She frowned. What had her old granny often warned with a knowing nod? *'A leopard never changes its spots, Eleanor.'* But it seemed to Ellie that human beings transformed all the time. Like free love and marriage. Look at them now, Sean and Cam, Cam and Sean. But as Cam always said, 'We were different people then.'

Of course it had been the two men who'd decided she should tackle her parents today. The plan was to turn up unannounced at Woodlands, but with Sean Walsh in tow. Completely bloody strange, or what. How would it go? 'Hello, Mum, I've come to challenge you about Dad and his weird behaviour. Oh, and let me introduce Sean, a student Cam and I once knew who's wormed his way back into our lives.'

But was that even true? Hadn't he always been there behind that closed door?

Not quite grasping her real worry, she sighed. Sean was actually being kind; the poor guy hadn't had a choice.

'You know it would be me if I was up to it,' Cam had said to her yesterday. Then to Sean: 'Is that OK with you, mate?'

Sean's eyes had flickered. 'Yes, of course. I can wait outside in the car.'

Making plans for Ellie. Like a child who had no say. She didn't know if she was riled or relieved.

In a final bid for autonomy, she'd insisted she try one more time to speak to her mum first. So she'd rung her.

'Hello, Mum, it's me—'

'Oh, hello love, I'm just in the middle of baking, my hands are all floury,' Marian had replied. 'I'll call you back in a bit.'

She hadn't phoned back in 'a bit' or at all, so that was that.

Ellie crept around the house in the budding light of the morning. Like a contented phantom, she was coming to enjoy these still and silent starts to the day. Though perhaps a 'contented phantom' was a contradiction. Phantoms, like her nightmares, weren't happy. She wished she didn't have the damned things, but if on waking she didn't immediately describe to Cam what had happened, they dissolved.

Like artificial sweetener, leaving a strange taste.

She put her head around Jake's bedroom door. He was in the bed, the two changeling girls on the floor. Liam Walsh had also stayed the night. He'd gone out with Toby and Daniel after dinner and they hadn't returned until half past ten. It wasn't so much the lateness of the hour that she wondered about, but what they'd been up to for so long. What did early teenagers do? They were too young to go to a pub, and would an off-licence sell to them? Although Liam was a little older and could pass for eighteen, Daniel looked boyish and ID was expected these days.

She stole down the creaking stairs. Toby's sweatshirt was still lying where he'd left it near the door. Even before she scooped it up, the acrid combination of tobacco and cider hit her nostrils. Oh hell. Liam Walsh was clearly a bad influence. Yet she remembered it well, Year Ten or even Year Nine, smoking menthol cigarettes and adding blackcurrant to help the bitter alcohol go down.

'What's happened to your old friends, Ellie? Tricia and Rosie? We don't see them any more,' Marian would ask nicely.

'She's in with a bad crowd; prefers the wrong sort. Just look at the state of her. And the language I overhear on the telephone. I don't know why you bother asking,' Maurice would comment, as though Ellie wasn't there.

'Well, you wouldn't hear it if you didn't eavesdrop. The "bad crowd" have more laughs, actually. But you wouldn't know about fun, would you, Dad?' she'd reply.

Now feeling a little underhand herself, Ellie dipped into the pouch of Toby's top. Save for a chocolate bar wrapper, it was empty. Sighing, she sat down on the bottom stair. She had to let him do all the things that teenage boys do, but she prayed it wouldn't involve crime or drugs. Or getting embroiled with the 'wrong sort', as Maurice had put it.

'It's really no big deal, Ellie ... We've both done it loads of times. And you won't get caught near the cemetery.'

Yes, the attraction of the bad crowd had continued through to university. And it hadn't ultimately been fun.

Suddenly thirsty for water, she lifted Cam's jacket to slot Toby's hoodie beneath. It swung open and revealed an envelope tucked inside. She stared. A letter. Not on the hall table, nor in the study as usual, but hidden in a pocket. Her fingers hovering, she swallowed. Should she look? Whatever it was, did she really want to know?

46

Peeping through the lounge window, Ellie groaned at the prospect of today's trip to Chorley. With Sean Walsh, of all people. Stupidly breathless with nerves, she glanced again at her watch. Cam hadn't looked impressed when she woke him for the boys and their sleep-over guests, but he'd groggily wished her good luck.

Was 'luck' what she needed right now? She had no idea, but her irritation with him was still there from yesterday.

'It's Sunday tomorrow, Cam; you can't expect Sean to drop his family commitments just to drive me to Mum's house,' she'd said once he'd left. 'I'm perfectly capable of going on my own.'

As occasionally happened, Cameron had swung from not taking the situation seriously at all to going overboard.

'You need someone there, Ellie. You may call it a cuff, but Maurice has been violent towards you. Anything could happen. Sean doesn't mind, so it's sorted,' he'd said. Then, with a shrug, 'Anyway, I've done him a favour: I've got him out of going to church.'

Not knowing whether it was just a quip, she'd stared at him.

What was it about their friendship she couldn't quite fathom? Did it include her? Making plans for Ellie? One thing was for sure, it made her uncomfortable.

At the beep of a horn, she looked again. Oh God; her carriage had arrived.

Trying to look suitably composed, she left the sleeping house and climbed into the Audi. She turned to Sean briefly. 'Thank you for doing this,' she said, pulling on her seat belt. 'I'm sure you have better things to—'

'It's not a problem,' he replied. But he was wearing sunglasses; she couldn't tell if he meant it.

Neither of them spoke until the SUV hit the motorway. 'Presumably no further word from your mum. Is everything else OK?' he asked.

'Fine thanks.' What else was there to say? Both of them knew that nothing really was OK.

Leaning against the headrest, she blankly gazed at the electricity towers. Motorways, pylons and the past, inexorably linked.

Perhaps she had snoozed or was lost in thought, but it took several moments to register the car had stopped. She glanced around, astonished to see Sean had pulled up in a country-road lay-by, not far from Woodlands.

'Oh, we're nearly there. Any particular reason why you've . . . ?'

Sean tapped a map. 'I'm just getting my bearings.'

She peered at the satnav. 'Oh right.'

His jaw seemed tight. 'You'd fallen asleep and I didn't know where you'd want me to drop you off.' He paused. 'Why are you grinning?'

'I'm not. I'm sorry. It's nerves.'

Seeming to relax, he smiled back. 'And . . . ?'

'Your aviators. They're a surprise. You look like an Italian taxi driver.'

'Not an erudite professor of psychology?'

'Well, exactly. Aren't they supposed to wear brown cords as a uniform?' Picturing the old Sean, she shuffled in her seat. 'What happened to the philosophy bit?'

He took off his shades and raked his thick hair. 'Ah, philosophy. Spouting crap far more than I should. Don't remind me. I was full of anger then.'

'Two of us, then.'

He tilted his head questioningly.

Ellie shrugged. 'You said I was angry too—'

'You remember that?'

'How could I possibly forget all those kind compliments you gave me?'

She unbuckled her seat belt, opened the window and breathed in a vanilla aroma – camomile or magnolia – the one that reminded her of holidays. She was procrastinating, of course. Facing her parents felt too uncertain. And if she was honest, a tiny part of her was afraid.

A memory filtered back. *Anger*. Something Sean had once said about *his* mum and dad. 'You said the same about your mum.' She squeezed her mind. She heard the words but couldn't place them. 'That you blamed her?'

'That too?' He stared through the windscreen. 'I did. It seems so unfair now, but I couldn't forgive her for not fighting back, for not protecting us and herself. Occasionally Dad drank too much, and then . . . Well, he used his fists.' He looked at his own hands. 'The sins of the father . . . ' He cleared his throat. 'Are you ready to go?'

'A few more minutes,' she muttered. Painful stomach cramps had suddenly hit. It was panic; sheer panic. Hoping he hadn't noticed, she tried for normality. 'Are your parents still around?'

He didn't answer for several beats, then he seemed to relent.

'Yes. They're still on the farm, almost unrecognisable from the people who brought me up. Dad had a heart attack a few years back and had to cut down the drinking. He'd had a "life of hard labour", the doctor said. I never recognised that. But you don't, do you, as a kid? You only feel your own needs.'

Ellie nodded. She understood it completely. But her childhood complaints seemed petty compared to his. She frowned. '*Watched the blood spurt from her nose.*' Sean's voice again. A dream or did he really say it?

She thought of asking, but a different question came out. 'Do you think you'll have more children?'

Clearly surprised, he lifted his eyebrows. 'Maybe. Kids make it all worthwhile, don't they?'

Her heart was still racing, but talking seemed to help. 'Do you see them much – your mum and dad?'

'Not as much since we moved but, yes, they can't get enough of the children. Spoil them, give them hugs and kisses.' His brows knitted. 'I can't remember being held or cuddled by either of them. Or perhaps I've forgotten. But I think that's the way it was. Three older girls, then me when they could ill afford it; hard graft, little money. I eventually learned that you can't change it. Just try to do better for your own.'

Staring ahead, Ellie played with a few strands of her hair. *Older* siblings. Was the 'Irish Beast' still doing what he did back at uni – sleeping around – and if her memory served her right, not just with women?

'You seem to have forgotten your younger sister, Sean.' Oh God, her attempted jokey tone had emerged loaded with sarcasm. She softened it. 'Samantha, I think you said.'

He didn't answer for moments. He eventually turned, his eyes hard. 'What are you saying, Ellie?'

'Nothing. Sorry. I'm just rambling, asking stupid questions

229

because . . .' She swallowed. 'Look, I don't think I'm up to seeing my parents today. I know I've wasted your time—'

'We're here; you should go. You need answers.' He turned on the ignition. 'Directions from here, please.'

The impulse to escape battered Ellie's chest. She reached for the handle, ready to bolt, but an overheard conversation from long ago filtered back.

'She's an adult now, Marian. She should be out looking for work, not acting like a lazy teenager—'

'Adult or not, she's still my child, Maurice. My child who needs me.'

Holding her breath, seconds passed. Sean watched her, saying nothing. Finally expelling the trapped air, she pulled on the seat belt. 'Through two sets of traffic lights, then it's the first on your left.'

47

Approaching Woodlands on foot felt strange, a throwback to sixth form, those half happy days when Ellie had looked forward to chatting with her mum before Maurice arrived and took over, well, everything. Pretty much like now. Ruling the roost with mother hen Marian scuttling to his every whim and want.

She walked down the road and entered the driveway. As she stole across the pebbles, two blackbirds flew off the bird table.

Yup, that old sense of dread was building. That same 'what will his complaint be today?' churning if her dad was home before her. She'd hidden it with her freckles behind her make-up mask, tramping past the Jag in her Docs, slamming the front door and bounding up the stairs to her still-pink bedroom, but the turmoil had been there inside.

Of course the walls had been whitewashed by the time of her teacher training studies. Both the elevations and her face. Though the apprehension was still somewhere deep within, it was much diluted.

Not wanting to disappoint her parents – or herself – she didn't mention her application to Edge Hill until the offer had arrived in the post. Maurice didn't say much at the time, but a few weeks later a man had arrived at Woodlands with a car, a brand-new shining Ford Fiesta. She'd assumed it was for Marian, but her dad had held up the keys with a smile. 'For you,' he'd said. 'For driving to college. We're proud of you, Eleanor.'

Now taking a deep breath, Ellie headed to the kitchen window. She had intended to stride to the front door, open it and walk right in as usual, but she felt winded and nervy, as though she was in trouble.

'Not this time,' she repeated to herself. 'Not this time.' Yet still she tapped quietly on the glass. Clearly listening to the radio as she prepared Sunday lunch, her mother looked up. She didn't appear surprised, but she lifted a finger to her lips and motioned to the back door.

Ellie sharply inhaled. It was too, too ridiculous; she'd done nothing wrong. Yet she did her mother's bidding, retracing her steps to the road side of the house.

She stood in the shadows and rubbed her bare arms, despite the hazy day and warm breeze. Taking in the vibrant, picture-book garden, she sighed. Unlike the woody wilderness of the half-acre, this area was pristine. The grass was manicured and the colour combination of summer shrubs and bedding plants was spectacular, the work of an artist. There were the two clipped ornamental bushes in a spiral shape too. Of course the designer was Marian, her mother, who finally emerged from the panelled door with a fond smile.

Slipping her arm through Ellie's, she gently but firmly pulled her away from the building. 'I've told Dad that I'm popping out for some Oxo cubes, so let's walk up to Spar,' she said. 'Then we can have a nice chat.'

Dumbly, Ellie complied.

'Such lovely weather,' Marian continued as they walked.

'Though the garden suffers, as you know. Let's hope there isn't a hosepipe ban this year. The neighbours will take no notice, of course, but you know Dad, he likes to play by the rules, so I'll be in and out with the watering can even before it's official . . . '

Mesmerised by her mum's strange but familiar behaviour, Ellie fell into step, heading for the cluster of shops on the main street. Then, as though waking from a spell, she abruptly stopped, extracted her hand and glared.

'Mum, this can't go on, you know. You're acting as though there's nothing wrong. You were upset on the phone the other day, you haven't answered my calls and now we're sneaking around like criminals. What's going on with Dad? We need to talk properly and sort it out.'

'There's nothing to discuss. Dad's settled down now, he's fine.'

'Then why all the pussyfooting? This Oxo ruse? This isn't normal behaviour.'

She isn't normal. Ellie cringed at the words. But it seemed they were bloody true.

Marian turned and put a hand on Ellie's cheek. 'Oh, love. Have we ever been?' She pulled away and looked at her wrist. 'The thing is, Dad's fine when—'

'When I'm not around? So what do we do? Pretend I don't exist?'

Picturing her blue Ford Fiesta, she breathed deeply. She wanted to cry – bloody sob, actually. The gift had been generous and unexpected. She'd been so touched she'd wept, holding out her arms to her father.

'Oh, Eleanor, don't be sad. The tears are behind us,' he'd said, accepting the embrace and patting her back.

The car lost its special shine eventually, but the hug never had.

She now stared at her mother's impassive face. She wanted to shake her. 'Have you forgotten, Mum?' she wanted to yell. 'I may be an adult, but I'm still your child. And I need you right now.'

'Have you considered how that makes me feel?' she asked quietly instead. 'Don't you think the boys will wonder why you don't come for lunch any more, why we don't visit? This isn't right, Mum; surely you can see that?'

Marian tapped her watch, like she did when Ellie was young. The 'time to go' signal.

'I know it's not ideal, love, but it's best to leave things as they are for now. Dad will come round soon, then everything will be back to everyday.' She rubbed the top of Ellie's arm. 'Really, love, it will be.' She smiled. 'Now I'd better buy the Oxo before Dad sends out a search party.'

Watching her mother's departing back Ellie stared, disbelieving. A small woman, but one who held herself erect and smart, which made her seem so much taller. Was her doggedness surprising? She wasn't sure. Marian had always appeared to be the compliant 'little wife', but that wasn't really her, Ellie knew that.

'You need to talk to the doctor, Mum,' she shouted after her. 'And if you don't do it, believe me, I will.'

48

Sean opened the car window and leaned over as Ellie approached.

His aviators were on, hiding him. 'How did it go?' he asked. 'Are we staying or leaving?'

Ellie glanced up to the shops. Her mum's rigid back was entering Spar. 'We're going,' she replied, realising they had walked straight past Sean's SUV; he'd probably witnessed the whole frustrating exchange.

Without asking more questions, Sean drove up the street and on to the main road, heading for the motorway. She thought they might stop again and chat, but he looked straight ahead, his expression concealed by the shades.

Sensing he was angry, she played with her watch strap, clipping, unclipping. 'I'm sorry about before,' she said eventually. 'I didn't mean to speak out of turn about your family. I was just curious, I suppose.'

'It's fine. What did you want to know?'

'Nothing really.'

She returned to her own head. The parent trauma incomplete,

she flipped to another – the letter in Cam's inside pocket, the one he hadn't seen fit to bloody mention. Was it just them or were all relationships the same? She clipped and unclipped, her mind juggling a hundred random thoughts. One fell in her palm. Turning and testing it, she wondered whether to broach it again. Why had Sean reacted so defensively to her question about his sister? And why did it bother her so much? She had believed him the last time they spoke about it, but his body language, his whole being, seemed so furtive today, it was difficult to judge. And he was distant, tense. Was he lying?

She eyed him again. 'How old is your sister?'

'Which one?'

'Samantha.'

He smoothly changed lanes, then finally replied. 'She's twenty.'

Bloody hell; so young. Turning to the passenger window, Ellie stared absently at the people in cars. If the girl was a lover, he'd have given up the pretence by now, surely? And there'd definitely been a resemblance between her and Liam. A thought suddenly struck, so shocking it pelted out as sound. 'Is Samantha your daughter?'

His jaw tight, he shook his head. 'She's my half-sister, Ellie.' He glanced at her then, his scowl turning to puzzlement. 'Why would you think that?'

Ellie covered her face and sighed. There it was again; her judgement so random, so skewed. But despite Sean's obvious irritation, she felt a trouble lift. 'I don't know. You just seemed . . .'

His *half*-sister. How had that happened? Oh God. 'Sorry, Sean; I'm poking my nose into something that isn't my business. I didn't mean to upset you . . .' She finally trailed off and went back to the sun-stripped countryside.

Sean was quiet for some time, then he snorted mildly. 'Maybe you aren't so wide of the mark; I didn't hold back on my . . .

romantic tendencies, so I could have fathered a child back then. But Samantha ...' He tapped the steering wheel and seemed to make a decision. 'My older sisters couldn't wait to leave the farm; the moment each of them hit eighteen they were gone, so Dad got in hired help. A girl from my class was one of them. Patricia. From the age of fourteen until I left for Leeds she was part of the family; me and her were close mates.'

He blew out a long breath. 'First year of uni she wrote to say she was pregnant and that my dad was the father. He'd given her money but didn't want to hear from her again. My emotions were all over the place – mainly selfish, of course: I had finally escaped and this was reeling me back in; how could my dad and Patricia have done this to me?' He glanced at Ellie. 'I know, contemptible. There was disgust, of course – my deplorable father and exactly how long had he been at it with her. Then blame – to my deep shame, I not only held Patricia culpable, but my mother too. How had she allowed Dad to stray? had regularly thumped through my mind. So I heroically dealt with it by ignoring the letter and staying away.' He paused. 'Then things happened; I grew up and I realised that a baby was a blessing. And whatever mistakes the adults had made, it wasn't the child's fault, so I finally got my act together and apologised to Patricia. She was unbelievably magnanimous and allowed me to become part of Samantha's life.'

Ellie reached out a hand and lightly touched Sean's. 'Thanks for telling me.' She thought back. 'You said it's something you don't talk about?'

'My other sisters don't know about it to this day.' He raked his hair. 'Perhaps it's the wrong call, but they'd invoke punishment, fire and brimstone on Dad and that would involve my mother, too. I can't risk her ever finding out. It would kill her. Despite everything, he's her ...' His expression darkened. Anger or sadness? It was difficult to tell. 'Her soulmate, one true love or whatever you'd like to call it.'

Thinking of her own parents, Ellie smiled wryly. 'I get that.'

'Do you?' Sean asked.

Feeling something slither inside, she cleared her throat. 'Yes, if my mum's behaviour today is anything to go by.'

'Her Eurydice to his Orpheus?'

She laughed drily. 'Something like that.'

Not wanting to dwell on those stupid feelings of rejection, she went back to her watch, clipping and unclipping thoughts of that bloody envelope.

Sean drove on steadily, glancing at the mirror, moving lanes smoothly. She closed her eyes. Life without bumps; if only.

He broke the silence eventually. 'You and your dad,' he asked. 'Were you ever close?'

Rousing herself to the question, Ellie thought of the long walks, just the two of them, naming birds. And the lovely fuss he'd made on birthdays and at Christmas when she was small. When did it all change? He'd always been strict, but at some point the affection simply stopped, like turning off a tap.

'Sometimes, when I was little. But then, as I grew older, he seemed so . . . so disappointed in me. I never felt good enough.'

'So you rebelled?'

'You could say that. It made life easier – I couldn't blame him for not loving me then.'

'And today?'

'I only saw Mum – as you probably gathered – and she's determined to ignore everything. I have no idea what to do next. Just the thought makes me feel tired, so I'm parking it for now. Besides . . .'

She clipped and unclipped. The envelope, the letter.

Suddenly, it seemed, they were on Didsbury Road, nearing

home. The need to say it rushed out. 'I found an envelope in Cam's pocket this morning. I know it was addressed to him but I . . . It was from the hospital,' she blurted.

She hadn't intended to say anything; she was alarmed by the letter's contents, embarrassed by her snooping. She'd promised herself to wait until Cam mentioned it first. 'He needs radiotherapy, Sean. He hasn't said anything to me.'

The car hummed at the traffic lights.

Sean removed his sunglasses and turned. 'It'll be a precautionary measure,' he said slowly. 'Are you going to tell him that you've seen it? It might be easier for him if you did.'

'Why does he do this?' she asked, covering her face.

Reaching over, he gently prised her hands from her eyes. He'd done this before, hadn't he? In another life or in a dream or just in her imagination?

'It's not just Cam,' he said, his expression cloudy. 'We all do it. Protection from our emotions, our hopes, our fears.' He gazed for a moment before replacing his shades. 'Sometimes it's just easier to hide them, to pretend something isn't there or isn't happening. It's too scary to face them. Don't you think, Ellie?'

49

Sean drove the SUV slowly along Ellie's road. To her right, familiar faces bobbed in and out of the park entrance. To the left, her door, all the windows and the garden gate were ajar.

'Looks like everyone is having fun,' she said. 'I hope the visitors are still in one piece.' Then, as an afterthought, under her breath: 'And those *damned rabbits*.'

She slipped from the car. She still felt winded and shy, the burgeoning friendship she and Sean had only days ago seeming fragile, unstable somehow. She couldn't quite meet his gaze. 'Thanks so much again. Please thank Ciara for letting me borrow you.'

Oh God, was that the right thing to say? Why she was on this see-saw of emotion with him and Ciara and his family, she didn't know. She couldn't express why, but he'd felt like a rock, the one solid thing in her sea of uncertainty. Now she wasn't sure; nothing felt safe any more: not Cam, her parents, not even her friends.

Taking a breath, she entered her house and popped her head in the kitchen. Every work surface was cluttered with dirty dishes and items of food – scraps of ham, grated cheese and tuna flakes – but mostly crooked loaf edges.

'Cam?' she called. 'Did you put the roast in the oven?' She glanced at the cooker; it wasn't on. The potatoes were still next to the sink, their jackets undoubtedly on.

'Hello, sweetheart, how did it go?' he replied from the decking.

'What happened to the beef?' she asked, raking a pile of crusts into one hand with the other.

Cam appeared at the door. 'Those little girls offered to make everyone sandwiches for lunch, so I thought, Why not?' He laughed. 'Are all girls that bossy? Thank God we don't have one.'

Thrown back to a long-ago conversation, Ellie gazed at him blankly.

'Wouldn't it be nice, Cam, a little baby girl? Just one more won't make much difference.'

'You're very persuasive when you're naked, young lady. OK, let's see what happens. But I'm never driving a people carrier. Promise?'

'Guide's honour, Cam.'

She pushed the memory away: no people carrier, no baby girl.

'Harry helped,' he added. Seeming to notice the disarray for the first time, his eyes swept the kitchen. He picked up a shave of bread. 'He was in charge of these babies.'

'Are all his fingers still intact?' she asked, flopping down at the table.

'Ah, good point,' he replied amiably.

She felt a shadow at the door, but didn't turn.

Cam sat too. 'Actually, while the kids are at the park, can I have a word, Ellie?'

The shadow spoke. 'Liam's not answering his phone. I'll go and find him, then I'll get off.'

'It's fine, mate. Come in. I wanted to talk to you, too. Close the door and grab a seat, will you?'

Cam ruffled his hair. He was wearing his glasses, which made him appear even more boyish. 'Right. Well . . . The thing is, I've had a letter from the consultant.'

Sean cleared his throat. 'Look, I'd better make myself scarce.'

Ellie glanced at him. It was funny how things changed. In days gone by, she'd have been angry with Cam for imparting such important news in front of someone else. Especially this intruder in their lives. Perhaps it was because she already knew what the correspondence said, but she found she didn't care any more.

'It's all right, Sean, please stay.' And with a faint smile, 'Cam would only tell you later.'

Cam's cheeks coloured. 'Yeah, so the letter suggested a course of radiotherapy, which freaked me out, but I've spoken to the doc and everything's good. It wasn't malignant, I don't have the Big C. It's just belt-and-braces stuff after the infection's cleared. So, that's that. Panic sorted.'

The moment's silence was broken by the thump of the kitchen door shortly followed by Toby, Liam and Daniel. All three unkempt youths glared at the adults and immediately retreated.

'Hell, are they only just up? Don't go far, Liam, we're going in five minutes,' Sean called.

Cam laughed. 'Like father, like son.' He scooped up a crust and lobbed it at Sean. 'You never got up before lunch.'

'Yeah, but I had an excuse. I stayed up all night—'

'Like a bloody vampire—'

'To write my thesis.'

'And the rest . . .'

Ellie watched the interaction between the two men. Strange; Cam rarely brought up their university days. But then again, today it had distracted them from the conversation at hand, so like madness, there had been method in it.

She picked her handbag from the floor. There were questions she'd normally ask – what exactly had the consultant said? When had the conversation taken place? What would the side effects of the treatment be? Could Cam still travel or work? – but the moment had passed and she was exhausted.

Almost spinning with tiredness, she stood. 'That's great news, love.' She kissed his hair. 'So brilliant to hear there's nothing to worry about for now. Are you OK keeping an eye on all the kids for a while longer? I'm really zonked; I need a five-minute lie-down.' She glanced briefly at Sean. 'Thanks again.'

'Ellie. Ellie? Wake up. You've been asleep for a couple of hours. Everyone's hungry.'

She shook herself awake. God, she must have been tired; no weird dreams, the room was still bright with sunshine and she hadn't stirred. Remembering a house full of kids, she focused on Cameron. 'Has everyone gone?'

'Yup. The bossy girls have scarpered and we've tidied up. The boys are watching a film. I've even cooked the beef, but no veg or potatoes. I thought sandwiches again?' He chuckled. 'With crusts this time.'

Smiling, she sat up. 'Peeling a step too far?' Then, 'Is the beef properly cooked? The boys don't like it pink.'

Cam settled next to her. 'Quite right. No boy should like pink. Worry not; I asked Sean how long it needed. It was in the oven for precisely two hours and eighteen minutes. It's now having – how did he put it? – "Standing time".'

'Hmm. Is there anything you don't ask the oracle?'

'Not much.' He grinned. 'Anyhow, you seem to get on better with him these days. You used to loathe him.'

'I'm sure I didn't *loathe*—'

'And you never bothered to hide it.'

Those hidden eyes today. Sean had opened up about his sister, but ... Ellie shook the discomfort away. 'Well, I have to admit that he's been very helpful recently, so he's growing on me. Slowly, very slowly . . .'

Cam put his hands behind his head. 'Good, because Ciara has invited us round for a posh dinner to celebrate their anniversary next weekend. Sixteen bloody years; Sean deserves a sainthood. It should be fun. Paul and Ruth will be there too.'

Ellie propped her head on her hand. 'They seem such an odd couple . . .'

'We know that. Jack Sprat, as you always say—'

'No, I mean Sean and Ciara.'

'Ah.' Cam took off his glasses and cleaned them with the sheet. 'I was surprised when I first met her, back in the day. Pretty enough, but not his usual type. But then, was there a usual type? Just female. And attractive. He never really said much about her. Except once, yeah, he once said, "she's my redemption" when I asked.' He raised his eyebrows and shrugged. 'I know, it's weird. But we weren't brought up with God, were we? That's something they have in common.'

'And lots of children.'

'Ah, well, Sean loves his kids and you know men will do any-thing to get a shag.'

He rolled to her hip and lifted his leg. 'Shit, that hurts. I think a good seeing-to is still on hold for a few days, which is a shame seeing as you're looking particularly gorgeous this afternoon.'

'No I'm not,' she replied with a snort. 'We do have mirrors, you know.'

Mirrors. The thought took her back. Though the wound had been livid, raw and ugly, the need to inspect it had been compulsive.

'It's horrible, Mum. I look so ugly.'

'Stop looking in the mirror so often. It won't heal any quicker.'

'I'll be scarred all my life.'

'Of course you won't. It'll heal, then you'll go back fresh to university, you'll meet someone nice, fall in love and it'll all be forgotten.'

Leaning towards Cam, she softly kissed him on the lips.

He looked at her thoughtfully. 'What's that for?' he asked.

50

She's on their private road with her dad, arm in arm and ambling for Oxo. His face is soft and she knows life is fine. Then suddenly she stumbles and falls to her knees. She tries to crawl away, but the pain is like a whip, thwack, thwack on her back. Burning fire sears through her torso, then up to her face.

Who is doing this to her? Who's hurting her like this? She turns. Oh God, oh no, it's her. Smoking a cigarette, she's nodding sadly. 'A whore, Ellie. Whether you like it or not, love, that's what you are—'

Gasping for air, Ellie burst from the bubbles. What the hell, what the hell? She snapped her head from side to side. It wasn't a dream within a dream; she was in the bath, the water still piping, the hollow globules slowly dying. Bloody hell; for an iota she must have fallen asleep. Her heart pelting with alarm, she pulled up her knees and rested her head.

The sprint finally slowed to a thump. Whore. Branded like a whore. The deep, deep shame. Why hadn't she thought of it before? *Whore.* Her dad's word, his description of his own daughter, had been staring her in the face. The one person she'd told; the one person she'd trusted.

Almost slipping in her haste, she stood and stepped out. She waited for the dizziness to pass, then scooped up her mobile from the bath mat.

With trembling damp fingers, she composed the text.

You told him. How could you? You promised.

It was the end of Ellie Wilson's second year at the University of Leeds. As the hot summer began, she moved in with new flatmates, Kim and Jade, two photography students from the 'Poly', girls Maurice would not have approved of had their paths crossed. Which meant they were interesting, 'alternative' and fun, willing to have a good time. Great artists, too. Their work had been exhibited in a secondhand bookshop when Ellie first met them, and she'd been amazed at their creativity. She and Kim had clicked immediately, their taste in music, men and fashion remarkably similar. Though Jade was moody and a little too direct at times, Ellie was in awe of her, especially her brilliant eye for detail and her dedication when she was working on a project. Some things Ellie wasn't so sure about, like the two women occasionally doing a runner from restaurants, shoplifting from the local Spar and nicking funky clothes from a nice guy in the market.

'Don't get all sniffy with us. Our dads aren't rich like yours,' Jade would say when Ellie dared to call them out on it.

But sharing with them suited Ellie. Her old housemates had returned home to stay with their parents for the holidays. There was no way she was going back to Woodlands for a whole bloody summer. Days here and there were bad enough, but the thought of weeks on end under her father's dictatorial rule was unbearable.

So she and her new pals had gone on social security for the break, 'sub-letting' a high-rise council flat near the centre of town.

Life was hunky-dory that humid August. They went to gigs in dank basements, to gatherings and parties that lasted several days, but they took their art seriously, hiring a small gallery, submitting to magazines, honing their skills. The autumn term soon came around, Ellie's dole money seamlessly stopping as Maurice's grant payments kicked in.

Or so she had blithely thought.

Realisation that no credits were going into her account was painfully slow. Though her debit card was declined a couple of times, she put it down to a blip or a fault in the plastic and borrowed money from Kim until she had chance to go to the cashpoint. When she did late one night, her card was swallowed. Then a 'red' letter from the bank fell on the doormat. She had exceeded her overdraft; her finances were now frozen. Puzzled and astonished, she stared at the statement. Her mind searched for reasons why no grant had gone in. A bank error? Forgetfulness on the part of her father? But she knew she was kidding herself. Maurice had stopped her monthly payments without any warning or explanation. What the hell? What the fucking hell?

'What's up, Ellie?' Kim asked. 'You look as though you've seen a ghost.'

'My dad has stopped paying my grant.'

'Bloody hell, why? He's loaded, isn't he?'

'Not exactly *loaded* but . . . '

Ellie tensed. What had she done this time? Maurice made no secret of his view that her art degree was a waste of time and money – 'even worse than an ology', as he put it – but why now? Sure, the last time she was at home she'd had a crisp exchange with him about various things over Sunday lunch; they'd ranged from social, economic and political male privilege to her disgust that he and her mum rattled around a huge house when there was so much poverty in the world. She'd told them to 'sell up, downsize and do some good with the money'. That it was what she'd do if Woodlands was hers.

Bloody hell; was that it? Her father's face had been white with anger. 'Dad does plenty of *good* with his money, Ellie,' Marian had quietly replied. 'He gives regularly to charity, and he's very generous to you ...'

Now gazing at Kim, Ellie tried to breathe though the shock and dismay. The disorientation too. She'd never been without money; it went into her bank account and out again without any thought. What even were her outgoings?

As though reading her mind, Jade spoke from the door. 'What about your share of the rent, Ellie? You know the deal: we shouldn't really be here. If Andrei gets wind you haven't paid, he'll throw us out.' She folded her arms. 'You need to sort this, Ellie. Like now.'

'Yeah, sure, I will. I'll talk to my dad. It's probably just a mistake ...'

'Like now, Ellie.'

Both girls looking on, she telephoned Maurice's office and spoke to his secretary.

'It's Eleanor. Is Dad around, please?'

Clearly embarrassed, the poor woman didn't speak for a moment. 'Sorry, he's ... too busy to talk, but ...' She cleared her throat. 'He left a message in case you rang. He said you should find employment to support yourself and when you are ready to show some respect and apologise, he'll consider his position on the matter of finances further.'

The distress turning to anger, Ellie ended the call. There was no point speaking to her mum – her dad's decisions were hers and besides, Marian had no independent money to give her. But *employment*? A bloody job? She was at university, for God's sake, she was learning a craft. Painting took time, stimulus and patience. It was creation, not something you could turn on and off to suit working hours.

Kim looked sympathetic. 'I guess that's a no from your dad, then?'

'Apparently I have to get a job ...'

'Well, you'd better get one pretty damned quick.' Jade's expression was truculent. 'I'm not moving all my gear out. If you can't afford to pay the rent then we'll have to find someone who can.'

Her heart thrashing, Ellie covered her face. Money; she had no money. The flat was pretty cheap because of their arrangement with Andrei, but it wasn't nothing. She had to eat and pay bills; she had to travel, buy books and materials for her course. And if she moved out, where would she go? Not Woodlands, for sure; even her mum had seemed angsty with her the last time she visited. Besides, she'd never grace that bloody house again.

'It's fine, Ellie.' Kim squeezed her hand. 'You just need some quick cash for now. Then you can look for bar work or talk your dad around later.' She raised her eyebrows and Ellie knew what was coming. 'It's the perfect answer. You know it is.'

Ellie shook her head. *That* was another thing about her new friends she wasn't so sure about.

Prostitution. It was something they both did to supplement their grants. In truth, it had deeply unsettled Ellie at first, but the rule was that no 'punters' came to the flat, so she'd been able to feign deafness whenever it was discussed. And it wasn't for her to be judgemental: until now, she'd had a ready income from her parents; they hadn't.

Kim wryly smiled. 'Look, I know it sounds horrible, but it's really no big deal if you stick to hand or blow jobs. We've both done it loads of times. And you won't get caught near the cemetery. Some of the punters are pretty disgusting, but it doesn't take long if you make a few encouraging noises. God knows why, but they pay more if you say you'll swallow. Mind over matter, girl! Spit it out when they're not looking. Let's face it, we've all been there and done it for bloody nothing. This way it's a really good earner.'

Her mind racing, Ellie stared. Why the fucking hell not? Her whole being was burning with pure rage. The enormity of her decision didn't touch her; instead, she was almost jubilant at the thought of Maurice's disapproval. It felt like spite, but she didn't care. She loathed that man; she had no idea what she was supposed to be apologising for. She'd support herself out of her earnings and if he asked what her new 'job' was, she'd take the greatest pleasure in telling him.

She nodded. 'Right, I'm going to do it.'

51

Determined to see through her first 'trick' that very night, Ellie hung on to her fury for the rest of the day. She chilled out with Kim, borrowed her skimpy dress, put on loud music and applied the brightest lipstick. Even Jade joined in, snapping open a cheap bottle of wine for them to share. It felt like a party night, even a blind date. In the few moments her resolve faded, she focused on her need for quick cash and floated above how the hell she'd find a 'punter' or negotiate the price of the deal and what was required. Like Kim had said, she had occasionally ended up in the bed of some randomer after a boozy party. Was this so very different?

'How about I start at the students' union?' she asked. 'There must be some desperate freshers . . .'

'You need money, Ellie,' Jade replied, not unkindly. 'A tenner isn't going to cover it. The better earners are in town. Plus, you have the warmth of a car rather than a grimy alleyway.' She topped up Ellie's glass. 'Get the first one out of the way, then you'll be flying . . .'

*

Pushing away the increasing prickles of danger, Ellie left the flat at midnight. She lifted her chin and skimmed over the prodding worry of being alone with a stranger. It was fine; blow jobs were pretty disgusting, but they were quick. She wouldn't think about whose dick it was, the man's age or shape or hygiene. Just get it done, take the money and run.

Her shoes chafing, she finally reached the road outside the cemetery. It was still and silent. What now? She glanced around, spotting her high-rise flat in the distance. Kim and Jade had said they'd wait up; they were good mates.

Wishing she'd worn a coat, she stood at the entrance and rubbed her arms. It was far colder than she'd expected, but relief was slowly spreading through her torso and keeping her warm. No one was here; she could postpone it to another day, maybe phone her mum first and see if she could soften up Maurice. Or go to the bank and extend her overdraft. Worth a try, surely?

A red Toyota pulled up. The passenger window opened. 'Looking for business?' a voice asked.

No. What the hell was she doing? Absolutely no. She shaped her lips to say the word, but the man spoke again. 'Quick. There's a police car coming. You don't want to get done for soliciting. Get in now and if they ask, just make an excuse.'

Barely breathing, Ellie sat in the car. The police, oh God, the police! It wasn't something she'd remotely touched on in her head. Suppose she was *arrested*? Would she get thrown out of uni? And what about her mother's disappointment and shame? Her eyes glued to the wing mirror, she watched the white vehicle park behind and a uniformed officer climb out.

The constable walked to the driver's side. 'Everything all right?' He peered at Ellie. 'A crematorium's an unusual place to park at this time of night.'

Her heart battering her ribs, she swallowed. It felt like a moment of no return. 'Yes, Officer,' she replied. 'We were just having a chat.'

Holding back the overwhelming need to vomit, Ellie stared at the shadowy weeping willow through the smeared windscreen. In awe of its beauty and symbol of nature, fertility and life, she'd painted one in the summer; she'd never look at one again.

Oh God; what had she done? Shutting her eyes tightly, she'd tried to block it out, *him* out, his smell, his grunting; his rough, bruising fingers. But it had still been more than repellent, and it hadn't been 'quick'.

She now heard him snort and zip up his flies. She just needed to hang on a moment longer; she could bolt very soon. But instead of handing over the notes he'd shown her and stuffed in the side pocket, he pulled out a lighter and lit a cigarette. Frozen for moments, she willed the panic to pass. She couldn't turn, let alone breathe, but she had to get the money. That's why she was here, traumatised, winded and disgusted with herself.

Her voice barely there, she held out her hand. 'The cash, please.'

'What was that? You'll need to speak up.'

She tried to glance at this middle-aged man. But she couldn't describe him if she'd tried; all she could see was her father leering back.

'Please can you pay what you owe me.'

'Payment *please*?' he mocked. 'You're joking. To a whore?' He leaned close to her face, his tobacco breath almost suffocating. 'You want payment? Here you go.'

For a second she felt nothing but astonishment, then realisation hit, swiftly followed by his laughter and words.

'Branded like a whore! Cos whether you like it or not, love, that's what you are.'

Disbelieving, she reached a hand to her face. Oh God, oh God.

This repellent man had just ground his cigarette into her skin. She had to get out, get away.

Adrenalin pumping, she scuttled from the car. Leaving her handbag behind, she stumbled in her platforms along the dark, sodden streets to her high-rise, eventually removing her shoes to pelt up the six flights of stairs. Finally at her flat and the usual stench of urine, she bent double to catch her breath. Razor-edged stinging hit. The reality, the sizzling grip had finally reached her consciousness. She'd been *burned*. That bastard had stubbed out a cigarette on her cheek. It felt as though the soft flesh was still searing and melting.

She battered at the door. No reply. She hammered again.

Jade opened it a crack. 'Ellie? You bloody scared us. Why didn't you use your keys?'

Then Kim stepped forward, her expression aghast. 'Oh my God, what the hell? Did the bloke . . . ?' Then recovering herself, 'It was just bad luck. It could've been one of us. Let's take a cab to the hospital. They'll know what to do to stop it . . . '

Dumb with shock, Ellie stared at this person who was supposed to be her friend. To stop what? To stop it stamping her? Branding her a whore?

She quickly turned away; she couldn't let anybody look at her now or ever. She had to get home to Marian and hide.

Her fingers almost refusing to obey, she packed her rucksack with essentials, pulled on a coat and fumbled with the laces of her trainers. Ignoring her flatmates' inquisitive eyes, she scooped a few coins from the 'milk' jar, then left without a word.

She hoped for a late bus but none came, so she tromped through the drizzle to the other side of town. Arriving at the motorway, she eventually found a bridge over it, then climbed down the ridged bank. Not knowing how one hitchhiked, she stood on the hard shoulder and held out a thumb.

How low had she come? She had appalled herself with her willingness to climb into a stranger's vehicle for prostitution, but never for the simple act of a free ride. Cars, vans and trucks hurtled by, blasting her with gravel, speed and fumes.

Cold and wet, her whole body shook, the power in her legs nearly gone. No one was stopping. What now? Staring at an oncoming lorry, she watched herself step out. As easy as that; she could end it if she wanted to. One effortless stride. Death would be guaranteed. But as though reading her mind, the driver slowed, pulled on to the hard shoulder and stopped.

Holding her breath, she climbed into the cab. 'Thanks so much.'

The man's accent was Geordie. 'Where are you going?' he asked.

'Chorley. So anywhere on the way, please.'

He frowned, his expression concerned. 'It's a bit out of my way, but it looks like you need to get home.'

'Thank you; thank you very much.' Remembering her Ps and Qs; Maurice would be proud.

Still icy despite the warmth, Ellie counted the pylons. From the family snap on the dashboard and his kindness, she guessed the trucker was someone's dad. But then so was *he*, probably, the man who'd scarred her.

'You take care, love.'

At the sound of his soft Geordie tones, Ellie opened her eyes. It took a moment to get her bearings, another for the deep, deep shame to strike. But the driver had kept his promise; he'd pulled up on the main road close to Woodlands.

'Thank you again. You've been really kind.'

Her limbs finding strength, she jogged down the street. Tiptoeing carefully on the gravel, she squeezed by her father's Jag, past the bird table and down to the greenhouse. Finally inside, she crouched down, spitting and spitting until no saliva was left.

She was safe; she was home, thank God. But home was him, too;

the man who'd cut off her money for some unknown slight. The nugget of hatred hard in her chest, she stared at the black night. Maurice Wilson, her dad; a *father* who was supposed to love his child. Looking down, she thrashed around the soily floor, finally spotting a glint of metal. Though fit to drop, she snatched it up and retraced her steps.

She longed to pierce the stillness, to yell and howl, but she didn't. Instead, she inhaled deeply and with all the strength she had left, she rammed the sharp nail along the glossy paintwork of the car.

Dragging her feet, she stumbled back to her hiding place and watched like a sentinel until her dad emerged from the front door at eight. Apparently oblivious to the scratch, he unlocked the Jaguar, threw in his briefcase and performed the usual three-point turn, before heading to his office.

Eleanor Wilson emerged then. Overwrought and frantic and finally crying, she called for help and her mum.

52

The antique village was busy for a Wednesday. Taking in the usual mix of 'old' aromas, Ellie pushed through the bustle to Marian's stall, but her mum was talking to a customer, so she removed her damp jacket and sauntered away. Her chest was tight with anxiety, but the intensity ebbed as she took in the contents of the other cluttered units.

Nostalgia swam before her eyes: each kiosk seemed to be a reflection of her childhood in some way. Annuals, comics and books; records, toys and ornaments, all so familiar. It was as though Marian had scooped them up from Woodlands and scattered them here.

She snorted at the thought; perhaps she had – they certainly weren't in her whitewashed bedroom these days.

Moving on to the larger booths, she almost salivated at the splendid variety of furniture, each design, embellishment and type of wood. A memory flashed in of her grandma's handsome mahogany. Her mum had stored it upstairs when the old lady died. Was it still there?

She strolled back to Marian's unit, her fingers brushing the past. The intimate smells and wistfulness felt warm but sad. Perhaps some of her belongings were hidden away in the 'junk' bedrooms at home. It would be fun to explore them with the boys now they were older.

Home. How easily the word slipped into her thoughts. She blew out the trapped, tremulous air. She wasn't welcome at Woodlands any more. That's why she felt sick; that's why she was here.

Her mum was still chatting, so she stood to one side, examining the items for sale on her stall. The display had been rearranged since Ellie last came, but the back wall was covered in paintings as usual. A series of eight or ten canvases dominated it today. She leaned in closer to inspect the small watercolours. Signed in tiny writing by Marian, they looked familiar but she couldn't place them.

'Norfolk. The River Bure,' her mum said from behind her. 'Yours are at home somewhere. Though one wouldn't know it was the same river. Yours were much better than mine, of course; your art came from within. I just painted what I saw.' She peered at her. 'Don't you remember Norfolk?'

Ellie shook her head. No; there was a vague recollection. A soapy smell of lavender. 'Did we stay in a cottage?'

'Yes! A beautiful thatched one at the top of a hill. So you do remember. We'll have to dig out those paintings. Oils, of course; you always loved your oils. You're looking a bit washed out, love,' she said, kissing her cheek. 'Are we ready for that coffee?'

Ellie gazed for a beat. As though there was absolutely nothing wrong. That was how this neat, smiling woman was acting. Pleasant, impenetrable denial. Something told Ellie it would be her mantra all day. She shook herself back to the question. 'Yes. Yes, I am, thanks. You lead the way.'

Slotting her arm into Ellie's, Marian guided her through rows of bric-a-brac benches, then down a wooden ramp to a café area. Maurice-like, she gestured to a small table. 'Will this one do, love? If you sit here, you can have the view of the mill.'

Ellie did as she was told. Marian sat, too, reaching out to the wax replica on the walkway. It was a gnarled creation somewhere between a pirate and a yeti. 'He's supposed to haunt the mill after dark,' she commented with raised eyebrows. She nodded to the units that specialised in war memorabilia. 'I wonder how he gets on with the Nazis,' she added with a smile. Then, picking up the furled menu, 'It's quite basic here, love, but the cakes are nice. Tea or coffee? Sandwich or a bun? My treat.'

Ellie swallowed. Yes, pleasant, impenetrable denial. 'I'll have tea and whatever takes your fancy, please.'

She watched her mum make her way to the food counter, talk to the staff, then stop and chat to an elderly couple at another table on the way back. She felt anonymous, but of course they all knew Marian. Agitation building again, she tapped her fingers on the rattan placemat. Perhaps that's why her mother had chosen here for their 'chat'.

Blowing out, she breathed through the trepidation. Marian had replied to her bath text almost immediately.

Of course I didn't tell Dad. Why would I, love? A promise is a promise.

Then why is he so hostile to me? What's going on with him?

It's nothing to worry about, love. Coffee on Wednesday after work? We can chat then.

Unlike Cam's brutal one-word replies, her mum had a knack

of making her texts sound like her voice. Ellie had felt reassured at the time. If mention of *that* had resulted in her mum agreeing to talk about Maurice, it could only be a good thing. But now she felt nervous, unsettled and queasy.

Apparently serene and untroubled, Marian sat down and presented a wooden spoon. 'Oh, look at the digits.' She laughed. 'Some places don't have a *thirteen* anything, but you were born on the thirteenth, so I'd say it's a lucky number. They'll call when the food is ready. I've ordered you a vanilla slice. You always loved them when you were little. Do you remember?'

'Of course I remember. I just don't particularly remember Norfolk.'

It came out too snappy, but Marian just smiled. 'The weather there was shocking,' she said. 'Perhaps that's why.'

Both staring at the cake domes, they sat quietly for some time. Finally, a young girl with cerise hair appeared with a tray. 'Here you go, Marian,' she said. 'Your usual and a homemade vanilla.'

Ellie stared at the custard slice and felt her stomach turn. The sense of foreboding was churning, which surely was silly when her mum was so calm.

'Thanks, Mum, let's share,' she said. Then, knowing she couldn't swallow if she'd tried, she put down the fork. 'You promised we could talk about Dad today. Are you willing to go to the doctor now you've thought it through?'

Marian lowered her voice. 'I have thought about it and I can't, love. I'm sorry to disappoint you, but there are things you don't understand. I have to protect Dad from himself just now. You know how important his reputation is to him. He would hate any gossip.'

Annoyance overcoming the nerves, Ellie leaned forward. 'Stop talking in riddles, Mum. If you think that I'll back off just because we're in your local café, then you're wrong.' Inhaling quickly, she continued, the words tumbling out. 'I feel hurt and rejected, Mum. It's horrible. Please just explain. I have a right to know what's going on. I know you and Dad are as close as any couple could be, but you are my parents, you're supposed to love me. I'm your only child, for goodness' sake.'

Carefully replacing the cup on its saucer, Marian reached for her handbag. For an iota Ellie though she was leaving, but she unzipped the bag and extracted a lacy handkerchief, which she clenched in her fist.

'Oh, Eleanor.' Her expression suddenly defeated, her mum's shoulders slumped. 'That's just the problem, love.' She sighed. 'I hoped I'd never have to say it ...'

'Say what, Mum?'

She gazed for some time before dipping her eyes.

'You're not my child,' she said, her voice husky.

Half laughing, half frustrated, Ellie sat back and folded her arms. 'Come on, Mum, we've been through this before at the hospital. Apparently I'm the spitting image of Dad, and the ginger gene's your fault, or at least Grandma's.' The humour lapsed. 'Please, Mum, I'm just asking you to be straight with me.'

Marian wiped a few crumbs from the table. She eventually looked up. 'This is the truth, Ellie. I'm not your biological mother; I didn't give birth to you. It's as simple as that,' she replied. 'You've always been my beloved daughter, of course, but you're actually—'

Ellie almost guffawed again, but as she stared at Marian's wretched expression, the truth slotted in like a bolt. 'Aunty Diana,' she stated. '*Diana* is my mother? And that's why Dad thought I was her?'

She squeezed her eyes shut. Musky perfume, elongated vowels, red hair and laughter. But she couldn't really picture her, the memories were nebulous. She certainly couldn't remember a time when she hadn't lived in her pink bedroom at Woodlands.

'*She isn't normal,*' flying in, the ground shifted beneath Ellie's feet. She reverted to her mum's worried frown. 'So where did I live before I came to you? And who was my father?'

'Dad is, of course. Who else could it be?'

Still feeling the sharp slap, Ellie touched her cheek; a burn on a burn. But she couldn't blame Maurice for the first. Not really. She had for many years, but it had been her decision, her mistake.

Quelling an urgent need to vomit, she swallowed. 'So I am Maurice's daughter, after all. So that must mean . . .' She peered at her mother's anguished face. Realisation struck. 'Oh God, that must mean Maurice and Diana were—'

'No, they were not,' Marian barked. The man on the next table turned his head. She lowered her voice, but the whisper was still furious. 'Don't you ever, ever say that, Eleanor. They were most certainly not. They did it for me.'

53

Once they'd sipped their tea in silence, Marian and Ellie left the café, the two halves of the vanilla slice untouched.

They sat in Ellie's car and watched the rain cascade all around them.

'Goodness, what a downpour. We were lucky not to get caught,' Marian commented. 'So unpredictable this summer. It's been . . .' Then, apparently deciding to change tack, she reached for Ellie's hand. 'Dad wanted babies as soon as we married, as many as we could manage.' Her lips twitched. 'With us both being from small families, we wanted a large one.'

Still staring through the windscreen, the smile fell away. 'Getting pregnant wasn't a problem, keeping it was. Our baby died. Not just the once but several miscarriages. Late on in the pregnancy, too. Six and a half months, seven, nearly full term. I think it was probably the placenta. They know so much more these days; they'd carefully monitor and deliver early now, I suppose.' Her eyes misty, she glanced at Ellie. 'I had to give birth, so I saw each perfect child and held them for as long as I was allowed.' She rotated her wedding ring. 'It was devastating.'

Ellie put a hand to her own belly. She had been lucky; she'd had her three healthy boys without any complications. Yet her mum's grief was so tangible she could feel it – the appalling, debilitating and cruel loss of a child. Her nose stung, but she took a huge breath to hold back the tears. She had to focus; as awful as it was, that deprivation wasn't the crux right now; the story was much bigger than that: this woman who was describing her suffering with such poise and dignity wasn't her biological mother. Marian Wilson wasn't her real mum; an aunt who she barely remembered was.

Shocking, unbelievable, surreal.

Marian sniffed and pressed Ellie's fingers, that same reassuring 'happy ending' squeeze she'd given her as a child. 'Then Diana appeared, out of the blue after a long absence. She was shocked to see my appearance. I was sad, to say the least, I'd lost weight, I'd lost colour, I'd lost everything. I had to go on for your dad, but life wasn't worth living; that's how it felt. "Oh darling, if I could have a baby for you, I would in a heartbeat," Diana immediately said when I explained what had happened. It was just a flippant comment, really; she wasn't maternal, she had neither the time nor the patience for children. But she'd planted the seed in my mind . . .'

Ellie finally found her voice. 'The possibility of you having a child?'

Marian nodded. 'Yes. Day and night I thought of nothing else.' She smiled. 'It gave me light; it made me human again.'

Trying to work out the logistics in her mind, Ellie took a breath. 'But Dad . . . You said he didn't even like Diana.' She thought back to their hospital conversation. '*Vain and shallow,*' she'd said.

Marian turned to the rain. 'Dad's reaction was even worse than I'd expected. He'd already dismissed adoption as a possibility, he absolutely refused to bring up another man's child as his own, so the thought of taking on a combination of Diana and a complete stranger . . . Well, you can imagine. So, I said to him, "But, love, there is a way this child *can* be yours. Be a true Wilson, inherit your looks, your admirable qualities . . ."'

They fell quiet again, Ellie's mind sticky as she contemplated the shocking reality behind her mum's words. What had she said at the café? '*They did it for me* . . .' *It* being the operative word.

'Are you angry with me?' Marian asked eventually, still clenching the handkerchief.

Breathing out long and hard, Ellie gazed at her mum's contrite face. Anger? No, she didn't sense that right now. Strange and unsure and stunned, for sure; but there was also an inkling of relief that there was a reason for Maurice's coldness, that it wasn't simply because she was unlovable. Or a whore.

'I don't really know how I feel,' she replied after a moment. 'I'm too gobsmacked, I guess.' She tried to put her thoughts in order. How had the rules of surrogacy worked forty years ago? It must have been rare, but presumably the surrogate mother was the legal parent, same as now, a right that had to be transferred. 'I don't understand why you never told me I'd been adopted. Maybe not when I was little, but when I was older. That's what people do, don't they? When their child is eighteen, if not before.'

Marian sighed and smiled a tight smile. 'Would it have made things any better if we'd told you? For any of us? Sometimes lies . . .' Straightening her back, she corrected herself. 'Sometimes omissions are for the best.'

She opened her fist and studied the crumpled cotton before speaking. 'We registered you as my child, Ellie. I'd had so many pregnancies that everyone accepted the new baby was mine, born at home. Perhaps we should have taken steps to make it more official when you finally arrived, but we'd already decided not to.' She flushed. 'In all honesty, it was embarrassing for all of us. I know young people have different views these days; they're happy to share their news on social media, whether good or bad. But Dad and I are old-fashioned; we're not the type to wash our dirty laundry in public, are we?' She smiled thinly. 'My failure wasn't something I wanted to talk about, let alone advertise. And as for Dad . . . Well, Diana's role was "needs must", something he wanted to forget, not note for eternity on a document.' She rubbed Ellie's shoulder. 'You see that, don't you? Diana's name would have been recorded on your birth certificate if we'd . . . And she didn't give two hoots; she was soon off on her travels again, telling me with a grin that I was to take very good care of you as she was not going to do pregnancy and childbirth ever again. So all was good until—'

'Dad's stroke.' Ellie nodded; the jigsaw was slowly building.

'Yes. I'm sure these unofficial arrangements happened all the time in the past, but your adoption wasn't by the book. Although it was what Dad wanted, it's always worried him.' She softly chuckled. 'Him and his need for paperwork, to dot the I's and cross the T's.' The anxious frown returned. 'But now that he's so confused, who knows what he'll say if he's pushed? As I said, I need to protect him from himself until he's better.' She peered intently at Ellie. 'So, now you'll understand why I can't risk going back to the hospital or see a doctor.'

Ellie gaped. There was so much to take in. Marian's anguish, her decorum, her lies. A reason for Maurice's hostility. And then Diana, her real mother, her incredible sacrifice.

'Poor Diana,' she said quietly. 'Being pregnant all those months, then giving away the child. All that pain. For nothing.'

Marian took Ellie's hand and grasped it tightly again. 'But it wasn't for nothing. That's important for you to understand. Giving away a baby is never for nothing. It's a gift to someone else. You gave me such joy, love. You and the boys still do. And it was what my dear sister had wanted: to give me something I couldn't have. It was a surrogacy, not for any payment, but for love.'

They remained in Ellie's car, Marian sporadically imparting information as they watched the rain spatter the window. Diana had gone back to her acting work after 'the conception' and she'd stayed away until the birth was very near.

'Weren't you afraid she wouldn't come back when the baby was born?' Ellie asked.

She had to remind herself that 'the baby' was her.

'The honest answer? Yes, I was terrified. Those months were hard – harder that you could imagine. Wanting something so badly, almost at your fingertips. But I had to bide my time; I had no choice, so I focused on my own growing bump.' She smiled weakly. 'Getting into character, I suppose.'

'So, your own parents . . .'

'No, not even them.' She sighed. 'I don't think they would have understood something so . . .' She seemed to search for a word. '"Modern". And they didn't travel over to Woodlands very often, so it was fine.'

Ellie gazed. Woodlands; the secrets of that house. An uncomfortable thought hit. 'Did she . . . did Diana give birth in my—'

'No, love, not your bedroom. In the junk room before it was packed with, well, junk.'

An image of red hair on a white sheet scuttled in. Oh God, the poor woman. Did Diana have pain relief? Did she have to stifle her groans?

As though reading her mind, Marian spoke again. 'I was a midwife of sorts. One of my own had been born at home, so I knew what to do; I had time to plan and research things like suitable sedatives, so I made sure Diana was as comfortable as I possibly could. The last thing I wanted was my sister in pain.' She patted Ellie's arm. 'So there it is, love. You know everything now.'

She put on her headscarf then, saying the familiar words: 'Goodness, look at the time. I'd better get home. Dad will wonder where I've got to.'

Still mesmerised with shock, Ellie watched Marian hurry to her car. Then the obvious question stuck. Jumping from her own, she rushed across the wet concrete and crouched down next to Marian's door. 'What happened to Diana? Where is she now?' she asked.

Marian didn't know: Diana had visited from time to time, but there'd been no regular pattern and generally no warning; she'd just turned up when it suited her.

'Other than the postcards, we never even knew where she was. A sentence or two from all over the world. We looked forward to receiving them. You loved the ones from Spain. They had flamenco ladies with their dresses stitched on the cardboard. Do you remember them?'

Ellie nodded. Yes, those spectacular outfits, a rose behind an ear and a fabric fan. But it wasn't just the layered red frock the young Ellie had admired, it was the dancer herself, her head and shoulders back, her chin lifted with attitude. A sense of connection between her teenage self and Diana swamped her chest, but that woman wasn't her mother. *This* person was her mum, the one who'd brought her up, the person who'd always been there, solid, strong and loving.

'Yes, I do,' she replied. 'So when was the last time you saw her?'

'A long time ago, love. The postcards stopped coming when, I don't know ... When you were eight or nine? Yes, you'd just started at the junior school and there was a change of uniform from infants and you donned it to show her. You gave her a twirl and a curtsey. It brought tears to her eyes because you looked so grown up.' Marian brushed her slacks. 'Would you want to find her?'

Suddenly aware of her teeming hair and wet coat, Ellie stood. The spread of emotion almost hurt, but her answer was definitive. 'No, Mum. No, I wouldn't want to find Diana.'

54

She expected to dream, she wanted to dream, to catch Diana's face as she breezed through her childhood, but Ellie slept solidly, only waking late when Cam shook her.

'We're off. The boys are stir-crazy and they need to get out. It's been raining but the forecast is fine. I thought Crocky Trail. It'll be muddy, but what the hell?'

She flung back the duvet and jumped up. 'Can I come? I'll be ready before you know it. Please?' she asked, knowing she sounded plaintive.

He shrugged. 'Absolutely; why not?' he replied. 'Though you might not approve of the picnic food.'

'You made it, so you won't get any complaints from me,' she said, breathing away the dizziness from standing so quickly. 'Tell the boys I'll be two minutes, I promise.'

Ignoring Cam's raised eyebrows, she dived into the bathroom. Avoiding her reflection, she squeezed stripes on the toothbrush with fumbling fingers and turned on the tap. But she couldn't resist a quick peep at the new person she was. She leaned closer to the mirror. Her father's nose and eyes, certainly, but the lips, the complexion and the hair?

Yes, shocking, unbelievable, surreal.

Cam hadn't asked much about her coffee with Marian and for once she was relieved. '*I can't do needy*,' he'd said years ago. Sometimes it had been extremely difficult, especially with Jake, but she had tried her hardest not to be. Then there'd been his strange outburst about her conduct when he'd come home from 'Vietnam'. He'd been ill, of course, but the memory was still tender. Anyway, she was glad of the distance, his lack of inquisitiveness today. She needed time to mull things over, but felt strangely afraid to be alone.

A day out with four action-ready boys was just perfect.

Jake sulked for the first few miles towards Chester. He'd been promised the front seat.

'It's OK, Jake, I'll sit in the back,' Ellie had said when he har-rumphed and folded his arms, but Cam had intervened.

'We can't have a rose between two thorns. Mum's place is in the front with me. Come on Jake, chop-chop, out you get.'

Harry's voice now broke the silence. '"Chop-chop" is a Cantonese word. It's something to do with sailors and means hurry up.'

Cam laughed. 'And you know this how . . . ?' he asked through the mirror.

Harry shrugged his reply.

Ellie glanced at Cam with wide eyes. 'Harry "the sponge" Hastings strikes again.'

She inwardly grimaced. The mention of anything related to Cam's work away would have brought her out in hives not so long ago; little did she know what was coming. But today was a good day; her family were together, just as it should be. She turned to the boys and smiled. 'How about a song? Harry?'

'God, no, anything but that,' Toby replied, even though he was wearing his huge muffler headphones. But Harry immediately sang, joined in eventually by Jake and then Cam.

Her mind flittered as they drove. The story Marian had told yesterday still felt imaginary, like a surreal fairy tale. Since then she'd tried to think it through from beginning to end, but her mind was too fuggy. Like a drunkard, her concentration had gone. Yet as the green Cheshire countryside flew by, she came back to the sheer hell Marian had gone through by losing all those babies. *Hers* were now up to thirty-three men mowing a meadow with a dog called Spot.

She was lucky, incredibly lucky.

The sky stayed grey at Crocky Trail, but at least it didn't rain. The boys clambered out of the car and viewed the wet equipment for a beat before hurtling towards it. The metal tubes, giant slides and obsolete farm machinery was basic, not made to look pretty. They'd been here before, and from Ellie's first glance, there seemed to be one or two new activities.

Glad to inhale the damp air, she ran after them, Cam trailing behind. He caught her up at the barrel run.

He cleared his throat. 'Actually, Ellie,' he said quietly, 'I'm glad you've come. I didn't think about ...' He glanced around the apparatus area and shook his head. 'I'm fine to walk, but climbing, tunnelling and ...' He nodded at the padded blue cylinders. 'Running the gauntlet. To be honest, I don't think I can manage—'

'Good job you've done the picnic. And that I'm wearing scruffs,' she replied. A comment about gender roles was on the tip of her tongue, but she thought better of it. She kissed his cheek. 'Think you can manage the playground swing, love?'

'Not funny ...'

Burrowing and dangling, spinning, slipping and mounting, Ellie joined the boys at every stage. Cam watched, shouting instructions like a sergeant major for them to go higher, deeper, faster, until he had to retreat to the car for a rest.

There shouldn't have been time to think, but Ellie did.

'There were no turkey basters then ...' was all Marian had mentioned about the mechanics of her conception.

The notion persisted in her head. What greater love was there? What greater love than to allow your husband, who you absolutely adored, to have sex with your beautiful sister? And what of the sister who'd agreed to do it?

She hadn't dared to ask, but where had the coupling taken place. In a cheap hotel? Or in her parents' bed, Marian covering her ears to block out any sounds of passion, enjoyment? And how often? Did sperm fortuitously meet egg on the first occasion, or did it take time, Maurice and Diana coming to know each other's smells and bodies and intimate preferences?

And then the other thought: Maurice. What greater love than to fuck someone you'd made no secret of disliking? But did *like* always matter? Was 'whore' a clue that her strait-laced father had secretly enjoyed it?

Exhausted and dirty, Ellie and the boys joined Cam at the picnic area for lunch. Foil-wrapped items were spread across a weather-worn table under a corrugated cover. Drinking coffee from a flask, Cam looked much brighter.

'Feeling a bit better?' she asked.

'Yup. Harry, are you hungry?'

Cam gestured to the lucky-dip assortment of food. 'I can't remember what they are now, so it'll be like Christmas. Eat up. And no moaning.'

'Jake won't like not knowing what's inside each—' Toby began.

'Jake can speak for himself, Toby.' Cam eyeballed his middle son. 'He'll man up for his dad. Won't you, Jakey?'

Jake bowed his head. 'Suppose I don't like it?'

Ellie tapped his shoulder with her own. 'Then you can swap with me, love. The surprise will be fun and I know Dad would only include fillings you all like.'

Clearly ravenous, Toby and Harry tucked into their sandwiches. She took a bite of hers. In truth, she wasn't keen on the chocolate-spread filling, nor the limp white bread, but she knew Jake was trying his hardest not to be daunted by the unknown. She chewed slowly, but it was a struggle to swallow. The shifting nausea was there. Every time her mind prodded a reminder of her shocking origins, she felt queasy, the soil moving beneath her.

The soft wind caught her hair. Why did she feel so claustrophobic in such an open space? Breathing deeply, she gazed at the slate-moody sky and willed the dreamlike sensation to pass. When she turned to Cam, he was looking at her quizzically.

'You haven't told me about your coffee with Marian yet,' he said. 'So, spit it out. What's going on with your parents?'

To give herself time, she bit her butty again. She was surprised Cam had remembered to ask, but she was anxious and uncomfortable too. How to reply when she hadn't taken it in fully herself? It still felt ridiculous, bizarre, just a story. Marian wasn't her mum. She was the product of some secret and illegal surrogacy arrangement. Her real mother was Diana, an aunty she could only remember in fragments.

Even if the boys hadn't been there, was she ready to share? How would she cope if Cam found it funny? She could clearly imagine his laughing response, belittling her news or comparing it to the *Jeremy Kyle Show*. 'Yes, flaming parents . . . ' she started, stalling again.

'Tell me about it,' he immediately replied. 'Dad sent me a text earlier. Apparently Mum's got another bloody kitten.'

Jake brightened. 'Wow, Dad, that's wicked. I love them. Can we have one?'

'It isn't actually, Jake,' Ellie quickly interrupted. 'Dad's allergic to them. Well, to the cat hairs. They make him chesty and he ends up feeling really ill.'

'Doesn't Jaqs know that?' Jake asked.

She and Cam glanced at each other.

'Don't call Grandma *Jaqs*,' she said lightly.

Standing abruptly, Jake threw his lunch on the sodden grass. His eyes burned. 'She tells us to call her Jaqs because she hates being a granny. That's what she said. I'm doing what the grown-up says, like you tell me to.'

'What about a dog?' Toby asked. 'We could get a puppy, Jake. They breed some with short fur. Non-allergenic, or whatever you call them, so they don't shed hairs like kittens—'

'Stop!' His voice raised, Cam banged the table with his fist. 'Stop stirring it, Toby. We're not getting a bloody pet. And yes, Jaqs knows full well that I'm allergic to cats. She's had them before and she doesn't bloody care. So, just let it rest, OK?'

Shocked by their father's anger, the boys fell silent, but Ellie was watching Jake's face. He was striving to hold it in, but he'd need to put the record straight. It finally burst out: 'But Harry's rabbits are pets.'

They all turned to Harry, but his end space at the bench was empty.

'Where the fuck is Harry?' Cam asked. He glared at Toby and Jake. 'How long has he been gone?' They both shook their heads, so he stalked up, cupping his mouth with his hand. 'Harry, where are you? Where the hell are you?' he shouted.

Though she'd seen him only a minute or two before, Ellie's

piercing fear was instant, a sudden and overwhelming premonition. She sprang from her seat, bolted to the playground and called his name. Scanning the spider trap and spinning disc, she searched for his blond hair. Trying to breathe back the inexplicable terror, she moved on to the sandpits.

'Harry? Harry!'

A hand on her arm stopped her in her tracks. She spun round. Oh God, thank God; it was Harry.

'Sorry, Mum,' he said, his face ashen. He nodded to a tunnel near the food shack. 'I'm really sorry. I was waiting to be found.'

Her heart slowing, she held out her palm and gripped his. The impulse was to shout, but she could feel her son's trepidation through her fingers. 'It's OK. But next time please tell me first, yes? Never go off by yourself, love. Ever. Even places like this aren't always safe.'

They rounded the corner to the picnic area. Cam immediately loomed, his face puce. 'Where were you, Harry?' he demanded. 'Where the hell were you?'

Harry waved to the tube, just a few yards away. 'Only there. I was hiding. It was for a minute, that's all. I thought it'd be fun. I was waiting until ...' Bowing his head, his wobbly voice trailed away. 'Sorry,' he mumbled, his tears splashing to the ground.

Almost snorting like a bull, Cam didn't move. Ellie stared. His expression was still livid, his fists clenched. What the ...? The alarm flaring as goosebumps, she stepped between him and her son. 'Harry knows, Cam. He won't do it again.'

Cam glared for a further moment. 'To the car now and stay there,' he bellowed, stalking away. 'All three of you.'

Their expressions fearful and shocked, the boys did as they were told, hunching in a group by the car. Her heart thrashing, Ellie packed away the food scraps.

With an eye on the boys, she waited at the table, her emotions

277

jangling with alarm and anger. Where the hell was Cameron? Though she understood his fear, running off himself was hardly an example. But a minute or two later he appeared and flopped down on the bench.

The colour had died down in his cheeks. 'At another time it would have been OK,' he said eventually. His voice was shaky. 'But not now, Ellie. I'm not up to it. If he'd gone far or if someone had snatched him, I wouldn't be in a fit state to . . .'

She was trembling herself but put her hand on his shoulder. 'It's fine. I'm with you. You're still getting better. But maybe explain that to the boys so that they understand why you were so—'

He shrugged off her arm. 'For God's sake, just forget it,' he snapped.

55

The first weekend in August and the Walsh anniversary dinner came around. Though Ciara had offered to host (indeed, had 'veritably insisted', according to Cam), Paul had taken the reins.

'One can't expect the poor woman to cook for her own celebration,' he'd said to Ellie on the telephone. 'She's done more than the usual honours by pelting out Sean's charming progeny. There are so many, I think I've lost count, but one shouldn't be surprised when one thinks back to the Irish Beast and his proclivities . . .'

Ellie had cringed, not only at the word 'pelting' – which could only be used by a man who hadn't had children – but at the memory of her car ride with Sean. So much had gone on since, she'd forgotten about her ridiculous suggestion that his sister was his daughter. Where that idea had come from, she had no idea, but she hoped he'd forgotten it. That and all the other times she'd let go of her dignity and exposed her stupid emotions to him.

'So I have booked a table for six at Cibo in Wilmslow,' Paul had continued. 'How do they describe it? "The finest Italian cuisine in a relaxing homely atmosphere." Just the ticket, don't you think,

Ellie? And I shall be footing the bill, so you may fill your boots until they flow . . . '

It did sound perfect; she'd have an excuse to dress up a little and there wouldn't be scope for Ciara's usual 'why don't us girls chat in the kitchen while the men talk?' session. The downside was the need for a babysitter. Adele from down the road was good with the boys; she had exactly the right combination of discipline and fun, but she occasionally phoned if Jake was playing up. 'Just for reassurance,' she'd say, but of course Ellie would rush home, Cam following much later with a 'told you so' look on his face.

Half listening to the chaos beyond the door, Ellie spent some time going through her wardrobe, pulling out frocks that hadn't seen the light of day since Cam started on his travels. The thought unsettled her. There were so many conversations to be had, from the recommendation of radiotherapy to when he'd return to work. Then there had been 'last week', as she'd come to term it in her head. On the one hand she had to keep reminding herself that her mum wasn't her *mother*, yet on the other, it was as though someone was shadowing her with a defibrillator; every time she happened to pass a woman with red hair – in the supermarket, through the car window, at the park – an electric jolt seemed to pass through her chest.

Weird, too weird; it still felt as though she was watching the drama from a distance; that it was happening to someone else.

She couldn't put her finger on why, but she hadn't ended up telling Cam. Another discussion it was easier to shelve? Or Marian's calm manner and the absence of drama? More likely it was Ellie's desire for life to continue smoothly without bumps. Besides, she hadn't known her true parentage for the first thirty-nine years of her life and had survived, so there seemed little point. And there was a niggle somewhere, questions that remained unanswered, nebulous memories that flittered in and out, something that hadn't been fully explained. She needed to sort it out in her head, to work it all through, and she doubted Cam would have the patience to listen.

Like déjà vu, Paul greeted them at the restaurant. Though his complexion was already florid, he looked dapper in a pink shirt and cravat. Giving Ellie the usual hug and kisses on both cheeks, he peered at her. 'Dearest Ellie, how lovely to see you.' He put a questioning finger to his lips. 'Something is different,' he said pleasantly. 'New coiffure?'

Ellie touched her hair self-consciously. To please Cam, she hadn't gone *over the border* to have it cut for some time. 'You're the girl in our family. Keep it long,' he always said. Besides, she hadn't had time for appointments. Life had slipped by with Cam's absences and Maurice's illness. And the astonishing rest.

'This way, dear amigos,' Paul continued. 'The guests of honour have already arrived.' He smoothed back his hair and grinned. 'Our private room awaits us, so jollification is compulsory.'

His hand light against the small of her back, he guided Ellie past a vibrant, bustling bar area to a spiral staircase. He turned to Cam behind. 'At the top it's left, then it's the annexe on the right. You'll find a rather sublime glass of Barolo in your place.'

Inhaling the garlic, basil and tomato aromas, Ellie smiled. God, she loved Paul and his ability to empty her head of all the clashing angst inside it. She felt good, too; she'd gone for a royal-blue fitted dress and red shoes. When she'd emerged from the bedroom, she'd taken the boys' initial silence as a good thing. 'Holy moly,' Harry had eventually commented. Jake had nodded and Toby had grinned, 'Wow, Mum, you look nice.'

'Here we are, Ellie,' Paul now said. But she already knew; at the top of the stairs, she'd caught Sean's appraising eyes through the sliding doorway.

Stepping in, she absorbed the marble tabletop, leather seats and elegant place settings. 'How lovely,' she said, focusing on Ciara. 'Happy anniversary to you both.'

Feeling Sean's gaze on her back, she made for the chair next to Ruth, but his voice cut in. 'I believe you're sitting here between me and Paul, Ellie.'

'Absolutely.' Paul cleared his throat theatrically. 'Rules of the evening: apart from eat, drink and be merry, adjacent couples are prohibited. But as you can see, the lovebirds are at each end of the table, so they can gaze lasciviously at each other all night.'

Ruth guffawed. 'Or not. It *has* been sixteen years, darling.' She stood to greet Cam and Ellie. 'Cameron, you look deathly pale. Where on earth have you been?' Then to Ellie: 'We arrived early and I've been sampling the gins. The blood orange is highly recommended.' She rubbed her hands. 'I know Cam will be on the vino with Paul, but get the social kissing done, then we can get stuck in.'

The food was delicious, the conversation flowed. Drinking gin and embracing the role of Paul's 'straight man', Ellie laughed and relaxed. He'd flourished a pair of wire-rimmed glasses to 'give one an air of respectability now one has taken silk'. It made her smile; no one appeared more *respectable* than Paul Paterson-Brown QC. He'd looked fifty when he was twenty, and no doubt he'd look the same when he was eighty.

He was now holding court, both literally and metaphorically, by mimicking the defendant, the junior barristers and the judge from his fraud trial that week. The defendant clearly had a stammer.

'Careful with that stutter,' Cam said. 'You could end up like Parnell.'

'Ah, a man greatly revered by the Irish People.' Paul looked at Sean and stroked his chin. 'I believe he had a heroic beard, too.'

With a polite cough, Ciara stood. 'Where will I be finding the Ladies?' she asked Ruth. 'Do I need to take the stairs?'

'Nope. To the left, you can't miss it.'

As though waiting for Ruth to accompany her, Ciara hovered for a moment before leaving.

Feeling a stab of guilt, Ellie glanced at Cam. Ciara had barely spoken all evening; Ellie had almost forgotten she was there. As though having the same thought, Paul smacked his forehead. 'I'm doing all the talking, aren't I? Sorry, chaps.' He turned to Sean. 'And the Irish Beast is so quiet these days. How I used to drink in your pearls of wisdom.'

Ruth chuckled and topped up the water tumblers. 'I think you're mixing your metaphors, darling.'

'But delicately put, Paul.' Sean smiled. 'Haranguing you all with my outrageous opinions was a more accurate description. I think I should be the one apologising.'

'Not at all. It all made sense when one was—'

'Completely out of it?'

'Possibly true, but as you know, my lovely wife here can drink me under the table. Plenty of practice at uni and beyond. I think the medics surpassed even us.'

Ruth lifted her glass. 'Medicinal purposes only. Interspersed with water, of course.'

Everyone seemed to fall quiet. Ellie glanced at Sean. Was his abstinence common knowledge? Or had she been the only one out of the loop? Feeling herself flush, she quickly looked away. Their 'social' embrace earlier was still with her. She'd never greeted him with kisses before. One cheek or two? had gone through her mind. His beard, too; would it feel bristly? It hadn't; it had been soft, like his lips.

Then his murmur in her ear: 'You look stunning tonight, Ellie. Truly stunning,' he'd said.

She turned to Paul. 'So why did you end up in our house for your third year? I never knew your excuse,' she asked to fill the silence.

His laugh emerged as a snort, showering his plate with wine. 'I couldn't stand the bloody toffs any more. Ten years at boarding school, two years at uni—'

Cam had been unusually reticent, but he seemed to rally with a grin. 'Er, Paul, my dear man, I'm sorry to break it to you, but you *are* a toff.'

'God no, Cameron. There are toffs and toffs. Secret clubs and societies. Special clothes and ridiculous rituals. Believe me, the Cabinet ministers will all be at it, even now as grown men.' There was the usual pause. 'I can't look at a hamster and not think about it.' Another beat. 'Or, indeed, a pig.'

Ruth pointed a plump finger at Sean. 'How about you, Mr Walsh?' she asked, her voice a little slurred. 'Why were you sharing with this lot? What was your crime?'

'Dangerous ground, Ruthie,' Paul whispered theatrically. He cocked an eyebrow. 'Good job his lovely wife hasn't yet returned.'

Ellie dared her eyes to Sean. Why was he there? Why had she never asked?

'I was young, hot-headed and very stupid.' He smiled, but his cheeks coloured and he raked his hair. 'As you can tell, Ruth, I'm getting in the excuses first—'

Cam laughed. 'Brawling,' he said. 'Is that the right word?' He stood up and demonstrated with a right hook. 'Fist fighting the fascists; scrimmaging for our freedom. No one else would have him. But we loved you, man. Didn't we, Paul?'

A pub conversation popped in Ellie's head: *'Peak experience, infliction of bodily harm. An essential quest of humans once basic needs have been met.'* But who had said it?

'We certainly did and of course still do,' Paul was saying. 'I wonder what became of Raj and Sylvie. Do you remember when Raj's parents turned up unexpectedly in the summer term, Ellie? It was early in the morning and you answered the door, saw them and closed it as though they weren't there.'

'I don't remember that!'

'Yes, you do. It was hilarious. We were having breakfast when the doorbell went. You answered it and then immediately closed it again because Raj and Sylvie were still asleep in her bed. We hid in the kitchen, convulsing with—'

'Think you're dreaming, Paul,' Cam interrupted. 'I don't remember that either.'

'Ah, that's because you'd done one of your disappearing acts.' He looked at Ruth. 'Every now and then dear Cameron would disappear – one night, maybe two – and we never knew where.'

'How interesting.' She leaned forward on her elbows. 'Fess up, then. Where did you go?'

Cam rubbed the table. A shiver passing down her spine, Ellie gazed. How would he reply? Even now she didn't know.

'Just a bit of time out—'

Paul guffawed. 'We gathered that. More specifically?'

Cam shrugged. 'Climbing, Muay Thai, bungie jumping . . .'

'Really?' Ellie said. Aware of Ciara's return and a waiter with a tray, she looked down to hide her surprise. At the snap of a cork, she glanced up again. Cam was pouring champagne.

'Here we go, ladies and gents,' he said, handing around the flutes. He pushed his chair back. 'To Ciara and Sean. Sixteen happy years. Here's to married life!'

Swallowing the irony, Ellie stood too. 'To married life,' she echoed.

Cam briefly hugged Ciara, then stepped over to Sean. 'Congratulations, man,' he said, patting his shoulder. He swigged back his bubbles. 'I meant to mention earlier – I'm taking the boys to the Aquatics Centre in the morning. A family session with the huge float and slides. Do you fancy bringing the team?'

'Ah, sorry – church.'

'Right; of course. Maybe another time? We could do a Saturday.' Cam squinted in thought. 'Maybe next? Not the following, though, I'm taking my woman away for a night of passion.'

Surprised, Ellie lifted her head; the weekend away hadn't been mentioned since she'd collected him from the hospital. 'Really?' she said, feeling as though that word was stuck in a groove with Cam today. 'It sounds a lovely idea but—'

'The boys?' She could feel Sean's gaze. 'They can come to ours with pleasure,' he said. He looked over to his wife. 'Is that OK with you, Ciara?'

'Bloody hell,' Ruth declared, her voice gravelly and garbled. 'Whatever happened to asking the women first? Seems to me you've been landed with a fait accompli, ladies. I, for one, would protest.'

56

She's in the hospital, charging through the whitest snow and searching for Maurice. She knows he's here, she saw him in the garden at the bird table, wearing a surgical gown. The corridors are endless. She's been walking through their maze for a long, long time, but she needs her daddy, she wants him to hold her small hand.

Badly needing to pee, she pushes a heavy door to a room. It's filled with cots, but they all look the same. Running from crib to crib, she peers at each dolly. They're all identical with red hair; how will she know which is hers?

A second hand moves and she remembers. The one with a watch! Pacing up and down, she finally finds her. Tears blinding her eyes, she lifts the toy to her face and breathes in the scent. Escape, escape; they need to escape. She runs to the door, but a doctor shakes his head and bars her way. And under his arm there's a pillow. Her heart sinking, she looks to the ground; it isn't snow, it's feathers—

Ellie broke through to consciousness with a heave of hot air. Just a dream, thank God. A tear seeped from each eye. Jake and pillows, inextricably linked. That intense spread of guilt, even after all these years.

Quietly reaching for a tissue, she glanced at Cam's side of the bed. He was turned away, fast asleep, thankfully. A dull shaft of light lit his shoulders. The rope mark was still there, now a silvery line, like a memory. What did he say about it, way back? Yes, that was it: he'd laughingly played out the scene from *Jaws* before admitting that he'd got caught up in the lines when releasing a sail; that he'd been stupid not wearing a lifejacket. So perhaps climbing, Muay Thai and bungie jumping weren't such a surprise, after all. Extreme sports made sense, but God knows why he'd been so secretive about it at uni. Though he hadn't mentioned the sailing trip until afterwards either.

Not quite knowing why, the thought of young Cameron's *other* life made her shudder. She pushed it away. Although the dream was alarming, it had prompted a memory. She wanted to see if she was right about that. Slipping out quietly, she opened the curtains a crack. It was already light outside, so later than she'd supposed, but it was Sunday of course, a lie-in morning. Every day was like that right now, though, with the boys home for the summer and Cam recuperating.

Getting better, convalescing, recovering? Supposedly. She snorted to herself as she opened the wardrobe and reached for her jewellery box. Cam's business partner had rung yesterday morning, asking for him.

'Ellie, you're up! I was sorry to hear you hadn't been so good. I take it you're feeling much better?'

Bemused, she'd inhaled. 'I am thanks, Tim. I'll pass you to Cameron.'

Cam had shrugged after he'd finished the call. 'I had to say something to explain my ... absence, sabbatical, whatever.'

'What about telling the truth?' she'd asked.

'It's embarrassing, Ellie. Bloody humiliating, actually,' he'd replied, his voice steely. 'You just don't get it, do you?'

Careful not to tug the duvet, she now climbed back into bed. Last night they'd stayed at the restaurant until midnight and Cam had been fairly pissed, the type of drunk you don't recognise yourself, but everyone else does. Those who were relatively sober, at least. Though she hadn't been driving, she'd paced the G&Ts, interspersed with plenty of water, in case the babysitter called. Sean offered them a lift home and she'd felt in strange accord sat next to Ciara in the back; after Ruth's comment it had felt as though they were in the same club. *The little wives' club*. Like Marian. Of course, Ellie wasn't even a wife, let alone that type of woman, but the idea of being subservient or managed somehow had rankled. God knows how she'd been laughing only ten minutes later.

'Why do we always have to talk about bloody university when we get together?' Cam had complained as he threw off his socks and collapsed on to the mattress. 'It was a year – no, not even a year – eight, nine months of our lives and nineteen fucking years ago! Haven't we got anything else to talk about?'

'Like booking a weekend away and instead of telling me personally, which would've been lovely, you announce it to the crowd? You like to keep your life private, but mine's—'

'For fuck's sake, Ellie, sometimes ...' he'd muttered before crashing out.

Now crossing her legs, she studied the silk-covered jewellery case. Pink, of course, to match her Woodlands bedroom. She took a breath before opening it. Like Pandora? God, she hoped not. The ballerina popped up, but as though knowing to be silent, she didn't make the usual plaintive ping.

Feeling a spread of nostalgia, Ellie gazed at the trinkets. They were mostly keepsakes from holidays and those sweet little gifts the boys had breathlessly brought home from school trips. There was also her cameo, on a thin gold chain, still on its plush cushion. When she was seven or eight, Maurice had spent some time in Malta on business. He'd presented it with a flourish on his return, a brown one for Marian, a pink one for her. 'Take care of it, love. It's real gold,' her mum had said. Thrilled at receiving something so grown-up, it had remained in its box and little Eleanor had peeked at it now and then with a buzz of pleasure, a reminder of her daddy's love.

She sighed. Because it had been there then, hadn't it?

Shaking away the sadness, she searched for the watch. Mildly panicked, she dug around the soft lining, but eventually her nails found the leather strap. The Timex was there, rooted and lifeless at the bottom. She laid it in her palm, closed her eyes and swept a finger across its face. Yes, there they were, the bumps and scratches of childhood, some hazy, but others as though it was yesterday. She turned it over and peered at the metal back. The engraving was tiny and a little worn, but with the help of her mobile, she made out the words.

Ellie is Eleven! Love always, Aunty Diana

The curtains fluttered. Certain someone was watching, goosebumps danced down Ellie's spine. Almost fearful to look, she turned her head towards the window.

'Cam! You surprised me.'

His arms folded, he was scowling. 'Satisfied?' he said. 'I could feel you itching to do something for the last half an hour. I'm shattered. Can we go back to sleep now?'

57

She's watching him watching her and her lips as they travel down the centre line of his torso. Her own body tingling, she kisses the trail of glistening dark hair on his chest, his abdomen and belly. Smiling, she looks up with a question. His green eyes reply. Stunning tonight. Truly stunning, they say.

With a sigh of contentment she turns back to finish her languid journey, but she stops in her tracks. The door is ajar; there's somebody there, watching them both—

The whole clan woke up late, Harry and Jake fumbling to get dressed in time for the family swimming session, Ellie searching in every drawer, bin and cupboard for Harry's missing trunks.

'Sorry – The Grinch again. You'll have to wear shorts, love.'

He rolled his eyes. 'As long as they're not Thomas the Tank.'

But as ever, he chuckled. Like his dad, Harry fell on the funny side. When Cam was fit and well, anyway. Unlike her eldest, who refused to get up. Resisting the urge to hold her nose, Ellie tried to persuade him. 'Come on, love, up you get. You can show off your front crawl. I bet you'll be faster than Dad now,' she said, stealthily opening the small window. 'You'll be disappointed if you miss the fun, and you love swimming.'

'No I don't. You just think that. You all make assumptions and never bother to ask. Just like you never tell me anything.'

'OK, fair enough, no armbands today.' She pecked his forehead. 'But if you're not up by half past, I'll set whatever she's called from next door on you. Tell her you're the thudding culprit.'

'Hilarious, Mum; I might die of laughter.' He pulled up the duvet and turned away. 'And she's called Valerie. You'd know if you listened.'

God, he had a point. She opened her mouth to reply, but the reverberation of the front door interrupted, so she rushed downstairs, grabbed a packet from the kitchen and tiptoed in bare feet to the car.

'Have fun, guys,' she said, shoving the cereal bars at Cam before he climbed in. 'Don't forget to eat them on the way, love,' she said meaningfully, not wanting to mention Jake and his blood sugar out loud.

As though reading her mind, Jake turned and threw her the special smile that made her heart swell.

'Do you think it's ADHD?' she and Cam had asked the child psychologist a few years back.

'There's no such thing in my view,' he'd replied. 'Just underlying causes.'

Ellie had wondered what that meant at the time. Was the psychologist making some point about them as parents? Was he criticising her son's upbringing? She had fretted about it for weeks, swinging from frustration to guilt and back again. Jake's hyperactivity from as young as three or four had been exhausting, and part of her had wanted to scream, 'Just prescribe him some damned Ritalin!' But on reflection she'd been glad of the psychologist's stance; from what she'd read, the side effects could be scary. Far easier and safer to follow his advice: 'Watch what he eats, give him plenty of iron, keep his blood sugar stable, make sure he has lots of sleep. Simple but good practice for us all.'

She sighed. And listen to your child; talk to them too.

A weariness hitting, she trudged back up the stairs. How nice it would be to slip back in the sack and sleep until noon just like Toby. But then she might return to that sensuous and embarrassing dream. She'd tried to it shake off as soon as Harry woke her and Cam with a sleepy 'Aren't we supposed to be at the swimming baths at ten thirty?', but the abashment had followed her around since.

She now stood outside Toby's bedroom and stared at the wooden letters glued on the door. He was too old for the colourful characters spelling out his name, but he hadn't asked her to remove them. Yet.

The clutch of guilt nagging, she inhaled deeply. She'd made light of his complaint, but he was absolutely right. No one had told him anything about Cam's illness. But what should she say when his dad had sworn her to secrecy? Then there was 'assumptions' and not asking . . . Oh, God; had she given Toby enough attention of late? It was undoubtedly tough as the eldest child anyway – siblings came along and demanded all the attention – but he was the older brother of a particularly troublesome boy. He probably spent much of the time torn between loyalty and jealousy, irritation and love; it couldn't always be easy.

Perhaps she'd been lucky to be an only child; blessed to have Maurice and Marian.

She sniffed at the rare loving thought. Then unease flitted in. Those few questions for her mum. They were nothing major, but like Pandora, she still hadn't decided whether to let them escape or leave things settled as they were.

She tapped on Toby's door and pushed it open. 'I'm back.' The room still reeked of sweaty socks and funky body parts, despite the thin breeze. 'They've all gone now. Shall we have a chat?' she asked his covered head. 'Come down when you're ready; I'll be in the kitchen.'

Smelling a whole lot better, Toby appeared with damp hair. He scraped back the chair and flopped down at the table.

Ellie turned from the sink. 'Morning, love. Are you hungry?'

His face shadowy and troubled, he played with the pepper grinder and didn't reply.

She inwardly sighed. He was too like her: he struggled to hide his unhappiness.

Opening a bottom cupboard, she peered at the astonishing selection of cereals. The first box was empty, and the next, so she continued her chore, extracting each one and lining them in front of Toby like a wall. When it was complete, she sat the other side, hidden from view.

She rapped on the table top. '"Is there anybody there?" said the Traveller . . .'

Toby pulled off a top 'brick' and relented with a smile. 'I get the picture, Mum,' he said.

She watched him help himself to the Shreddies. Why did all her boys pour milk to the very brim of the bowl when they only ate the cereal? A mystery, like so many things. She waited until he'd fished out the very last lattice.

'So what's up?' she asked. 'Just be honest.'

Lifting his head, he glared with burning eyes. 'Honest? That's a joke.' His Adam's apple bobbed. 'Why won't anyone tell me what's going on?'

'In what way do you—'

'Dad for starters. I'm nearly thirteen and no one tells me

anything. I'm not a kid like Harry. You all fucking whisper. You with Dad. And Sean, too. What's *he* got to do with anything?'

She shook away Sean's expression in the shadows last night. 'Come on, Toby, don't swear—'

'And then there's Grandma and Grandad Wilson – what's that all about? We haven't seen them for weeks. I'm not stupid or deaf, Mum. You spend half the time looking worried or in a daze, and Dad never listens, he thinks everything's a joke.' He swallowed. 'Do you know how scary it was to come home from school and see him carried out of the house on a stretcher and put in an ambulance? Even Jake didn't believe the bloody flu story.'

'Toby—'

He put his hand to his forehead to hide the tears. 'You have no idea what it's like to know stuff is going on, mumbling and sneakiness, and no one is telling you.' His voice cracked. 'You just assume the worst. Dad was taken to hospital in an *ambulance*, Mum. That isn't normal!' A sob bubbled out. 'I don't . . . I don't even know if . . . if he's going to die.'

'Of course not!' Ellie closed her eyes. Half-truths and secrets. So familiar from childhood, she could taste them. Both scary and safe. But it wasn't just back then, was it? It was still happening now.

She stood and wrapped her son in her arms. After a moment, she pulled away. 'I'm sorry, love, we were trying to protect you and stop you from worrying. Just ask me right now. Tell me what you want to know,' she said. 'And I promise I'll give you a straight answer.'

58

Spying another cigarette butt between the wooden slats, Ellie squatted down on the decking. Was it Toby's, the babysitter's or her boyfriend, friend or whoever had been under her roof last night? One of the latter, she hoped. Though it could have been there for yonks, and she'd only just seen it. She tried to pull it out with her fingers. Nope, it was a touch out of reach.

Yup, those stubs felt like a huge bloody metaphor – hiding in plain sight but a little too distant to grasp. Like everything else right now.

She gave up and flopped back on the bench. Cam had not been impressed when she told him about her conversation with Toby.

'What exactly did you say?' he'd asked crossly when the boys belted upstairs, the smell of chlorine in their wake.

She'd held out her palms. What else but the truth?

'That you had a lump in your testicle, that you went to the hospital to have it removed. That you definitely don't have cancer but they've offered to give you further treatment to make sure there is nothing left that could cause any future problems.'

'Why mention the radiotherapy? That's just belt and braces. The consultant protecting his own back. I haven't even decided—'

'I asked you to talk to him, Cam, to explain everything. You didn't. He thought you might die, for God's sake.'

'Well, that's stupid and now he'll worry about the radiotherapy—'

'So what was I supposed to do?' she asked. 'Just be half honest?'

She now groaned and shook her head. It was so difficult to judge with children. Was it better to protect them with lies or to frighten them with the truth? Most parents sheltered their kids with white lies to some extent. The agony of childbirth, prevalence of paedophiles and terrorists, their own fear of spiders or snakes or the dentist. And what about Father Christmas, the Tooth Fairy and the Easter Bunny? Lies for fun.

She shook away the worry and replaced it with another: this morning's weird and sensual dream. Why her mind was pecking it to pieces, she didn't know. It was just her malfunctioning subconscious. And the goodbye kiss? It was nothing, really nothing; more humour, a joke.

She sighed and replayed last night yet again. After virtual silence throughout the meal, Ciara had made up for it on the way home, prattling non-stop to Cam until she realised with some indignation that he was snoring. God knows why, but it tickled Ellie and pulled her from her temporary malaise. She and Ciara would never be in the same club; only Cameron Hastings could fall asleep mid conversation. Life was actually just grand.

There had been further palaver when they arrived at their house: clearly disorientated from his snooze, Cam only just managed to stay upright when he lurched from Sean's car. Moments later the babysitter stormed out of the front door with an agitated-looking young man in tow, who almost collided with Cam.

Though Sean had followed, Cam flicked off the hall lights and groped up the stairs. 'Weebles wobble, but they don't . . . ' he said over his shoulder. 'Off for a long piss while I'm still standing.'

Yes, it was funny, that was all. Still chuckling, and clearly more tipsy that she'd realised, Ellie had turned to Sean. 'Thanks for the lift and happy anniversary! I would give you a social farewell kiss, but I still haven't mastered the etiquette so . . . ' She'd held out her hand.

Taking it, he'd lightly tugged her towards him. He'd gazed intently. Sure that he would kiss her, she'd held her breath, but he'd eventually smiled. 'You just need to practise. This is how it's done,' he'd said, his lips brushing her cheek, yet lingering for several beats.

It was just a goodbye. But why did it feel as though he had properly kissed her on the mouth? Why had she wanted him to? After a few moments he'd turned away. 'Night, Ellie,' he'd said. 'Sweet dreams.'

The house cleaned and in some semblance of order – the downstairs at least – Ellie pulled out the old deckchair and sat in the garden. Taking a breath of summer air, she gazed at her colourful bedding plants and shrubs before closing her eyes. Those few questions for Marian . . .

Sighing, she looked up at Toby's bedroom window. Childish fears were magnified for all the reasons he had described. But Eleanor Wilson was a grown-up now. She was nearly forty; her two youngest sons were creating an ineffectual rabbit run from table tennis netting and cricket wickets, and from what she could glean, Valerie and 'the blonde' next door were having an argument about dicks. Whether it was Dick's, dicks, *dicks* or private detectives, she had no idea, but the humour made her smile. And she'd had such fun at the restaurant last night. Life didn't have to be serious. Maybe Cam tended to the other extreme at times, but it was a glorious, bright afternoon. Like her advice to her eldest, she just needed to *ask*.

She scooped up her mobile and pressed the tiny icon of Marian's face. She answered straight away.

'Woodlands 6275.'

'It's only me, Mum. Have you got a minute or two? I have a couple of questions about Diana,' she said, sounding braver than she felt.

Her mum hesitated, but only for a moment. 'Well, yes, if you're quick. I've just come in from the lawn to get Dad a glass of water. It's such a lovely day. We're both sitting outside to read the Sunday supplements.'

'Yes, I am too. Admiring the gorgeous flowers and watching the boys . . . ' God, she was turning into Marian! Get to the point, Ellie. She cleared her throat. 'When we talked the other day, you said we didn't see Diana after I went into the junior school, but I'm sure she came later, when I was older. I can vaguely remember things . . . '

A long pause. Had Marian left the conversation? 'Mum, are you still there? Did you hear—'

'Yes, you're right, love. Diana did visit a couple of times after that,' she replied slowly. 'But we hadn't seen her for two or three years, so it was a bit of a shock. She just rang the doorbell one day and there she was, looking frightful. She wanted to see you, of course, but it was late and, well, she was high or inebriated, I don't know . . . '

Ellie blinked. *You're drunk and you're embarrassing yourself.*

A memory rather than a dream? Her palms suddenly sweaty, she took a breath. 'Is that when she . . . when Diana . . . brought me the watch? The Timex watch for my birthday?'

'Yes—'

'You told me it had come through the post.'

'We didn't want to frighten you, love. You were only just eleven and she'd changed so dreadfully. She was slurring her words, her teeth were rotten; it was awful. Your dad and I thought it was better for you to remember her as she was, bright and beautiful.'

Lies to protect children. Ellie felt strangely numb. 'What had happened to her?'

'We couldn't get any sense out of her. She'd fallen on hard times, I suppose. And she'd suffered from . . .' Marian stopped speaking.

'Go on, Mum, don't tell me half a story.'

Marian audibly sighed. 'She'd suffered from . . . well, everything was termed as depression in those days. Mental health blips or just the blues, I don't know, but I did wonder if it had come back. Sorry, I didn't want to say that, really. I don't want to worry you.'

Making plans for Ellie. 'So what happened in the end?'

'Dad was concerned for you, so he threw her out each time she came back and eventually she stopped. We hoped the healthy, vibrant Diana would return one day, but she never did. I'm sorry, love. She was my sister and I felt truly guilty, but you were my priority, you had to come first. And it was such a long time ago, I can't remember each detail.'

Finishing the call, Ellie absently stared at the sky. She couldn't recall everything either. But snatches were there. Desperately needing to wee in her lovely pink bed. The doorbell late at night and then hammering. Scrunching her eyes and willing sleep to come. Whispers, doors closing, her dad in striped pyjamas. And his shouting: *You're drunk and you're embarrassing yourself. Think of the child asleep upstairs. This has to stop.*

What she could recollect very clearly was the fear.

59

It was Wednesday, a day at Grandma and Grandad Hastings' today. Harry's backpack was stuffed; he was taking no chances.

'They do have a television, stupid,' Toby said, lightly smacking his head.

Refraining from the urge to say, 'And don't we know it!', Ellie slicked back a strand of hair that had fallen from her youngest's sculpted quiff. Also resisting the word *Jaqs*, she smiled. 'You'll have fun with the new kitten. Remember to take lots of pics. Grandma is cooking burgers for lunch, apparently.'

'Served with candy floss, no doubt,' Cam said through the corner of his mouth. He turned to the boys. 'Right, everyone in the car. Over the border is a-calling.'

Ellie followed them out and watched the usual scuffle at the passenger door from the porch. 'Good luck with that,' she called to Cam with raised eyebrows.

He stepped back. 'I'm not hanging around with that blasted cat, so I'll only be half an hour. What are your plans for today?' He tapped his temple. 'Because you do have a plan, I can tell.'

She laughed. What was this? Had Cam suddenly discovered intuition? 'Thought I'd have a drive out.'

'A *drive out*?'

'Yeah, to Leeds.'

His grin was replaced with a grimace. 'Why would you want to go to Leeds of all places?'

It was something she needed to do. She didn't really know why. Perhaps it was the Alston Terrace chatter at the anniversary meal or that unexpected, tender kiss – which she was most definitely not thinking about – but she'd never been back after uni and that felt incomplete, a missing piece.

Closure, she supposed, the need to tick at least one final box in her life. The Diana box was still open a crack, but she was trying her best to sit on it and squash the lid shut. *'Mental health blips or just the blues'* was a notion she did not want to dwell on, so she'd avoided phoning her mum over the last couple of days. Not that Marian had called her either.

She came back to Cam. 'Just a mooch around. I don't know; the shops, maybe have a drive past Alston Terrace. Do you fancy coming?'

His frown deepening, Cam inhaled to say something, then seemed to change his mind. 'Nah. I've a backlog of paperwork. A day in the study for me. If I don't see you before you leave, have fun.'

She lifted her hand to the boys and chuckled. Clever little chap: clearly pleased with himself, Harry had managed to bag the front seat. Feeling an odd sense of loss, she turned back to the sunlit hall. Her resolve was already slipping. Badly. Why *would* she want to drive fifty miles on a dusty, packed motorway, just on a whim? The abrupt peal of her mobile seemed to reply. She scanned the stairs and the sideboard. Oh heck, where was it? Following the sound, she scooped it up from the ironing pile and peered at the screen. Alleluia! It was Hen.

Hen's voice was breathy. 'I need to get out of the house,' she said without preamble. 'Are you in?'

'I am indeed.' Ellie paused. She could stay here and drink too much wine with Hen in the garden, or . . . 'Though I was thinking about a day trip to Leeds. Have a look around my old uni haunts. Do you fancy it?'

'Perfect,' she replied. 'Old haunts and Harvey Nicks sound just perfect. See you in half an hour. I'll drive you.'

'Is it OK if I open the window a crack?' Ellie asked once Hen had taken the slip road towards the city centre.

The smell of warm leather in Maurice's Jags had always knocked her sick as a kid. Hen's brand-new Bentley had the same effect.

'Sure.' Hen finally turned off the radio. She had listened to, and intermittently belted out, songs on Capital FM the whole length of the motorway. But Ellie had been glad. Though it was the journey in reverse, the old memories of self-loathing and disgust were still battering her chest.

Sucking in the fresh air, she closed her eyes. The thought of the girl she'd been back then still winded her. Yes, she'd been angry, petulant, spoilt and naive, but how had she been so blasé, so louche, so casual about selling herself for a sexual favour? Climbing into a stranger's car. Allowing that abhorrent man to roughly force her mouth to his penis. Incredibly putting herself in that vulnerable, dangerous position. Thank God she'd had her mum, the *safety* of her mum.

It's really for the best, I promise.

Frowning, she tried to place the words. Definitely Marian's, but when had she said them?

'Earth to Ellie! So, where are we going?'

She snapped back her head. Hen had pulled down her sunglasses and was studying her quizzically. What on earth would she or Nina think if they knew what she'd done that night? They'd be revolted for sure. 'Sorry? Oh right; we're going to Headingley. Two miles along the A660.'

'For t'cricket, lass?' Hen asked in a dreadful Yorkshire accent.

Ellie laughed. 'Something like that.'

Glad to leave the Bentley and breathe, Ellie gazed at the large detached house. Number eleven Alston Terrace. Even before clocking the new front door and window frames, the neatly trimmed privet told her it was privately owned now. It looked cheerful, somehow. Had the brick always been this red or was it just the sunshine?

A wistful sorrow spreading, she pinched her nose. What a handsome building. Why had she never seen that? Maybe today was its proud summer look. Or perhaps she'd projected her unhappiness on it back then. Had she always been sad? Not all the time, surely? There had been laughter; yes, belly-aching convulsions with Cam and The Judge over nothing at times. And sometimes Sean, too, though that inscrutable gaze had never wavered.

'*Cam doesn't know what he wants yet. You've got to pick yourself up.*'

Hearing a dog yap, Ellie turned to the pavement. An *Oodle* of some sort. A Schnoodle or a Yoodle? She smiled at the pretty crossbreed. But then her gaze slipped to the profile of its owner. Glossy dark hair and that smile. What the hell? It couldn't be. Why would Sean's sister be here, of all places?

Breath stuck in her throat, she watched the young woman crouch, collect the dog poop in a bag and tie it. But then she stood and raked her long locks behind her ears. It wasn't her; it wasn't the girl who'd looked at Sean with adoring eyes.

Almost laughing to herself, she blew out the relief. But there was a tinge of disappointment too. God knows why, but she would have liked to speak to the girl again, look at her closely so she'd *know.* Know what? If Sean was really her brother or if he was playing away with one of his students? He wasn't; she trusted him. And it was none of her business. Absolutely none. That goodbye kiss had to be looked at in context. It wasn't even a kiss, for goodness' sake, just a friendly, funny peck on her cheek.

'So . . .' Hen's voice made her jump. She'd climbed out and was leaning artfully against the car. 'So this is where you lived in your third year. Lovely; you should see the hovel I rented. Mice. What's the collective noun? A group? A nest? Millions of the buggers, anyway. Oh, and slugs in the grotty bath. Most charming.' She squinted at the façade. 'Very nice; put that in Hale and you'd be talking well over a million. Which room was yours?'

Exhaling the last of her agitation away, Ellie pointed to the sash window. 'The smaller one in the middle. The box room, though even that was a fair size.' Picturing the high walls, she smiled. The Johnny Cash poster! What on earth had become of that?

Hen raked back her shades. 'Is that where true love blossomed? You and Cam at it like . . . well, like undergraduates.'

'Actually no, not at all.' She turned to Hen and smiled wryly. 'Not for want of trying on my part. I never even saw him fully naked.'

Hen laughed. 'Played hard to get, did he? Doesn't sound like Cam.'

'That's true . . .'

What *does* Cameron sound like? Ellie wanted to ask her. But not in a challenging way. Though she'd had that stupid paranoia weeks ago, she didn't for a moment think Hen had or would go after him, but her old thoughts of how we perceived ourselves and how others saw us struck again. The two seldom matched.

You are special, you must know that.

It was actually quite unsettling.

As though reading her mind, Hen spoke again. 'And what

about the handsome professor? Where did he sleep?' she asked with a high laugh. 'Did you ever see *him* in the buff? I certainly wouldn't mind a quick peek. Or even a very long one. Hairy in all the right places, I'll bet. What was he like? Didn't you fancy him just a tiny bit?'

Ellie didn't reply for a beat. Her mind was pushing at a door. Stripped pine, a dark knot in the wood staring back like the face of *The Scream*. Sean's bedroom, of course. Yes, she had seen him at least partially naked. Why she'd been there, she had no idea, but he was with a guy.

She shook the uncomfortable image away. The long-haired, derisive Sean Walsh experimenting with another man was hardly a surprise; she had to get over it.

Going back to Hen's question, she laughed. How had The Judge once put it? *The answer to womankind. The Beast's bevy of beauties.* 'Sean had his own private harem. And no I didn't; we never hit it off.'

Yet she remembered those strong arms when she'd needed them. And that kiss? Well, she wasn't thinking about that.

Hen had lifted her slim wrists and was gyrating. 'And that is . . . ?' Ellie asked.

'A belly dance. Think I'll qualify for Sean's gynaeceum?'

'Hmm, I'll give you a seven. Come on, chauffeur, let's go. One more stop and then lunch.'

Hen pulled up opposite the willow tree. 'You want me to park here?' she asked.

Ellie nodded.

'Right here in this joyful spot?'

'Yup. Just for a minute.'

Breath stuck in her chest, Ellie squinted through the windscreen and shivered. She'd never been here in daylight before. Like the

Twin Towers, the skyline was empty, yet the grey high-rise flats seemed to loom in the distance like phantoms. But when she finally allowed her eyes to focus, the grounds of the crematorium were surprisingly friendly, grassy and bright, the trees glowing green, the borders alive with wild flowers.

Scraping back her sunglasses like a headband, Hen frowned. 'Well, *this* I didn't expect on our grand tour. Not exactly evocative of student life.' She peered at Ellie. 'Or is it?'

Feeling the sizzle, Ellie searched for the scar on her cheek. *Whore.* Yes she had been a whore that night; she'd made a choice, an extremely bad one. But she'd been so young then and she *had* been punished. Was it finally time to forgive herself?

'It is, actually,' she replied. 'It's reminiscent of disgrace and self-loathing. Shame of the deepest kind.'

Silent for many seconds, Hen eventually spoke. 'None of us are perfect, Ellie. We're all ashamed to some extent.'

Something in the way she'd said it made Ellie turn. Hen was dabbing her eyes with her elegant fingers. 'Oh, Hen. What's wrong?' she asked.

'Nothing,' she replied. 'How could there be?' She gestured towards the Bentley's high-tech wooden dash. 'I have this, don't I?' She dangled her hand. The huge diamonds glinted, the gold bracelet shone. 'And these and this and plenty of cash,' she added. 'If I want *company* for an hour, I know how to get it.'

She took a shuddery breath. 'But it doesn't *touch* me, Ellie. There's no intimacy. I *feel* nothing, life's so very empty.' Digging in the glovebox, she pulled out a tissue and noisily blew her nose. 'I love only the man I married and he's never there. It's a beautiful summer's day but where're he and my only child? They're together on a golf course somewhere, whereas I'm sitting with you in a bloody Yorkshire graveyard!' She reached for Ellie's hand and squeezed it. 'No offence meant.'

Ellie's lips twitched. 'None taken.' But the smile fell. She'd been selfish again, hadn't she? She hadn't for a moment stopped to wonder, let alone ask, why Hen needed to get out of her house today, nor where Giles was during the school holidays.

'Come on, lovely friend, let's get out of here. I'm treating you to lunch and a proper chat. Whatever takes your fancy is yours.'

Hen lifted one eyebrow. 'Anything?'

Ellie laughed. 'Absolutely.' She took a last look at the weeping willow. As though in supplication, its branches scraped the ground. And beyond it a car was parked. A red car as it happened, but it was just a red car. Perhaps Cam was right; she had been self-obsessed. But that was fine, actually, she could put it right now. She'd been stupid once, but that was years ago and the closure was there, she could feel it.

And as Cam had put it so succinctly, they were different people then.

60

It was Friday. Infused with ridiculous energy, Ellie had been up since dawn, washing, cleaning, ironing. Vacuuming her grumpy boys awake:

'Mum! Go away and do that somewhere else.'

'Come on, Toby, rise and shine. It's a glorious day.'

A glance at his mobile, then a groan: 'No day is *glorious* at half past eight.'

'What's that horrible noise?' from beneath Harry's pillow.

'It's an alien from Minerva.'

A bounce from the bed to the floor in one movement: 'Really? Coolio.'

As for Jake, he had slept through it. His face was so peaceful, it had almost pierced Ellie's own contentment.

She was now in the back garden. She'd been on her knees for the last hour, furiously pulling clumps of grass and weeds from the arid flower and shrub beds. She should've done it months ago, but after waking from a deep and dreamless sleep, she'd put it at number seven on the chore list.

Wiping her sweaty forehead with the back of her hand, she looked at Cam. 'This is harder than it looks. I'm boiling and *parched*...'

He glanced over his newspaper. 'Good work. Keep it up, young lady.'

'Why thank you for the *young*, if not the offer of a ...' That joyous feeling of *holiday* hit her. 'Do you know what I fancy?'

He scrunched his face. 'Baba ganoush? Veggie crisps? Cillian Murphy?'

'Well, obviously all three, but not right at this moment. I have a penchant for a beer.'

'What? Not chilled wine or an icy gin and tonic?'

She sat back on her heels. 'No, lager straight from the ice box, like on hols. Cold beer, hot weather, or perhaps the other way around.' Her hands on her hips, she looked at Cam with raised eyebrows. 'A nice refreshing drink, just the thing for the *workers*.'

'This *is* work,' he replied, flicking the paper. 'Sport, stocks and shares, lying bloody politicians; in that order.' He stood from the deckchair and rubbed his hands. 'Well, my love, we have the weather, we have beer. What about a few people to join us? It *is* a Friday, after all. I know you'll be getting piss-up withdrawal symptoms if we're not very careful.'

'Cheeky sod.' She leaned forward to inspect a bunch of half-eaten shrubs. 'Flaming bunnies! I wouldn't mind their free pruning services, but it's the wrong time of year. Do you think this plant has had it, Cam? No leaves at all. Should I dig it up?'

'What you *should* do is get rid of those bloody pests. Take them to Alderley Edge and release them to a life of freedom. It's what I'd want if I was cooped up, living a life of ...' He thought for a moment. '*Entrapment.* Maybe they'd live a long and happy rabbit life or maybe they'd get snapped up by the first fox in town, but they'd be free. And there are so many now that Harry wouldn't miss one or two.' He stretched and yawned. 'No idea about plants. Trading boxes is my thing. And organising Friday piss-ups. Leave it with me.'

Wearing astonishingly high heels, Hen arrived first with Giles. He'd changed so much since Ellie had last seen him, she found herself gawping.

'He's grown so handsome and what a lovely voice. Shame I don't have a daughter,' she quietly quipped as she helped Hen negotiate the steps from the decking to the grass.

She gave her friend a tight, meaningful squeeze. During lunch at Harvey Nicks, they'd had a long chat about Hen's loneliness and the possibility of her getting a job, even volunteer work. As Ellie had pointed out, there were so many opportunities when one dug just a little – from donkey sanctuaries to mentoring disadvantaged kids; from park maintenance to visiting the elderly. Or even starting her own charity: with her efficiency, gregarious personality and charm, Hen would be brilliant; she just needed a cause.

'You're not suggesting I become a *do-gooder*, are you, Ellie?' she'd asked, her face a picture of disdain. 'Lord above! Takes me back to the vicarage and my parents. Look how they turned out. Think I'll stick to my other *charitable* causes.'

Yet Ellie had seen a light, a glimmer of something hopeful in Hen's eyes. She'd also suggested that Hen talk to Edward and tell him how she felt. It was rich coming from Ellie Wilson, of all people, but she was pretty damned contented right now. True, it was helped by shelving her parent debacle, but there had been no nightmares for days and their absence made her feel unencumbered, as light as a kite. Or perhaps it was just a full night of sleep.

Followed by their mum, Faith and Noah soon clattered down the steps. 'Nina, sit here,' Hen called, patting the seat next to her. 'And for God's sake tell me you're walking or getting a taxi home.

I don't want to be pissed and dangerous alone. Ellie is drinking lager of all things.'

Nina lifted her eyebrows. 'Ah, that continental sensation?'

'See,' Ellie said. 'Nina gets it.'

Nina nodded at Giles. 'Flipping heck, Hen, he's going to be a stunner.' She leaned closer and whispered, 'Are you sure he and Edward are related? Not the model-cum-whatever?'

Ellie held her breath, but Hen just guffawed. 'Carpet fitter. He was cute until I realised that I had a mouthful of his chewing gum. Edward is coming later. He likes to remind himself of how the other half live. And of course, I'll need a driver to take me home.' She nodded to the cooler. 'Is that wine I see before me? Are you pouring or shall I?'

Hunched on a picnic blanket, Giles, Faith and Toby were picking at a bowl of crisps and swilling cans of Coke at startling speed.

'It'll be alcohol before we know it,' Hen commented. 'Then inevitably sex.'

'Don't! They've known each other since the womb, which makes them siblings of a sort,' Nina replied. The women watched for a moment. 'I wonder what they talk about.'

'Wowee! They're tiny.'

Ellie turned to the young voice. Harry and Noah were at the rabbit hutch, their hands sticky with droppings, sawdust and straw as they handled the latest batch of baby bunnies. How *that* had happened, she didn't know. She had intended to segregate the boys and girls, but as Hen put it, the inevitable had occurred before she'd had chance.

'Don't let them out, Harry,' she called. 'You know Dad won't be pleased. And don't forget to wash your hands.' Then, reverting to Nina, 'Yeah, I wonder too.' She thought back to Toby's upset and anger. 'We think they're still toddlers, but kids see and know a lot more than we give them credit for.'

Like at eleven.

Shrugging the discordant chime away, she lifted her eyebrows. 'Would we really want to be a fly on the wall, though? We'll probably hear things we can't unhear.'

'Absolutely. Especially when they're *doing* a lot more too, judging by the state of Giles' sheets since he's been home, anyway.'

'Hen, you can't say that!'

'What? Say that my son masturbates whenever the opportunity arises? Come on, Nina, all boys do it. Even little Noah will be at it soon, day and night, just you wait.'

Ellie leaned forward with a grin. 'While I am not prepared to accept that any of my sons will ever do anything like that, I think Toby is smitten. It's—'

Her words were cut off by the creak of the side gate. 'Bloody hell.' She lowered her voice and laughed. 'Talk of the devil.'

As solemn-faced as ever, Katrina Walsh floated in, soon followed by four of her siblings, who fired into the garden like bullets.

Hen fanned her face and sighed. 'Oh, do tell me these ragamuffins belong to the handsome professor.' Sucking in her cheeks, she turned to Nina. 'You haven't met him, girl. Herbal pill alert. You're in for a treat. Have a good gander and let me know what you think.'

As the balmy afternoon breezed into evening, the garden slowly filled with adults and children. Relaxed in the warm sunshine, Ellie stayed outside. There was no point inspecting the state of the kitchen or ascertaining whether Cam had done anything about food. Each child had appeared in the garden with a can of fizzy something and a bag of crisps, so she figured everything was in hand. After all, if the kids were happy, so were the grown-ups. That's how it worked, didn't it?

Turning to the decking, she took a quick breath. Bloody hell, it was 'the blonde' from next door. Was she here to complain? She peered at her hand. She was holding a glass; perhaps shouting was unlikely.

Ellie chuckled. Only Cameron Hastings was sufficiently brazen to invite her. But then again, the woman had accepted. She beckoned. 'Hello!' she said, wishing she had the balls to ask about the *dick* argument. 'How are you?' she asked, as though they hadn't been silent neighbours for over two years.

'Fine thanks. I'm Amy, by the way.'

Young and attractive, she was still wearing her tailored work suit. After a stilted start to the conversation, Ellie topped up her glass and soon discovered Val was her civil partner, that they were both in the law, she a criminal defence solicitor and Val a barrister.

'I don't suppose you know Paul Paterson-Brown?' Ellie asked.

'Mr Paterson-Brown *QC*?' Amy emphasised the 'QC' with a grimace. 'He sits in the Crown Court as a Recorder. He'll be a judge soon, no doubt. Very respected but irascible and scary, too. A hanging judge he'll be, that's for sure.' She put her hand to her mouth. 'Oh shit. You know him, don't you?'

Ellie laughed. 'Close friends since uni.'

'Oops,' Amy replied. 'There go a few more of my clients to the gallows. Too many glasses of wine as usual. Better get off and see what there is to eat for dinner. But now we're acquainted you must come round to meet Val. Let's exchange numbers.' She pulled out her mobile. 'She's the telephone dragon, by the way. When you come round I'll feed her a few children first to ensure she's not breathing fire . . . '

Ellie waved her away. Still smiling, she shook her head. What a small world. And there it was again; the veneer of the human, no one really knowing what's inside. Who'd have thought her apparently prissy neighbour would be so likeable and funny? And the avuncular Paul? Well, *that* was a surprise.

314

'A lovely smile.'

She spun to the voice. His arms folded, Sean was leaning against the frame of the decking. He tilted his head. 'You seem bright and happy.'

Oh God, the kiss. Aware of her deep blush, she tried not to look at his lips. 'It must be the effect of sunshine and weak beer.'

He took off his sunglasses and studied her for a beat. 'So everything's fine?'

She lowered her eyes to deflect that green gaze. They fell on his shirt; the top two buttons were undone. The dream and the slick, dark hair flashed in Technicolor. And where it tapered to. She laughed away her embarrassment. 'Of course, why wouldn't it be?'

He shrugged. 'No reason at all. I just wondered how your parents were faring.' He replaced his shades. 'Thanks for the anniversary rosebush, by the way. It was a very enjoyable night. One to remember . . .'

'It was.' Impulsively, she reached for his hand. 'Come on, Professor. Hen won't forgive me if I don't drag you over to say hello again.'

Feeling ridiculously proprietorial, she pulled him to the cluster at the centre of the garden. 'Hen? Nina?' she asked, interrupting the chatter. She watched her friends' faces as they turned. 'Sean, I'm sure you remember Hen,' she said. 'And this is Nina, the other founder member of . . .'

Nina eyes widened, then she chuckled. 'The Friday piss-up,' she replied.

61

Ellie pulled up the car outside the kitchen window where Maurice's Jag was usually parked. The house was silent, the lights off, but she wasn't surprised her parents were out. She had finally steeled herself to telephone yesterday.

'How's Dad?' she'd asked Marian, the pound of disquiet loud in her ears.

'He's fine, actually, love. Back to normal, I'd say.'

'That's great, Mum. Can we visit this week?' The thump even louder. 'The boys are asking after you both; they're missing you and your chocolate flapjack.' She took a quick breath. 'Or you could come here if that works better.'

'That would be lovely, but can we take a rain check for now? We're out and about most days before Dad goes back to the office. We thought we'd revisit all the places we take for granted. Haigh Hall, Rivington Pike, the tea rooms at Anglezarke Reservoir. The fresh air and the walk will do us both good.'

And provide a perfect excuse not to see me, Ellie had thought. But when she woke this morning, she decided to drive up to

Chorley anyway on the off-chance they'd be in. Cam was taking the boys and a friend each to snowboard at the Chill Factore.

'Fancy coming with us?' he'd asked her at breakfast. 'After your impressive performance at Crocky Trail I might even let you join my team.'

'Eleventh man? Thanks, but no thanks,' she had replied, surprised that he'd offered. 'Snow in August doesn't feel right. Like those shops that sell Christmas decorations all year round.' Trying to sound normal, she'd added: 'I might nip over and see Mum and Dad instead.'

'Fair dos,' he'd replied. 'Have fun. Oh, and Better Call Saul if Maurice misbehaves. I will come running.'

Cam still hadn't properly asked about her mum and dad. Which was fine. But odd, surely? Sean had. She'd been 'shelving' her concerns about her parents at the piss-up on Friday, but if he asked again, how would she describe the secrets and the surrogacy, the benevolence and profound love? And also the anxiety: the sketchy recollections and the need to know more, yet fear of those memories too. She'd been mulling over it all weekend. Like those damned cigarette butts; now that she'd glimpsed them, she had to dig them out.

She came back to the present, inhaled deeply and climbed from the car. Checking the kitchen was empty en route, she made her way to the front door and studied the 'Woodlands' plaque. The letters had been gouged out of a slice of tree trunk. Though more invasive than her usual light touch, it was a Marian creation, of course.

She peered at the brass handle. Though she was doing nothing wrong, she felt stupidly furtive. This was her home too, wasn't it? Yet still she pulled the key from her back pocket and fingered it for a while. Eventually taking a sharp breath, she slipped it in the lock, turning it left and right, somehow sure if she persevered, it would turn. It didn't. Perhaps not surprising; she hadn't used it for a decade at least.

Sighing, she tried to bat away the sensations of paranoia and rejection. Life here had improved dramatically once she'd started the teacher training at Edge Hill. She had her new car, which gave her freedom when she needed it, and Maurice was pleased she was taking a 'useful and vocational' course after her 'disappointing degree'. The spare room was hers again. She even invited friends round for dinner or drinks, both the ones she'd abandoned at thirteen and other trainee teachers. And when she re-found Cam, he became an almost permanent fixture, the son Maurice and Marian never had.

Then look at her life now: she was blessed with three wonderful boys. She didn't need to look back.

Yet she still itched to enter the house. Lifting the pots each side of the door, she found worms and woodlice but no key. Where would they hide the spare? She tapped her fingers in thought, then headed for the greenhouse. The wooded area was luscious, the shrubs thick and high, the laurel bushes towering around its perimeters. They gave privacy to the plot, but blocked out the sunshine. It kept the grass moist, the air slightly dank. She liked it that way, though. A spicy, verdant smell, the aroma of both woodlands and 'Woodlands', the fragrance she always associated with home.

She yanked back the sliding door and inhaled a distinctive, sharp scent. Tomatoes. She smiled, pleased to replace the usual dark nudge with a much fonder memory. She could picture it so clearly: her small hand cupping the tiny fruit. 'They'll grow much bigger if you leave them, but go on, Eleanor, just one,' her dad was saying, popping it in her mouth like a pill. 'The birds and squirrels will have them if we don't keep them in here.' Then with keen eyes, 'What's the verdict, love? Is it sweet enough for my sweetie?'

Sniffing back the emotional burn, Ellie searched under tubs and trays of burgeoning bedding plants. Beneath pots of rosemary, basil and parsley. No luck. Then she clocked a box of gardening tools: secateurs, trowels and forks, twine and a small plastic tub. She opened it. Bingo.

The old guilt surfacing, she listened to the crunch of her footfall as she retraced her steps to the house. It wasn't a rusty nail today – or malicious intent – but her fingers trembled just the same. Taking another shuddery breath, she inserted the key, turned it and let herself in.

As though she'd been running, she found herself panting. What the heck was wrong with her? The hallway was the same as always: scrupulously tidy, with a tang of home cooking in the air.

She swallowed. It was stupid to feel so nervous; she was thirsty, that was all.

She made her way to the kitchen, stood at the sink and ran the tap. When she was on her second glass, realisation hit: she was aping the first thing she had done all those years ago. Only then she'd had an excuse: she hadn't consumed any liquid for hours and she'd needed to get rid of that taste, that man's disgusting taste. Along with the compulsion to examine her cheek, she'd drunk water obsessively for days. But today it tasted odd; different from Heaton Moor. Hard water or soft, she could never remember which.

The kettle seemed to stare. Could she make a hot drink? No; somehow it seemed wrong to brew up without the occupants there, a step too far. She was a stranger, an imposter, the uninvited. Even her sandals felt intrusive, so she retreated to the mat and kicked them off.

The house was silent, deathly so. What now? The spare room? Well, it had once been hers.

She snorted at her own timidity. This once was her home! Yet she still tiptoed up the polished wooden staircase, the sweat between her toes leaving invisible prints.

Passing the other doors, she continued to her corner entrance and walked in. She took a pace back. Of course she'd slept here as an adult, but had still expected to be greeted by an array of pink. Pink, pink and more shades of pink. From the pale flowery wallpaper to the matching cherry curtains, cushions and duvet.

She stepped to the window and looked out. Though the walls were sanitary white these days, her favourite place was still there, a deep sill that Marian had lined with velvet-covered pads, creating a settle. With the low radiator below, it had been a warm and snug place to read books and listen to music, or just watch the squirrels dancing. And, of course, name the birds.

Taking in the scene, she sat in her old cushion dent. 'The best view in the house,' her dad always said, and he was right. From here she could see the tall Sessile oaks, the bench and the greenhouse beyond. Or peer into the next-door neighbours' plot. An elderly couple had lived there then; they'd look up with fond smiles and wave, but the garden was empty now. Dead long ago, she supposed.

A scold of sparrows on the table caught her eye. Their feathers puffed, they appeared to be squabbling over food. It used to be bacon rind or even lard, but maybe that wasn't PC warbler food these days.

With a jolt, a memory surfaced. Little Ellie standing here in her flamingo-pink nighty, rubbing groggy sleep from her eyes, then running down the stairs, her bare feet slapping the parquet.

'Daddy? The bird table has moved! Have you moved it?'

Marian at the kitchen sink, answering for him. 'The birds don't like too much sunshine. We can't have their wings melting like Icarus, can we, love?'

Unsettled by the sudden flashback, Ellie turned away. For God's sake, what was she doing here? There was no sign of her mum and dad, it was best to retreat.

As though they might be sleeping, she crept past her parents' bedroom, intending to leave. But when she reached the lacquered balustrade, her eyes caught the closed doors on the far side of the landing. She hadn't been in either room for years.

'The boys can go in my studio, but tell them to be careful, love,' Marian had said when they were small.

'Thanks, Mum. But better safe than sorry,' she'd replied, glad of an excuse. Easier to ban them completely; she had almost visualised the precious breakages and her mum's stoic disappointment.

She looked at her watch. Did she have time? Did she even want to peep in? Berating herself for her cowardliness, she strode to the first and turned the ceramic knob. The cool smoothness against her palm took her back. Stepping in, she glanced around. The lofty room was still in a basic state – the paisley wallpaper peeling and the stripped floorboards bare – but it was much brighter than she recalled, probably because the shutters had been removed to let in more light. Her mum's workshop, of course. The potter's wheel in the centre, it was packed with her ceramics on wooden pallets in different stages of creation.

An easel and several watercolours were propped against one wall, but there was no sign of larger canvases or oils. What had Marian said about her Norfolk river paintings that 'came from within'? Perhaps they were amongst the clutter in the 'junk' room opposite.

Anxiety nagging, Ellie stood at the second door. Her heart seemed to clatter against her ribs. Why this one felt daunting, she couldn't say, but she puffed out the hot air, slowly turned the cold handle and pushed. Nothing happened; the bloody door was stuck. She chuckled despite herself. It might have been a sign to back off, but it had always been this way. Remembering the old technique, she gave it a shove, put her hand to the left wall and fumbled for the switch. Dull light lit the room. She breathed a smile; even dim illumination was a good thing – when she was young, the central bulb wouldn't be replaced until her dad 'had the ladders out anyway' and that had been pretty rare.

Her fond smile still hovering, she pictured little Ellie with a torch, the glow as shaky as her hand. Looked on by the looming dark furniture, this room had felt scary with electricity, but with a weak battery gleam, it had been even more so. Corners and shadows, fingers and eyes. Imagined movement and scrapes. And always that stale, fusty smell of old things. Just short of being haunted in her mind, it was both thrilling and terrifying for those childhood games of hide-and-seek.

'I wouldn't let the boys play in here, love,' her mum had said of this space. 'Grandma's belongings are stacked high. Something could easily come flying. I'm not bothered about the junk, but I would hate one of them to get hurt.'

The shutters were closed, but even in the feeble light, Ellie could see why her parents hadn't cleared out the antiques. The huge mahogany and ornate walnut pieces were pristine. A matching sideboard, Queen Anne table and hat stand lined one side; double wardrobes, huge divan, dressing table and drawers the other. Then there was a whole host of smaller items: books, furs and ornaments piled haphazardly on the bed, many more on the Indian rug covering the teak floorboards.

Taking care where she stepped, she strolled around. She traced her fingers across the cheeks of the pale china dolly that had freaked her out as a girl. And there was the fox stole with staring glass eyes. Yes, some things she remembered, both thrilling and chilling, but other contents had held no interest for a child: the discoloured ornate potties, the framed sepia photographs and old tomes; an embellished wooden writing box, an ancient Holy Bible, a bundle of wartime newspapers.

She pictured Cam's face, the rise of his eyebrows and the jab in her ribs. 'Get them to your mum's antique village; they'll be worth a few bob, Ellie.'

She shook her head at the thought, but another recollection was prodding, not quite there. Something about this room. In her flamingo-pink nighty and standing at the door? Like a dust mote she tried to catch it, but it wafted away. Perfume. Yes perfume. She remembered the floral scent. That's right; she used to read and chat in here with . . . with Aunty Diana.

She turned her head to the three-mirrored dressing table. God, yes. There had been gloves, Grandma's gloves, like treasure. Long, medium and short; silk, leather, cotton and lace; some with pearly buttons, others with clasps. And in every colour one could desire . . .

Perching on the piano stool, she gazed at the slim drawer, then gingerly pinched the glass hilts. Her heart ached as the warm recall flooded back. She and Diana used to sit here, thigh to thigh, and play shop.

'Hello, madam. Welcome to Ellie's Boutique. How could I help you today?'

'I'd like to buy some of the finest gloves, please, my dear. I'm going to a grand ball and my dress is of the most exquisite turquoise chiffon. With a duke, don't you know? What would you recommend, my dear? Perhaps I should buy two pairs, perhaps even three.'

Her smile abruptly fell as another memory snapped. Red hair and snow . . . Red hair and snow? Picturing the image, she whipped her head to the mattress.

Was that where she was born? Yes, it must have been in that very bed. Why hadn't she twigged before? Almost haunted, indeed. Goosebumps stabbed her skin as she stared. No, it wasn't that.

The recollection was a scene she saw with her own eyes. A happy sensation ripped away moments later by sheer horror.

She tried to blink it away. It was just an old divan, covered in bric-a-brac. Her imagination was overwhelmed, like a dream within a dream, that was all.

Battling the surge of nausea, she returned to the mirror.

Flame haired and beautiful, Diana gazed back.

62

The window open a crack, it's a balmy night, not long after Eleanor
Wilson's eleventh birthday. Her favourite selection of greetings
cards are still on the bedside table with the usual glass of water.

She abruptly wakes and unravels her flamingo-pink nighty. She
yawns and holds out her wrist to catch the time in the soft, seeping light beneath the door. It's her new shiny Timex. She hopes
Mummy won't know she hasn't taken it off before bed like she's
supposed to.

A sound from outside. Scariness creeping, she pulls in her arm
and stills to listen. The rattle of pebbles, shuffling, tapping. And
quiet talking. Though she drags up the duvet and covers her ears,
she can still hear them. Murmuring, whispers and sighs. A low
moaning, too. She's heard it before; it makes her heart clang, but
she doesn't know why.

Snatches of Mummy's hushed words fly in. It's her kind-yet-firm
voice. But today it sounds strange: steely, determined and cold.

'She'll hear you.'

'Be reasonable.'

'But she's not your daughter.'

'The watch, of course I did.'

'You agreed.'

'Come on now.'

'You don't mean that.'

'What's best for her?'

'We know it's been hard.'

'You wouldn't; you know that.'

Then finally: 'Oh love, you're so tired and overwhelmed. Come in and sleep on it, eh? I'll lie down with you, keep you company until you drift . . .'

The house eventually falls silent and despite the need to pee, Ellie squeezes her eyes and wills sleep to come. She's almost nodded off when the wee prods again. It's hurting her tummy; it won't go away and suppose she wets the bed?

Pulling back her cherry cover, she slips from the mattress and opens the door. It's dark now, but she has to be brave like Mummy says. She pads towards the bathroom, but a noise or a movement stops her in her tracks. Her heart thrashing, she squints across the landing. What's going on? The door of the spare bedroom is ajar, hazy light's glimmering through.

A sudden sense of celebration replaces her fear. Her fingers and toes tingling with that 'special day' anticipation, she inches to the door and gently pushes. She holds her breath and peeps in. How strange. His face turned away, Daddy's standing next to the old ugly divan. He's wearing stripy pyjamas and clutching a pillow to his chest. Is he sleeping in here tonight? But his head is bobbing, his shoulders are shaking. He's making no sound. Is he laughing or crying? Mummy's at his side, her palms covering her cheeks.

And there're feathers, white feathers are everywhere.

Like snow, she thinks, smiling. How exciting. But as her daddy steps away, her gaze falls on the bed. There's hair, a thick spread of russet red, glowing like a sunset against the white of the sheets.

Daddy suddenly turns, then Mummy does too. 'Ellie?' Her shocked expression is replaced by her reassuring smile. She holds out her arm. 'Come on, love, back to bed. I think you've been sleepwalking.'

'I needed the loo . . .'

'Well, that's probably why!'

Wearing her patient look, Mummy waits while she pees. 'No need to wash your hands now, love. Just this once, you can do it in the morning.'

Her fingers tight on Ellie's shoulders, Mummy guides her back to bed. She straightens the duvet and feels her forehead. 'Oh Ellie, you're hot, love. You're not very well and you've had a bad dream.'

Though they are scrunched, tears ooze from Ellie's eyes. Something was wrong with Daddy's stare. Was it her fault? Was she in trouble? 'But Daddy. Daddy's face when he . . .'

Mummy laughs. 'What face?' She pops out two aspirins and hands her the water. 'A quick swallow, then straight back to sleep. Horrible mean dreams. It'll all be forgotten by morning.'

63

'Eleanor? Love? We've just got back. We saw your car in the drive and your sandals on the mat ...'

Her mouth dry, her head groggy, Ellie lifted her chin. She must have fallen asleep. But it couldn't have been for long. She was still on the floor next to the old divan, her arms around her knees, her fist clenched.

A spot of pink on each cheek and breathing heavily, Marian was standing at the door. 'How come you're in here? It's a bit chilly. You look pale. Are you all right, love? You should be careful; anything could fall. Are you coming downstairs? I'll put on the kettle ...'

Holding out her hand, Ellie unfurled her stiff fingers.

'Mum, I've remembered,' she said.

The sunshine beaming in through every window, her parents shuffled to the lounge. Like conjoined twins, they sat together on the sofa, their faces ashen, their eyes wide. Maurice was wearing frameless spectacles Ellie hadn't seen before. They made him appear insubstantial and frail.

So childlike, so innocent, so afraid.

Her heart squeezing, she stared. Was she really going to do this? Would it be better to leave and say nothing?

As though she was in charge, she perched stiffly in the armchair opposite. Like a boss or a teacher, ready with reprimands. More like a bloody judge. But she didn't feel angry, just inordinately weary and sad.

She brushed a tear from her nose. 'I've remembered that night, the night you . . .' Clearing the clot of emotion from her throat, she looked at her father. 'The night you suffocated Diana, Dad.'

Opening her fist, she held out her palm and showed them her treasure. A soft feather, a single white plume, dancing from the tremble in her hand.

The silence heavy, her parents gazed and said nothing. The world swayed and Ellie searched for air. Perhaps she'd got it wrong. Maybe it had been a dream.

But the feather; this feather was real. Wasn't it?

The disorientation dizzying, she took a quick breath, but before she could speak Maurice let out a piercing yelp. 'It's not true! It's not true.' His cheeks spattered with sudden tears, he turned to his wife. 'Tell her, Marian. Tell her!'

Marian patted his knee. 'There's nothing to tell, love.'

But he jerked away and pointed at Ellie. 'Didn't you hear what she just said?'

Marian sighed. 'There's nothing to tell, love,' she repeated, peering at Ellie. 'As I said on the phone, Dad sent Diana away. She was becoming a nuisance, turning up most weeks, asking for you. She even slept in the greenhouse one time. We didn't want to scare or upset you. Dad didn't like having to do it, but he had to for you.' She squeezed her husband's shoulder. 'You just sent her away, didn't you, love?'

He didn't appear to hear. He'd taken off his glasses and was examining his hands. Though his heavy tears were still falling, he was turning them forwards and back, peering at his nails.

Intense anger flew in; Ellie gritted her teeth. Her bloody mother was still doing it. Even now she was covering for Maurice and making excuses for him. It wasn't a dream, she knew that. She *saw* him; she saw his pale guilty face, she saw his bony white knuckles gripping the pillow. And she heard Marian's words: *'It'll all be forgotten by morning.'*

Rage clogged her chest. Her father had done something deeply, deeply dreadful and yet her mum was still protecting him and not her only child. Always Maurice, bloody Maurice, claustrophobic Maurice. It was no surprise Marian had needed her breather holiday every year; no wonder she'd been desperate to escape.

She exhaled long and hard. But these people were her parents; this man was her only birth family. She had to stay calm and think it through.

Taking a steadying breath, she looked at her mum. 'I saw him,' she began, her voice emerging staccato. 'I saw him, Mum. I clearly remember it now. You can't excuse him this time . . .'

But Marian had turned to Maurice. 'Come on now, love,' she was saying, rubbing his back. Then to Ellie, 'Oh dear. He's upset, as you can see. You know he hasn't been well, he's meant to be resting, so . . . I'm sorry, Eleanor, but I think it's best if you leave. We can talk about it another—'

Abruptly lurching from her touch, he fell at Ellie's knees, the words rushing out. 'She was already dead. I was asleep when Marian came for me. It was too late to do anything.' He gazed with imploring pale eyes. 'I thought she was messing, a silly game, but she wouldn't wake up.' He smacked his ear. 'I listened for her breath; put my head to her chest. Nothing. So I shook her and shook her, praying for a gasp of air. She wouldn't move; she wouldn't breathe, not even when I begged.'

Covering his head with his arms, he rocked back and forth. Finally he spoke, his voice high and querulous. 'I was left to sort it all out.' He lifted his shaking hands. 'Have you any idea what it's like to touch a dead body, limp and warm and heavy and lifeless? Then to dig and dig, to pick up every damned feather? Not a night has gone by without seeing her. Her dead accusing eyes staring at me.' He keened again. 'And if they unearth our garden, they'll find her.'

A weight of shock, her mind sluggish, Ellie struggled to think. Already dead? But the pillow and the feathers . . .

And her mother's soft voice through the crack in the window: *'Oh love, you're so tired and overwhelmed. Come in and sleep on it, eh? I'll lie down with you, keep you company until you drift . . .'*

Ellie tried to exhale. Like a grip on her throat, realisation was choking her. Marian, her mother. Of course it was her: steely, determined and cold.

Marian stood. Her back was poker straight, her expression wan but placid.

'Diana came here that night. She was drunk and wouldn't listen to reason. I persuaded her to sleep on it. We lay down together on the old bed and when she passed out, I pressed the pillow on her face until it was over,' she said calmly. 'She was in such a state it was best for her, really; best for everyone.' She looked towards Maurice. 'She didn't know and it was quick. I didn't tell Dad until afterwards.'

Ellie gaped. More excuses? Another lie? But her dad was still quietly whimpering as he examined his nails. No, this was finally the truth. And the bird table, of course. She had gone to bed one night and in the morning it had moved, the soil freshly dug beneath it.

Kissing Maurice softly on his forehead, Marian helped him to the sofa. 'I've told you a hundred times, love. Neither the new high speed train nor the tram will come near here. We're not moving anywhere and it'll be Eleanor's house one day. She'll look after it; the woods, the birds and the garden. You've got to stop worrying; everything will be fine.' She turned to Ellie. 'Won't it, Eleanor?' she asked softly, but that steeliness was there.

Folding her hands, she leaned forward. 'I had no choice, love. I had to do it for you and for us.' Her gaze was clear and untroubled. 'You see, she ... Diana ... she'd been in a car accident and she'd lost both her lover and her unborn child. It deranged her, the grief, the hopelessness and the loss. It was terrible. But she wanted to take you away from us. Not just for a holiday, but for ever. Of course it wasn't what we'd agreed or good for you, but she wouldn't listen to reason. She said she'd lost everything already, so had nothing more to lose by creating a scandal, going to the police or the courts. I couldn't have that, love. I wasn't going to risk losing you. And of course there was Dad. I couldn't put him through the humiliation of people knowing, could I?' She smiled a small smile. 'Diana was in a very bad place, love; it was best for her, too.'

At a surge of renewed sobbing, they both turned to Maurice.

'I'll put on the kettle, love. A cup of tea is just what we all need.' Her eyes glossy with tears, Marian looked at Ellie. 'Will you tell Dad that the train won't come through here, just like the motorway didn't? He's been so very worried. It's been on his mind most days. For a long, long time.'

Almost frozen, Ellie stared at her father's wretched face. He'd missed a feather. Just one escaped feather hiding between the cold wooden floorboards.

What now? Was her parents' secret hers, too? Though the truth had been acknowledged, would it be hidden again, deeply buried like Diana? She didn't know; she didn't know. But she had to say something.

She stepped to her dad and reached for his trembling hand. 'Mum's right. The train won't come through here, I promise.'

Tears had washed the colour from his eyes. 'Promises,' he said eventually, as though the word had just landed. He touched her cheek. 'I made you a faithful one.'

She looked at him enquiringly.

'All those years ago I promised you a pet. I truly meant it, Eleanor. You'd been such a good girl and you'd waited so patiently.' He glanced at his fingers. 'I'm so sorry I couldn't keep it.'

His keening started again. 'But dogs have heightened senses, don't they? They sniff and explore and dig,' he said between gulps of air. He looked at her pleadingly. 'You understand, don't you? Bones; they like bones, too. Suppose she was brought to the surface . . . '

Shoving away the dreadful imagery, Ellie swallowed. 'I understand, Dad. I do.'

64

Though almost paralysed by shock, three halting days of Ellie's life had stumbled by. What to do about Marian, Maurice and her terrible discovery had been an overwhelming cycle of worry and indecision. Disabled by anxiety, she'd struggled to absorb anything else. It hadn't been helped by repeated phone calls from Marian. Her last words before Ellie left Woodlands on Tuesday were: 'Everything is all right now, isn't it, Eleanor?'

Ellie hadn't been able to reply then or since. She didn't know what she should or would do.

Today was the start of her and Cam's 'maiden' weekend away, as he described it. To guarantee a full day in Derbyshire, they had set off for Marple Bridge 'first thing', but once they arrived at the Walshes' bungalow, Ellie asked Cam not to rush her; it was important to settle in Jake before they whizzed off to Cam's secret location in the Dales. She hadn't spent a night without all three sons before, and while she was very much *up* for their trip, it felt strange and unsettling to leave them behind.

Harry and Jake pelted to the back garden, shortly followed by

Sean and Cam, but Toby hung back with her, as though there was something he wanted to say.

'Are you all right, love?' she asked him.

'Yes, it just feels weird and . . .'

He looked teary. But he was her eldest; he probably felt responsible for his brothers. 'I know. I feel a bit odd too,' she replied. 'But it's only for one night, so I'll see you tomorrow.'

'Mum?' He abruptly clutched her around the chest. 'You're not ill, are you?' he said into her shoulder.

'Of course not! Why would you—'

'When we came home on Tuesday, you'd been crying. And since then, you've been really sad and—'

'Hi, Toby. Do you like coconut cookies? You know, while they're still hot?' a soft voice cut in.

Toby spun to the sound. Holding a tea towel, Katrina had appeared in the hallway.

He looked at his feet. 'Yeah, sure.'

Neither child moved. 'You've let your hair grow longer. It suits you,' Katrina said, sounding remarkably like her mum.

Toby rubbed his head. 'Yeah, thanks.'

Ellie smiled at Sean's eldest. 'They smell delicious, Katrina.'

She breathed out her relief at the interruption. Cam had been blind to her inward struggles, but her sensitive Toby had noticed, bless him. The thought brought a burn to her nose, but she sniffed it away. She was a little more with it today, thank God. And whatever she decided about her parents, it could wait. Right now, she was determined to be positive for her son, her family and herself. She nodded to the kitchen. 'Shall we go and inspect them, Toby?'

'Yeah, sure.'

She followed them into the sweet-scented room.

'Mum and I just took them out.' Her expression serene, Katrina

335

stood at the counter and detached the dough from the baking parchment. Toby looked on dumbly, his eyes on her slim fingers.

You are special, you must know that.

With a jolt of discomfort Ellie focused on Ciara's slim back. It was time to say her goodbyes and start her weekend adventure with Cam.

'Ciara? Thank you so much for—'

'Shall we take these outside and see what the others are doing?' Katrina said to Toby.

'Yeah, sure,' he replied.

'Have a great day, love. See you tomorrow,' Ellie said, catching his worried glance as he sloped out. Then to Ciara: 'It's very good of you to have the boys, thank you so much.'

Still turned away, Ciara was washing a mountain of baking equipment and oven trays at the sink. Apparently absorbed in her task, she didn't reply for several beats. Then, as though finally registering her presence, she twisted around. 'Oh Ellie.' Her glance was tense and distracted. 'Yes, that's fine; don't you be worrying about it,' she said, returning to her chore. 'I've got so many children running in and out of here, another three won't make any difference.'

Feeling rather shamed, Ellie looked at the shambles on the breakfast table. Scattered cutlery, half-eaten bowls of cereal, egg cups and shell, plates smeared in setting yolk. And at its centre there were freshly baked rolls. She'd never stopped to think how tough it must be for this poor woman to cope with six children. Bloody hell; the daily grind of making meals for *eight*, the washing, the ironing, making beds and changing nappies, let alone the school run and grocery shopping.

Selfish Ellie. She should've brought a bunch of flowers; she *must* buy Ciara a thank-you gift in Derbyshire; be kinder, more charitable too. Bending to the table, she began stacking the soiled crockery.

Ciara jerked back and wiped her hands on her apron. 'Oh, no, Ellie. Don't trouble yourself with the dishes.' She looked exhausted, her usual Trojan spirit all gone. 'You don't want to be getting that nice top dirty.' As though visualising a stain, she stared at Ellie's T-shirt. Then her eyes focused again. 'Have you got time for a coffee?'

Charitable, Ellie. Yet Cam's instruction to drop the boys and leave 'without pissing about' thumped in her head. But Ciara continued to speak. 'You'd do me a favour if you stayed for five minutes. It'd give me an excuse to sit down.'

Though she said it in a bright way, there seemed a desperation behind her words, so Ellie pulled out a chair. 'I'd love one, Ciara, thanks.' And though the mix of food aromas was almost cloying, 'It smells lovely in here. You have been busy.'

Ciara fired up the hob, placed the old-fashioned kettle on the flames, then sat down heavily. She put her head in her hands before sitting up straight. 'Oh yes, the baking. The bread rolls are fresh. Help yourself if you're peckish.'

She looked on the verge of tears. 'Are you all right, Ciara?' Ellie asked. 'Three children is tough, but six! You do so brilliantly, but you must get fed up at times.'

'Keeping the children happy is easy,' she blurted. She pressed her fingers to her mouth.

Bloody hell; what was coming? Ellie silently gazed.

'Well, I don't suppose it's any secret that Sean just about tolerates me,' she continued. 'I try my best, I really do, but days go by when he hardly says a word to me. He's fine in front of the children, of course, but when we're alone, he has nothing to say.'

Large tears rolled down her pale face. She roughly wiped them with her palms.

'I know he doesn't love me, but he adores his kids, so I say: "Wouldn't it be lovely if we had another child?" I fall pregnant

337

and while I carry the baby he's tender towards me. For those nine months I exist. Then the little one is born, and he's gone again, withdrawn back into himself.'

Somewhere beyond the kitchen, a baby began to cry. Panicked at the sharp bawl, Ellie made to stand, but Ciara reached out to stop her. 'It's all right, Katrina will see to Georgie.'

Now she'd begun her tale, she seemed determined to go on.

'I didn't want to move from Ireland. Why would I? My home, my family, my sisters ... But he applied for the job here, said that would make him happy.'

Stunned at the revelations, Ellie searched for reasons. So, Sean had upped sticks to Manchester because it would make him happy. Why? Confusing images flashed in her head. Sean's dark-haired sister – was it something to do with her? Then one of him behind the knotted-pine door. Had there been more men at uni? Was he bisexual? He and Ciara had lived in a remote Irish village ... Perhaps a leopard – or an Irish Beast – didn't change its spots after all. Did Ciara know he was unfaithful? Was that the reason for the intent set of her jaw?

She felt a guilty flush. That non-kiss; God, how she'd craved more.

But Ciara was still speaking. 'So I agreed and for a while things seemed to change. But he's been so distant again, so restless when he's here. Even church on Sundays ... Well, he's reluctant. So last night I suggested that we try for another child.'

Almost hypnotically, the tears dripped again. Ellie leaned forward to say *something*, but Ciara continued, her voice almost a whisper.

'But Sean said no. No more babies. And he was kind. That was the worst of it. He held me and he said he was sorry but there wouldn't be any more babies.'

Wiping her face with her apron, she took a deep shuddery

breath. Then, her eyes hollow, she nodded. 'I know he'll never leave me, but he'll never love me again either.' She grasped Ellie's fingers. 'Oh Lord, oh Lord. I've no idea how I'll bear it.'

Dazed and emotional, Ellie quietly left the kitchen and stepped into the cool hallway.

What happened just then? As though it would give answers, she peered at a Walsh family photograph on the sideboard. The kettle had whistled like a shrill scream in the silence, then Ciara had snatched back her hand and abruptly stood. 'Look at the hour. No time for coffee; you'll be needing to get off.'

Ellie had opened her arms to offer some comfort, but Ciara shook her head and stepped away. She'd lifted her chin, that heart-rending stoicism firmly back in place. 'It is as it is. I'm sorry to have troubled you with my woes. You're on your way for a lovely weekend, so you are. You don't need me putting a cloud over it.' She'd briefly touched Ellie's arm then. 'It's just my silly chat. Time of the month, probably. Forget that I said anything, won't you? Cameron doesn't need to—'

'Absolutely. I won't. Of course not.'

'Close the door on your way out, would you?'

Disorientation hitting, Ellie leaned against the wall and tried to breathe away the nausea. The past and swimming memories were making her dizzy again. They frightened her, if she was honest. She *had* to shake them off and get back to positivity. The *hour* was indeed here; it was time to start her maiden weekend with Cam.

She strode to the decking, looked down to the sloping garden and absently counted the kids she expected to see. Harry was with Sean's middle three boys, Toby with Liam, Jake was carrying the cat. Who else was missing? Children were missing. Oh God, where was the baby? That's right: Katrina had the little one; she'd heard Georgie's cries earlier. It was fine; he was somewhere, he was safe.

Her eyes swept the grass again. No sign of Sean and Cam. Where were they? They must have come in when she was having *that* conversation. Returning to the house, she listened. Yup, voices from the lounge. Blithely pushing at the wood, her heart almost stopped. What the . . . ? His head back, his legs spread, Sean was lolling in the armchair.

The scene almost blinding her, she dumbly gawped, then today and reality snapped back. It was that flash from the past yet again, but this time so much clearer. A man giving Sean oral sex. Almost expecting Ciara's pallid face behind her, she stupidly looked over her shoulder.

Cam's voice broke through from his place on the sofa. He stood. 'Finally! Ready to go? I'll just say bye to the boys.'

She pulled back to let him pass, but couldn't drag her eyes away from Sean. She could almost *taste* the memory and it hurt.

His eyebrows knitted, he stared. 'Are you OK, Ellie?'

The image sparked again. Dark belly hair, slick with sweat. Eyes closed, face caught in rapture. And the other man? Yes, kneeling on the floor, his arms muscled and taut, and that bobbing motion she'd dreamed of.

Languid, too languid, too slow, too *meaningful*.

God, it had been more than youthful experimentation. And the other guy's back – his spine, the slats of his ribs either side – there were welts and bruising, old and new. What had Cam said of Sean before they met? *Brawling . . . fist fighting.*

And those words: *Peak experience, infliction of bodily harm.*

Had Sean used other men as punchbags? For *pleasure*? Oh God. 'Ellie?'

As he walked towards her, another memory tumbled in. Her box room at Alston Terrace. The Johnny Cash poster. The torn canvas, Sean's soft, emotional expression. And the feel of his strong and safe arms.

'*You are special, you must know that.*'

His voice broke through again. 'Ellie? What's wrong?'

Deep disappointment. 'Nothing.'

'Talk to me, Ellie.'

'I thought I was . . .'

'Was what?'

Special, she almost whispered, but she shook her head. God knows what was wrong with her. Sean's past and present life, his relationships, his business was not hers. He'd been a supportive, helpful friend of late. To both her and Cam. That was all.

And it was fine, it really was. She had what she'd wanted from the moment she met him: Cam, her lovely Cameron. He was hers and he had been for years. They had three beautiful boys.

She smiled as the happy images flooded in. Cam in a plaster cast that very first day; chucking snowballs and belly laughing; feeding her food from Iranian to Indonesian; listening to music in the early hours and cuddling; the sheer look of delight when they reconnected in the wine bar. '*Come here, kiss me. Promise you'll never run away again.*'

As though reading her thoughts, the man himself appeared and pecked her lips. 'All set, my beautiful girl?'

Unable to look at Sean, she reached for Cam's hand and tugged him away. 'Come on, then. *Chop-chop.*'

A Cam laugh behind her. 'See you tomorrow, mate. Keen missis, or what? Looks like I'm in for a bloody hot night.'

65

It was odd, just the two of them travelling along the leafy country roads in the car. Ellie found herself turning to make comments to the boys in the back as the world outside became larger and greener.

'*Look, there's the entrance to Lyme Park. Remember the picnic with the Walshes?*' she almost asked, but Cam hadn't been there that day. He'd been working away. Absent.

His *absence* and the consequences. Her stupid insecurities and the way she'd stopped thinking straight about all sorts of things. Her 'connection' with Sean, in particular. She hadn't even recognised it was there until this morning. But it was fanciful and illusory, simply born of her temporary dependency. He'd been there when she had needed him, but it was over now.

'It was convenient to drop the boys at the Walshes',' Cam commented, as though reading her mind. 'Halfway there. Well, maybe a tenth, and it beats leaving them for a weekend of sugar and television with my folk. Though Dad told me a funny joke in the pub last night. How did it go?' He scrunched his face in thought, then laughed as he repeated it.

'Only racist and homophobic this time, then?' she replied drily.

He grinned. 'Don't knock it. His gay mate from Jamaica was laughing the loudest. It's the way he tells 'em, as they say.'

Shaking her head, she returned the smile. 'I'll give him that. Stuart's a very good mimic. I think he might be a loss to the acting world.'

'Praise from Ellie! I must remember to tell him. Though we wouldn't want to bring on another heart murmur from the shock.' He reached for her hand. 'Seriously, though, I'm glad you're in fine fettle for our maiden voyage. The first weekend of many.' Then after a beat, 'Was Ciara OK? She seemed a bit strained when we left. Quiet and subdued? Not even one sermon today.'

Surprised that he'd noticed, Ellie pictured the poor woman's broken face. Who'd have guessed she hid such deep, deep unhappiness? 'I think she's a bit fed up. You know, feeling unappreciated.'

She almost added, 'Which, in my testosterone-rich home, I get!' to lighten the abrupt change in mood. But she wouldn't go there, even as a quip; she had no intention of being the *me, me, me* Ellie Wilson Cam had described, ever again. Besides, she was lucky to have him in her life. They weren't man and wife and he never declared his love, but she *felt* loved today.

Lost in thought, she absently gazed at the passing countryside. Ciara and her need for another baby to validate their relationship, to secure tenderness; like her own desire for the girl she'd never had, she absolutely 'got' that, too. The thought taking root, she glanced at Cam. He was clearly making an effort . . . Sure, she was in her late thirties, but maybe it wasn't too late to try again.

That old sensation of hope seemed to swell in her belly. 'Perhaps Ciara needs some of this,' she said, trying to control it. 'A magical mystery tour to Matlock of all places.'

'Don't knock it, woman. Not everyone gets treated to a night in a Grade II listed hotel. Wait until you see it. It has a resident ghost, apparently.'

'Really?'

She inwardly sighed. Haunted by the past. It would be funny if wasn't so true. What the hell would she do about her parents? Since Tuesday, her mind had swung like a pendulum – from brushing it under the carpet to doing the 'right thing'; from euphemisms like 'smothered while sleeping' or 'put out of her misery' to the brutal reality: Marian Wilson had *murdered* Ellie's birth mother. She'd ended the life of her own sister, for God's sake. Ellie's father had covered up the crime; he'd dug a hole and buried the body in their garden. Part of her wanted to share her appalling discovery, but she couldn't do that. Not yet; not until she knew it was absolutely the right decision. And, anyway, who would she tell? Hen, Nina? Hardly. And Cam? Where would she even start? Sean had been the first person she'd considered. He'd felt like her security net, a safe pair of hands, and perhaps more than that. But this morning and that blinding realisation ... She'd been a fool; he wasn't who she'd thought, he wasn't the man she'd started to—

Cam coughed. Had she fallen weirdly silent? She glanced over and smiled. 'I hope Casper isn't sleeping with us tonight.'

'The bed will be big enough, by all accounts.' He beamed. 'So here's the lowdown for this evening. We're having a six-course à la carte dinner with a taster wine for each course. Just you and me in a private dining room. We'll sit at a posh table and watch chefs prepare the food through a window to the kitchen; we'll eat until we're fit to burst, drink too much fine wine, then relax in a deluxe suite with a four-poster wide enough for the whole Walsh family. Who could ask for more?'

'No one. Thank you, dearest Cameron; it sounds wonderful.'

A surprising choice, but a client of his business had recommended it. And they would be walking, too: now Cam was fit enough, they'd do a 'long trek' in the Derbyshire Dales with 'no kids trailing behind us and moaning', as he put it.

Ellie sharply inhaled. Oh God, the boys. At times she forgot her ultimate decision about Maurice and Marian would impact them too. They were their beloved grandparents after all. It was far easier to say and do nothing; they'd never find out. But then again, they might; one day Diana could surface; a long-dead woman with their DNA . . .

Trying to ignore the damned pendulum, she gazed through the window as they sped towards Bakewell. The landscape was lit by morning sunshine. Undulating green fields, drystone walls, scattered sheep, cows and horses. '*Look, Billy-goats, Harry*,' she almost declared. Instead, she turned to Cam. 'Jake will be OK, won't he?'

'He will. Do you hear that?'

'No. What?'

He grinned. 'Silence. Close your eyes and make the most of it.'

Bordering on sleep, she jerked back from oblivion as the car abruptly swerved.

'Sorry. I nearly missed the turning,' Cam said, slowing down as they climbed up a driveway lined with thick, glossy evergreens. A stately home popped out at the top. Dark and handsome, the hotel was surrounded by pristine sloping lawns and colourful flowerbeds. Cam followed the signs to a side car park and pulled up.

Clearly pleased at the setting, he whistled. 'First impressions?' he asked.

Ellie gazed at the glistening mere behind the old building. 'It's perfect, Cam.'

She climbed out and inhaled the heady blend of aromas – the pine trees, cut grass, flowering shrubs and summer blooms. She stilled and listened. Yes the chirrup of skylarks, too. Batting away the nagging image of the bird table at Woodlands, she turned full circle. For the first time in years, she itched to paint the stunning scene.

'Look at all the vibrant colours, Cam. And the topiary. It's as though they've used nail scissors they're so perfect.'

She pictured Marian's neat side garden and felt a sickening jolt. That was the woman who'd murdered her real mother. But she'd been a solid, loving and attentive mum; the only one she'd ever known. She tried for a smile. 'I had a go at it once, when I was a girl. Mum tried to guide me, but it isn't as easy as it looks.'

Though allowed a peep in, their suite wasn't quite ready, so they left their overnight bags with the concierge, changed trainers for walking boots and collected a selection of rambling routes from reception. They headed to a bench overlooking the lake. The breeze ruffling his hair, Cam carefully studied each map.

'Which one are we going for?' Ellie asked, stretching out her bare legs.

'This one looks good. We walk along the Derwent path to Darley Dale. There's a pub stop halfway.' He chuckled. 'We won't walk past it. You'll see why. We can work up a thirst and be rewarded with one of your holiday lagers.' He kissed her nose. 'See? I was listening.'

'So you were. Who knew Cameron Hastings had such hidden talents?'

The sun warm on their faces, they set off. Holding hands, they chatted amiably about the news and the boys, last night's television drama, which country for the family holiday and whether to try wood flooring in the lounge. Absorbing the colours and smells, the butterflies, the birds and honeyed air, they tramped along velvety green pathways, the perimeters of rough fields, then across a stile to a shady track that ran the length of a fast-flowing stream.

Cam didn't talk about Sean; he didn't ask about Ellie's parents or mention his working future. Ellie breathed; freedom from that constant cycle of angst was sublime.

An hour into their amble, they climbed a low hill that finally led to a lane. Cam pointed to a white-rendered building in the distance. 'Not far now.' Then when they got closer, 'What do you reckon? Is this the right one?' he asked with a grin.

The Halfway Tavern was more than just toasty inside.

'An open fire in August is a new one on me,' Ellie commented as she shedded her thin jacket. 'Still, I'm thirsty and starving, so I'm not complaining.'

Cam snorted. 'More Djibouti than Derbyshire, it would seem. This one?' He stepped to a rustic table and pulled out the heavy chair. 'Your seat with the view of the room, madam.'

A nod to Maurice. Oh God. Was Cam going to ask about him now? She held her breath, but he didn't. Instead, he sat opposite and scooped up a dog-eared menu. 'Holiday lager for two, methinks.'

'And a jug of tap water please.' Water; how insignificant that experience seemed now. She studied the food options and laughed. 'Will it be steak or steak?' she asked.

'I might surprise you and go for the fish,' he replied. 'It's probably to keep the werewolves at bay. The roaring fire, that is, not the cod.'

'Ah, so you're keeping the *stake* in case of vampires?'

He laughed. 'Funny. Not bad for a girl.'

'Actually, if we're being technical, I think werewolves roam the Yorkshire Moors, not the Derbyshire Dales. I'm going for the ploughman's.'

'What? Not the garlic mussels?'

She stuck her boots out from under the table. 'I feel it matches my attire.'

Cam ordered the beef, rare. 'That's actually bleeding,' she laughed. 'Raw meat. Perhaps you *are* the werewolf.'

'Nah, not me,' he snorted. 'What you see is what you get.'

She nodded. Yes, her straightforward Cameron. Perhaps he could be carelessly insensitive or unreliable at times, but he was still that open and uncomplicated boy she had adored. Not evasive or guarded, even disingenuous . . . But she was over that now.

Finally replete, they made their way to the exit. A handsome German shepherd and its owner were coming in. Ellie stood back and swallowed. There it was again, that damned pendulum. However negatively she tried to think about her father, her mind always came back to the last thing he'd said. He hadn't forgotten his promise to buy her a dog; he knew he'd let her down. It hadn't been the casual, unloving change of heart she'd supposed. The poor man *couldn't* keep his vow; he'd lived in terror of Diana being unearthed for nearly thirty years.

She reverted to Cam's quizzical gaze. 'That fire has deceived me,' she commented, rubbing her arms. 'The wind feels a bit chilly now.' Looking up to the horizon, she pointed. 'That must be Oker Hill. The story goes that when two local brothers left the village to seek their fortune they each planted a tree. One of the brothers never returned, so only one tree survives, hence the nickname One Tree Hill.' She laughed at Cam's incredulous expression. 'Don't worry, I'm not the fountain of all things Derbyshire. I just read about it in the loo. It looks a little lonely all by itself.'

He patted his belly. 'God, I'm so stuffed I need to lie down.' He squinted at the skyline, then gesticulated to a row of trees so tightly knitted that they resembled one toothbrush-shaped tree. 'Whereas that's a close ménage. I guess that must be—'

'The Toothbrush Tree.' Yes, a tight and loving family. Perfect. Smiling, Ellie held out her hand. 'We can't not walk there. Come on, dearest Cameron; let's lie under the Toothbrush Tree.'

66

The rays warm on their shoulders, they strolled down a stony pathway and across a thistly field. Finding a shallow area of the river, they tested the mossy stepping stones with the tips of their boots before crossing it. Then they climbed up the soft hill towards the dense flora at its peak.

The temperature abruptly dipped at the top. Though the 'family' trees did indeed hug, the lack of sunshine cooled the sweat on Ellie's skin, like a shiver. She stopped to catch her breath, then leaned in to read the memorial plaque attached to a pine bench.

Like a bird table of remembrance.

A wave of sadness swooped. No wonder she'd carried an overwhelming sense of loss throughout her adult life. That constant feeling someone was missing, had died or been taken away. The tears burned behind her eyes. She had lost her aunty and friend; she'd never get to know her birth mother. And that dank, familiar scent of timber, vegetation and rotting leaves ... Oh God; she could never return to her childhood home. How many times had she blithely fed the sparrows and inhaled that redolent, happy smell?

No, neither she nor her children would ever go back to Woodlands; a body was buried there.

She breathed through the sharp emotion and turned to Cam. 'Shall we sit here for a minute?'

'Yup.'

Listening to the tussle of breeze through the thick foliage, Ellie sipped water in silence. Then Cam reached out an arm and she rested against him.

'You know I'll have to get back to work proper soon,' he started. Then after a moment, 'Sean thinks I should keep foreign trips to a minimum, share the load with Tim. He's right; it's only fair.'

Hmm. Sean *and* work. 'That's good to hear.'

Indeed it was. The hope popped again. If another baby came along, Cam would be around more. And in fairness to Sean, his suggestion meant she wasn't the one asking or showing her *neediness*. Another thought landed. 'So what about Susie and her anxiety when Tim isn't around?'

'They're getting divorced. Apparently she met someone else walking the chihuahua or whatever that ratty canine was. Ironic, eh?'

'Cam! You didn't tell me—'

'Only just found out myself,' he replied easily. He looked up. 'I think we're sitting under the Toothbrush Tree. Are we going to lie down?'

It was the usual swift change of subject, but she'd let that one go. 'I guess we should now we've made it.'

Cam fired out his waterproof like a man with a cape. 'Fair Queen, do sit.'

She laughed and climbed on it. 'Hmm. Didn't Sir Walter Raleigh end up beheaded for treachery?'

He hunkered down too. 'It's nice to have some time together. Just you and me,' he said, pulling her close and pecking her hair.

Ellie gazed at the patterns of cloudy blue through the gaps in the leaves. She took a quick breath. Under the *family* of trees it felt right. She propped her head on her hand. 'Cam . . . before I'm too old, can we try again for another baby? I mean, properly try.'

He pulled a face. 'Come on, Ellie, I don't think so, do you? Having to start all over again. Nappies and tantrums and no sleep. Nah, we're good as we are. The boys are happy and even Jake seems settled so . . . '

'All the more reason why the timing is perfect.'

His expression was dismissive. Could she tell him about that hole in her heart? The new imperative to fill it? 'Please think about it, Cam. It's hard to explain, but it's something I need—'

'Stop.' He pulled himself up. 'Stop, Ellie, I'm not going there.'

'Going where?'

'Into another of your pregnancy fantasies.'

Ellie sat up too. 'That's a bit harsh. Sure, I've asked you to consider another child from time to time, but it's hardly a *fantasy*.' Anger flared. 'It's bloody insulting, actually.'

He snorted. 'Come on, Ellie, it isn't as though you don't have a history.'

'History of what?'

'Fantasies. Saying you were pregnant when you weren't.' He glared, the easy-going Cam abruptly gone. 'Don't act all innocent. At university. Making it up to get attention. Like the black moods, black make-up and stupid black paintings. The arty piercings and angst and bitten nails, too. I've no idea why I didn't twig for so long. But I sure did that night.' He shook his head. 'Just freaky, pathetic attention seeking. It was embarrassing, humiliating—'

'I didn't—'

'Yes you did. Why do you think I hate talking about those

fucking days?' He lifted a finger to stop her talking. 'No, just don't. You weren't pregnant then and you're not going to be again. Ever. So that's it. OK?'

Her heart thrashing, she stared at his flickering eyes. 'Ever. What does that mean?'

He stood and shook his head. 'Let's get going.'

Dread sizzled like acid in her chest. 'Ever,' she repeated. 'What the hell does that mean, Cameron?'

He strode away, but turned back. 'Leave it, Ellie.'

'I'm not going to—'

She flinched as he stepped close to her face. He mimicked her voice. *'Let's have another, Cam. A baby girl would be so nice.'* His spittle splashed her cheeks. 'Doing my head in. Constantly pecking. Did you never work it out? Did you never wonder why you hadn't got pregnant again after Harry? Because I didn't want any more. Three was already too many. Like those fucking rabbits, it was entrapment, a life sentence.' He stared. 'I had the snip, a sterilisation, a fucking *vasectomy*, Ellie. Do you understand now? Can we move on?'

She stood frozen for seconds. As though swaying with the trees, her mind was floaty, refusing to focus. A *vasectomy*? Cam had had the snip on the quiet? Realisation crawled through her body. Month after month he'd let her anticipate another baby. The tears had gradually dried up, replaced with resignation, but not a period had gone by without that sharp slash of disappointment and the thump of deep loss.

He hadn't told her; he hadn't told her. Self-centred and cruel. And so bloody unfair.

Shock was replaced by sudden outrage. 'How could you, Cam?' she yelled. 'How could you be so utterly selfish?'

'No, Ellie. No. No. No! Don't you fucking start—' he roared, his fists clenched, his face puce.

Afraid he'd strike out, she cowered and scrunched her whole body. But a blow didn't come. Instead, he closed his eyes and breathed loudly through his nose. Then he turned tail and stalked off.

67

The cold hitting, Ellie came round with a jerk. What the ...? A rock as a pillow, she was lying on the mossy, rusty ground. Certain someone was behind her, she sat up and slowly rotated her head. A sycamore. God, that was right. After Cameron tromped off, she'd gone back to the bench and stayed there for some time, trying to work through her anger, her incredulity, her confusion.

Something irreversible had just happened. A shift in dynamics that could never be put right.

The shock now slapped again. Cameron, her partner, the father of her kids. The man who was *entrapped* and serving a life sentence. Who the hell was he? It was as though he had ripped off a mask and revealed a completely different person. But in truth she'd seen glimpses before, snatches of an enraged and frustrated being trying to climb from his skin. One who was ready to pounce and ...

Trying to breathe through the anxiety, she lowered her head. Cam lunging and ready to strike ... Yes, she could now picture it clearly, but that incident hadn't been today. And other images from the past were seeping in. Too disturbing and overwhelming, she pushed them away.

So why was she still under the toothbrush canopy? She felt the earth beneath her legs and her bum. Exposed tree roots. That was right. Stiff from the cold, she'd finally got up from the bench, gathered Cam's waterproof and slung it around her shoulders. She hadn't felt ready to retrace her steps to the hotel, so she'd briskly walked in the other direction, then suddenly tripped, lost her footing and fallen on to her outstretched hand.

Lifting her left arm, she stared at her wrist. It was swollen already. As though demanding acknowledgement, the dull, throbbing pain abruptly hissed. Yes, she went flying and . . . She looked at the jagged stone. Had she bumped her head and been knocked unconscious? Or was it the upheaval and that desperate need to block it out by sleep or by hiding or by . . . She frowned. *Forgetting?*

Panic hit. Lost snatches of memory were now firing back. They didn't all make sense, but they frightened her.

Forcing her achy bones to work, she knelt and unzipped her bumbag with trembling fingers. Her mobile wasn't smashed, so that was something. A face reflected back as she stared at the screen. *Yes, Miss Eleanor*, that black-haired Goth girl who'd sat cross-legged at a candlelit coffee table, drinking shots and telling truths.

Tears seeped from her eyes. Her recall was fractured, but she could feel that girl's deep unhappiness, her devastating sensation of abandonment, of loss. And in truth, nothing had changed. She was still so alone; there was no one to turn to, neither her parents nor Cameron. And no longer Sean.

As she stood on jelly legs, she pictured the Goth girl testing the sharp point of her Stanley knife. Was this a breaking point? Was she back to that moment of sheer desolation? Perhaps. But she had three beautiful sons now. For them she'd pick herself up and go on.

*

Up hill and down dale, Ellie tromped. Half lit by evening sunshine, the rear of the hotel finally emerged beyond the pines. Weary beyond belief, she stopped for a breather and gazed. Ivy-clad elevations, smart balconies and panelled casements. A scintillating lagoon and neatly trimmed gardens. And a phantom, like Woodlands. But there was more than one ghost, wasn't there? The second, she'd forgotten, but she'd been haunted just the same.

She leaned against an ash tree. Could she lift another foot? Her walking boots had been so comfortable when she'd headed out hopefully, but they now felt like lead weights and her ankles were grazed where the leather had chafed.

Closing her eyes, she shuddered. She had to face the man in the mask. Though it had slipped before, she'd been cowardly and insecure – far easier to ignore the 'other' Cam and pretend the blips hadn't happened. His many 'omissions', too. But an omission was deception as much as a lie was, and this one was too huge to ignore.

She sighed. How good it would be to hide. Or sleep a thousand sleeps. During the roam back, her mind had been drowning with images and sounds, sensations, tastes and aromas, but she was floating above them for now. No, not bobbing on the surface, but paddling furiously like a swan. Some memories were too stunning; others didn't yet make much sense.

Numbness was easier.

She stumbled on, past a pretty bower and the topiary. Seeming to understand her completely, the sightless lion stared. Finally at the pillared front entrance, she stepped into the cool lobby. Would Cam be waiting in their room? Though she didn't glance his way, she sensed the concierge was watching inquisitively. Her muddy legs, she guessed, and perhaps windswept hair. Still, the guy worked at a hotel; he'd probably seen worse.

Not bothering to ask for a key, she made her way to the suite.

The heavy door was wedged ajar, so she took a resigned breath and walked in. Propped in an art deco armchair, Cam was facing the French windows. The voile beneath the thick brocade wafted a greeting.

He snapped around. 'Where have you been? I've been looking out . . .' He frowned. 'What happened?'

She didn't reply. She'd already caught herself in the wardrobe mirror and moved closer to look. Her hair on one side was matted, her temple smeared with clotted blood. She touched her skull. Yes, a lump and quite tender; she must have gashed it on the rock. Her wrist was still throbbing and smarting too. But that was fine; external pain she could handle.

She glanced at Cam. 'I tripped and fell.'

As though he'd actually hit her, he looked at his right palm. 'I suppose you want to talk?' he asked.

'Right now I really want a long soak.'

He nodded and stood. 'And I need a drink.'

Cam was back in his seat when she'd finished her bath. A bottle of spirits centred the Queen Anne table.

Jack Daniel's, of course.

Fighting the nausea, she closed her eyes. That sweet, liquorice smell; that overripe, earthy taste. The front room at Alston Terrace and the truth game, of course. Like Cam, she didn't want to go back there, but that's where it had all ended. No; where it had started.

He watched her towel dry her hair. When she gave up her attempt, he spoke. 'So what do you want to know?' He'd already quaffed a good inch and a half of the bottle, but didn't seem particularly drunk.

Tightening her robe, she sat on the bed, cross-legged like a girl. What *did* she want to know? Until now, she had suspended all contemplation save for her need for the loo and a bath; she'd absently watched the water spurt as the tub slowly filled and kept her mind shallow. Should she add bath oil? How to use the shower attachment for her hair. What could she manage with only one hand? Once she was in, would she be able to climb out?

Other thoughts had been too deeply traumatic to dwell on.

She came back to Cam's question. 'Just why, really.'

He sighed. 'Why, what?'

'Why the vasectomy? The snip. No. Why—'

No; he'd already told her that. She didn't want to hear his derision about her sons and what she'd thought was a happy life. But he'd already started to speak.

'What I said before ... I'm sorry; I didn't mean it.' He rubbed his face. 'I love the boys very much; you know that. It's just ... sometimes it gets too much. The domesticity, lack of freedom, autonomy. I feel resentful, I suppose, pissed off at being in a situation I didn't sign up for. And the thought of ending up squashed on a sofa, staring at the TV with nothing to say ... It does my head in. So I need to go out, get away from the drudgery.' He smiled thinly. 'Then I miss it.'

End up like bloody Stuart and Jaqs? Wanting to protest, Ellie frowned. But he was right in a way; she had been the baby instigator each time, and he had never put his scrawl on a wedding certificate. He hadn't deceived her about that.

Yawning, he continued. 'Even before we met ... a fucking geology degree? I was supposed to go to the States, a whole new life, adventure.' He snapped his fingers. 'Like that. In a split second, a tear and a pop, my sporting dreams were down the pan. Then other stuff happened ...'

He trailed off, so Ellie took a quick breath. 'Why a secret vasectomy?' she asked. 'Why not just talk to me, explain?'

He poured more whiskey and drank. 'I didn't want a drama.'

He spread his arms and laughed drily. 'Like this. Exactly like this. I'd had a belly full of . . . of *scenes* in my life already.'

He seemed to drift, inebriated after all, and she waited.

Eventually opening his eyes, he leaned forward and pointed. 'Ellie, my Ellie. You're such fun when you're well, but I didn't want to risk—'

'Well? I'm always well.' Fingering the word, she frowned. '*Well*. What's that supposed to mean, Cam?'

He stared for a beat before replying. 'You had two breakdowns at uni, Ellie. Both in that third year. Marian told me about them. She swore me to secrecy like a fucking Boy Scout.' He took another slug and squinted. 'First one at the beginning, before we met, before you moved in with us.'

She took a breath to put him straight, but he lifted a hand. 'You asked, so I'm telling you.' He ruffled his hair. 'Yeah, so . . . you must have lived somewhere else in Leeds first, with other students, I guess. You were ill. Went home to Woodlands, to your mum, for a bit. Then you came to us, to me and Sean and the others in Headingley. Yeah, a nervous breakdown, she said; that's why you arrived later than everybody else.'

'What? No, I . . . ' She instinctively touched her cheek. 'You know what happened, Cam. Someone burned me with a cigarette outside a nightclub. I came *later* to Alston Terrace because I was embarrassed to show my face. I wanted it to heal first.'

Rocking back in the chair, Cam shook his head. 'Then again – after that final, bizarre night. Another meltdown, or whatever your mum called it. I should've guessed from your freaky behaviour that evening . . . '

Falling silent, he narrowed his eyes as though picturing the scene. 'End of exams. All of us there, supposed to be happy. We drank, laughed, smoked, played the truth game and by morning you'd gone. You'd packed up during the night and fucked off home without saying a bloody word to any of us. We were your friends, Ellie. Me and Paul, Sylvie and Raj. Even Sean. Your *friends*. You just pissed off and dumped us.'

Ellie froze at the thought of Marian's words: *'Mental health blips or just the blues.'* Like her mother, Diana?

Cam didn't speak for a time. 'I was shocked, confused you'd gone. But when I thought about it, perhaps I was glad. The weird stuff you said that night. It was horrible.' He rubbed his skin again. 'God, I don't even know why I'm talking about it. We were different people then. All of us. Nineteen fucking years ago. You don't even remember—'

'I do, mostly I do . . . ' Closing her eyes, she breathed deeply and put the scrambled memories in order. Faces and pictures and voices. And the stench of weed mingling with the Tennessee malt. 'I did leave that night,' she said slowly. 'I was upset, I packed up my stuff and left the house. Yes, but not before— I needed to talk to Sean, so I—'

Oh God, it was then. The knot and *The Scream*. Pushing the pine door was then.

Bewildered, she blinked. 'So I went to Sean's bedroom and I saw—'

Pitching forward, Cam gawped. 'You saw us?'

'What? *Us?* No. I don't understand . . . '

But Cam had covered his face. When he lowered his hands, his expression was gobsmacked. 'Fucking hell. You saw me doing . . . that. Fuck. Fuck! Why did you never say anything?'

Dumb with shock, Ellie stared. The man with the welts and the bruising was Cam? She took a gulp of air. Oh my God. Sean and Cam; Cam and Sean. It was never simple friendship; they were lovers. Had it continued? Were they still? But Cameron Hastings . . . *gay?* Of all the people . . .

Surprised at the fresh anguish, she put a palm to her chest. But perhaps it made sense. 'You said you were in love with a person in the room,' she said slowly as the recall seeped back. 'That's what you said, Cam. You said you were in love with someone there. Your truth, that night.' Her throat swelled with emotion. 'Everyone laughed, thinking you meant me. And perhaps I did too, a morsel of hope because I wanted you so much. But you didn't fancy me, you never had, because you were gay.'

'No, not gay,' he protested. Then more quietly, his voice slurred, 'Not gay at all. No one else, ever. Just Sean.'

Swamped with fatigue, Ellie reached for a pillow and rested her head. Her mind was too scrambled to think straight. So Sean was . . . and Cam's injuries . . . what did it all mean?

Abruptly animating again, Cam topped up his tumbler and held it unsteadily aloft. 'Here's to the most humiliating night of my life,' he said, swallowing the contents in one gulp. He coughed, then guffawed. 'What would my dad say if he knew?' Though his voice was becoming increasingly garbled, he tried to mimic his father's gruff tones. '*My son tried to give his best mate a blow job, to turn him, to make him love him.* That'd go down a treat in The Sportsman.'

The words finally reaching her, Ellie sat up. What exactly was Cam saying?

He turned to the French windows and was silent for a time. Then he came back with a weary snort. 'Poor fucking Sean,' he muttered. 'Never spelled it out, not until then, but he knew. Wasn't interested in me, or in men – not like that, anyway. He'd gently rebuff me and I'd take off for a night or two, get the frustration and anger kicked out of me. Self-flagellation of sorts.' He laughed drily. 'But I got him, Ellie. Got Sean. A challenge he couldn't refuse. An intellectual exercise: existential love, opening his mind to a new experience, all that bullshit. And for some reason that night he gave in.'

His eyes drooping, he groaned. 'I tried; he tried. Couldn't get him hard, not even a semi, let alone ...' He slumped further in the chair. 'Cried, Ellie. Declared love. Needy and pathetic. Disgusted myself.'

Slipping into sleep, his words were sluggish and muddled. 'Held me then ... arms tightly around me, but too ashamed, too humiliated.'

Seeming to pull himself back, he smiled weakly. 'Worked it out, though. Worked Sean out. Those women he fucked. Never made sense ... didn't fit in with his politics. Looking for someone to save, he was. Atone for his mum and his sisters. For not saving them.' He gave a last sigh. 'Fucking pathetic. Love. Doesn't go away,' he mumbled, before passing out.

Ellie gazed for a moment longer. Self-flagellation. *'Infliction of bodily harm. An essential quest of humans once basic needs have been met.'* So it was Cameron who had said it.

Despite her aching wrist, the empty tiredness was inordinate. But she had to check on her sons. Reaching for her mobile, she sent each a text. Replies fired back:

Missing you, Mum. I hope you're OK.

We had baked potatoes with tuna for tea, but Liam says they have marmalade (with bits in) at breakfast. Do I have to eat it?

Love you too. Sooo much xxxxxxxx

Wiping her tears, she thanked God for her blessings. But she couldn't let oblivion take over just yet. Like agonising stomach cramps, the most searing, painful memory had been pushing through since she came round from the fall. She'd shelved it while speaking to Cam, but it was there, devastatingly whole and complete.

For years she'd tried to bury it deeply, but it had always been present, just under the surface. And now it was here, it had to be acknowledged.

Taking a shuddery breath, she typed a message. Just two simple words.

I've remembered.

68

Time slows as Ellie stares at the large canvas. Too cheery, too jolly, too full of fucking hope. The tears finally flowing, she lunges. Wishing it was flesh, she rips from corner to corner. Ready to tear it again and again until it's obliterated, she takes a deep breath.

'Ellie, don't!' The door has burst open. 'What are you doing?'

She stops in surprise and spins around. She thought she was alone in the house, but from his tousled hair, dark stubble and soft face, Sean must have been asleep in the bedroom opposite.

Shaking her head, she turns back to her mission. Needing to slit and slash again, she lifts her arm, but a strong hand catches it firmly, peeling her taut fingers away from the knife.

'Just stop, Ellie, stop.'

She covers her eyes. 'I have to. It's too painful, too much of Cam. I can't bear to look at it.'

'Then I'll take it,' he replies.

She hears him move the canvas, but knows he's still there, watching, waiting. For what? Lowering her trembling palms, she looks.

His green eyes are blazing.

'Cam doesn't know what he wants yet. You've got to pick yourself up. Paint the sorrow on canvas. You're a beautiful girl Ellie. Don't let it beat you,' he says, and there's a catch in his voice. 'You are special, you must know that.'

She finally meets his gaze. It's not mocking, but cloudy with emotion. Her body knows before her mind catches up. His desire, deep desire. And it's exhilarating—

Ellie snapped open her eyes and sat up. It was daylight. Where was she? That was right. In a hotel in Derbyshire with Cam. She looked to his side of the bed. It was empty.

'Sorry, I didn't mean to startle you.'

She turned to the voice. Not Cameron in the chair, but Sean.

He sat forward and spread his hands apologetically. 'Sorry, I did knock but . . . you've been out for the count since I got here.'

Dull throbbing in her wrist filtered through. Then the recall of yesterday hit like a punch. Cameron; the vasectomy argument, her fall, his drunken confession.

But more than that, even more than that – the tumble of memories she'd fought so hard to suppress, the loneliness and isolation, her debilitating loss.

She tried to breathe through the sheer dismay. In the space of a few days, her life had imploded. Her parents and Cameron and the past. But Sean was here; thank God he was here.

She flicked away the errant tears. 'How come—'

'I got your text.'

His eyes were deep pools of concern, but she couldn't, she just couldn't go there right now. Instead, she glanced around. 'Where's Cameron?'

His jaw tight, Sean looked to the ground. 'He's at my place. That's how I was able to let myself in.' He grimaced. 'He's in the garden shed, actually. I don't think the cherry tree will make it. Still, it could've been the kitchen window.'

'Right.' Then his words sank in. 'Cam's in Marple Bridge? How did he . . . ? Oh my God, he *drove*?' She put a hand to her mouth. 'He was blind drunk. So much so, he'd passed out.'

Sean nodded. 'I pretty much guessed that. The car's bashed up.' He raked his hair. 'His face is too. I don't think he was wearing a seat belt. He'll live, though. He refused to move out of the outhouse this morning; said he was fine, just needed to sleep it off.'

Fighting her emotions, Ellie covered her face. 'It's not something he can sleep off, Sean. Not this time. Everything's broken, smashed into little pieces.' She put a hand to her breast. 'I don't think I can fix it in here this time. He . . . '

'I know; I'm sorry.' Anticipating her question, he pulled out his phone to show her. 'He sent me this in the night.'

I've fucked up, man. I've fucked up big time.

'I didn't see it until this morning.' He paused for several moments. His eyes were dark, the green almost turned black. 'I read it after yours. Do you want to talk—'

'No.' She dragged back the bedding and stood. 'I just . . . ' The need to sob hurt her chest. 'I need the bathroom.'

Avoiding her own reflection, she cleaned her teeth and washed her face with fumbling fingers, but the bubbling, corrosive grief eventually took over, so she sat on the loo, trying to catch air between spasms.

A knock at the door finally roused her. 'Ellie?' Sean asked, looking in. His face was shadowy. 'Are you all right? You've been in here a long time.'

Unable to speak, she shook her head.

'Everything's fine.' He knelt and held her tightly. 'We don't have to talk about it now. Or ever. Only if you want to. OK?' After some time he pulled away and passed a wad of tissues. 'Do you want to get dressed? Then I'll take you home.'

Ellie closed her eyes in the car, but the tears wouldn't stop. The raw agony was still there, fierce in her throat, her breast and belly. The gut-wrenching loss of her baby.

Silent, unmoving, dead.

Stillborn, yet beautiful, perfect.

And that unforgettable newborn smell.

Her mouth abruptly found words. 'Sometimes I thought I had spotted her. Babies, toddlers, little girls. Always with dark hair.' She sharply inhaled at the realisation. 'That's why when I saw you and Samantha at the art gallery ...' She shook her head. 'My stupid questions. I had no idea why, but part of me hoped she was your daughter. Our daughter.'

His face tight and pale, Sean nodded. 'On reflection, I thought it might be that.' He sighed. 'I'm so sorry, Ellie.'

After a while, he glanced over. 'In all likelihood your memory loss was a disorder called dissociative amnesia ...' He reached out a hand. 'Brought on by deep trauma and stress. Although consciousness can't access the blocked-out events, it can continue to influence behaviour. It's different for everyone, but it can be similar to PTSD. Flashbacks and dreams, confusion, anxiety. It's tough, it really is.'

'But I forgot so very much.' She swallowed. *She isn't normal.* That was the harsh reality; she wasn't. 'That can't be how most people ... It isn't normal, is it?'

'There isn't any normal, Ellie. The amnesia can range from being unable to recall a specific period of time to forgetting only some of the events; it can last from minutes to decades.'

An inkling of relief. 'Can it happen more than once?' she asked.

'Yes. More than one episode is typical, actually.'

Nodding, she gazed through the passenger window. At eleven. Deep trauma. And yes, overwhelming anxiety and fear.

She came back to Sean. 'How did you know about everything?'

'Your mum. After you'd gone, she turned up at Alston Terrace to collect your paintings. She's a nice woman; she was very kind when she could have been angry. Then she contacted me again when you . . .' He paused and blew out. 'When the amnesia set in. Though it was a shocking blow, it was good of her to tell me that the baby had . . . died.' He frowned. 'So at least I knew and had that closure.'

Ellie tensed. Marian, her 'nice' mum. So Sean had met her; no wonder he'd been so cagey the day he'd driven her to Woodlands.

Though she scrunched her eyes to stop it, the reel of memories played again. Hiding from Maurice in her bedroom at Woodlands, numb, abandoned and alone. Sleeping but barely speaking, hardly eating as her belly expanded with a will of its own. Then a holiday to Horning with Marian against her dad's wishes. *I need time to paint and Ellie isn't well. She needs a break and fresh air. We're going to a scenic village in Norfolk. You'll just have to do without us for a few weeks.*

The dreadful weather, her bitten nails, her unhappiness; the thatched cottage and the surge in the size of her stomach as she slept. Her only release painting; oils of the River Bure, smearing on layer after layer of hopeless dark colour. Then at the bench on the village green without Marian, her swollen belly pitching, a sudden onset of discomfort and that leaking sensation she'd always feared. Climbing the long hill to the cottage, doubling up with the shocking, sharp pain. Crying out for her mum. And for Sean, for Cam, even for Maurice.

A room swamped with disinfectant, disapproval and whispers.

The unexpected length and agony of childbirth, her pleading for relief as she glared at her mother between contractions: *'It hurts, Mum, it hurts so badly. You had me. You must have known. Why didn't you tell me?'*

A midwife with a frown: *'It'll be over soon.'*

Sudden liberation from torment. The unmitigated, instant joy as she held her newborn; a perfect baby, a beautiful girl. Her daughter. Then panic, worried faces, the child snatched from her arms.

And finally the searing loss. *'She's gone. They tried their hardest, love. I'm so very sorry. Put this behind you and look to a happy future. It's really for the best, I promise.'*

Her breaking point.

Then nothing. For a long time, nothing.

69

'It has to be the truth, the honest truth. Everyone agree?'

'But what is *truth*?'

'It's only a game, Sean. Besides, another slug and we'll know.'

Six young adults in the high-ceilinged room, two cuddled on the sofa and four on the floor. A girl and two guys sit around a candlelit coffee table. Though late, it's still balmy, the leaded windows ajar. They're drinking Jack Daniel's from shot glasses.

Ellie snaps open the second bottle and pours. Her nails are bitten, her nose pierced, her short hair dyed black. Her attention is focused on Sean stretched out on the floor.

Lifting his dark head, he glances at her. 'Isn't there anything other than that American shit?' he asks, his Cork accent distinct. He goes back to his spliff and takes a deep drag. 'OK. Then we'll use the correspondence theory of truth,' he says. 'A belief is true if there exists an appropriate entity – a fact – to which it corresponds. If there's no such entity, the belief is false.'

Cam laughs. 'OK, genius, I'll start.' Blue-eyed and neat featured, he looks younger than his twenty years. 'A secret. A true secret . . . ' He knocks back the whiskey. 'I'm in love with some-body in this room.'

Ellie whips up her head, her stark make-up barely hiding her shock.

'Tell us something we don't already know!' Paul is huge, his voice booms Home Counties. 'Come on, Cameron, old chap. What did you say? The honest truth. Something you haven't told anyone before.'

'Right; here's one. My mum tried to snog me once,' he says.

Everyone but Ellie laughs.

'No, it's true, I'm not joking. Dad had buggered off, so she spent all the time drinking and crying—'

'And snogging you?'

'Yes, Judge, Your Honour.' He guffaws. 'The truth and the whole fucking truth, eh? Only the once, thank God, when she got close enough. I can't do needy. Fucking disgusting.'

A silence of drunk embarrassment, then Paul's eloquent voice again: 'Raj, Sylvie? Are you two lovebirds playing?'

They turn to the couple on the sofa. Sylvie is asleep. 'We're living our secret,' Raj says. 'But one you don't know . . . Let me think. My brother and me, we used to spit in the take-outs. Special treat for the racists we knew from school.'

'Nice.'

'Nah, Raj. Good try, but it won't put me off your delicious—'

'I saw my father beat up my mum.' Sean looks fixedly at the ceiling. 'Badly. Watched the blood spurt from her nose. Did noth-ing to stop him.'

Ellie stares, but doesn't speak.

Cam leans over. 'Fuck, Sean,' he says. 'How old were you?'

'Still a kid. But I blamed her. Probably still do.' He sits up and throws back his shot. Then he squints through the smoke at Ellie, still sitting cross-legged and silent. 'What about you, nice middle-class Miss Wilson? You're not saying much. What's your secret?'

Everyone is watching, all eyes are on her. 'A secret truth?' she asks, turning to him. 'With an actual *fact* to which it corresponds?'

Sean snorts. 'Yeah. Come on, then; try me.'

She opens her inky lips. 'Today I found out I'm pregnant with your baby, Sean. It's too late to abort.'

'For fuck's sake, Ellie, that isn't even funny,' Cam says. 'It's a truth game, not "let's wind up Sean, see if he explodes" game.'

She pulls up her knees and holds them tightly in her arms. 'OK. I did a blow job for money last year. A disgusting middle-aged man in his car at the crematorium. He said he'd pay more if I swallowed, which I did, but he—'

'Stop! Fucking stop.' His face flushed with anger, Cam is on his feet. 'What the hell is wrong with you, Ellie?' he shouts. 'Why are you saying all this crap?' He steps away, then he turns, his fists clenched. 'What the fuck are you doing?' He suddenly lunges and she cowers, but Paul is up, holding him back. Yet still he points, his spittle flying. 'There is something seriously fucking wrong with you with all this attention seeking. It isn't normal. You aren't normal. Do you know that?'

70

Ellie peered at her home through the passenger window. Sat in Sean's SUV felt like life on repeat, but today she didn't want him to leave. Though the tears had finally stopped, she felt lost. What would happen now? How would their futures be? Cameron, her boys and her parents? She had absolutely no idea.

She turned back to Sean. 'The torn canvas,' she said, stalling for time. 'It's still upstairs in the spare room.' She smiled thinly. 'It seemed to encapsulate everything, my hope and hopeless love for Cam, and us, the day we made our baby.'

He nodded, so she continued, 'After that final night I went home to Woodlands and told my mum about the pregnancy. But as the days went by, hiding there, abandoned and lonely, more than anything I wanted the painting back. So Mum drove to Leeds, to the house and she met you. "The man who wanted to keep a canvas safe, even though it was damaged," she said.'

She sighed. Damaged. Such an ugly word, but true. Not just the painting, not just her face, but her soul.

She touched her cheek. 'You already knew about this, didn't you?'

'Not at first. But at some point I met Jade, we discovered our mutual connection and she told me what had happened.'

'And you didn't judge me?'

He frowned. 'Who was I to judge anyone? The bullshit talk was a cover. I was hiding my own deficiencies, my insecurities, my past.' He smiled faintly. 'Besides, I loved you. I tried extremely hard not to, but I loved you.'

She stilled at his exquisite words, but after a moment she spoke again. 'But I condemned myself. I thought saying it out loud and confessing it as a truth would make me feel better, but it didn't. Then I came to your bedroom to talk, to explain properly about my situation, to ask what I should do next. But you were . . . ' She blinked away the image. 'You were busy, so I left.'

Sean's eyes blazed with pain. 'I'm so sorry. I should have listened when you said it, but we were all so tanked up and coming out with all sorts of weird stuff. I can't tell you how many times I've relived the evening, trying to make it all different, wishing I'd never met bloody Jack Daniel's.' He sighed. 'But Jack wasn't all bad. Looking back on that night and the havoc it wreaked in all sorts of ways, well, it helped me give up the booze.'

Ellie nodded. Havoc indeed. Cam's disgust with her, his attempt to be 'loved' and his own self-loathing, her fleeing from the house.

The silence was broken by the sound of children's laughter from the park. Sean dug in his pocket and lifted the house keys. 'You'll need these.'

Oh God, he was going.

His brow furrowed, he didn't speak for a beat. 'I'll check the state of Cam and the car when I get back, but another night might be better if he's driving. Or I can bring the boys over this evening. Whatever suits you best.' He cleared his throat. 'What does suit you best, Ellie? Shall I come in for a while?'

She couldn't help smiling. 'Yes please.'

He followed her in and stretched in the hallway. It revealed an inch of bare belly above his jeans. 'A bracing game of squash yesterday,' he commented. 'I feel as though I've strained something.' Then, stepping towards her, 'Talking of which . . .' He lifted her wrist and examined it with gentle fingers. 'I noticed you struggling with it. It's swollen, bruised. How did you hurt it?'

Conscious of his proximity, she peered at it too. 'I tripped on a tree root and bumped my head.' She laughed to deflect her discomfort. 'I didn't realise it had bled until I looked in the mirror. It was not a pretty picture.'

He released her arm and studied her. 'Always a pretty picture. Should I look?'

'I'm sure it's fine, but . . .'

His breath against her ear, he gently explored her hair. His aftershave or deodorant smelled nice. And he must have been to the barber's now she looked properly. His hair was shorter, his beard trimmed.

She carefully stepped away. 'Will I live, Doctor?'

'You will.'

Moving to the kitchen, she opened the decking doors, flicked on the kettle, then sat at the table opposite him.

'Two teas coming up.'

They listened to birdsong from outside.

'Are you OK now?' Sean asked eventually. He breathed a smile. 'Stupid question, but you know what I mean.'

She gazed. This man had said he loved her. She'd been right all along. It had been fudged by paranoia, forgetfulness and loss, but she had been special, she had traced his body with kisses. Though only that one time in the box room, it had been sublime, a whole afternoon of intense and intimate lovemaking before the others came back.

'Do you want to talk about Cam?' he now asked.

She continued to study him. Beautiful eyes, full lips, a hidden dimple in his chin? 'Nope.'

He tilted his head. 'So ...' He laughed. 'Have I got dirt on my nose or—'

She felt the blush rise and looked down. 'In the car you said you'd loved me back then.' She rubbed the table top. 'Do you still?'

She heard the scrape of his chair. Was he leaving or ...? No, he was taking her hands and gently tugging her upright. Cupping her face, he gazed intently. Then he smiled and kissed her softly, again and again.

'What do you think?' he finally replied.

Lying against Sean's shoulder, Ellie sighed out the exquisite waves of release. Eventually she pecked those full, clever lips. 'Why did you never tell me – I don't know, remind me – shake out the amnesia?' she asked.

He stroked the length of her spine with gentle hands. 'God knows, I wanted to at times. Wanted to remind you – of us, of this. That you'd desired me, really needed me.' He dipped his head to meet hers. 'But you'd blocked out the ... the grief and I was afraid of hurting you, bringing back your dreadful loss.' He sighed. 'Maybe today there'd be treatment at the outset – psychotherapy, cognitive therapy, clinical hypnosis – but your mum made the decision not to seek medical help. She thought you'd had enough trauma. More damaging to force it back than to leave it alone. Does that make sense?'

She nodded. A secret, silent and buried beneath a bird table. Of course it made sense to Marian.

'And before then ...' He blew out. 'Well, I got your message and for a long time I was angry and hurt.'

Ellie hitched up. 'What message?'

'Well, not a message as such, but a communication, if you like.'

376

'I have no idea what you—'

'When Marian came for the canvas and told me your news, I put two and two together – what you'd said at the truth game and us together in the February. I wanted to see you, talk to you.' His expression clouded. 'Hold you, love you, take care of you. But she said you'd decided to go it alone; that you didn't want me – or "the father" – involved. She was kind but firm. She made it clear I wasn't to contact you.'

'Marian said that?'

Of course she did.

Anger fired through Ellie's whole being. She pictured her mother's straight back, her calm yet fixed expression when she wanted her own way. And those childhood 'aspirins'. They'd been bloody sleeping pills, hadn't they?

Making plans for Ellie. She'd been controlled and manipulated her whole bloody life.

No more; no more. Two resolutions popped in one. She voiced the first.

'About Cam and me . . .'

'Yes?'

'I'm going to . . .' She almost used Marian's expression. 'I've decided to stand on my own two feet. Be me instead of . . . an add-on, an accessory, I suppose. Cam and I will work better apart.' Heartache sprang to her eyes. 'Apart but close for the boys. Friends. Or at least friendly. Do you think that could ever work?'

'I hope so, I really do. You can only try.'

She reached for Sean's hand. She was just borrowing him, she knew. He'd never leave Ciara and his kids, which was fine, she wouldn't want him to. But that 'connection' was there. He'd fathered her first child; on some level he was hers and had been for a long, long time. Was it love? She didn't know. But whatever it was, she could feel it like a bright, burning coal in her chest.

'Will you be around to look out for us?' She took a sharp, fearful breath. 'For me?'

Pulling her close, Sean wrapped her in his arms. 'You should know that by now. Always.'

She smiled through the tears. 'Always' was just perfect.

The second decision was to finally face her mum.

71

Already missing Sean, Ellie meandered down the stairs. The house felt echoey and empty. Not just of people, but furniture and furnishings. She was projecting, of course, her mind anticipating the worst. God, she hoped Cam would be reasonable and do the right thing for their sons. If he found accommodation nearby, it wouldn't be so different to their lives for the past eighteen months. It would give him the freedom he wanted – his 'autonomy', as he'd put it.

His words still stung, but at least he'd been honest, finally honest. She understood self-loathing and it didn't make for good company. Maybe one day he'd forgive himself like she had.

As though reading her mind, a message beeped. It was Cam.

Too many apologies to list, so I'll just say sorry. Boys are all good. Are you OK if we come home in the morning?

Ellie snorted and sent a yes reply. A 'sorry' was progress, but the message was otherwise pretty standard, dismissive Cam-style. She flopped down on the sofa and curled up her legs. How did that make her feel? Nothing, actually. Which was a relief. She never wanted to feel that uncertainty, paranoia and insecurity ever again.

Her phone rang. Expecting a Cam follow-through, she scooped it up. Bloody hell, it was Marian. She stared at the screen. Yes, she'd made her decision to confront her, but she hadn't had time to think it through. Her heart thrashing, she quickly pressed the red icon and turned to the window. What *was* she going to do about her parents?

She gazed through the bay. The possibilities ranged from doing nothing to calling the police. Burying her head again was not an option. But would she really do something so extreme as to involve the authorities? She pictured her father's whitewashed face. There would be police officers, pathologists, tents and excavators in the garden at Woodlands. Would she really make his worst nightmare come true?

But she had to do something; there had to be a middle ground. Distance herself and the boys? Make it clear to Marian that there would be no further contact, that their relationship was over.

She sighed. That felt like the easiest choice, but was it the right one? And would it even work? Would her mum really stop ringing her mobile and the landline? And how would Ellie explain it to the boys? Tell them another half truth? Do to them what had been done to her throughout her childhood?

Then there was the separation from Cam. That would be upsetting and unsettling for them all. Wouldn't it be better to keep other aspects of her sons' lives – especially their relationship with their grandparents – on an even keel?

But Ellie had to be practical. Suppose Diana's bones did get unearthed somehow? As Marian had said, she'd inherit Woodlands one day. She could never live there herself, so she'd sell it and be in the same position as Maurice – terrified a body would be found. It didn't seem so unlikely either. It was a huge plot; there was plenty of room to build another house if not two. And what about the boys? How would they feel then as grown-ups? Surely traumatised – and angry – that she hadn't had the guts to deal with it now.

She scrunched her eyes. Oh God. Maurice and Marian had brought her up; despite their faults, they'd both loved her. But there was really no other solution. Now wasn't the time for more cowardliness, she had to protect herself and her sons; reporting the crime to the police was the only way forward.

She picked up her mobile. What did one do? Call 999? But an idea popped. There was another answer, one that would be kinder to everyone. She quickly pressed her mother's icon.

'Ellie, how are you? I've been worried. I must have telephoned three times . . .'

It was actually sixteen calls at the last count. Ellie flinched at the easy lie. Her mum's misdemeanours were many, but telling Sean that she didn't want 'the father' to get in touch hurt the most right now. The isolation and loneliness for those four months had been unbearable, and this woman, who was supposed to care, had instigated it. But she had to stay focused on the bigger picture of what was best for her children.

Marian was prattling, so she interrupted. 'Mum, stop and listen please.'

'What is it, love?'

She took a deep breath. 'I want you to do something for me and the boys.'

'Of course, anything.'

'I want you and Dad to hand yourselves in to the police.'

'Eleanor—'

'Just listen. If you report it yourselves, you can explain what happened in your own way.' She blinked away an image of Diana's fond, smiling face. 'From your point of view. Only you and Dad know what happened, so you can prepare yourselves first. If it's done quietly like this, there'll be far less scandal and you'll get credit for coming clean. I will support you and we can explain it to the boys in language they'll understand. If the worst happens and you have to go away for a while, we'll be there for you and visit you both.' She swallowed. 'In truth, I think it will do Dad good, too. He needs to face those dark—'

'Oh Ellie. Why would you say that? He's right as rain now, just like you will be when you've calmed down. You're just overwrought; you need to give it a few days. It'll all work out, it always does.' Then with a smile in her voice, 'Now, is Jake there for a little word? I've found him something he'll—'

'Stop.' That calm and reasonable bloody tone! The anger abruptly boiled. Ellie's blocking out, her amnesia and mental health issues; her deep-seated feelings of insecurity and rejection; her constant sense of having done something wrong – they had all started the day this woman chose to kill her own sister. 'You do it or I will,' she snapped, ending the call.

72

Sitting on the decking, Ellie gazed blankly at the garden. Though an hour had passed, she was still breathless and trembling from earlier. Anger, nerves and sheer bloody frustration.

Her anxiety wasn't helped by Cam's second text:

PS I do love you

'Too bloody late!' she had wanted to reply. But that wouldn't have helped her resolve. Going forward she needed to rely on herself. She'd spent a lifetime seeking love and approval. Neither Cam nor Maurice had given it. Perhaps they weren't to blame: Maurice had been shaped by his upbringing, then crippled by guilt and fear; Cam by his childhood too, in all probability. But those things weren't her fault.

Nor were her parents' criminal acts. But would she really report them to the police? In all honesty, she just didn't know.

Tobacco fumes and conversation filtered over from next door. God, she wished she still smoked. But the chatter was comforting;

it made her feel less alone. And after the offer from Amy, she could pop over if she needed to. Another thought hit: both Amy and Valerie were lawyers, she could ask for their advice in a roundabout way. Though in retrospect, she wished she'd confided in Sean this morning. He'd know what to do.

She smiled despite her agitation. They'd had other compelling things on their minds. She stirred at the thought of that body, those kisses. And he'd said he loved her; he'd always be here for her.

Like an answer to her prayers, the doorbell rang. Smoothing her hair, she dashed to the hallway and opened the door. But it wasn't her lover. Her head erect and expression composed, Marian Wilson was waiting through the glass. For an iota, Ellie considered stepping away to hide, but she had to be brave; she needed resolution.

'Hello, love.' Marian made her way to the kitchen and sat. 'Shall we try to clear the air?'

'Clear the air', as though they'd had a frivolous spat? Pulling out a chair, Ellie rubbed the disbelief from her face. She took a deep breath. Shouting wouldn't achieve anything; she had to be measured, get her mother to understand what was best for everyone.

'Look, Mum, I've thought it through carefully. I'm sure you'll agree that the boys – my children and your grandchildren – are the most important thing here. There's a dead body in your garden. One day it will be discovered. It might be in ten years or thirty. It might be when we're both dead. But the point is that your grandsons will find out. They'll discover your crime and my lies. They may never forgive us; we might not be around to help them understand. If you and Dad report it now, you can explain it to the police however you wish; I can do the same with the boys. But at least we'll stick together and support each other; we'll still be a family. No more secrets, Mum. Surely you can see how destructive they are?'

Relief blew through Ellie's chest. She'd said her speech and her mum had listened intently. She was now reaching out her hand. 'You're right, love. We are family, which is precisely why it happened: we did it for you.' She smiled. 'For *you*, love.'

It took a moment for the words to land. When they did, Ellie found herself shouting after all. 'Don't you dare put this on me! I was just eleven, still a child. You killed a person – your sister, my birth mother.'

'A woman who barely bothered to take any interest or visit you. A woman who was out of control. Who knows what might have happened if we'd done nothing to stop her? You could have been snatched or harmed, even killed. There was no talking to her; she wasn't being rational—'

'Why did you tell Sean to stay away when I was pregnant?'

Clearly thrown by the change of subject, Marian sat back. She shook her soft curls. 'You had told him you were expecting, Ellie, and he didn't believe you. He reeked of tobacco and alcohol when I met him. Quite honestly, I think he was relieved. I promised to keep him in the loop, which I did. And it all ended up for the best, didn't it? You met Cameron and had your beautiful boys. Why are you worrying about it now? That's just plain silly.'

The rational Ellie had gone; rage was now charging through her whole body. She was not going to let her mother use that reasonable voice to get away with homicide. She was not.

'You *murdered* another human being. You should and will pay for your crime. There's nothing more to say.' She scraped back the chair. 'Now go.'

Marian dipped into her handbag. She was leaving, thank God. But she didn't pull out her car keys as expected. Instead, she was sliding an envelope across the table. Almost laughing from exhaustion and this woman's sheer tenacity, Ellie stared at it. What was this? A bribe? A big fat cheque from Maurice to keep her quiet?

Marian tapped it. 'You'll be pleased. Go on, love, open it.'

With a sigh, Ellie did. She glanced at the single content – a photograph of herself. 'A photo of me before uni. So what?'

Marian didn't reply, so she looked again. 'What am I supposed to see?' she snapped. 'Other than a child whose real mother has been—'

Not breathing, Ellie stared. This young woman had her auburn locks and big smile, but not her other features. She had a dimple in her chin; she was taller . . .

Realisation cracked. Oh God, oh God; her baby girl wasn't dark haired after all. Heaving, she flew to the sink. When the retching finally stopped, she turned.

Her voice was a croak. 'My baby was born dead.'

Marian folded her hands. 'Yes, she was. But a miracle happened; they were able to revive her shortly after. By then they'd given you a sedative to help with . . .Well, you were hysterical, to say the least. When you finally came around . . . well, you'd already "lost" her, so I didn't want you to suffer twice.' Her eyes welled. 'Nobody knows the agony of a stillborn child more than me.'

Through the fug, Ellie frowned, trying to shape words.

Her expression sympathetic, Marian cocked her head. 'Don't you remember, love? Those long, unhappy weeks at the cottage in Horning. You weren't in a fit state to look after a child, so we'd already agreed to adoption. Plans were in place. I was hardly going to tell you the baby had lived, then have her taken away from you again. It was kinder to let you believe she had died; it gave you more closure.'

Ellie's temples throbbed. Adoption? No, she couldn't recall that, nor signing any papers. And bloody closure? This woman had no idea – the ghost who'd followed her around; the constant feeling of loss; the ragged hole in her heart. 'Closure? I haven't had closure since she was born. And not knowing why . . . You thought that was *kind*? How could you be so cruel? How could you?'

But something else was nagging. She strode back to the snap. The familiar backdrop behind the girl, the small village store ... Almost smelling the lavender, Ellie breathed through the nausea. Windmills. Eighteen waving windmills on the dresser at Woodlands. Marian's visit every October to her 'gift shop friend' in Norfolk ...

My God. The annual week without Maurice had been to see *her* child; to celebrate *her* daughter's birthday.

'You've been visiting her?' A loud sob bubbled out. 'For all these years you've held and touched and talked to *my* baby?'

The heartache was so savage, Ellie struggled to breathe. But Marian's neat fingers were on the photograph, carefully tugging it back. The sense of loss flooding again, Ellie tried to reach it a moment too late.

'No, no don't put it back. Let me look at her again.' She needed more than a glimpse. She needed to study every inch of the image, absorb every contour of her child. She needed to know everything about her. Oh God, she needed to meet her in person. 'What's her name? Where is she? Is she living in Norfolk?'

No reply. Instead, Marian slipped the envelope in her handbag and snapped the clasp shut.

'Mum? My girl. Where is she? Can I see her?'

Her mother stood, straightened her slacks and made for the door.

Panic hitting, Ellie blocked her way. 'Tell me. I'll call the police right now if you don't!'

'Come on now, don't be silly, love.' Marian lifted her hand and softly touched Ellie's face. 'She's precisely the reason you wouldn't dream of doing that. You want to meet her and get to know her, don't you? As you said yourself, your children and my grand-children are the most important things here. You wouldn't want her to suffer or be sad.' She smiled. 'Like your boys, she loves her grandma very much.'

She tapped her watch and shook her head. 'Goodness, look at the time. I'd better get home to Maurice, but just think of the future and all the lovely gatherings we'll have. A family party in the garden at Woodlands would be a nice start, wouldn't it?' She kissed Ellie's cheek. 'Oh love, you look tired. But there's really no need to worry about anything; sometimes lies ... no, not lies. Sometimes omissions are for the best.'

ACKNOWLEDGEMENTS

Much love and thanks to:

My gorgeous family – Emily, Charlotte, Elizabeth and Jonathan.

Alison, Beth, Brionee and the Piatkus team, particularly Anna Boatman and Hannah Wann, my fabulous, intuitive and wonderfully collaborative editors.

My excellent literary agents, Kate Johnson and Rach Crawford.

Insightful early readers Elizabeth Ball, Hazel James, Robert Peett, Charlotte Levin, Dominic O'Reilly, David Beckler.

My fellow writers and appraisers at the South Manchester Writers' Workshop.

All the supportive and hard working bloggers who have championed my books. There are too many to mention, but particular thanks to Steph Lawrence of StefLoz Book Blog, who chose *Betray Her* as one of her favourite reads of 2019!

So many brilliant friends. You all know who you are from our #lockdown WhatsApp and Zoom chats, but special thanks to the GNO faithful – Belinda, Yvonne, Janet and Adele, and the Psych Thriller Killer authors – Carolyn, Libby and Sam.

Last, but not least, the fantastic reading public! Thank you so much for buying my books, investing hours of your time reading them and posting such heartwarming reviews.

May 2020